Armored Fleet

Sovereign Stars Book 3

Blair C. Howard

Library of Congress Control Number: 2022921193
Cleveland, TN
ISBN: 979-8-9862563-7-5

Dedication

For Jo, as always

Prologue

New Hope

Planet Typhon

Eta Persei Star System

Date: 3279 11 25 Standard

Dense columns of smoke were rising above the small city of New Hope, huge columns of gray that glowed eerily against the backdrop of the night sky. Somewhere, several streets away, a fire was raging. One of the larger buildings near the town center had been hit by a *halo ship* strike a few hours earlier and the flames cast an eerie orange glow over the ruined city. The superheated concrete crackled like a vat of frying meat.

Kyne Minnah kept low as he ran across the street, aware that the glow from the nearby inferno would make him easier to spot. He scampered into an alleyway, straightened up and pressed himself against a wall, sinking into the shadows.

He held his breath, his heart thudding in his chest, counting the excruciatingly long seconds, certain the hum and whine of a *halo ship* would fill the night air any minute. Either that or he'd hear the hammering of a trio of blue-armored *stalkers* rushing down the street to fry him with their plasma weapons.

But, as the seconds rolled by, Kyne let out his breath. Other than the crackling concrete, the streets were silent—no hint of any impending danger. He took a couple of steps forward and looked carefully around the corner into the alley. There was a hole in a wall a few meters away where a gravcar had crashed through it. Little was left of the gravcar. Just a black heap of melted metal.

Kyne glanced quickly over his shoulder, then turned to look across the street and motioned for his comrades to join him. The coast was clear, at least for the moment.

Four figures rose from their hiding places among the shadows, dashed across the crumbling pavement and joined Kyne with their backs against the wall: two young men, a young woman, and an older man, all eyes on him.

"All right," Kyne said. "This is the building I was telling you about." He flipped a thumb over his shoulder.

The woman turned away, keeping watch, eyeballing the burning building, then she turned again to Kyne and said, "How do we get in? Is the door locked?"

Kyne smiled, peered around the corner and pointed at the hole and the remains of the gravcar. "Somebody already took care of that for us. Come. See?"

Carefully, they moved quickly into the alley, picked their way through the rubble and entered the building to find themselves in a large, open warehouse. Eighteen months earlier, before the Swarm attack, the building had been used as a factory, processing blocks of osmium and dutrinium from a refinery next door.

Kyne had been in the building once before, on a scavenging mission shortly after the first Swarm attack. Most of the machinery was useless for the needs of the New Hope survivors, but there was one item he'd kept in mind.

And now, almost exactly a standard year and a half later, it just so happened that the one-time factory was perfect for what he needed to do.

Kyne pointed at a stack of metal crates, each filled with scraps—offcuts—of dutrinium ore and said, "Set up your firing positions there. Those crates should be able to take several hits before they melt through. Mozzley, you can set up behind those machines over there. You copy?"

All four of his comrades nodded. "Copy," they said in unison.

Kyne grinned. A true military commander would have said something like, "Is that understood?" or "Do you copy?" But while Kyne was no military commander, he was a game designer; so he used what he thought was the correct term.

Kyne Minnah was an agile young man aged about thirty —exactly how old he was he didn't know. His parents had died before his first birthday and he'd been brought up in a series of foster care homes. He was tall, slim with a wild mop of hair over a less-than-handsome face, a pair of piercing green eyes and a small nose and mouth. He was dressed in a tight-fitting, hunter green body suit under a red and green patterned coat that hung almost his knees. Kyne Minnah was also a geek and a genius, a technological wizard.

He'd been designing strategy games since he was in high school and that had given him an edge. The plan they were about to carry out was his, and it had to work. If not, his little group of survivors probably wouldn't last another week.

The three younger members of the group made their way to the crates. One young man, his name was Drave, was carrying a large duffel bag. He set it down behind one of the crates, opened it and passed out the rifles, railguns, weapons they used only when they absolutely had to. Ammo was scarce. So were power cells. But Kyne had managed to convince the others that the use of their precious resources would be well worth it.

Let's just hope I'm right, he thought.

Mozzley, the old man, shuffled over to the machines and settled down out of sight behind a laser shimming machine. He was thin and balding, with a few wisps of white hair sticking up off the back of his head. Mozzley was a hundred and thirty-two and was beginning to show his age, but he was essential to the mission.

Once everyone was in place, Kyne crossed the open space to a spot near the loading doors, looking for the thing he'd noticed all those months ago. He pushed several empty crates out of the way, wondering if someone else had beaten him to it, then he spotted it: a small grav lift hidden behind a stack of steel pallets.

The lift was less than half the size of a gravcar, little more than a box on four large wheels with a seat and control panel perched on top. Kyne took a moment to inspect the mechanics and controls. He tapped the power icon on the dusty screen. The icon lit up green. He grinned. "Yes!" he said and tapped the start icon. It too turned green and the grav engine came to life, humming quietly.

Kyne checked the power levels and smiled. *Perfect. The*

power cell's low, but it still has enough juice for what we need.

He hopped up onto the seat, not bothering to strap himself in, and looked over the controls. It took him less than thirty seconds to figure out how to work the machine.

He tapped a couple of icons on the control screen and slowly backed the lift out of its parking spot, taking great care not to hit anything. Driving a vehicle with wheels, especially when you're not used to it, is a pain: you can't just spin in place like you can with a gravcar or similar machine, but Kyne didn't mind. In the last game he'd designed, before the world went to hell in a hurry, he had included virtual chariots pulled by teams of horses. The turn radius on this thing was amazing compared to that ancient vehicle.

Kyne thumbed the grav controls. The humming grew louder as the grav engine generated an invisible tractor beam and lifted a large crate filled with scrap dutrinium.

He drove to the loading doors, looking around to confirm his comrades were in position. The three shooters were behind the line of crates, guns at the ready. Mozzley was half hidden behind the shimmer machine opposite them on the far side of the vast room.

Kyne nodded to Mozzley, who raised his hand, palm first, and closed his eyes...

The large doors in front of the lift slid open slowly, their rusty wheels screeching like a herd of stuck-horned hogs.

That was why the old man was there, why he was so useful. Physically, he had trouble moving around. But shortly after the Swarm attacked, the old-timer discovered he had a level of TK that was straight out of the fairy tales of the days of The Purge.

Mozzley opened the doors just enough for Kyne to drive the lift through.

Outside, the night was darker now, the wide street a crazy world of flickering shadows. The fire a few blocks away had burned down some; either that or the glow was being obstructed by the surrounding buildings. Not that it mattered. Kyne was thankful for the darkness. It would make it easier to spot the glowing blue armor of their enemies.

He waited, his eyes darting back and forth.

The plan was simple. They needed to tease an alien, maybe even two or three, into the building, and one of them had to be a stomper. They had enough firepower to handle three or four aliens, but not more than that. And certainly not a *halo ship*.

Outside, it was quiet, deathly quiet, the silence broken only by the deep hum of the grav lift. He tried to relax, breathe easy.

The nearest building, some twenty meters away across the street, was in ruins, little more than a pile of blackened rubble. Next to it, another building was still standing, mostly intact, but there were large holes burned through its front, side and roof.

Plasma blasts... Kyne thought. *The life of a pioneer, they said. An adventure, they said. Get away from the crowded worlds and the big cities, they said. Embrace the quiet life of a colony. Oh yeah, that's what they said.*

His thoughts were suddenly interrupted by the unmistakable thud of alien boots echoing off the walls. Kyne held his breath, eyes wide, and he was oh so scared, but he took a deep breath and gritted his teeth. *This has to work,* he thought. *It has to!*

He spotted a faint blue glow on the walls across the

street some sixty seconds before he saw the armored troopers. As always, there were three of them marching in a loose V-formation. The first was a stalker, sleek, its armor blue and pulsing, holding a plasma rifle.

Kyne knew from experience that stalkers had gray aliens inside the armor, armor that wasn't too hard to penetrate with kinetic weapons or TK-accelerated projectiles. Gray creatures with huge, lifeless black eyes.

The two that followed the stalker were what Kyne had been hoping for, a pair of stompers. Stompers were a recent addition to the alien troops, and they were different. They were larger, heavier, and their armor was harder to crack. They were self-regenerating robots.

He tapped the warning icon used to warn fellow factory workers to get out of the way. A hollow and weak beep sounded from the vehicle. The power cell was beginning to fail. He tapped it again and again.

The three aliens turned in unison. The stalker spotted him, turned and headed his way.

Got your attention now, you bastards.

He tapped the grav controls and the tractor beam raised the crate higher. He put the lift into reverse and retreated back toward the open doors.

A brilliant beam of intense blue energy struck the crate, now in front of Kyne's seat. The crate glowed dull red hot and crackled. But the dense dutrinium inside remained unaffected.

He heard the rapid stomping of the approaching aliens. A second then a third energy blast struck the crate, and another hit the side of the lift. Yet another hit the front wheel, which instantly exploded and then melted.

The lift lurched to one side, dragging its melted wheel screeching across the concrete. It began to rip. The crate, still in the grip of the tractor beam, swung upward as Kyne leapt out of the seat and into the air as the lift toppled over.

"Three incoming!" he yelled as he scrambled back inside the building.

A beam of shimmering plasma punched through one of the doors, striking a heavy machine inside. Another lit up the opening in the doorway, burning a hole through the wall opposite the doors.

Kyne dodged to his left and took cover behind a crate full of dutrinium. Everything went quiet except for the thumping of the armored boots approaching the doors.

Then the stalker entered first, followed by the two stompers. They marched into the factory and stood for a minute just inside the doors, seemingly studying the vast interior, looking for Kyne.

Kyne and his little group held their breaths and waited. For a long minute nothing happened, and then all three of the aliens turned and lumbered out into the open area.

"Now!" Kyne yelled. "Get the stalker first!"

The three members of his group who'd taken cover behind the crates opened fire. The streams of 6mm projectiles from the K9 railguns traveling at more than a thousand meters per second—four times the speed of sound—filled the factory with an ear-shattering sonic roar. Hundreds of rounds ripped into the stalker, shattering its armor. Its knees buckled and it collapsed before it could even bring its weapon to bear.

The two stompers, however, raised their right arms, upon which—instead of hand-like five-digit claws—were small plasma canons. The two stompers turned in place, pivoting at the torso, and unleashed a barrage of plasma beams.

Fortunately, the newcomers, the stompers, were slower

than the original blues. They were also not as smart. But they were larger and tougher and their weapons, larger than those carried by the stalkers, were much more powerful. The survivors had learned over time that the stompers could fire at two main settings: a large, powerful beam that was nearly as devastating as the weapons on the *halo ships*, and a full-auto setting, which fired a stream of needle-like beams. The needle beams were nowhere near as effective, but they were still deadly.

Bright blue waves of plasma washed around the room blowing holes in the walls, melting the factory machines, and burning into the steel crates but doing little damage to the dutrinium within. It was obvious the stompers didn't know where their attackers were, because they were firing seemingly at random.

Kyne's comrades waited for a break, then opened fire a second time, filling the factory with an unremitting, earsplitting sonic boom as hundreds of dutrinium projectiles punched holes in the closest stomper's armor. The glowing blue robot staggered backward, its weapon still emitting streams of plasma in all directions.

A block of raw dutrinium larger than a human head, guided by Mozzley's TK, flew across the room at close to the speed of sound and smashed into the damaged stomper's head, tearing it from its shoulders and the headless body keeled over and hit the concrete with a crack.

The metal block that had removed the stomper's head rose from the ground and traveled upward into the roof. The second alien robot was swinging around, this way and that, staggering under the impact of the railgun rounds, desperately trying to find its attackers.

In the far corner, still half hidden by the shimmer machine, Mozzley waved his hand and the dutrinium block, now directly above the robot, fell on top of its cranium, collapsing it.

The survivors stopped shooting and watched as the stomper stood frozen for a long moment until finally, it toppled over backward.

Kyne slowly emerged from behind the crate he'd been using as cover. He stood for a second, staring at the three downed aliens, then ran first to the headless stomper, then to the other. Then he put his fists to his head and groaned. They'd both been hit many times in the torso. The plan was to make sure they left at least one torso intact. Otherwise, it was all for naught. He chose the robot with the least damaged chest, the one with the caved-in head, and pointed at it, looked at Mozzley and said, "This one."

The old man was slowly walking toward the two still-glowing machines. The other three members of the group came out from behind the half-melted crates, their rifles raised, ready for the least sign of movement from the two stompers.

Good, Kyne thought. They knew from experience that these things could regenerate themselves.

Mozzley stood closer to the stomper Kyne had selected. The old man's body went rigid. He balled his hands into fists and... shards of scrap dutrinium of various shapes and sizes rose from the piles on the floor nearby, snapping to attention like a squadron of starfighters. Then, as Mozzley raised a hand and opened his eyes, the pieces of scrap flew with deadly precision and struck the stomper's arms and legs.

Kyne had to step away to avoid being hit, even though he knew he was in no danger. This was what Mozzley did best. It was his *forte.* Lifting large objects with TK drained him, but smaller objects he could hurl easily and with deadly accuracy.

The squadron of scrap dutrinium targeted the shoulder and hip joints, shattering the strange, glowing glasslike armor. Then, with a brushing motion of his hands, the arms, legs, and even what was left of the head were swept away, leaving only the torso behind. As each appendage was separated from the body, it instantly stopped glowing, turning a grayish, somewhat translucent color.

Kyne lifted his boot and smashed it down on the stomper's no-longer-glowing hand. It crumbled easily beneath his foot. He stared down at it, smiled and turned his attention back to the torso. Something was going on inside it.

Through the cracks and holes, he could see a bright blue shimmering light. Tiny ribbons of light, live luminescent threads, writhed and wriggled, moving along the inside of the glowing, translucent armor. Whenever those live wires touched a crack in the armor, something extraordinary happened: the damaged section healed itself. The hole grew smaller as the armor flowed into the wounds. Even the joints and neck were starting to rebuild themselves.

Kyne and his friends knew that, given enough time, the stomper would completely regenerate itself, but only as long as the core was still intact within the torso.

"Look," Drave said, pointing to the second of the two downed stompers. It, too, was self-repairing. One of its feet twitched. Drave yelped and reflexively jumped back.

"Let's finish up here," Kyne said. "Mozzley, would you do the honors and crack this bastard open, please?"

The old man nodded. He motioned at the torso in front of him. It lifted some ten meters into the air, then slammed down onto the concrete floor with incredible force. Spiderweb cracks appeared in its armor. He did it again.

The noise when the torso hit the floor was... thunderous. The cracks grew larger. Again the damaged torso rose into the air and came crashing down.

Mozzley put his two hands together and shut his eyes. When he spread his hands, the armor split wide open revealing the glowing innards. Bright threads snapped in the process, writhing like headless snakes as their glow slowly dimmed and died away. A blue orb, about the size of a pineapple, lay exposed, wrapped in wires, tubes and nodes, pulsing slowly. Mozzely lifted his hands slightly. The core rose several centimeters.

Kyne was ecstatic. This was it. A core. This was what they'd come for. He grabbed the duffel bag from Drave, then knelt down beside the remains of the torso, reached inside with both hands and slowly withdrew the core, slipping it into the bag and zipping it closed.

Mozzley heaved a great sigh and let his arms drop to his sides, and Kyne staggered under the full weight of the core as he hugged the duffel bag to his chest.

"We need to move," the woman said, her eyes wide as she watched the slowly regenerating stomper just two meters away. Already, the torso had produced a new neck, and the first slivers of a new head were beginning to grow like a time-lapse holo of a grava vine.

Kyne hefted the duffle bag, threw it over his shoulder, and said, "Right you are!" Then he turned to Mozzley. "You good to travel, old timer?"

The old man looked exhausted. Sweat was beaded on top of his bald head. But he nodded slowly, breathing heavily.

"Good," Kyne said. "Then let's get the hell out of here and go somewhere safe. We've got what we came for."

They ran to the far end of the factory floor where Drave

stopped, turned and dropped to one knee, pressing the butt of the Z9 rifle into his shoulder. He thumbed the trigger button and a stream of rounds slammed into the core of the remaining stomper.

Kyne and the others cowered against the wall, knowing what was about to happen.

Blue energy snapped and arched around the robot and, a split second later, what was left of the stomper exploded in a brilliant flash of blue energy.

Kyne covered his face with his forearm, trying to shield his eyes from the blinding light.

"Well, that's one that's not coming back," the woman commented.

Kyne nodded. The one weakness the stompers had was their core. Damage it and the stomper was done for; it would explode.

"Whew!" Drave blew out a huge breath as he stood up and joined the others. He looked at the duffel bag in Kyne's arms and said, "I hope that damn thing was worth it. I hope it will do what you think it will."

I hope so too, Kyne thought. But he didn't say it. Instead, he put on a brave face and said, "Don't you worry. It will work." *It has to*, he thought.

Chapter One

Orso Royal Palace

Planet Caerus

Orso System

Date: 3279 11 29

Tenilo Barum straightened out his tunic, adjusted his spectacles and took a deep breath. He hated these meetings, these official sovereign proceedings. As a commoner and a scholar, he could usually dodge them, but his friendship with Prince Padric Felder often meant he was expected to tag along and play nice with these Westerner royals. On top of that, his decision to stay long-term in the Orso System meant he'd have to carry out certain duties on behalf of the royal family of the Alastor System.

He was a... small man, a little overweight, but not terribly so. He wore his shoulder-length brown hair styled in the way that was popular with the royalty, but his did not have the volume or length of his prince's wavy locks. His face was... unremarkable: high forehead, sharp cheekbones, brown eyes, cleanshaven. But his looks belied his superior intellect and tenacity. He was the quintessential man for all seasons.

Two robot servants with strangely human-like upper torsos and oval faces glided forward to greet him as he and his entourage approached.

"We are here to escort you to your meeting, Mister Barum," one of the servants said.

"Right," Tenilo said after a deep sigh. "Well, lead the way, I suppose."

They both gave a slight bow and spun around, motioning for Tenilo to follow.

Orso's royal palace was huge and exquisitely decorated. A lush red carpet covered the floor of the hallway, which gave Tenilo the feeling he was sinking deeper with each step. The lighting was completely hidden, giving the impression that the illumination came from everywhere and nowhere, as if the walls themselves were glowing with a golden radiance.

Two great wooden doors opened automatically as they approached. The room beyond the hallway was large and circular. Servant and guard robots stood at attention around the perimeter. The centerpiece of the room was a huge, round table, a ring of polished iron wood set with padded chairs, most of which were already occupied.

One of the servant bots led Tenilo to one of the few empty chairs. He sat, or rather perched on the edge of the seat, fearing the excessive padding might swallow him.

Tenilo looked around the room. Many of the men and women already seated wore the attire and markings of dukes and duchesses of the Orso System. Several Marshals were present, only one of whom he knew personally. The others? Well... most seemed interested only in their fore-arm-mounted data screens. Those that noticed Tenilo's gaze responded only by hastily looking away.

Two of the guests, however, seemed to be completely unabashed by staring at Tenilo. They were seated directly opposite him. By their attire and demeanor he knew they were royalty.

The man, an imposing figure with shoulder-length hair, a well-oiled beard, and a short but muscular frame, appeared to be in a foul mood, for he spent most of his time staring at the holo generator on the floor in the space inside the ring conference table, glancing up at Tenilo now and then, scowling at him.

The woman, obviously his wife, wore a black satin dress tight enough to tastefully reveal her shapely figure. Her hair, a deep reddish-brown, fell in voluminous curls over her shoulders. She too stared at Tenilo, her emerald-green eyes fixed on him, her lovely face twisted with fury.

Instinctively, Tenilo moved back in his chair, wondering who they were and what he might have done to upset them.

Of course, he thought. *I was invited to sit after them, which means the palace AI deemed me to be more important than this obviously royal couple. No wonder they're upset. It's unheard of for a commoner to sit down after royalty. But what royal couple could possibly be lower on the social ladder than me, a royal historian from a faraway world in the Galactic East? Who are they?*

Tenilo thought for a moment that perhaps he should introduce himself to the royal couple, but then changed his mind; he didn't have the nerve.

Mentally he kicked himself for not being more prepared. A seasoned diplomat, like his friend Prince Padric, or the long-dead Duke Steren, would have done his homework and built a file on everyone scheduled to attend. Padric would know them all, would have recognized them, known everything about them, every personal and professional detail: their names, what system they were from, their family and professional ties, and, of course, why they were attending the meeting.

Tenilo resisted the temptation to look them up on his data screen. If they figured out what he was doing... *Whew!* Well, he'd just be asking for more anger, more scrutiny.

His thoughts were interrupted and, thankfully, all eyes were drawn to the opposite side of the circular room, where a golden robot announced in a baritone voice and with an ancient, Old-Earth accent, "Pray stand for King Orson Lorne, the seventeenth of that name, and Prince Elio Lorne of the Orso System."

The king, just over two meters tall and heavily muscled with a trim blond beard and a flowing mane of blond hair, strode into the great room with all the confidence of a grand royal: long steps, arms swinging gracefully by his sides, his scarlet cape fluttering behind him like the wings of a great red condor. He was the image of grace and power.

The king was followed by Prince Elio, who was almost the opposite of his father in more ways than Tenilo could count. He was thirty-two years old, just as tall as his father but not quite as heavily muscled. It was easy enough to see that he was his father's son, and that the Heroic bloodlines flowed in his veins. But it wasn't Elio's physical appearance that set him apart; it was his demeanor. Where his father, the king, strode confidently into the room, Elio's gait was... casual. His long blond hair was straight and fell over his shoulders like a golden waterfall. His eyes were electric blue, sparkling, but somehow, he seemed less... confident.

Some things never change, Tenilo thought. Elio, unlike

Padric, was not a diplomat. He hated these meetings almost as much as Tenilo did. He was a gamer, a hacker, and an adept in TK and Psy, a happy-go-lucky individual trying his best to be what his royal status demanded, and he struggled with it. Whenever Elio had to make a public and royal appearance, especially when he was with his father, he seemed to shrink. It was only when he was alone or with friends that he came out of his shell.

After both were seated, the king nodded to a man seated next to him, the one man in the room other than the king and Elio that Tenilo recognized: Marshal Ugo Tan, commander in chief of Orso's military forces.

Tan leaned forward, clearing his throat forcefully to make sure he had everyone's attention, then said loudly, "Well, ladies and gentlemen. We might as well begin."

He tapped an icon on his data screen and a holo image appeared in the center of the conference table, floating a meter or so above its generator. It was a large and comprehensive global map of the United Sovereign Systems.

"As you all know," he continued, "over the past two standard months, Swarm activity has increased significantly. What began as a series of small skirmishes has become an ongoing stream of attacks. To date, nineteen outlying worlds have been completely cut off. Twenty-four more have been evacuated. Almost all of these systems were colonies, sparsely populated and vulnerable. But now, even the larger, more developed worlds are suffering from these seemingly random attacks. But you already know this. What you don't know is that only three days ago the United Sovereign Fleet—the USF—completed the evacuation of the Odin System, a world with more than a billion inhabitants."

The royal couple across from Tenilo shifted in their seats, and the man grunted.

Tenilo's eyes lit up. *So that's who they are.* He couldn't resist. He tapped his data screen. The angry couple were indeed King Wulfrick Tudor and Queen Zara Tudor of Odin.

Marshal Tan manipulated the holo control via his data screen. The map zoomed in on the systems nearest Orso. Faint purple lines spread out from Orso to the distant systems, tracing the routes of the Slipstream and its branches. In many cases, the Slipstreams were single lines while others branched out; in some cases even the branches had branches, all connecting the systems all across the galaxy.

One slipstream glowed brighter than the rest. It was the route connecting Orso to Odin.

"With the collapse of the Slip connecting Odin and Orso," Tan continued, "we've eliminated one path the Swarm could have used to enter the Galactic Home Systems. But this, unfortunately, has made us, Orso, a pinch point for the Swarm invasion."

Another grunt sounded from the seat opposite Tenilo.

King Orson turned his attention to the royal couple from Odin. "Is there a problem, King Wulfrick?"

Tan discretely leaned back in his seat, effectively giving his King the floor.

"By the stars, you know there is," Wulfrick replied. "My world has been abandoned. That's a problem, Orson."

The room went quiet as the assembly watched the two kings. Tudor stared at Orson, snorted in derision and continued, "On top of that, we don't even know for sure that collapsing the Slipstream—which was hastily done and without my approval—will have any effect on the Swarm movements at all. It's long been thought that they could have their own FTL travel technology."

King Orson shook his head. "Forgive me, your grace, but that subject is beyond the scope of this meeting and will be discussed at another time. The representatives of the Sovereign Worlds chose to do what they felt was best for all of humanity. Nothing was decided behind your back, I can assure you."

Tudor glared at Orson Lorne, his eyes half closed, his fury plain to see, but somehow he managed to control himself. He sat back in his seat and said nothing. The tension around the room eased, and Orson nodded.

Finally, after a long pause, Orson told Tan to continue, which he did, and things began to move quickly.

Tan showed the latest reports of Swarm attacks, as well as a status report on the building efforts on Freyja in the Sheratan System, where, only two months earlier, Prince Elio had established an alliance with the Free People of Freyja.

The report didn't exactly inspire hope, but it wasn't all doom and gloom, either. The Swarm was growing, both in numbers and strength, and they were adapting. Still, no one knew where they came from, only that they came from another reality and were hell-bent on destroying humanity. All efforts to communicate with the aliens, except for two short conversations, had failed and had resulted in instant aggression.

Tenilo, bored by the technicalities, stopped listening and his thoughts drifted to Elio and the two conversations he, Elio and Richard Morian, had had with the *grays* shortly after first contact. To Tenilo's knowledge, those were the only times any alien chose to communicate with a human, and only when they were dying. Tenilo made a mental note to ask Elio about those conversations again. *Perhaps there's something we've overlooked.*

It was at that moment that Elio looked across the table at Tenilo and nudged him with his Psy.

Knocked out of his train of thought, Tenilo looked around, realizing that all eyes were now on him and the holographic map had disappeared.

Tenilo's mouth fell open and he started to stammer.

Your message, Elio whispered in Tenilo's mind. *You're supposed to give the royal message now.*

"Mister Barum," Tan said a bit impatiently. "Did you hear me? What message do you have from Alastor System?"

"I... I..." Tenilo mumbled. *Oh hell. Get a hold of yourself, Tenny.*

"Of course, my apologies," he said loudly, rather a little too loudly. "King Felder of Alastor and the esteemed Prince Padric wish all to know that the Alastor System and the coalition of Sovereign Systems of the Galactic Far East pledge their ongoing support in the conflict against the Swarm. Our resources and the full might of our military are at your disposal."

Once again, King Wulfrick Tudor grunted, drawing attention to himself. "Hah! How gracious of the Easterners to offer their help."

King Orson put his finger to one temple, massaging it, obviously frustrated by the king of the Odin System.

But Tudor and his wife were both staring at Tenilo.

"Of... of course we want to help," Tenilo said softly. "This is about the defense of all humanity."

Tudor slammed a fist on the arm of his chair. "And what has Eastern help done for us so far? My system is in ruins while your worlds prosper."

Tenilo opened his mouth to respond, but he hesitated. What was he supposed to say to this?

And then he felt a mind probing his. Not the familiar Psy of Elio. Tenilo, caught off guard, looked around the room. Someone was probing his mind; he was sure of it. But, if not Elio, then who?

Prince Elio leaned forward and said, "The Alastor System has been incredibly helpful, King Wulfrick, as have all the systems in the Galactic East. You're just bitter because the Swarm chose your sector of the Known Systems to begin their invasion, and understandably so. But, Your Grace, it cannot be helped, and you can rest assured that the Sovereign worlds will do all they can to restore your kingdom."

Wulfrick folded his arms in front of him, as if he was a small child pouting because he didn't get his way.

Tenilo decided to jump in and defend his world. "Your Grace," he said kindly. "I am deeply troubled by the fall of your home world, as is my king. Odin is a bright gem among the Known Systems—"

Queen Zara Tudor rose to her feet, her hands balled into fists resting on the tabletop, her face red with fury. "Fall?" she snarled. "There was no fall! Odin was abandoned. You gave the system to the Swarm; that's what you did. Perhaps if we'd had a modicum of support from the systems east of Homeworld, things would have—"

"Enough!" King Orson's booming voice silenced everyone. "We achieve nothing by bickering like children. Zara, Wulfrick, control yourselves or I will have to ask you to leave."

Several of the people seated around the circle gasped at the way Orson spoke to his fellow royals, but it had the intended effect. Zara sat slowly down, her teeth clenched.

Wulfrick leaned back in his chair, lowered his chin and folded his arms.

Well, I would have liked an apology, Tenilo thought, *but I'll take it, whatever it is.*

"Mister Barum," King Orson said. "Please continue."

"Of course, Your Grace," Tenilo said, giving the king a slight nod. He glanced at Elio who was doing his best to hide a grin.

Tenilo cleared his throat and continued. "The very best engineers from all parts of Sovereign Space—east and west alike—have been working day and night to complete the final designs for the newest generation of USF warship: The Avenger Class, which we hope to begin building on Freyja within the month."

Prince Elio leaned forward in his seat, sending a Psy message to Tenilo: *Let me jump in here.*

Tenilo paused, then nodded.

"Avenger Class ships are designed from the ground up with just one purpose in mind: to fight and destroy the Swarm," the prince said, "using technology and strategies that have been field tested by brave USF officers."

Elio grinned, obviously very proud of the work both he and Tenilo had put into the project.

Tenilo spoke up once again. "That's true. Thank you, my prince. Extensive resources from my home system and others in the Eastern Coalition are being funneled into the project. And, I have been given permission to offer the personal assurances of King Felder of the Alastor System, that a full-scale mobilization of all USF resources in the sector will be brought to bear against our common enemy. Humanity cannot be allowed to fall."

The King of Odin, still scowling, raised a hand, calling for the attention of everyone in the room. "That's all well and good, Mister Tenilo, but what of the worlds that have already... *fallen?*" he spat the last word as if it were a nasty taste in his mouth.

Tenilo bowed his head to the king, summoning every gram of grace he possessed and said, "Then, Your Grace, we will take the fight to the Swarm. We will push them back to whatever infernal dimension they call home. We won't rest until every world ever touched by human feet is reclaimed and rebuilt. That, Your Majesty, is the solemn promise of the Alastor System."

King Tudor stared at him for a long moment. His expression softened a little and he nodded his thanks.

Tenilo leaned back, now happy for the luxurious chair to swallow him up.

More was said, but Tenilo barely paid attention. When King Orson Lorne called the meeting to an end, he was glad to leave, looking forward to returning to his office on the opposite side of the palace to continue his work.

The datapad on his left arm buzzed. He glanced at the screen. It was a message from Elio.

Meet me in my suite.

Tenilo smiled and changed direction, striding down a side hallway to the north side of the palace where Elio had his suite of rooms. He was looking forward to chatting with his friend.

Chapter Two

Orso Royal Palace

Elio's Suite

My stars, *what a day*, Elio thought once he was back in his own suite. All the excitement had made him anxious and... a little hot.

"Dinka 2.0," he called to his upgraded robot. He couldn't part with the name of his late robot. Everything about his new one was the same, except for the voice which was maybe an octave higher. He told himself it gave the robot its own personality, so he couldn't bring himself to change it.

The robot awoke, engaged its grav-drive and came silently to his side as he flopped down on this plush sofa, sinking into it.

"Yes, my prince?"

"Set the thermostat to 21.7 degrees Celsius, please."

"As you wish, Your Highness." Dinka 2.0 bowed slightly and did what was asked of him.

Elio sighed as he instantly felt the air cool. And all was well again. He was getting better at these political engagements, but he'd never be a Felder, nor did he want to be. He was growing into himself, and he hoped that his mother would be proud of the man he'd become.

The door slid open and Tenilo strode in, tapping his datapad. "Sorry to keep you waiting, my prince."

"Not a problem," Elio said, shaking his head.

"I was just analyzing the footage again," Tenilo said distantly, his eyes locked on the screen jacked into his forearm.

Elio raised an eyebrow. "You were granted access?"

"Courtesy of Ugo Tan. Ten hours only, then the footage will be wiped from my personal pad," he said, holding up his arm. "I thought it would just be handy to see again—how the bombs worked." He lowered his arm and walked over to Elio. "You know, we were able to disable our own Slip points. Maybe we'll be able to disable the Swarm's using the same technology."

Elio smiled and gestured for him to sit with him.

Tenilo plopped down beside him. "It's only a theory of mine," he said, shrugging. "I'd need to do some research, of course."

"You are a genius, Tenny, truly." Elio patted Tenilo's arm and smiled at him.

Tenilo smiled tentatively. "I try my best, my prince. Anything I can do to help defeat the Swarm." Tenilo sighed. "I fear the alien race is multiplying exponentially." His voice was grave.

"Yes," Elio said, nodding. "To that point, we must talk more about our latest endeavor, the Avenger Class Ships."

It was their hope that this project would be their saving grace. They had to advance, stay one step ahead of the Swarm.

"Oh, yes," Tenilo said, bobbing his head enthusiastically. "The officials at the meeting seemed to be open to some good news." He sighed after some thought. "Well, all except for *His Majesty* King Wulfrick." He said "His Majesty" with some bitterness.

"Ah, yes. Well, that's to be expected... I've been in contact with Captain Morian," Elio said, changing the subject. "He's informed me that the engineers and fabricators have all the updated stats on the original *Avenger* so that her new and upgraded sisters," Elio said and laughed, "can match her order. The biggest being the installation of Big Charlie's and the latest version of the 88 and 120mm railguns." He paused, tapping his finger against his chin. "Oh! And the new-and-improved torpedoes as well... Mark 99s, I believe they're calling them."

"How exciting," Tenilo said morbidly.

Elio shook his head, smiled, slapped his friend on the shoulder and said, "We will win, Tenny. We'll beat them."

Tenilo turned his head to look at him, returned the smile and said ruefully, "I hope you're right, my prince."

Elio could see the hope in Tenilo's eyes. Hope that they would take back their Systems, their dignity, their lives... Elio closed his eyes and said a silent prayer to the heavens that, in time, they would indeed be able to do all of that. The vision that the dying alien had shown him so many months ago as fresh in his brain as ever, and he couldn't let it come true. *I mustn't.* Elio, his eyes still closed, was deep in thought, his fists clenched.

"Are you all right, my prince?" Tenilo asked, furrowing his eyebrows.

Elio relaxed, allowing the blood flow to return to his hands.

Dinka 2.0 heard the concern in Tenilo's voice and floated over. "Would you like a body diagnostic scan, my prince?" he asked.

"No, I'm quite all right. Thank you."

The robot bowed slightly, then turned and floated away. It was at that moment that Elio received a message on his datapad. *Elio, we need help ASAP! The Swarm—*

He paused the message.

Tenilo saw Elio's face. "Are you sure you're all right?"

Elio, pale as a ghost, nodded. The message was from Kyne Minnah, his long-time hacker friend.

"My friend on the planet Typhon needs help," he said.

Tenilo's mouth dropped open. "Typhon?" he asked, shaking his head. "That planet is out on the Rim, deep in Swarm Space." He shuddered involuntarily.

"I know," Elio replied. "Watch." He played the rest of the message, and they watched the holo together.

Chapter Three

Field Test

Swarm Space

"You are a go for launch, Ranger Squadron."

"Copy that," Danis Morian replied as the hangar doors opened. She touched the screen on the panel where once the armrest had been, increasing power to the grav-engines. The F32A Mark 3 fighter lifted off the hangar floor. Danis enjoyed the feeling of the adrenaline rush coursing through her body as she rocketed out into the blackness of space, disengaged the gravs and engaged the fusion engines.

Lt. Commander Danis Morian, Ranger Squadron commander, was forty-three, almost two meters tall, dark-skinned with green eyes and raven-black hair, and was Commodore Richard Morian's twin sister, younger than her brother by four minutes.

"Take the lead, Joker," she said. *What the hell...* she

thought, *he needs the experience.* Gian was doing well with his training, and moments like these only made him better.

"Copy that, Domino," Gian said. She could hear that he tried to conceal the shock in his voice.

"I think I hear someone cryin'. Is that you, Joker?" Jackknife teased him. He was half a kilometer away on Danis's port side.

"Keep it quiet," Danis ordered. "It's not too late to take that Visa back, Jack," she said, more to herself than to Jackknife.

"Copy," Gian said, stifling a laugh.

After a moment, Jackknife said, "Yes, ma'am."

"Ahhhh." A sigh came from the co-pilot's seat behind her.

Up until then, Danis had willed herself to forget he was back there.

"If I'd known there'd be so much commentary, I'd have stayed aboard the *Avenger*," Grell Dunn said, adjusting the straps of his harness. "I'm here for action, not drama," he said with a huff.

Danis rolled her eyes.

"Approaching the asteroid cluster," Gian announced. "Stay alert."

Pieces of rock—some many kilometers in diameter, others tiny like pebbles—were scattered across the blackness of space. A globular cluster more than a million kilometers in circumference.

Danis was adjusting her velocity, slowing down, when her proximity alerts sounded.

Jackknife had already streaked away. He knew.

"Incoming," Gian yelled into the comms. "Three enemy craft. Port. Vector three-seven-zero."

"I've got this one." Jackknife went for the one farthest

away. His copilot, Skyla, used her TK to force the Swarmie ship into an asteroid.

"Nice work," Danis said. "Watch Joker's six."

"You got it, boss," Jackknife said.

Danis's fingers fluttered over the screen. The ship's inertia dampeners enfolded her and Dunn as the F32's engines went to full power. Her fingers danced over the screen as she hurtled through the asteroid cluster.

She could hear Dunn breathing. She glanced at the diagnostic readout. His heart rate was increasing. He sounded like he was hyperventilating, then he heaved.

Oh, for stars' sake, please don't let this man throw up! She knew Dunn lacked the capacity to sit with the vomit even for a few minutes... He'd panic, take off his *helmet.* Then she'd be left with a medical emergency and a mess in her fighter.

Well, that's one way to get him sent back home in a hurry... She quickly pushed the thought away. Focusing right now was critical. She got a lock on her target and waited for the right moment to fire... Nine seconds later her fighter's railguns fired twin streams of 50-caliber dutrinium projectiles. The enemy craft exploded in a blaze of blue fire.

She looked at her screens. *Where the hell is Gian?*

"Ranger one to Joker. Come back."

"Joker here," Gian replied.

"Where are you?"

"Right behind you, Ranger Leader." Danis could almost see the smile on his face.

"Did you get him?" she asked.

"You betcha," he replied. "How about you, Jacko?"

"What d'you think, funny man? All clear, Domino."

"No, we're not," Danis snapped. "Incoming, behind

you. Vector one-three-nine. Three enemy craft. *Watch out, Gian!*"

She glanced quickly at her targeting screen. It turned red, flashing. The three enemy craft to the rear were already within weapons range and she knew a targeting lock was imminent. She flipped her fuselage, then did a one-eighty roll, shut down her upper starboard engine and poured on the power to the other three engines. The F32 rocketed away in a terrifying, spiraling turn, increasing its speed to a blistering Mach 32. The second she hit the throttles, the fighter's inertia dampeners enfolded her and Dunn and, for the most part, negated the crushing G-forces generated by the tremendous acceleration and the spiral turn.

She brought the upper starboard engine back online. The enemy craft was still chasing her but losing ground.

Her cockpit and weapons systems were now facing the enemy. She brought her targeting systems online, reversed her engines, slowed her speed and waited.

She didn't have to wait long. The blue ship closed the distance between them rapidly.

She smiled. "Gotcha, you bastard," she muttered as her targeting systems turned green.

She tapped the firing button and two Mark-7 Harpoon missiles streaked away and were rapidly lost in the distance, but only for a second, until they both impacted the Swarm fighter. It instantly exploded in a blinding ball of cobalt blue fire.

She grinned to herself and, not realizing she was on an open channel, said out loud, "Nice one, Domino. One down, two to go."

"You took your time, didn't you, Domino," Jackknife said. "We took our two out hours ago. We've been watching you. What took you so long?"

But before she could answer, a transmission came over her comms.

"Avenger to Ranger One. This is tactical. Do you copy?"

"Ranger One," Danis said, "all clear."

"Very well. You're cleared for landing in... seven minutes."

"Copy that. Domino out!"

She'd expected more activity, but the asteroid cluster was clear. It was time to go home.

"Back to *Avenger*, guys," she said, "and well done."

As they turned to head back, Danis tried to use her Psy to calm Dunn's mind... She did not want to have to clean up whatever it was he'd had to eat that day. *Not on my chron,* she thought savagely.

* * *

"Take it easy, why don't you!" Dunn's voice was more annoying than the high shrill of an overly demanding, in-need-of-an-update AI robot. "You're comin' in way too hot." He groaned dramatically. It was clear to Danis that her Psy hadn't done much to curb his complaining, or his temper, much to her chagrin.

"Just sit tight," she said as she glided the F32 into the hangar bay and settled it gently on the minodutrinium deck.

Jackknife came in even faster, his F32A turning on its axis as it floated at high speed across the hangar to land neatly in its designated spot. Gian, somewhat slower than Jackknife, tried to emulate the veteran pilot but with a notable lack of success.

Danis bit her tongue, not wanting to say anything to her newbie co-pilot as she climbed down the ladder.

He's not worth it, she thought. *Remain calm. Focus on your breathing.* She tapped her datapad. Her heart rate was starting to slow as she'd hoped. *Ninety-two beats per minute and decreasing...* She took off her helmet and watched as Dunn descended the ladder. He took his sweet time, moving slower than pre-Purge net speed. *Does this man have any sense of urgency about him at all?*

Finally, Dunn was on the deck, stumbling toward her. He stopped in front of her, struggled with his helmet until he was able to tug it off. A thick tuft of red hair sat atop his head. He was fifty-two, but his features and disposition made him look much older. And not in a good way. His face was heavily jowled, his skin blotchy. On the bright side, though, he didn't look as if he was about to puke.

"For goodness' sake, woman!" he yelled in between gasps. He had the audacity to get in her face. "How long exactly have you been flying?"

Danis could feel her blood begin to boil, but she didn't flinch. *How dare he ask such a question? I'm the leader of this squadron, dammit!*

Danis's piercing blue eyes glittered. She didn't give him the answer he wanted. "Long enough to throw you off my ship." Her voice was stern with a sharp edge to it. She didn't back away. Instead, she drew herself up to her full height and glared down at him.

By then, Gian had disembarked and was standing at the foot of the ladder, watching, a half-smile on his lips.

Dunn snorted. "Ha! Not likely. You know that's not going to happen as well as I do."

And he was right. And she knew it. He was there ostensibly because of his TK abilities, which she considered mediocre at best. The real reason, though, was because he was related to the Holder family. That's "The" Holder family. His ancestor was Mark Holder, the inventor of the Slipstream Drive.

Grell Dunn, Danis assumed, made his money by means of nepotism and an endless stream of trust fund money. His family, however, had made their money in the tech industry and planet development. And they'd invested a large sum of money into "Operation Freyja," which mostly entailed the recommissioning of the shipyards on said planet.

Dunn was there, on *Avenger*, to "find himself." For him, it was a voyage of discovery. At least that's what his family said. "It will be a wonderful experience for him," his mother and older sister had said at the introductory holo meeting. And of course, Captain Morian couldn't say no. They were a huge benefactor and Dunn did, after all, have abilities, of sorts.

Maybe they wanted to be rid of him just as much as I do right now, Danis thought, then she took a deep, soothing breath. "Mr. Dunn," she said in her most professional tone, "please go to your quarters. Thank you."

Dunn blinked a few times, then walked away, muttering to himself.

Danis walked over to Gian, shaking her head. He gave her a sympathetic look. "That guy's something else, Domino."

"You're tellin' me..." she said. She was going to say something else but was distracted by Jackknife. He jumped down from the USF-regulated fighter. His own ancient Veridian Mark 9 fighter was undergoing an extensive overhaul.

There was something about Jackknife that Danis found alluring... He was a giant of a man, mysterious, rough around the edges, and had a give-it-to-you-straight, no-

nonsense attitude. He also had the Sight, though he'd never admit it.

Jackknife's co-pilot, Skyla, hopped out of the fighter behind him. The girl, just a year or two older than Gian's friend, Andra Graynir, had been flying with Jackknife for several months.

She pretended to stumble so he could catch her and hold her up. She was much too graceful for that.

"Thanks, partner," she said with a giggle, her wavy brown hair still tied up perfectly in a USF regulation top knot. She didn't look drained from the Swarm encounter; her caramel skin glowed.

She was from the Alastor System, and while her flying was good, her stats were even better. "She's one of the best we have," Prince Felder had said. And Skyla wanted to be with the best. Her TK abilities were good, too. *Seems to me like she just wants to screw around with*—Danis's thoughts were interrupted.

"Um," Gian said. He tapped her shoulder. "Avenger to Commander Morian... You all right?"

"Uh, yes," she said, her eyes still glued to the pair.

Gian sighed. "Any word about Andra? I miss her."

Danis turned to Gian at the mention of their friend. "She'll be here soon," she said. "Elio's expediting the process. If only I had that advantage with the Academy." It came out a bit more harshly than she'd intended, but Gian didn't seem to notice.

"Anything else, Gian," she said. "No? Good. I have things I need to do." And she turned and quickly left the hangar. She was done watching Jackknife flirting and she didn't want to hear about Gian's budding relationship. *What's wrong with me?* she wondered as she hurried down the hall. *Get a grip, Danis!*

* * *

On the command bridge, Commodore Richard Morian, captain of the *Avenger,* paced back and forth along the rail as the ship made her way towards another Swarm cluster. Manda Haal, his first officer, had been using her Sight to place *Avenger* in the most advantageous, strategic locations. Her recently discovered talent was proving to be invaluable.

"Lieutenant Fargo?" Morian called to his chief weapons officer.

"Yes, Captain?" Corin Fargo was a soft-spoken woman, but she wasn't meek. She did her job, and she did it well. The freckles scattered across the left side of her face gave her character.

"What's our status on the T-torpedoes?"

She checked. "Eighty-nine percent, sir," she replied.

"T" stood for training. They were Tenilo's brilliant idea: the T-torpedoes, like the railguns, were kinetic weapons designed to destroy or disable multiple enemy ships per missile. Like Big Charlie, they carried warheads designed to explode and scatter eighty-eight-millimeter solid dutrinium orbs over a wide area. The official designation for them was still to be determined, though he'd heard through the grapevine that it was to be M99.

"Very well, Lieutenant. Let's see what they can do in real-time, shall we?"

"Aye, Captain," Fargo replied and turned back to her console. The testing of the new weapons systems was, after all, the reason why they were there in Swarm Space.

Morian stood at the rail, his first officer, Manda Haal, beside him, and together they stared at the giant, globular hologram generated on the well deck just in front of and below the command rail. It was showing a one-million-kilometer-diameter global view of the surrounding space. The view included *Avenger's* avatar in green and the individual Swarm ships in blue. The cluster of sixty-seven blue ships was ranged at thirteen-hundred and two kilometers off the port bow at vector 341.

"Come to three-four-one, Mr. Sen," Morian said, both hands on the rail, gripping it tightly.

"Aye, Captain. Three-four-one it is."

"Load forward tubes one through four, Ms. Fargo, "and nine through eighteen and prepare to fire," Morian said, concentrating on the hologram.

"One through four and tubes nine through eighteen it is, Captain."

"Distance to target, Mr. DeLong?"

"Eleven hundred kilometers and closing, Captain," DeLong, *Avenger's* chief navigation officer, replied.

Morian glanced up at the forward screens. The distance was still too great to see the cluster.

"Morian to Domino. Stand by to launch fighters."

"Aye, Captain," Danis replied over the comms. "Ranger Squadron standing by."

"Shields up, Mr. Kingston."

"Shields at one hundred percent," the senior tactical officer replied.

"Point defense turrets one through thirty-two stand by," Morian said.

"Acknowledged, Captain," Fargo said calmly.

"Increase speed to Mach 10, Mr. Sen."

"Aye, Captain."

Morian felt the ship surge slightly as the ship's inertia dampeners engaged and the six fusion engines increased power momentarily and then eased off again.

The view on the forward screen changed as the cluster suddenly appeared and quickly grew larger.

"Reverse thrust!" Morian snapped. "Reduce peed to Mach 1."

Again, the ship surged and slowed almost instantly as the six giant engines reversed thrust.

Avenger was now almost at the center of the cluster. Morian could see them spread out across the holo display and on all seven view screens. The ship was surrounded, and she was already taking fire.

"Fire forward tubes, Ms. Fargo," he ordered. "Bring point defense online."

"Aye, Captain."

The great ship shuddered as all forty-eight point defense railguns opened fire in unison.

Morian and the crew on the command deck watched four of the new torpedoes streak out of the forward tubes. Less than ten seconds later all four warheads exploded at their preset proximities shooting twenty-four, 88mm laser - guided projectiles into the heart of the enemy cluster.

Morian smiled. The crew broke into cheers as they watched nine of the blue ships explode in balls of brilliant blue fire and four more drift away disabled, their blue halos fading away to nothing.

Morian nodded, smiling grimly. "Belay point defense. Fire tubes nine through eighteen. Reload tubes one through four."

Again, he gripped the rail and watched as ten more torpedoes streaked away—five to port and five to starboard—and enemy ships in every direction began to explode. *Tenny,* he thought, *you are a genius!*

Twelve more Swarm ships exploded and five more were

disabled. The remaining Swarm ships quickly destroyed the disabled craft then turned tail and ran.

In all, counting the nine disabled ships, now no more than clouds of gray dust floating in space, the new torpedoes had destroyed thirty enemy craft. The exercise had been a resounding success.

"Excellent," Morian whispered. "Just... excellent. Morian to Domino. Stand down, Danis. You won't be needed."

"Copy that, brother. How did it go?"

"It went well. We'll talk later."

He turned to his first officer, Manda Haal, and said, "That was something to watch, don't you think?"

"It was," she replied. "But a little disappointing."

"How so, Commander?" he asked, puzzled.

"We launched fourteen of the new torpedoes. I counted thirty Swarmies either destroyed or disabled. At least three of them was taken out by point defense. That means the T's accounted for twenty-seven... which is only one-point-nine-three per torpedo. Good, but not outstanding. Big Charlie does better for a fraction of the cost."

"Hmm... yes... well, if you put it like that..." Morian said.

"May I speak freely, Captain?" Morian's XO, Lt. Commander Michael Jadern, had come up from the well deck and was standing at the rail next to him on his left side.

"Of course, Michael." Morian couldn't help but smile. He thought of Jadern as a younger brother, an officer he could count on to do things by the book.

"I think the experiment went well, sir," he said, sounding almost apologetic. "There may be an end in sight."

We will exterminate all sentient life in this universe.

Morian recalled what the alien had shown him with Psy

nearly twenty months ago. It filled him with dread. The thought passed, and the expression on his face remained stoic as he watched the holo display.

"I'm afraid this war is far from over, my friend." He turned to Jadern with a hint of a smile. "This was but a small victory and, yes, the experiment did indeed go well."

Morian could tell that Jadern's spirits were high. He reached out with his Psy and scanned the well deck; everyone was in good spirits, and that was always a plus.

"The enemy cluster has retreated, Captain," Kingston called out.

Morian surveyed the holo. Kingston was right. They were gone. All of them.

"What's the status of the T-torpedoes, please, Ms. Fargo?" Morian asked, placing his hands behind his back.

"Eighty-one percent, sir."

"Very good. Take us home, Mr. Sen," Morian said, letting out a heavy sigh.

"Aye, aye, Captain," Haltar Sen replied, then looked up at Manda, expectantly.

She smiled shyly. She loved that the command crew, especially Sen, trusted her Sight. He had been the most skeptical when she first discovered her gift, but now...

She left the rail and took the six steps down onto the well deck, then stepped over to the helm.

"Do you have the route, Commander?" he asked and smiled. The glow of the screens and the small hologram hovering over his console gave a soft sheen to his olive skin.

"Hmm," she teased, tapping her index finger to her temple and closing her eyes. Then, serious but still smiling, she said, "Go to vector..." And she gave him the coordinates of the Slip gate. They arrived seven minutes later with pinpoint accuracy.

"Amazing," Sen whispered as he leaned back in his chair. "I'll never get over how you do that." He looked up at Manda in awe.

"It's a gift, I suppose." She averted her eyes. She never liked the attention to stay on her for too long. She wasn't used to it and thought she never would be.

Six more jumps and nine standard hours later, they were back home in the Orso system with minimal damage and zero casualties.

"Give me a ship wide channel, please, Ms. Lowry," Morian said as the ship docked at the orbital spaceport.

"You have it, Captain."

He raised his wrist, tapped the icon on his datapad and said, "Now hear this. This is the captain. We're home again. Well done, everyone. Except for the watch of the day, you have a forty-eight-hour pass. Enjoy yourselves, but don't do anything I wouldn't do. Morian out."

Chapter Four

Distant Signal

Orso System

The high of the earlier success was beginning to wear off. Morian's body and mind were tired. The necessity to always be on high alert had, by the end of the day, taken its toll. And his were long days. Long days of tension masked by a façade of calm. Long days made bearable with the help of protein bars and caffeine tabs.

Back in his cabin, he took a hydro and then checked his chron: it was after eleven standard time. He'd been up and working for more than nineteen hours with little rest or food. *Two hours of sleep should do it*, he thought wearily. *Haal and Jadern can handle it for now.* He lay down on his bunk, turned on the audio sleep aid, closed his eyes and, within seconds, was sound asleep.

Barely twenty minutes later his dreams were invaded by his sister's thoughts. His Psy link with her was strong.

She was rushing along the hall toward his cabin. Her thoughts were a jumbled mess of confusion and frustration. He caught a glimpse of Jackknife's face, and Gian's, but the strongest emotions she was emitting were anger and contempt, and those feelings were all aimed at Grell Dunn. It was... as if her thoughts were tinted red.

Whoa, sis... He sent his thoughts to her as he sat up on the bunk, turned on the light, then swung his feet to the floor but remained sitting on the edge of the bunk. *Take a breath, Danis.*

His attempt at calming her didn't work, and moments later, the double-paneled, opaque sturmglass doors slid open.

"I want him out," Danis shouted as she stormed into his sleep center. "He's got to go! Grell has to go!"

Sister or not, she was ignoring all military protocols: no request to be admitted to his quarters. No "May I speak freely, Captain?" No standing at attention. She just needed her brother to hear her out. At that moment, she didn't give a toss about his rank or protocol. After all, who else did she have to talk to about such things?

Morian rubbed his eyes with his right hand, then slowly lowered it to his chin. He stared up at her, massaged his jaw muscles, then said wearily, "Danis, we've gone over this before. You know why he's here. We're still field testing the use of the emerging special abilities." He dropped his hand into his lap. "He's a TK, and we have to know how effective those abilities are, and will be, during battle."

Danis laughed mirthlessly. "He's a civilian who wanted to come aboard the *Avenger* to check it off his bucket list."

She stepped closer to him. "Richard, *Avenger* was going to be put into retirement... But now, after what she's accomplished during the last twenty months, new ships are being designed in her image." She spread her arms wide to emphasize her point. "This ship has become a celebrity in its own right. Everyone across the far reaches of the galaxy wants to be a part of her. That's what this is all about. Dunn is disruptive, disobedient, disrespectful and... and... he's an idiot."

Morian didn't answer. He just watched her as she made her case. Inwardly, he was smiling, recognizing they were more similar than she realized. They had the same prominent cheekbones and full lips, the same dark skin. He was older than his sister by four minutes, and he never let her forget it, always in jest, of course. It was as if he was watching a blue-eyed, female version of himself having a tantrum.

"He's not helping the cause," she snapped. "Ugh!" She spun a full three-sixty on her heels in frustration, put her balled fists on her waist, and stared down at him. Then she must have suddenly realized she was ranting at a fleet commodore...

She sighed, closed her eyes for a second or two, took a deep breath, opened them again and said, "I apologize, Captain, but you know I'm right. He's used his TK only once during this entire assignment, and I had to help him finish off the enemy craft." She sighed. "Sir..." she added.

"I've seen his stats," he said. "His ability is new to him. He needs time and practice to develop it, as did we all. Look at Andra and Elio." Morian saw Danis flinch when he said Elio's name. She couldn't hide her feelings for the prince from him. Their telepathic bond was too strong. He knew her feelings for the prince were developing. He also knew she was confused by those feelings, and she knew that he knew. At times like those, they both wished they weren't such open books.

Danis tisked then said, "Those two are an exception. They were under extreme stress when their abilities emerged... So were we all, for that matter. I don't think Dunn's experienced any real hardship in his entire life, and he's not even trying to do better. He's been a thorn in my side from the moment he stepped off the shuttle. A constant complainer and he criticizes my every move." Danis crossed her arms. "Civilians with new-found abilities shouldn't be thrown into battle."

He nodded, his face pensive. "Well, maybe on our next trip for provisions, we can see what he says about it... but if he wants to stay, my hands are tied." He shrugged. "His being here can do a lot of good for the Freyja Operation. And I signed the contract between his family and the USF. As long as he doesn't endanger the crew, I can't just... send him away."

Morian's thoughts turned to Prince Felder and how desperately he'd wanted the young but enthusiastic prince off his ship... but he couldn't do anything about it. Having to deal with civilians, especially a prince, and an unknown enemy was a huge responsibility. Fortunately, it worked out for the best. Prince Felder had saved his life and his ship.

Danis nodded, feeling deflated and defeated. "Well, I'd better let you get some rest, Captain. Thank you for listening to me, brother."

Morian chuckled. "Oh, I'm wide awake now," he said. "I think it's time I went back to the bridge."

Danis nodded and turned on her heels, leaving him alone with his thoughts.

Morian sighed. His sister was troubled. But he knew she'd do what she had to do regardless of her problem co-pilot and her burgeoning feelings for prince Elio. She was, after all, one of the best fighter pilots in the entire USF.

* * *

Morian arrived back on the command deck to find the *Avenger* still traveling on the outer rim of the Orso System. They'd entered the system several minutes earlier and were only some ten-thousand kilometers in. The holo display revealed a fleet of more than eight hundred ships of various sizes and designations—giant Class-A super carriers, battleships, cruisers, frigates, destroyers and gunships—surrounding Orso's sun, a blue-white star some one-and-half times the mass of Sol. Not just ships from the Orso system, USF ships from across the Sovereign Systems. Orso's two slip gates were vulnerable, and so it was all hands on deck to keep the Swarm at bay.

As much as Morian wanted to be reassured by the fleet's presence, he couldn't shake the overwhelming feeling of uneasiness. The Swarm was a fluid entity and they were multiplying, almost exponentially, developing, improving, and he wasn't sure if humanity could keep up. They'd won battles, but as he'd told Jadern, the war was far from over. Everyone knew there was a confrontation coming—a cataclysmic clash between humankind and the alien race. But nobody knew when, not even the seers. Morian could feel it in his bones. The battle to end all battles could not be avoided, so it was essential that everyone stay on the alert, ever ready.

His datapad lit up and the nerve jack tingled in his forearm. It was a notification of an important message.

"Prince Elio requests a private meeting, Captain," Krista, the ship's AI, said over his personal comm. "As soon as possible, sir. He's waiting for you."

Morian walked briskly to his ready room and closed the door behind him.

What could it be that's so urgent? he wondered. He felt an uneasiness begin to crawl through his nervous system, an uneasiness that wasn't his own. Even though he was planet-side he could feel Elio's distress. Something was terribly wrong. Was the invasion coming sooner than anyone expected? He didn't know, but Elio's troubled thoughts that Morian could sense even from so far away seemed to confirm it.

He sat down at the large table, placed a halo on his head, and felt the familiar tingling of his nerve endings vibrating in his temples as he jacked into the meeting. He found himself seated at a table in a large, ornate conference room. He knew it was somewhere in the Orso Royal Palace, but he hadn't seen it before.

In the halo-generated meeting, Elio was sitting opposite him. Tenilo Barum was at his side.

"Captain Morian," Elio said, nodding his hello.

Tenilo smiled an obligatory smile.

"Hello, Captain. You look..." he trailed off. The captain looked fatigued. His eyes were bloodshot and heavy bags darkened the skin under his eyes. "You look... well," he said finally.

Tenilo also had Psy abilities. Not as great as Elio's, but he could sense an emotion and pick up on other people's thoughts if he needed to. He couldn't sense the captain's thoughts from where he was, some one-point-two billion kilometers from where they were seated, but he could see the look of concern on his face he also knew that the ending to this conversation was likely be an unfavorable one.

"Greetings, my prince, and to you, Mr. Tenilo," Morian said, resting his arms on the virtual table. "There's something urgent we need to discuss?" He directed the question to Elio.

* * *

Elio tried to hide his nervousness with a smile. He could feel Morian's skepticism, and he hadn't even said anything yet. "I have a mission for you." He tapped his fingers on the table, trying to figure out how to best continue. "The Typhonians have need of you." He looked at him earnestly.

Morian stared at him, bewildered. "I'm sorry, my prince. Did you say the Typhonians?"

Elio cringed. For one, he hated his title, but he knew that it was inevitable that people would use it, must use it. Two, he saw Richard's face. He didn't want his request to be shut down, so he knew he had to tell him about it quickly and assuage his fears.

"Yes, Richard, Typhon still stands. A friend of mine from New Hope has informed me there are survivors and that help is needed... I thought he was long dead." Elio felt guilty for not reaching out to his friend after the first wave of battles for Typhon. *Maybe if I'd reached out, contacted him sooner, we wouldn't be dealing with this now.*

Morian could tell by reading Elio's thoughts that his feelings were genuine and he felt sympathetic. But there were serious questions that had to be asked and answered.

"Are you sure this isn't a tBalto? Remember Clintok... how he fooled us."

Clintok, a member of the Free People of Freyja, had been stranded on an asteroid and had broadcast a distress signal. When the *Avenger* came to his rescue he pulled the poor-lone survivor act, and then tried to steal the ship's data logs with the intention of selling them to the IMFP, the Independent Militia of Free People.

Elio rubbed his chin. "No... Captain," he said. "I don't

think so." He turned and gestured to Tenilo. "Tenny and I have the original holo."

Morian pursed his lips. "Those can be fabricated."

"I believe I'm savvy enough to spot a fake," Elio said confidently. "Unless there's someone out there using advanced Swarm technology to produce a false hologram message, I'm sure what I saw was rea—"

"And precisely what did you see, son?" It was King Orson. He'd jacked into the virtual room.

Elio sucked in a breath. "Father..."

Tenilo looked back and forth between Elio and the king, like a trapped crabrat.

"I'm sorry, my prince," Tenilo couldn't quite look at Elio. "I forgot to tell you that His Majesty would be joining us."

"Don't fret, Tenny." Elio's voice was steady. He didn't want his father to see him stumble. "It's all right."

"Father," Elio said as he turned his head to look at the king, matching his unwavering stare. "I was just telling Captain Morian that there are survivors on Typhon."

Even before Elio had finished speaking, the king was vigorously shaking his head.

He glanced at Morian and acknowledged him. "Good day to you, Captain Morian. I'm sure you're extremely busy, so we won't be keeping you long. This meeting will be over shortly."

"And good day to you, Your Majesty," Morian replied with a respectful bow of his head. He knew that last statement by the king was his way of showing his authority over his son. Morian bit his lip and took a deep breath. He could tell by the angst Elio was emitting that he was prepared for another father-son power struggle, and he wondered who was going to win.

Elio was becoming a great speechmaker, persuasive in his arguments. He was also learning how to stand up to his father. He didn't have Sight, but he was one of the very few gifted with both Psy and TK. All of that being so, Morian felt that eventually, even if it was a long and arduous conversation, Elio would be able to persuade his father to do as he wished. The king, however, loved to assert his royal will. He was a stubborn man. *Elio's stubborn too, just like his father*, Morian thought, *but when it comes to doing the right thing, it's good to be unwavering, to stand your ground. We'll see...*

Elio looked at Morian and nodded slightly. Even though Morian wasn't actively reaching out to Elio with Psy, the prince appeared to get the message.

Elio turned to face the king. He had to win this argument. "Father, the USF fleet in the Persei System is severely depleted, barely holding their own."

"No, son. It's too risky." The king sounded resolute. "There are far too many ways a rescue mission could go wrong. The USF must remain focused on the inner Sovereign Systems."

"I don't need the whole fleet, just the *Avenger*," Elio said.

"The *Avenger* is otherwise occupied, testing new weapons. We need all her resources here, to protect the systems we know have survived."

Elio's eyes widened. "I *know* for a fact there are survivors on Typhon; in New Hope... We must go to their aid. We can't leave a single human behind."

The king slammed his fist down against the table like a gavel. "Absolutely not," he shouted. "I will *not* allow it. The *Avenger*... No ship in the USF fleet will venture into

Swarm Space without my express permission. Do you understand, Elio?"

Elio clenched his teeth, ready to deliver a stinging retort, but then his father's face turned red and his eyes bulged. Elio thought the king was about to explode with anger, but he didn't. He staggered, clutched desperately at his throat, gasping for air.

Before Elio could take a step forward to help him, the King's avatar disappeared from the virtual room.

Elio stood still, staring at the empty space his father's avatar had occupied.

Tenilo looked helplessly at Morian. Morian could do no more than raise his eyebrows in alarm. Something was very wrong.

"My apologies, Captain," Elio said in a low voice. "I'm afraid you'll have to excuse us, for now." Then he looked at Tenilo, and they both hastily removed their halos and left the meeting.

* * *

Morian was left alone, concerned about the king's condition, anxious about the possible mission, and... exhausted.

He removed his halo and returned to reality. He was tempted to stay there in the conference room and sleep, but with high rank comes great responsibility. *Things to do...* he thought. *The laundry list never ends.*

* * *

Back at the palace, Elio and Tenilo were running through the maze of adjoining hallways, their shoes slapping against the marble tiles. Elio's face... panic-stBaltoen. He and the king had had their disagreements, but Elio would never wish for anything bad to happen to his father. The king's death would bring great grief and newfound responsibility... Elio would become the King of Orso. And Tenilo knew that Elio wasn't ready for the weight of the crown. Elio wanted to make a difference in his own way, by using his abilities and hacker skills to defeat the Swarm.

Tenilo pushed his grim thoughts about the king's possible demise out of his mind. He didn't want Elio to read his thoughts and think ill of him. So he focused, engaged his Psy and was able to detect the thoughts of a nurse, a member of the royal medical staff.

Keep him steady... Hold up his head. He needs to be sedated.

Tenilo felt a rush of relief. He grabbed Elio's arm. "The king's alive, my prince. He's in the infirmary. He's being sedated."

Elio looked confused, but Tenilo could sense the prince's mind and knew he was receiving the same thoughts as he was. Now that they knew where he was, they quickened their pace.

Jenson Myster, the lord physician, head of the king's personal medical team, was waiting for them at the infirmary. He bowed slightly as the prince and Tenilo approached.

"What happened to my father?" Elio asked. "Has he had a heart attack?" It was unlikely. No one in the Sovereign Systems had had a heart attack in almost three hundred standard years. Illnesses and diseases of the heart and vascular system had become a thing of the past due to diet, evolution, and medical advances.

"We're not yet sure, Your Highness," Dr. Myster said

and glanced at his datapad. "But it appears his nervous system was on the verge of shutting down."

Elio paled as he saw the group of nurses gathered around his father.

"How... How is he?" Elio asked.

"He's stable, but his condition is critical," Dr. Myster replied.

Elio looked at him, then back toward his father.

"We got to him just in time and had to sedate him quickly. Had we not, he would have... died." The doctor avoided making eye contact with Elio. "Was it is, he's in an induced coma and we're still running tests."

Elio shook the doctor's hand graciously. "Thank you, Jenson," he said, then took a deep breath, closed his eyes and then quickly opened them again. His mind was in a whirl. He closed it, blocking any attempt to read his mind. He stiffened his back, bit his upper lip, looked at Tenilo, and then at Myster.

"When will you know something, Doctor?"

Dr. Myster shrugged, made a face and said, "I honestly don't know, Your Highness. I've never seen anything quite like it. The king's condition is a mystery. As I said, we're running a battery of tests. We'll just have to wait for the results. Why don't you go back to your quarters? There's nothing you can do here. I'll send for you as soon as we know something."

Elio nodded, thanked him and... his datapad flashed green. "We must go, Tenny," he said. "I've been called to another meeting."

* * *

The holo message Elio received was from Duke Rutta, and he looked a little too happy, considering the circumstances. He wanted a private meeting with Elio, and he also wanted a meeting of the royals.

Elio, however, wasn't in the mood for the duke's blathering, so he ignored the invitation. He did, however, call for Dinka 2.0. If Elio was to assume the mantle of regent, he had to stay one step ahead of Rutta.

"Yes, Prince Elio?" the robot responded quickly.

"Send a formal message to all the dukes and marshals of Orso. Inform them they are to attend a royal briefing in one hour, and that all are expected to be present."

An hour later Elio jacked into the meeting to find the virtual room packed with dignitaries, including Duke Rutta, sour-faced that he'd been preempted.

Elio called the meeting to order, read through his preprepared preamble and was about to speak when Duke Rutta held up a finger and said, "May I speak, my prince?"

Elio knew if he was to maintain control of the meeting and take over while his father was disabled, he had to remain calm, hold his temper in check. "You have the floor, Duke Rutta."

The duke cleared his throat. "I wanted to bring this up with you privately, but now is best, I suppose." He looked around the room, then back at Elio. "I'm more than happy to take your place as regent, my prince."

The dukes and marshals around the room gasped. Elio had not yet told them about his father's situation.

"I know... We all know," Duke Rutta said and waved his hand in a sweeping gesture, "that you prefer to stay away from..." He paused and looked directly at Elio. "Shall we say, the political loop." The angelic smile on his face could not cover the venomous, patronizing words he spat.

"I assure you, sir." Elio held his gaze. "I'm completely willing and capable of holding the position of regent while my father is incapacitated." He paused, then continued, "It appears my father has suffered some sort of attack to his nervous system. He is presently in the infirmary under sedation and will remain so until his doctors can determine the full nature of the attack. In the meantime, until he is well enough to return to his duties, I will, of course, assume the mantle of regent. This is not up for discussion. Any questions?" He looked around the room. There were none, though there were some unhappy faces at the table.

"Good," Elio said. "Item number two. I have received a communique with critical intel from Typhon in the Persei System. It appears there are survivors. It is, therefore, my intention to send the *Avenger* under the command of Commodore Morian to Typhon to investigate the situation there and pick up any survivors."

"But Typhon is in the middle of Swarm-controlled space," Marshal Crandon snapped.

Elio raised an eyebrow. "All the more reason to go," he said firmly. "We cannot leave them to the Swarm." He turned to look at Marshal Ugo Tan and said, "I have decided. As regent, I intend to order the *Avenger* to Typhon."

Ugo didn't say anything. His face was a blank slate. He knew the prince, as regent, had the right to make that decision. But Tenilo, reaching out with his Psy, knew that Tan wasn't happy about it. He also knew that when Elio had made up his mind about something, there was no convincing him otherwise.

"Mr. Tenilo?" Duke Rutta addressed him directly.

"Yes, my lord," he replied, leaning closer to the table.

"I think it would be wise if you were to accompany

Commodore Morian aboard the *Avenger*. He may have need of your extensive knowledge and expertise."

There was something about the timber of Rutta's voice that Tenilo didn't like. The suggestion seemed... odd to him. "Thank you for the offer, my lord. But I think, considering this extraordinary turn of events, that my place is here," he said and looked at Elio, "with the prince."

Chapter Five

Flight Pattern

Orso system

It was five o'clock standard time when Captain Morian received a holo from Elio.

"The mission is confirmed, Commodore. I've received another message from Kyne Minnah on Typhon. He tells me the Swarm is evolving. There are now two types of Blues; what he calls Stompers and Stalkers. Apparently, the Stompers can regenerate. He has captured a Stomper energy... core. He also states that the Swarm now has a second-generation ship that carries a crew of nine. Richard, we need that tech. You are to make best speed to Typhon where you will confirm, or not, the presence of human survivors. If there are indeed survivors, you will pick them up and bring them back to Caerus. They have information and tech critical to the war effort. Understood?"

Morian could see the stress on Elio's face. Whatever

was going on at the palace with the king had him very worried, and for good reason.

"Understood, my prince. We'll do everything we can to find and rescue any survivors and bring them home."

Elio nodded and said, "I'll send you all the information I have. And I can't stress enough the urgency of this mission with regard to the survival of all humanity. Good luck to you, my friend. May God be with you."

"And to you, my prince," Morian said. "And, on behalf of myself and everyone onboard the *Avenger*, we hope the king makes a speedy recovery."

"Thank you," Elio said, bowing his head. "By the stars, I hope we have good news soon."

The holo closed and Morian was once again alone in his ready room.

Even though he'd heard the king forbid the expedition, as soon as he'd received the news that the king was incapacitated, and knowing Elio as he did, he'd already begun to make preparations. The ship had been rearmed and reprovisioned. The crew had been put on high alert, and all leave had been canceled. The *Avenger* was ready to depart at a moment's notice.

"Krista," he said.

"Yes, Captain," the ship's AI replied. "What can I do for you?"

"Alert the crew and have the ship brought to readiness. We leave for Typhon at nine o'clock standard."

"Yes, Captain."

"Now hear this. Now hear this," Krista broadcast on the shipwide comm. "All hands to stations. Secure the ship for imminent departure. Command crew report to the bridge. We leave for the planet Typhon at nine o'clock standard. Now hear this..." Krista repeated the message three times.

"Thank you, Krista," Morian muttered under his breath when she was done.

"My pleasure, Captain."

* * *

Dagon Jax, *Avenger's* senior shuttle pilot, was aft on the training deck, seated at the controls of the Type-C heavy cruiser flight simulator.

The Defender C-class heavy cruiser is a mighty ship. Slightly smaller than a Class-B battleship, the Defender Class—of which *Avenger* is one—is fourteen-hundred meters long, two-hundred meters wide at the bow, two-hundred-and-fifty meters at the stern, including the two wings, and two hundred from topside to keel. The two rear wings are each seventy-meters long, thirty-five meters wide and twenty-two meters from skin to skin. She is propelled by six GX fusion engines and is equipped with fourteen gravdrives. The ship is fitted with up to two meters of dutrinium armor. She is equipped with twelve heavy DEW cannons, forty-eight point defense DEW lasers, forty-eight 88mm point defense railguns firing either solid shot or explosive rounds and a single capital railgun capable of firing a range of twenty-five-kilogram projectiles from depleted uranium to nuclear. She also carries Mark 47 Saber and Mark 59 Lance missiles. The ship's hangar can accommodate up to four shuttles and twelve fighters (a squadron), and she carries a contingent of sixty Marines—six squads of ten—under the command of a major. She is designed to act either as a support vessel as a member of the fleet or to act independently.

Jax, a seasoned shuttle pilot, was learning to pilot the

Avenger and act as back up for Haltar Sen if ever the need should arise.

"We prepare for the worst," as Commander Manda Haal would have put it, "and hope for the best."

Dagon Jax was at the helm and the simulation was in progress. The *Avenger* itself was parked in a synchronous orbit above Orso's capitol, the planet Caerus. Even so, the simulation was no different from the real thing. Jax had been a pilot for almost ten years, but the nerves still got to him. *Adrenaline and excitement*, he told himself. Thinking about it could only make it worse. His palms began to sweat as Simon DeLong, the chief navigation officer, gave him his flight instructions.

The instructions were complex, and Delong didn't slow down to wait for Jax to catch up. Jax had to stay on his toes to keep up. In moments like these, he wished that he had Sight like his commanding officer, Manda Haal. *Maybe then my nerves wouldn't be so frayed...* he thought, but he couldn't focus on his nerves or his pounding heart. His training had taught him to deal with this kind of pressure... outwardly, at least. His fingers danced over the hologram as Delong continued to call out instructions.

"Alert, alert!" Krista's voice intoned in the simulation, red lights flashing all over the console. "System failure. System failure."

"Damn," Jax whispered under his breath. He knew DeLong was pushing him hard. That was the point of the simulation. He had to do a manual override. The grav-engines were all at one hundred percent. He had to handle them, all fourteen of them, by himself.

He could feel the G-force weighing him down. He had to get a handle on the grav-engines, or the ship would be torn apart. Beads of sweat dripped from the tip of his chin.

He slowly tried to adjust one of the grav-engines. *This should do...*

But the gravitational forces were too much for the *Avenger*. The ship shuddered, pitched, then cracked, and was torn in two by a gravitational tide.

Jax sat back in his seat, defeated, and wiped the sweat from his face.

"Simulation over," Krista announced. "Mission failed."

"Krista does have a way of rubbing it in, doesn't she, Jax?"

Jax jumped in his seat, then straightened up. He hadn't realized that Commander Haal was standing behind him, watching the simulation. *Stars, how much of that did she see?* he wondered as he wiped his sweaty palms on his flight suit. "Yes, ma'am, she does," he said, taking a deep breath and trying his best to hide his disappointment.

He knew Manda could likely see how dejected he was, but she smiled and said, "Come now. Don't be so hard on yourself. You can do this."

Jax sighed. He'd been flying for more than half his lifetime. Unfortunately, though, he'd become so used to using the AI that he felt handicapped by the need for the technology. Would he ever be able to fly the *Avenger* unassisted? The thought had never really occurred to him, not until now... Until the onset of their battles with the Swarm, all of the training had been... just routine.

They hadn't been in a war in... forever—more than two hundred years. He'd never experienced even a skirmish with pirates before the Swarm invasion. Now, all of this was more than just procedure... Manual operation had to be mastered. As the helmsman, he could find himself in a myriad of dangerous situations, like the one he'd just failed. If he didn't pass the simulations, he would not be able to fly without DeLong or the Commander looking over his shoulder. He felt... out of his league, useless.

DeLong patted his shoulder. "It's all right, Dagon," he said with a smile. "It happens to all of us. It may take some time, but you'll get it. You're an excellent pilot."

"Thank you," he told them both. "Thank you for your support." He smiled, showing the gap in his teeth. "I'll keep trying."

Manda glanced at the datapad on her forearm, then looked at Jax. "Dagon, you have a pickup to make." She looked down at her datapad and tapped it again. "I've sent you the information. Take shuttle two; it's fully charged. You may leave now," she said.

"Yes, Commander," Jax said. He stood up. Stood to attention, saluted, turned on his heel and hurried away to the hangar.

* * *

Jax walked quickly into the hangar and was astonished to see Grell Dunn. On any other day, Dunn would be in the mess hall complaining about the food, but here he was, his eyes closed, his hands at his sides balled into fists.

Jax couldn't see what the man was doing, not until he got closer and realized that his Shuttle was hovering a half-meter above the hangar deck. Dunn was using his TK to levitate the ship.

"Hey! You!" Jax shouted.

Dunn's eyes snapped open. The shuttle dropped to the deck and bounced on its shocks. Thankfully, he'd barely lifted it, and the USF shuttles were designed to take a lot of punishment.

"What the hell d'you think you're doing? That's not a toy. Don't do that!"

"I was just practicing," Dunn said, backing away.

"This is not the place," Jax said, shaking his head. "If you want to practice your TK, go to the designated area in the gym... Where you can't do any damage." *Civilians*, he thought, *so aggravating!*

Dunn ambled away, head down, hands in the pockets of his jumpsuit, muttering to himself.

Jax watched him, shook his head, climbed into the shuttle and took his seat at the helm.

He checked his datapad to see what his orders were. Two companies of Marines—sixty men in six platoons of ten—were waiting for him on the USF ship *Orion*.

The *Orion* was a light carrier, more modern than the *Avenger*. Armed with energy-based weapons and shields, nuclear missiles, and two squadrons of F32A fighters, the Angel Class ships, equipped only with magnetron shields and lacking the heavy dutrinium armor of the old Defender Class-C ships, were practically useless against the Swarm.

Jax had heard of the Marines' commanding officer, a large man with an attitude. Dubois, recently promoted to major, was known to be something of a jerk.

Jax sighed and shook his head. He just knew he was in for one of those moments.

He docked with *the Orion* some fifteen minutes later, lowered the ramp and stepped out onto it.

He greeted the Marines with a nod and waved them aboard.

"Good morning, sir," he said as their CO stepped onto the ramp. "I'm—"

"Yes, yes," he snapped as he rushed up the ramp. "Good, good, I'm Major Dubois," he said as he stopped at the top of the ramp and studied the shuttle's stubby wings. "Quite an old model, isn't it?" The Marines, now seated by the open hatch, just looked at him, not bothering to answer.

Jax bit his tongue, said nothing, showed the Marine major to his seat, then returned to his own.

He lifted the shuttle and flew smoothly out of *Orion's* hangar into the black. *I'll be out of his way in just a few minutes,* he thought as he circled the ship and headed back to *Avenger.* The sun's rays were illuminating her hull. She looked stunning, a beacon of bronze against a backdrop of darkness and twinkling stars. He set the auto pilot, smiled to himself, and was soon lost in thought. *Yes, my shuttle's old, and the Avenger's even older, but just look at her. She's... magnificent, and she's reliable, dependable.* He held onto the yolk lovingly, even though she was on autopilot, as Krista guided the shuttle into the hangar.

Chapter Six

Ground Rules

The Avenger

"All right, everyone," Danis said, "gather around."

She'd called a meeting in the hangar. All fighter pilots, including Gian, Jackknife and their TK civilian copilots, and Marine Major Dubois were in attendance. Jackknife and Skyla looked like the power couple that they were. It was their attitude. They looked as if they were getting ready to perform a music holo... And of course, Jackknife was out of uniform. He was wearing the loose-fit, mismatched clothes of the Free People. "It's itchy and constricting," he'd said when he first tried on the USF suit.

Danis tried not to focus too much on how the two kept making eyes at each other. Instead, she counted, making sure that everyone was in attendance before she started her speech.

Dubois looked smug, and Danis thought the look was likely permanent. When they'd met an hour or so before hand, he began the conversation on a condescending note she didn't appreciate, but it came with the territory. It was, after all, even after twelve hundred years, still a man's galaxy.

Dagon Jax was at attention. As senior shuttle pilot, he too was expected to attend the briefing. Danis smiled at him and told him to relax and continued the count; someone was missing. She sighed and furrowed her eyebrows, *Dunn... Damn it!* She reached out with her Psy. He was moseying along, as if he had all the time in the world. She shook her head and swore to herself that Orso's sun itself would cool down before he made it to the hangar. *Damn it, Grell! Move yourself. NOW!* The thought reached him, and she could see that he just, ever so slightly, quickened his pace.

He finally sauntered into the hangar with a sheepish grin on his face. "Don't hold things up on my account," he said and yawned.

Danis tapped her foot impatiently. "This briefing is for the entire squadron and that includes you, Mr. Dunn."

He lowered his head and went to the back of the group, out of sight of Danis's vengeful gaze.

"Very well, now that everyone is here," she said, placing her hands behind her back, "let's begin." She began to pace back and forth in front of the group, making eye contact with each of the key fighter pilots.

She was impressed by Gian's attentiveness. He'd matured. She hadn't gotten sass-back from him in a while, and she had to admit that Jackknife's influence had contributed to his growth. He stood up straighter when she looked at him directly.

Danis checked the files on her datapad and said, "The *Avenger* will be leaving for planet Typhon at 0900 hours." She stopped pacing, turned to face them and continued, "As you know, Typhon is deep inside Swarm-controlled space. Once we enter Swarm Space we will be at full readiness at all times. We'll deploy in flights of three or four with our TK copilots. Gian, you and Jackknife will fly with me." Danis looked pointedly at Dunn, but said nothing.

She began to pace again. "For those of you who haven't yet faced the Swarm... they're good, very good, and they're continually improving, evolving. Fortunately, so are we. The new laser-guided railguns are a great improvement, and so are the new hellcat torpedoes... We can expect heavy resistance from the Swarm fleet. I'm not going to sugarcoat it; some of us, maybe all of us, are not going to make it. But we can improve the odds if we stay together in our flights. So no catting around on your own. We protect each other... Got it?"

She waited for a response and then continued. "How and if we deploy will be determined at each Slip point, and by how many enemy craft we expect to encounter." She stopped pacing and raised her voice. "The enemy is unpredictable, merciless—"

Major Dubois scoffed audibly.

Many in the group, including Danis, looked at him.

"Excuse me, Major?"

He stepped forward. "Pardon me, Commander, but don't you have a so-called 'seer' on the bridge? Shouldn't that take care of when you'll need to have fighter pilots 'on standby,'" he said using air quotes, "or not?"

Danis took a deep breath and glared at him. She knew she was going to have to get a handle on the cocky major before he undermined her authority. "Major Dubois," she said. "May I remind you that I invited you to attend this briefing as a courtesy. But I'll answer your question. Commander Haal's visions are helpful, yes, but they are not always crystal clear, and she cannot access them at will. It's better to prepare for the worst than to be caught unprepared. Wouldn't you agree?"

His face flushed. He wasn't used to being talked back to, let alone put in his place, even gently, as Danis had done.

She looked around the rest of the group. "We win by doing our jobs," she said. "We win by being prepared. Is that understood?"

There was a resounding "Yes, ma'am!" and "Yes, Commander!"

"Good," she said, nodding. "Dismissed." She made eye contact with Jackknife as he and Skyla were leaving. "Be in uniform by the time we arrive at the first Slipstream," she told him.

"Aye, aye, boss." He replied and winked at her.

Dunn, of course, was one of the last to leave the hangar.

"Mr. Dunn," she said. "A word, please?" She beckoned him to her.

Reluctantly, he stepped forward, stifling a yawn.

"You don't mind, d'you?" she asked. Danis didn't care if he minded or not, but she wanted to begin the conversation on a polite and professional note.

"No, no," he said shaking his head. "Is something the matter?"

"Well, Mr. Dunn," she said with a heavy sigh, "to be frank, yes."

The lines in his forehead creased. He truly looked distressed. "Is it about when I used my TK on that?" He pointed at Jax's shuttle. "I could barely lift the thing, anyway."

"What?" She'd heard about the incident from Jax, but it had slipped her mind. "No... but don't ever do that again." She took a deep breath. "It's about your behavior. Your flippant attitude. You were late today."

Dunn shrugged. "Only by a minute or two."

"That's not good enough," she said. "Timeliness in everything." She locked eyes with him. "You do realize that if it was up to me, you would not be here? But, as you well know, that's not for me to decide. It's the captain's decision and, for some reason, he sees some use in you." She stepped closer to him and continued, "Grell, you need to get this through your head once and for all. We're going deep into Swarm Space and I will *not* tolerate your continuous bitching in my ear. Do you understand?"

"You're right, you're right," he replied, holding up his hands in surrender. "I'll do better, I promise."

Danis didn't detect any sarcasm in his voice, so she nodded and stepped away, then said, "I don't need promises, Mr. Dunn. I need compliance. Now go."

He backed away, gave her a half-hearted salute, turned and headed for the elevators.

* * *

Danis remained in the hangar for a few minutes more, checking her personal sim stats. She was up to date, and other than a few spikes here and there she'd done well. *Not bad*, she thought.

She was about to leave when she heard chatter at the far end of the flight deck. She looked up from her datapad, frowning, knowing it couldn't be any of her people. It wasn't. It was a group of about ten Marines. They were in a ring around another soldier.

"...where the hell did the USF find this guy?" she heard one of them say.

"Look at him," another, a big husky fellow, said. "I never seen anyone scare so easily. Let's get outta here before he pisses himself."

The group broke up and they left, laughing as they went.

Danis shook her head and walked over to the harassed soldier. "Hey," she said, extending her hand. "You okay? I'm Lt. Commander Danis Morian."

He looked at her almost in a daze and took her hand. "I know who you are, ma'am. It's nice to meet you. I'm Frede-Balto Balter. They call me Balto." He let go of her hand, embarrassed. "I'm... kinda new. I got out of boot camp less than a month ago."

Danis smiled warmly. "What was all that about, Balto?" she asked as she pulled up his file on her datapad.

She scanned quickly through it. He'd been recruited primarily because he had Psy abilities, but he'd still had to pass through the Marines' rigorous twelve-week training, and he had, and he's scored well, so he had every right to be there.

He was young, about Gian's age, and smaller than most of the other Marines. But that didn't mean he was weak. She saw the embarrassment on his face and in his thoughts. And she knew he wished she hadn't seen the interaction between him and the other soldiers. *Cheer up,* she thought, reaching out to him. *Don't let them project their insecurities on you.*

Is that what they were doing?

"Oh, yes," she said out loud. "That's what bullies do... You're here because you earned the right. You're where you're supposed to be."

She knew only too well how it felt to not fit in. She'd had to deal with it at the Academy. Being one of only a few women and the only woman of color in her intake, she'd constantly had to prove that she was good enough. It had taken its toll sometimes. But she'd learned and grown from the experience. Now, as one of the top fighter pilots in the entire USF, she could laugh at all the nay-sayers. It all seemed so long ago now.

"You really think so?" Balto asked.

Danis was jerked out of her reverie. "Absolutely," she said, patting him on his shoulder. "Don't lose heart, soldier. You'll be fine."

He nodded and started to reach out to her with his Psy, but before he could project the thought, she blocked him.

"Balter?" Major Dubois' voice echoed across the flight deck. He was standing just inside the entrance of the hangar.

Balto tore his eyes away from Danis and stood at attention. "Yes, sir?"

"Don't you have somewhere else you need to be?" Dubois said, his voice betraying his irritation.

"Uh… yes, sir," he said, looking back and forth between Danis and Dubois.

"Well, then, stop slacking and hop to it, son!"

"Yes, sir, Major Dubois!" He nodded to Danis, saluted, turned and jogged away out of the hangar into the ready room.

Dubois followed him, not bothering to acknowledge Danis.

Perhaps he's still sore that I put him in his place, she thought. *Maybe I bruised his ego. Hah, I know his type. I wonder if he's ever been bullied…*

Chapter Seven

Royal Right

Orso Palace

Tenilo felt as if he'd been back and forth to the palace's infirmary a dozen times since the king had fallen ill. It was just after six-thirty in the morning, standard time. No one had gotten any sleep. Everyone was running on fumes.

Tenilo was with Elio in the infirmary. The king was surrounded by a group of nurses and doctors. Outside the infirmary door, the king's personal guards stood watch.

"They still don't understand how he could have sustained such a devastating shock to his nervous system," Elio said, his voice strained. "They're looking for anomalies in his brain, but they've found nothing... so far." Elio shook his head.

Tenilo felt a great sympathy for the prince. He'd not had the pleasure of meeting the queen, Elio's late mother, but he could tell by the way he spoke of her that she was truly an amazing woman, and he didn't know how the prince would be able to cope if he lost his father as well.

Becoming regent under such circumstances was pressure enough to destroy a lesser man, but Elio seemed to be handling it well enough, although Tenilo could see the strain was ever present, just below the surface.

Tenilo could feel how the dukes and marshals at the briefing resented the young prince, but they kept their decorum. It was their duty to do so. Only testy Duke Rutta and Marshall Ugo Tan seemed to be disappointed in the turn of events... Both Rutta and Tan expected Prince Elio to respect and comply with his father's wishes. *Avenger's* mission to Typhon planet would *not* be happening if the king were able to give the order. And both Tenilo and Elio knew it.

"Don't worry, my prince," Tenilo whispered. "You made the right decision."

Elio's thoughts were a jumbled mess. He was worried about his father and he had no idea how he'd be accepted as regent, if at all. He didn't reply. Instead, he continued to stare at the king, willing him to get well.

Tenilo wished that he could offer more than just words to comfort the prince. But that and his presence were all he could offer. "Your Highness?"

"Yes, Tenny?" Elio said without looking at him.

"Perhaps you'd like me to ask Dinka 2.0 to bring you some food?" He tried to keep his tone light. "And then maybe you could get some rest? You've had quite a long morning."

And the morning had only just begun... Orso's sun had just risen, its rays casting a blue glow on everything it touched. Elio had temporarily linked Dinka 2.0 to Tenilo's datapad. Tenilo turned away and whispered a command into his datapad that Dinka 2.0 was to join them.

The robot glided silently into the room. "Yes, Mr. Tenilo? How may I help you?"

"No," Elio said, his voice devoid of emotion. "No, thank you, Tenny. I'm fine."

Tenilo sighed. He felt defeated. It was difficult for him to see the prince in such a state. "Never mind, 2.0," he said, "But thank you and... stay close."

"Yes, of course, Mr. Tenilo." And the robot glided away.

Tenilo was suddenly aware... he felt something; anger... no, rage. Several people were approaching along the hallway, and they were in a hurry.

"My prince," Tenilo began to warn him.

"I feel them, Tenny."

Suddenly, there was a disturbance outside the door: loud voices. Unwanted guests. The king's guards tried to turn them away. They were unsuccessful.

"Do you know who I am?" King Wulfrick's thunderous voice demanded. "I'll have your heads if you don't remove yourselves from my presence. I demand to speak to Prince Elio this instant!"

One of the guards opened the door, stuck his head inside, looked apologetically at Tenilo and Elio and said, "The king and queen of the Odin System wish to speak with you, Your Highness."

Elio nodded, thanked the guard and, together, he and Tenilo stepped out of the room.

"Follow me," Elio snapped and marched swiftly along the corridor to a nearby parlor, Tenilo at his side, having noted the scowls on the king and queen's faces. Though he couldn't read their thoughts, he could feel the wrath emanating from them.

"What's the meaning of this, King Wulfrick?" Elio asked in a hushed tone. "You barge into my father's infirmary, which is most inappropriate, and demand to speak to me." He pointed in the direction of the infirmary. "My father is not well. Where is your respect, sir?"

King Wulfrick glared at him. "Respect? You young welp. I am here out of respect for the kingdom, the Orso System."

"How dare you—"

Tenilo put a hand on Elio's arm, effectively cutting him off before he could say something he might regret.

The king and queen were accompanied by their equerry. He appeared to be diligently taking notes on his datapad.

"I'm sorry, King Wulfrick, I don't follow." Tenilo could see that Elio was furious and wanted them to leave, that he was anxious to return to his father.

Queen Zara, a tall, slim woman of forty-one, just centimeter short of two meters and twelve years her husband's junior stood stoically beside her husband. She was a beautiful woman, regal, the quintessential royal wife, and she was master of the art of Psy.

Tenilo couldn't read her dazzling green eyes. He *really* couldn't read her at all; she was blocking him. It was clear she had powerful Psy abilities. Tenilo stopped pushing so she wouldn't suspect him.

"My Queen and I," Wulfrick said, taking a step closer to Elio, "have the right to rule the Orso System. We demand that you stand down."

"In your dreams, Wulfrick. What gives you that idea?" Elio asked, squinting his eyes. "I am the king's firstborn *and* I am of age; thus I am regent."

"My claim is in accordance with Sovereign Law," the king said matter-of-factly.

"Hah!" Elio snorted. "You think—"

"We want to put it to a vote," the queen snapped, cutting him off.

"We *will* put it to a vote," the king corrected. "I have called a virtual meeting with the dukes and marshals of the Orso System. Ten o'clock, standard. You have three hours." He turned to leave; Queen Zara and the equerry followed. "We will vote with or without you, Prince Elio," Wulfrick said as he stomped out into the corridor and away without looking back.

"Come, my prince," Tenilo said. "We must get back to the king."

But Elio just stood there, staring at the open doorway.

"Can they do that, Tenny?" he asked after a moment of silence.

"It would appear so," Tenilo replied. "Come, we'll go to the king." He took Elio by the arm and led him back along the corridor.

Tenilo spoke to the king's guards. "You are not to let anyone into this room other than Prince Elio, myself, and the medical personnel without checking their credentials. If need be, you are authorized to use deadly force."

The guards stared at him, stunned.

"No matter if the person is royal or not. *No one* is to come near the king."

They looked at Elio. He nodded slightly.

"As you command, sir," the guard who had introduced the Orion royal pair said. Elio probed his mind. The man was resolute. He would do as he was ordered.

"Elio," Tenilo whispered, pulling him to the side. "I think something very sinister is going on. I tried to read

Queen Zara's mind. I couldn't. She was blocking me." He pursed his lips, then continued, "I believe what's happened to the king was done *intentionally*... to overthrow the government."

Elio sucked in a breath, horrified, his eyes wide. "I should have been more aware. I should have—"

"You've been under enormous stress, my prince," Tenilo said. "It's not your fault. But you must go prepare for the vote," he said. "And please... try to get some rest."

Elio took a deep breath, nodded, then said, "You're right, Tenny. Let's get through this and then we'll talk. Have Dinka come to my suite."

"Yes, my prince."

But Tenilo knew that though the prince had indicated he would rest, it would be impossible. He could tell that Elio was too unsettled. He would be unable to sit still. He would spend what little time he had before the vote scouring the documents concerning sovereign law... Forming his argument in a way that would make the dukes and marshals see him as more than just the wayward son of the king. He would do what was necessary to keep the Orso System under his and his father's rule.

Tenilo waited until Elio had made the turn at the end of the corridor, then turned and said, "Excuse me, doctor. May I have a minute of your time? I need to ask you some questions concerning the king's condition."

Chapter Eight

Meeting of the minds

Orso Royal Palace

At nine-fifty-five, Elio and Tenilo jacked into the meeting.

King Wulfrick looked genuinely surprised to see them. "Ah, Your Highness... You're right on time."

Elio smiled slyly. "One must always be punctual, Wulfrick, especially when someone is trying to steal his throne."

King Wulfrick cleared his throat. Queen Zara puckered her lips indignantly.

There were more than thirty dukes and marshals in attendance, including Duke Rutta. He seemed almost giddy; he could barely sit still. His attitude and bearing were similar to that at their previous meeting nine hours earlier.

"Well, then," King Wulfrick said, standing. "Let us begin the proceedings." The queen stood with him.

"Sovereign Law states that a ruler of another system may take over when the current monarch is demised."

Wulfrick ignored the gasps when he spoke of King Orson's death so lightly. He continued, "The Queen and I have been accommodated by this system for some time now," he said and sighed, "after the... devastation that occurred on our own planet."

Tenilo and Elio exchanged a look. The Tudors and the inhabitants of Odin had been in the Orso System for less than a week.

"We therefore feel that it is our duty," he said, placing his hand on his heart, "to give back to the system that offered us comfort and support in our time of need. We are rulers of a neighboring system. Odin's government is comparable to Orso's. Our rule would be similar to..." He paused and bowed his head dramatically. "Or greater than that to which you're accustomed. I therefore exert my right to rule the Orso System until such a time as Prince Elio is deemed fit to inherit the throne... if ever."

Elio stood up. He was furious, veins protruding from his neck. "Might I remind you, Your Grace, that my father is *not* dead?" He looked at the dukes and marshals around the table and then continued, "I would hope that you are all as appalled as I am, that this... this... *foreigner*," he spat, "would put the king, my father, in the grave before his time." He sat back down and folded his arms across his chest.

"My apologies, Your Highness." King Wulfrick sat down. "But my argument and my claim still stand."

Queen Zara remained standing. "Misfortune has befallen the king... It is unlikely that he will survive." She forced a tear from her eye. "He has suffered a nerve burn, very rare," she said. "And the survival rate is less than six percent."

Now Tenilo was certain something was amiss. The doctors hadn't discussed any such malady with him or Elio.

He leaned over and whispered in Elio's ear, "I fear the king, your father, is the victim of an attempted assassination."

Elio stood up again, ready to officially state his case. Tenilo used his Psy to encourage the prince.

Thank you, Tenny.

"I repeat, my father is not dead. He is only temporarily incapacitated. I am fully capable of fulfilling my duties as regent." He looked around at the prospective voters. "Do you really want to hand the kingdom, our system, to someone who doesn't know us? You are Orso-born. All of you. Are you not? Are you going to allow these ancient laws to sway you? I think not."

Some of the voters nodded. Some shook their heads. Some remained stoic. *Well, at least some of them appear to be with me,* he thought.

"No, your father is not dead," the queen said. "Not yet... But the law also states that if a young ruler is deemed unfit, another ruler can take over if its current monarch becomes incapacitated."

Elio shrugged. "I am not a child. I'm thirty-two and fully capable of carrying out the duties of regent."

"Are you?" the queen asked. "The laws state that an heir under the age of thirty-five can be challenged in such circumstances."

Elio paled. He'd missed that detail.

"And, yes, the laws are 'ancient,' as you put it, but how else are you to rule a system? We are bound by the rules we set. And they must be upheld." Queen Zara glowered at

Prince Elio. "And if we're to stick to the facts, my prince, you would never have had anything to do with the administration of this system were it not for your father's ever-present watchful eye." She looked around at the voters. "Elio hates politics. We all know it."

Duke Rutta and some others nodded.

"Would you have the Orso System administrated by a boy more interested in playing with his virtual games?" Her green eyes flashed. "His only concern is how quickly he can become the next great hacker."

There were rumblings amongst the dukes and marshals. The vote was beginning to sway in the Tudors' favor.

Tenilo stood up, unable to stand the disrespect being thrown at the prince.

"That's quite enough!" he snapped

"Don't you dare interrupt me, you duplicitous little Galactic Easterner!"

There was a tense, momentary stare down between the two while Tenilo gathered himself for the fray. He was not intimidated by the angry queen and he intended to make sure she knew it, but he didn't get the chance because, at that moment, someone else jacked into the meeting.

Captain Sasha Crowe... Elio had met her previously on the *Avenger* when he convinced Captain Morian to enter negotiations with the pirates.

She looks so familiar, Elio thought. He'd had the same thought when he first saw her file.

"Marshal Ugo Tan informed me of this meeting," she stated, pulling up a chair and sitting down next to Elio. "I felt it necessary that I be here." She looked around the room. She had no fear in her voice. "For those of you who don't know me," she said, "I'm Captain Sasha Crowe of the *Golden Condor*."

"Excuse me, my dear," King Wulfrick said, "but why exactly are you here?"

Sasha smiled; her teeth gleamed brilliantly. "I didn't think I needed an invitation." She looked at Elio. "I am of Orso royal blood. I am Elio's older sister... his half-sister." She continued to speak calmly, ignoring the incredulous looks from around the table. "I'm King Orson Lorne's daughter."

The room exploded into an uproar.

Elio was no less shocked than everyone else, but as he stared at her, his eyes wide, he knew without a doubt that it was true. They had the same eyes, the same hair, and, apparently, the same spirit. And the memory came flooding back to him... He had seen Sasha even before that day on the *Avenger*. She had attended his mother's funeral, her face covered from the nose down by a veil. But he had seen her eyes, eyes that were so like his own.

His father had said she was a distant relative and had called her by another name. And then Elio recalled the late-night arguments between his father and mother when he was a small child... *They were arguing about her*, he thought. And he felt ashamed. He wished he had known sooner. The affair between his father and Sasha's mother must have gone on after he was born. *How long?* he wondered. He reached out, took her hand, squeezed it and smiled at her.

She nodded and smiled back at him.

Queen Zara clutched her jeweled necklace. "King Orson's indiscretion is a disgrace," she said to Sasha. "And you have been living outside the Sovereign Systems. On Freyja... with heathens!"

Sasha smiled at the queen. "My father's indiscretion is of no consequence," she said sternly. "It makes no difference whether this system knew or cared that my father lay with my mother or not," she said. "Nowhere in the law does it say that a king's heir has to be born in wedlock."

Elio had mixed emotions. He didn't really know how he felt about his new-found sibling or the fact that she had a right to the throne before he did.

"I am not here to assert my right to the throne," she said, reading his mind. "Though I will if you decide to vote against Elio. I *am* of age, and I have the experience. I command a ship of the line, a Defender-class heavy cruiser, and I am a member of Freyja's ruling council."

She glanced sideways at Elio, her expression softening as she said, "I am here to vote; in my brother's favor." She placed her palms flat against the tabletop as she continued.

"You see, The Free People's Fleet, including my ship, the *Golden Condor,* is defending the Orso System against the Swarm. That agreement was made between the Prince and one of our most trusted captains, Tiger Wok. If Prince Elio is voted out"—she nodded towards him—"the arrangement with The Free People's Fleet will, on my authority, be dissolved... We'll go back to our God-forsaken, heathen-run Freyja," she said the last part sarcastically, sneering at Queen Zara as she did so. "I must warn you," she continued, "if we leave, the defense capability of the Orso System would be reduced by more than seventy percent."

The dukes and marshals looked worriedly at each other.

"That would leave a mere handful of USF ships to defend your system," Sasha continued. "Is that what you want?"

The dukes and marshals were already shaking their heads before she even finished.

Sasha had them, and she knew it. She lifted her chin with an air of confidence. "All in favor of Prince Elio retaining his position as regent, say 'Aye.' All against, say

'Nay,' but..." She cocked her head toward the king and queen of the Odin System and said, "Understand that if you put these lovely people in charge... you do so without the backing of The Free People's Fleet." She shrugged.

It did not take long for the voters to come to a decision. Elio could hear that most said "Aye" for their vote. And the virtual ballot box confirmed it via the holo screen: Elio had twenty-seven votes, the king and queen of Odin only six.

"Thank you," Elio mouthed to Sasha. He knew that without her help, the outcome could have been much different.

Queen Zara sulked in her chair. King Wulfrick's face was flushed with anger.

Sasha giggled, covering her mouth, then said, "Well, I guess that concludes the meeting. Congratulations, brother."

Elio took her hand again and said, "We should talk."

And they did, for the rest of the day and into the night, alone in Elio's suite with only Dinka in attendance.

* * *

After the meeting adjourned and Elio and Sasha had gone to the prince's suite, Tenilo returned to the infirmary. The guards allowed Tenilo to pass. He knocked on the door and entered the room. The doctor turned, saw who it was and immediately came to him.

"Doctor," Tenilo asked, "do you believe the king could have suffered something called a nerve burn?"

"No, not at all," the doctor replied without having to think about it. He looked at the king's chart on his datapad. "When a person suffers from nerve burn, the patient first receives a shock to the brainstem and spinal cord. This then causes a seizure, and, in almost all cases, kills the patient within minutes." He looked down at Tenilo. "The king did not suffer a shock to the brainstem or have a seizure. His nervous system simply... shut down. It stopped working." He furrowed his eyebrows. "And we have not been able to find a reason as to why."

Tenilo nodded slowly. He was correct in his thinking that Queen Zara had concocted the king's malady. "I see..." he said thoughtfully. "Could I ask a favor of you, please?" He checked his datapad. "Ah, here it is." He showed the doctor. "Could you look into this, please?"

The doctor took a closer look at Tenilo's datapad. "This content is from the planet Canis?"

"Yes. I believe this file may hold the answer to what happened to the king."

The doctor raised his eyebrow. "I'll look into it... of course. What did happen, do you think?"

"Something I've read about in the old records, following the Purge. Something we've never seen in our lifetime," Tenilo said gravely. "I believe His Majesty is a victim of attempted Psy assassination."

Chapter Nine

Swarm Space

The Avenger

"Two minutes to Slipstream, Captain," Haltar Sen called from the helm.

Richard Morian stood on the bridge at the command rail, hands gripping the bar, leaning forward, his eyes focused on the now blank holo display, Manda Haal at his side. The holo showed only swirling darkness. He could feel the gentle tug as the ship drew closer to the exit.

"Very good, Mr. Sen," he said, taking a deep breath and several steps back to his command chair where he sat down, rested an elbow on the arm and put his hand to his chin.

The entire ship's crew had been on-mission for almost seven hours. It was almost noon, standard time, and they were about to exit the third jump. With the help of Manda's sight, they'd been able to avoid the Swarm almost entirely when exiting the two previous Slipstreams.

Using the coordinates she'd provided, they'd exited at points of least resistance—points where few enemy craft were present—with the ability to maneuver quickly and efficiently to the next point of entry. Thus far, it had not been necessary to launch fighters and the ship had taken minimal surface damage. All of the ship's weapons systems were still almost at full capacity, slightly more than ninety-three percent.

Through the use of his Psy, he could feel the crew's optimism, and he wondered for a moment if what Jadern had said to them on their field-test run might be coming to fruition. Was there an end in sight? Was this almost over?

"Exit in thirty seconds," Sen announced.

Manda took her seat beside Morian. "We should only need Mark-99s and eighty-eight-millimeter cannons," she said. "I only see a few dozen enemy craft. Many of them more than five hundred thousand kilometers out from the exit." She pressed her hand to her forehead and took a deep breath.

"Are you all right?" Morian asked.

She nodded her head and forced a small smile. "It's just a slight headache," she replied. "My brain... it gets a little fatigued, is all. It will pass." Her smile widened. "I shouldn't complain. The ability of Sight is a wonderful gift, but it does come with side effects." She shrugged. "I'll be fine." What she wasn't telling him was that she'd recently begun to develop Psy along with her ever-developing Sight. Dr. Dowd reassured her, telling her that it was because the Sight had already prepped her brain and it was becoming receptive to telepathic abilities.

Morian nodded. "Take it easy, Manda. I appreciate what you're doing." He'd learned to trust Manda's Sight over the months since it had manifested itself. Her accuracy was bordering on ninety percent; it was that final ten percent that worried him, and for that he trusted his own instincts.

"Ten seconds," Sen said. "Nine... eight..."

As Sen continued the countdown, Morian took one last look to make sure that the crew was ready, then he contacted Danis via his private comms channel. "You ready, sis?" he asked.

"As we ever will be," she replied.

If Manda was correct, they would only need to use their eighty-eight-millimeter railguns to fend off the enemy craft.

Morian was grateful that they'd been able to get a shuttle out and pick up a shipment of two thousand of the new-and-improved T-torpedoes—now designated Mark-99 torpedoes—just before they left the Orso System. They would, he hoped, be able to continue the testing in real time, on the battlefield.

Manda had called it correctly. They exited the Slipstream. The hologram sprang to life to reveal thirty-six blue dots, each representing an enemy craft scattered over a wide area. All within a five-hundred-kilometer global radius of the ship.

Morian stood Ranger Squadron down. The enemy seemed to be taken off guard. The Mark-99s and the 88-millimeter railguns would be sufficient to handle them. The new 99s, designed to explode on proximity and scatter a payload of 88mm, solid dutrinium orbs over a wide area, were able to take out as many as three enemy craft in a single shot, provided they were closely grouped. The warhead had been designed with known Swarm tactics in mind. To date, they were known to operate in flights of three, as did their ground troops.

Big Charlie would not be needed. Morian decided he

needed to save the big guns for when they were deeper into Swarm Space, closer to the Persei System and the planet Typhon.

The battle was brief. Only twelve of the enemy craft engaged the *Avenger*. Five of them fell to the eighty-eights. Three fell to a single Mark-99, and twenty-four, obviously seeing the fate of their comrades, turned tail and fled for the hills... In this case, the asteroids.

Morian sat back in his chair and smiled to himself. Things, thus far, couldn't be better. He glanced sideways at Manda. She had a self-satisfied smirk on her face.

"Well done, Commander."

"Thank you, sir," she said, rising to her feet. "If you'll excuse me, I should go give Mr. Sen the coordinates for the next Slip entry."

The new coordinates took *Avenger* to the far side of the sun, a trip of some fifty-five minutes at one-quarter light speed.

Manda and Haltar Sen were quickly developing a sort of symbiotic relationship. This due to her ability and his burgeoning trust in her. "Thank you, ma'am," Sen said. "You really are making my job easy." He glanced at Dagon Jax who was receiving on-the-job training.

Haltar, at the age of one hundred and seven, was fine with the young blood learning his job. Most of *Avenger's* command crew had backups. Sen was one of the few that didn't. It made sense, then, that he train someone to be ready in case he became, stars forbid, incapacitated.

* * *

They'd been in the Slipstream for almost forty-five minutes with as many more to go when Manda, at the command rail, suddenly put her hands to her temples and staggered two steps backward.

"What? What is it, Commander?" Morian asked, rising to his feet.

He knew that when Manda had graphic visions—those that affected her brain and balance—something big was coming. He reached out to her. He could feel her pain, the anxiety, but as the vision passed, her mood turned to one of tenacious grit. She opened her eyes, took two steps forward and gripped the rail with both hands.

Morian joined her at the rail. Her face was pale. Her knuckles white. She looked at him, locked eyes with him.

"What is it?" he asked. "What have you seen?"

"It's... bad, Captain," she replied. "We'll need to deploy the squadron." Her voice was flat, emotionless. "There's a large enemy fleet deployed around the exit," she said quietly so the rest of the deck crew couldn't hear the conversation. Morian responded in kind.

"How many?"

"Three hundred, maybe more," she said, gazing up at the forward screens into the swirling blackness of the Slipstream.

"Three hundred? Are you sure?"

She nodded, never taking her eyes off the screens.

"We need to take them by surprise," she said. "They are closely grouped. We should begin firing the new 99s as we exit the Slipstream."

"How long before we exit, Mr. Sen?" Morian asked.

"Forty-nine minutes, twenty-eight seconds and counting, Captain."

Morian nodded. "We'll be ready."

Manda didn't acknowledge him.

"Give me a ship-wide channel, Ms. Lowry, if you please," Morian said.

"You have it, Captain."

Morian returned to his seat, opened the channel and said, "Now hear this. Now hear this. This is the captain. All hands to battle stations. I repeat, all hands to battle stations. Forty-five minutes to Slipstream exit. Inbound enemy craft."

He closed the channel, stood up, stepped up to the rail and said, "Lieutenant Fargo. Load all tubes with Mark-99s and prepare to fire multiple broadsides on my command. Bring point defense online—eighty-eight-millimeter kinetic rounds—and open fire upon Slipstream exit."

He turned to look down at Lt. Commander Omario Kingston, senior tactical officer, and said, "Shields up ship-wide except for the hangar bay, Mr. Kingston. Bring those up as soon as the squadron has deployed."

He could have reached out to Danis, but he had to do it verbally for the ship's log. He tapped his datapad and opened a channel to her.

"Morian to Domino, copy?"

* * *

"Exiting the Slipstream in seven... six... five..." Haltar Sen counted down.

Good luck out there, Danis, Morian reached out with his Psy to communicate with his sister. *Stay safe.*

The entire squadron was about to be deployed and he prayed that everyone would make it back to the *Avenger* safely.

All good, brother, Danis replied. *Keep the ship in one piece, okay? I'll see you soon.*

Morian sighed. *I will*, he thought as he took a deep breath and increased his grip on the rail.

The holo display came to life, a glowing orb of black punctuated by millions of stars and a single green icon that represented the *Avenger... and hundreds* of blue dots that represented enemy craft. They were surrounded. Once again Manda had been right.

"Fire point defense, Mr. Kingston," Morian shouted. "Fire all tubes, Ms. Fargo, and keep firing."

The great ship shuddered as all forty-eight computer-directed point defense railguns opened fire as one.

Avenger shuddered again as she launched twenty-four laser-guided torpedoes.

Morian watched as, one by one, more green icons appeared on the holo as Ranger Squadron launched.

He watched as the computer-generated trail of twenty-four torpedoes streaked toward their targets.

And he watched as dozens of blue dots began to disappear.

A second salvo of M-99 torpedoes left the tubes, then a third and a fourth. All forty-eight railguns were sweeping space in every direction, creating a vast screen of solid dutrinium orbs.

For several minutes, the battle raged on and then the ship shuddered... once, twice... three times. She was taking fire.

"Damage control, Mr. Volkov?" Morian shouted as the ship rocked.

"Shields at seventy percent, captain," Maxim Volkov replied. "Turret two is gone. There's a fire on deck four, section seven. Damage control crews have been deployed to deal with it."

Morian nodded, stared down at the holo, then up at the

screens. Space to port, starboard, topside, keel, aft and forward was alive with blue craft. They were fast, faster than he remembered.

The ship shuddered as Fargo's crews fired another double broadside, and he watched as the twenty-four torpedoes streaked away from the ship, and as their proximeters exploded their payloads… and the devastating effect they had on the enemy craft: too many to count. He would have to rely on Krista for the numbers.

"Shields at sixty-percent and falling," Kingston shouted.

Damn! Morian thought. *We'll soon be down to nothing but our armor.*

"Damn it, Mr. Kingston," Morian shouted. "Is there nothing you can do to bring the shields back up to full power?"

Morian glanced up at the forward screens. He counted nine enemy fighters coming in fast.

Point defense opened fire, spewing thousands of rounds. Five of the enemy craft exploded in brilliant balls of blue fire. The remaining four broke through and continued their attack run.

Stars… here we go, Morian thought.

Three F32 fighters appeared on the forward port screen, railguns blazing. One of the enemy fighters exploded. A second went spinning away, its starboard weapons platform shot away. The remaining two enemy craft, however, were now well within range and both opened fire on the *Avenger*.

The forward screens flared brilliant white as eight bolts of plasma impacted the shields. Morian shielded his eyes with his hand. The ship rocked, shuddered. The lights on the bridge flickered, dimmed, then brightened again. The forward screens cleared. He could see one of the two Blue fighters floating dead in space some five hundred meters off the port bow. The other was engaged in a running duel with two F32s... and then all three disappeared into the black.

Morian looked down at the holo. Two green dots were chasing a single blue dot. Three seconds later the blue dot blinked out, and the two greens turned and headed back toward the *Avenger*.

"Damage report, Mr. Kingston," Morian said.

"Forward shields at thirty-two percent, Captain. Turrets one and three are down. One of those beams managed to break through, but didn't breach the hull. My crews are working to bring turrets one and three back online."

Haltar Sen, eyes wide, mouth open, face pale, sweat rolling down his face, turned to Jax and said, "You're going to have to take over."

Jax turned white. "What? No... I'm..."

"You must," Sen said, rising to his feet. He swayed unsteadily. "Do it. Do it now."

Jax swapped seats with him, looking at Sen with wide eyes as he helped his mentor to sit down.

"It's all right," Sen said weakly. "Krista will do most of the work."

Jax shook his head, stared at the holo floating above the console, then took a deep breath and nodded.

Morian, some two meters above the well deck, saw the exchange between Sen and Jax. He had no idea what was happening, but he trusted Sen implicitly.

He looked at the giant hologram. *Yes!* The enemy was retreating. The remaining blue dots were moving away, out of the system. It was over.

"Recall the squadron, please, Ms. Lowry," he said. "Aye, Captain."

She opened a channel and said, "Avenger to Ranger One. It's over, Domino. Bring your birds home. Copy?"

"Copy," Domino replied. "We're heading home."

Morian reached out to his sister. He could feel Danis coming down from her adrenaline rush as she and her squadron entered the hangar. Fortunately, they had not suffered any casualties. *Thank the stars*, he thought.

Manda, who had been sitting quietly in her chair next to Morian's, stood, went down to the well deck and gave Jax the coordinates for the next slip. She patted him gently on the shoulder and said, "You can do this, Jax."

Then she looked at Sen. His face was pale and bathed in sweat.

"What's wrong, Haltar?"

"...Nothing. Just a little dizzy. I'm fine."

She stared at him for a long moment, then nodded, turned away and returned to the command bridge and joined Morian and the rail.

"There won't be much resistance this time," she said.

"Good," Morian said. "What's wrong with Lt. Sen? He looks unwell."

"He is," she replied. "I asked him what was wrong, but he just shook his head and said he was fine, that he'd had a dizzy spell. I'm not sure I believe him. I think he should go to the sick bay."

"Mr. Sen... Haltar," Morian said. "You're relieved. Please go to the medical bay and get checked out."

Sen stood and came to attention. "Yes, Captain," he replied, then turned and left the bridge. He knew Morian well enough to know it wasn't a request.

Jax watched Haltar leave, then looked up at Manda worriedly. He couldn't believe that he was at the helm, alone...

Morian hoped that Dr. Jyra Dowd would quickly figure out what was wrong with Sen. True, he was an older pilot, so maybe it was just a routine issue. But Morian couldn't help but wonder if there was something else going on.

He turned from the rail and took the steps down to the well deck.

"You're going to be fine, Jax," he said and put a hand on his shoulder.

"I don't know," Jax replied, his voice trembling.

Morian probed his mind. He was indeed under stress. He could almost see the young pilot's heart racing.

"Commander Haal assures me there'll be little to no resistance at the next exit," Morian said. "I trust her. You should too. All you need do is take us in." Morian smiled down at him, squeezed his shoulder and continued, "Just a few more jumps and we'll enter the Eta Persei System."

Chapter Ten

Conspiracy

Orso Palace

The morning seemed to pass slowly after Tenilo had told the doctor of his suspicion, and he was worried... more than worried. He wasn't sure, but he felt a Psy attack could be the only explanation for what had happened to the king.

What else could it be? he thought as he waited for the doctor to confirm his theory. The hours felt like days, until finally, at two in the afternoon, he received a message on his datapad that the doctor wanted him to come to the infirmary.

"It's true," the doctor said as Tenilo entered his office. "The articles from Canis... The research is minimal, but there are other victims." The doctor scrolled through his datapad, then continued, "Please sit down, Mr. Tenilo.

There have been six-hundred-twenty-one confirmed cases reported across the Sovereign Systems."

The doctor pursed his lips. "It's extremely rare... Doctors were unable to find the cause and are still speculating, but there was an uptick in cases a little over a year ago." He looked at Tenilo. "Since then, researchers have found that there's a correlation between these mysterious cases and the gifted population; people with Psy and or TK."

Tenilo stared at him, then said, "So what you're telling me is that the king is the victim of a Psy attack?"

"I am. He has all the symptoms. I see no other explanation."

"Will he recover, doctor?"

The doctor sighed and shook his head. "That's a question I wish I could answer. He's stable, but I see no real improvement in his condition... We know so little about it. All we can do is keep him comfortable and hope for a miracle. Not what you want to hear, I know, but it's the best I can do... for now."

"Thank you, doctor," Tenilo said, rising to his feet. "I'll inform Prince Elio... I know how you must feel, Doctor, and I sympathize. I will make sure the prince is aware of your devotion to the king."

Tenilo sent Elio a message, then continued, "Please keep me informed if the king's condition changes, Docter. I would like hourly updates... Is there any way to protect the king from future attacks... or anyone else?"

The doctor drew in a deep breath and shook his head. "Not that I know of. As far as I know, there's no way to shield the human mind from telepathic intrusion."

Tenilo nodded. It was what he'd expected. The new abilities were vital to the fight against the Swarm. But it now appeared that these same abilities could be just as deadly as their alien enemy.

"Tenilo," Elio said as he entered the doctor's office, "I came as soon as I could."

Elio looked exhausted. His always-perfect hair was disheveled and there were dark circles under his eyes. It was obvious that he hadn't slept since the meeting with the dukes and marshals.

Tenilo explained what he and the doctor thought had happened and ended with a warning: "It seems, my prince, that there is no defense against such an attack." He looked at the doctor, who nodded. "My own thoughts are that the only possible defense is to keep our minds closed to intrusion... at all times... except in an emergency, of course, and even that may not work against a determined attack." He looked again at the doctor and said, "How is it done, Doctor? How does one attack another using Psy? It would seem to me the old adage holds true: The best form of defense is to attack."

"I don't know, Mr. Tenilo, but I will certainly try to find out."

Tenilo nodded and looked at Elio.

"I'd like to see my father, please, doctor," Elio said.

"Of course, my prince. If you'll follow me..." He rose to his feet and took them to the king's suite.

Tenilo could sense the prince's thoughts and emotions through their strong Psy link. The prince, too tired to hide the fear in his eyes, took the king's hand in his and stared down at his face. His thoughts turned again to his mother and how she withered away before his eyes. In his teenage and young adult years, his mother had been his only confidant. His only comfort when his father thrust politics and duty down his throat. Now, he wondered if he would lose his father as well, lose him before he had a a chance to prove himself. Elio had always prided himself in that he'd never actively sought the king's approval, but that was then, and he prayed that his father would live. Live for Orso, and live to be proud of his son. *You can't go, father... Not yet.*

"What are we going to do, doctor?" Elio asked without taking his eyes off his father's face.

"There's nothing we can do but wait and pray," the doctor replied.

"Nothing?" Elio said as he released his father's hand and stepped away. "Is there really nothing you can do to shield him from another attack?"

"My prince," he replied, "Mr. Tenilo has given me a file that may offer some hope. It involves some new research. I will study the research. That's all I can do... for now, I'm afraid. The good news is that your father is stable."

"Unfortunately," Tenilo said, "we don't know who did this. Once the culprit is found, my prince, how do you wish to proceed?" Tenilo could see the rage in his eyes and he had to wonder: *Who could the culprit be? Was there a bigger target? Was there more than one attacker, a terrorist group perhaps?*

Tentatively, Tenilo again probed the prince's mind. Elio was thinking about the king and queen of Odin. Vengeful thoughts.

Tenilo quickly exited the prince's mind, leaving him unaware of the intrusion. *The doctor's right,* he thought. *There is no defense against such an incursion. As to the king and queen of Odin... Yes, they have to be the prime suspects, but Elio can't make the accusation without sufficient evidence.*

"The culprits?" Elio snarled, interrupting his thoughts

to answer the question. "They will be put to death. Their trial will be anything but lengthy."

And then Elio strode out of the room, his body rigid as he marched toward the east wing of the palace, where the Tudors were housed.

Tenilo almost had to jog to keep up with him. "My prince..." Tenilo tried to catch his breath. "We are not certain."

"Oh yes, we are. It's them. I can *feel* it," Elio said through clenched teeth without looking back at Tenilo. "You know it as well as I do."

Tenilo couldn't deny it... He did indeed believe the king and queen must be involved in the attack.

Elio ran up the marbled steps two at a time to the guest suite. He quickly and easily overrode the security code and unlocked the door, threwit open, and marched into the room.

The king and queen were relaxing. Their royal robes exchanged for more casual attire, were taken by surprise.

King Wulfrick stood up from the oversized couch, his eyes wide and a look of outrage on his face. "How dare you!" he shouted, the loose skin of his neck shaking. "Have you no decency?"

Elio was not to be deterred. Hearing Wulfrick shout at him only made him angrier. "Admit it!" He pushed the king back with his TK.

The king stumbled backward and almost fell on the queen.

"Admit that you tried to kill my father!" Elio said.

"Stand down, Elio," Wulfrick said, holding up his hand as he made an effort to sit up straight. "I tried to kill your father? Are you mad? What in the Sovereign Systems are you talking about?"

Elio was too angry to see that the king was confused and didn't know what Elio was talking about.

Tenilo probed the king's mind only to find that he really didn't know anything. The queen, however... Her mind was almost completely blank. She was blocking him. He stared at her. She locked eyes with him and gifted him with a mocking smile.

"You two," Elio said as he looked first at Wulfrick, then at Queen Zara. "Both of you. You used Psy to try to kill my father." He balled his fists and snarled. "An attempted assassination of any member of the Orso royal family is punishable by death."

"Have you gone mad?" King Wulfrick asked.

The queen glowered at Elio and said, "You young fool. Your baseless accusations only further demonstrate that you are unfit to rule."

"Elio?" Tenilo said, gently grasping the prince's shoulder. "May I speak to you in private?"

"Not now, Tenny," Elio replied, still staring down the king.

"Please...Your Highness. I insist."

Tenilo turned to look at him, then turned again to glare at the king and queen, his eyes mere slits, his lips clamped together.

"You will die for what you've done," he whispered, then turned to Tenilo and said, "What is it? What do you want?"

"I need to talk to you, my prince, in private, now."

Elio took a deep breath, nodded, then spun on his heel and walked out into the hallway, followed by Tenilo trotting along behind, the doors automatically closing behind them.

The prince stopped outside the door. Tenilo grabbed his arm and pulled him further down the hall.

What is it? Elio asked, probing Tenilo's mind.

"I read the king's mind," Tenilo whispered. "He has no idea what's going on... He's totally unaware of the Psy attack," Tenilo said, speaking rapidly; something that only happened when he was either very excited or stressed. "I suspect Queen Zara is behind the attack. I tried to read her mind, but she knew it and blocked me. Her mind was a total blank. I couldn't get through."

Elio's rage began to subside as he listened to Tenilo.

He was quiet for a moment, thinking hard, then he said, "I believe you. I don't think the king has it in him. Zara, however... What are we going to do?"

"I don't know," Tenilo replied. "We can't have her arrested... Not yet. We don't have proof. Until we can figure out exactly what happened... how she formulated her attack, we have to sit tight, stay on guard. Elio, I think she'll come after you next. You must keep your mind closed at all times. You are vulnerable. I was able to read your mind with ease. You must be on your guard at all times, especially when you're asleep."

"Don't be ridiculous, Tenny. How am I going to do that?"

"I don't know, but I do know that your Psy and TK are the strongest I've ever encountered. Even so, you're going to need all the security you can get. Your most trustworthy guards only."

Elio nodded. "Yes, but what of my father?"

"You both can share my security detail. You need them more than I do," Tenilo said. "Prince Felder provided me with eight members of his personal guards."

Elio took Tenilo's hand in both of his and shook it.

"That's gracious of you, Tenny. I appreciate it, and I accept your offer. I'll contact Ugo Tan. He'll know what to do."

Tenilo nodded. The sooner they had a plan, any plan, the better. "You're welcome, my prince," he said. "Yes, I agree. Ugo will know what to do."

Elio was silent for a moment, then lifted his arm and sent Ugo Tan a message requesting an immediate meeting.

* * *

Elio returned to his suite, leaving Tenilo to return to the king's bedside.

He took a quick, ice-cold hydro to waken himself and clear his mind, then he put on his halo and jacked into his meeting with Marshal Ugo Tan.

For almost five minutes, Elio laid out the facts as he knew them for the marshal. Ugo Tan was not surprised by what he heard but somewhat skeptical, his expression pensive until Elio had finished his speech.

"And you believe Queen Zara is behind this... supposed attack? Because if you're wrong," Ugo said, stroking his chin, "the Tudors could well file a complaint against *you*, Your Highness. They could accuse you of treason against them and the Odin System."

Elio hadn't considered that, but he was steadfast in his decision. "She's behind the attack," he said, placing his elbows on the table. "I'm certain of it. What are we going to do, Ugo? The king is vulnerable to another attack... and so am I."

Ugo rubbed the back of his neck, twisted his head from side to side in an effort to ease the stress, pursed his lips, turning his huge white mustache into a row of bristles and Elio couldn't help but be reminded of an aging walrus on Homeworld.

"Your safety, and the king's safety, are of the utmost

importance," he said. "I'll assign two platoons of Marine Guards to protect you and His Majesty."

Elio nodded, but he couldn't help but wonder if all these guards would be able to provide protection or simply draw attention. *How could they possibly prevent another Psy attack? What happened to Father was without any warning.*

He didn't refuse Tan's offer, though. He decided he'd take every precaution necessary to protect himself and his father. Even if it meant being surrounded day and night by more than two dozen guards. Would they merely provide a false sense of security? He didn't know.

"I'll also open an investigation into the matter. I'll assign a team of our best detectives," Ugo continued. "Queen Zara will be thoroughly investigated."

"Thank you, Marshal Tan," Elio said, happy that Ugo appeared to be taking the matter seriously. He was already hopeful that it would soon be resolved and the guilty party punished, though he couldn't see how he could have the queen executed without starting a full-blown war between the two systems.

He took off his halo and collapsed onto his bed. He was tired, and the royal load he'd taken on was already beginning to weigh heavily upon his shoulders. There were other things on his mind besides the attack on his father. The Swarm was still out there. Humanity's survival still hung in the balance, and would continue to do so as long as the alien enemy's presence remained.

He closed his eyes and wondered if the *Avenger* was making headway on her trek toward the Eta Persei System. *I hope they're all right...*

Chapter Eleven

Persei System

New Hope

Kyne Minnah

Kyne Minnah and twenty-nine survivors of the Swarm invasion of Typhon, now established in a small canyon northwest of New Hope, were... jittery. It had been six weeks since Kyne had sent the probe containing his transmission requesting help to Elio.

The probe, programmed to use the Slipstream network and send the transmission on exit into the Orso System, should have arrived more than three weeks ago, but he'd heard nothing back and was wondering if the probe had even made it through.

It was only a matter of time, he knew, before the Blues found him and his small group. Rescue was their only hope for survival.

Kyne, seated in the wreckage of a second-generation Swarm ship, had been working diligently examining the downed alien ship for months and had made some minimal progress hacking into its systems but, for the most part, the ship was dead. Some minor systems were drawing power from somewhere. Where, he didn't know, but he had his suspicions.

The ship was almost a third larger than the first-generation ships that had led the attack on Typhon all those months ago. Its stubby wings and all four weapons platforms had been torn away when it impacted the canyon walls. Only the upper section of the fuselage remained intact. Its primary power source, however, whatever it was, wherever it came from, was no more. Kyne believed the power source, like the early Swarm ships, and Blues themselves, was drawn from the invader's own reality—wherever that was—and that included what little power was still present.

He'd thought the core he'd taken from the stomper might be used to reenergize the ship, but it was a forlorn hope soon discarded. He didn't have the technical knowledge to make it work. The core now sat on what appeared to be the ship's console, glowing, pulsing, tantalizing.

Kayne knew the core was, in itself, a source of power—it did, after all, power the stomper he'd taken it from. But Kyne also knew—at least he thought he did—that the core was a highly advanced, sophisticated computer capable of communicating not only with the Swarm ships, troopers and the grays, but also with its alternate reality, and that intrigued him. For seemingly endless days and nights he'd worked on the thing, trying to break through its defenses. To date, he'd made little progress and what progress he had made, made little to no sense to him. He needed the aid of a

Class 1 AI, and there wasn't one on Typhon; never had been, not even before the invasion. New Hope was a mining town.

He was seated in what he assumed had once been the pilot's chair and was staring thoughtfully at the glowing orb. He'd managed to open its transparent skin and probe its innards, but all he'd found were nine small nodes connected to and equidistant around the inside of the outer skin and a swirling mass of pure energy seemingly generated by the nodes.

So... he thought, *you're still connected to... something, but what, and how, and how can I get you to talk to me? Are you receiving and transmitting, I wonder? Are you analyzing me, breaking me down, studying me, as I am trying to study you? Are you a spy reporting your findings to your masters in another universe? What secrets do you hold, my little ball of blue fire?*

His datapad chirped. The nerve jacks in his arm tingled, signaling an incoming transmission, jerking him out of his thoughts.

He tapped the sensor. A small hologram sprang to life, hovering above the pad.

"Kyne," Elio said. "I hope you're still alive and able to receive this message. *Avenger* is on its way to get you and any survivors you have with you..." The avatar paused, then continued, "Kyne. We need to know what's going on out there. You indicated you'd captured some sort of enemy technology and that you're trying to decode it. We're losing the war. Kyne. We need a breakthrough. We need intelligence. By the time the probe reaches you and you get this transmission, *Avenger* should be in the Persei System. Prepare yourself and your survivors for extraction. Goodbye, my friend. I hope we can be together again soon." The hologram flickered and disappeared.

Kyne grabbed the glowing core, stepped out onto the rocky canyon floor and quickly made his way back to the cave he and his survivor friends were using as a shelter-cum-workshop.

It was dark inside the cave opening with no indication it was occupied, but the further he strode down the rocky trail into the interior, the lighter it became. Deep underground, the cave became a huge cavern that had been turned into a haven of light and semi-comfort. The thirty survivors had, over the sixteen months since New Hope had been destroyed, gathered together a vast array of technology, including a micro fusion reactor that provided energy, heat and light, along with tools, computer cores, food, water and weapons. They had become a small but well-equipped secret colony.

For fourteen of those months, Kyne had worked nonstop developing a half dozen breakthrough ideas and inventions, and for nine of the fourteen he'd been trying to solve the secrets of the Blue core. But without the help of a Class 1 AI, he'd found it impossible, and that irked him intensely.

"Mozzley, Drave, Ussef, everyone, gather round," he shouted. "I have news."

"You cracked the code," Drave yelled in excitement.

"Sadly, no," Kyne replied. "But what I've just learned affects us all. Is everybody here?"

He looked around. They all turned and looked at each other—fifteen men, eight women and six children—shaking and nodding their heads.

"We're all here, then," Kyne said. "Good. I've received a message from Prince Elio. Help is on the way. The *Avenger* should be here in the next couple of days or so. We must be prepared to leave as soon as they arrive, if they arrive. As we all know, Persei space is crawling with Swarm ships, as Typhon is with Blues.

"Pack only what you need and be ready to leave at a moment's notice. Drave, Mozzley, you must help me get ready. What we have here could possibly change the outcome of the war."

Chapter Twelve

Eta Persei System

Swarm Space

The *Avenger*

Jax was slowly beginning to settle into the job that had been so suddenly thrust upon him. He was handling the helm well, but Morian could see how nervous the young pilot was.

Working with Krista, he was making minor course adjustments and blessing the stars that Swarm encounters had been minimal since Haltar Sen had been ordered to the medical bay. It was four-thirty, standard time, day eleven of their journey, during which they'd made fourteen Slipstream jumps. The boredom of Slip travel and the rigors of the constant battles with the enemy, small though most of them had beem\n, were beginning to take their toll on the ship's company, especially the crew of the command deck.

Manda had assured the captain that it would be relatively clear, with very little resistance from the Swarm as they approached the Eta Persei System. They were now only two jumps out—one into the NGC884 System and the final jump into the Eta Persei System. Thus far, all of her predictions had been accurate, and Morian had no reason to doubt her abilities as they prepared to make the jump to NGC884.

Morian stood at the bridge as they flew deeper and deeper into Swarm Space. The distant stars he saw on the forward screens were varying shades of blue, reminding him of home, but also reminding him of the Swarm ships and their array of weaponry.

The ships, surrounded by a glowing blue halo, were equipped with four weapons platforms. Two on each stubby wing; two above and two below, each multi-directional and each capable of operating individually or together. Those weapons had devastating firepower. Each could fire a withering bolt of brilliant blue plasma. Morian had seen the damage the alien weapons could cause, not only firsthand, but he'd also seen it in his sister's mind, and the minds of his fighter pilots, the Marines and refugees rescued during the past sixteen months. Psy was, is, an amazing gift, but sometimes it could play havoc with the minds of the gifted.

Because of his Psy abilities, he saw, through the eyes of those he was close to, the destruction the Blues were capable of. In her weakest moments, he saw the images of utter destruction that plagued Danis's thoughts. Images of her fighters being blown apart, reduced almost to dust by the power of the plasma beams. He'd seen the images of the Seers slaughtered back on Freyja as they circled through Manda's mind. Morian, in turn, was haunted by those same images. So much so that just the sight of the color blue, at times, would make his heart race.

He took a deep breath and told himself to stay in the present...

Thus far they'd been successful in their quest. And he was certain that if they stayed alert, their good fortune would continue and they'd make it to Typhon unscathed. *Two more jumps. We're almost there*, he thought.

Manda gave Jax the coordinates, and they entered the Slip that would take them to the NGC884 System, all that stood between them and the final jump into the Eta Persei System.

"This will be a short jump, Jax." She stood at the helm next to him, her hands clasped behind her back.

Jax nodded, a hint of a smile on his lips. "Entering slip to NGC884 System in three... two... one."

For the penultimate time, they felt the gentle shift of the ship as the Slipstream *pulled Avenger* into its embrace.

Morian nodded to himself. Part of him wanted to rest, to relax peacefully in the moment. He placed his hands on the rail and stared at the black, undulating depths of the giant holo display. It was hypnotic. He closed his eyes and willed himself to stay vigilant.

"Exiting Slip in..." Jax looked at Manda to be sure. She nodded, giving him the go-ahead, "thirty-seven minutes."

Manda went back up to the command deck and joined Morian at the rail.

"It should be smooth sailing from here on in," she said to Morian as she joined him at the rail. "After this jump, we should be able to enter the Eta Persei System without any problems."

"Thank you, Commander," Morian replied and visibly relaxed.

* * *

"Twenty-two minutes until exit," Jax announced.

Second by second, Manda counted down as the minutes ticked by. Try as she might, she couldn't stop her heart from fluttering. Even with her Sight, the anticipation always wore her down.

What if I got it wrong? She thought. *What if I miscalculated?* She clutched the rail, gripped it and hung on for dear life. That rail represented a virtual lifeline, for the captain, for herself and for Jadern. It was built from black osmium steel and was an integral part of the command deck. She was sure, at times, that had it not been made from osmium, her handprints would have been etched deep into its surface, a reminder of the stress they had to endure on a daily basis.

She breathed deeply, tried to slow her heart rate, but then, she was suddenly overwhelmed by a wave of light-headedness. She would have fallen to the floor had she not been grasping the rail. As it was, she moaned loudly and sank to her knees, still grasping the rail.

"Commander Haal?"

She heard Morian, and she could feel him grasp her arm, but she couldn't respond...

The dizziness normally passed quickly when her Sight activated, but this time, it got worse. She closed her eyes as her head began to throb. A stab of pain seared her brain.

"Ah! Oh..." she cried out, then clenched her teeth... And then, she could see it. Cloudy at first, but the pain in her head seemed to make the vision clearer:

They were only minutes away from exiting the current Slip and entering the next Slip to the Eta Persei System, their ultimate destination. She saw *Avenger* exit the Slip into the Eta Persei System, where they were ambushed. Swarm ships. Hundreds of them—more than they'd ever encountered before—surrounded them near and far. She could see the holo display aglow with their ships.

She saw Danis and the squadron deployed. The enemy craft were waiting for them. Half the squadron's numbers were destroyed within minutes. Danis was forced to make a run for it. "I've lost too many," Danis shouted, her voice filled with anguish.

The holo screen lit up red, each dot representing a lost fighter and pilot.

Jackknife was gone. Joker too.

"Fire all tubes," Kingston shouted.

The fusion engines were at full power, but *Avenger* could not outrun the enemy craft. They were everywhere. It seemed space was alive with them. *Avenger's* hull shuddered as blast after blast of plasma broke through the quickly diminishing shields.

"Engines two, three and six are gone, Captain," Manda heard Volkov shout. "We have a meltdown in reactor two. We can't contain it. She's going to blow any minute."

"Abandon ship," she heard Morian shout.

It was total chaos as the crew scrambled and fought to reach the escape pods, but it was too late... There was an almighty explosion, a brilliant flash of light and the ship was consumed from bow to stern... and then, *Avenger* was gone.

* * *

Manda gasped, coughed, and retched, her face covered in sweat. Morian and Jadern were kneeling beside her. "Captain..." she whispered.

"You passed out, Manda," Morian said as he and Jadern

helped her to her feet. "We'll take her to my ready room, Michael." And, together, they led a wobbly Manda from the bridge.

"What was that about? Morian asked as they helped her to a chair. "What's going on? He sat down facing her. "Are you well? Do you need to go to the med—"

"Please, Captain, if I may?" Manda interrupted him, holding up her hand.

He raised his eyebrows. Whatever it was that she'd seen, he knew it had to be serious. Manda's Sight attack was the worst he'd seen her endure. He nodded, allowing her to speak.

"When we exit the final Slip into Eta Persei, we'll be heading straight into an ambush, an ambush we won't survive. How long before we exit?" she asked. "We have to be ready for an attack."

"We exit to NGC884 in... seven minutes," Morian said, checking his chron. "We'll be on track to enter the Slip to the Eta Persei nine minutes later." He looked at her as she slowly shook her head. "Talk to me, Manda."

"It's... complicated. You'll have to trust me," she said. "We'll have to make a loop back around." Manda briefly closed her eyes, then opened them. "We cannot enter Typhon space at the present coordinates. I have new ones for you," and she dictated them to Krista.

"Please confirm the new coordinates, Captain," Krista said.

"Coordinates confirmed by Richard Morian. Commodore commanding *Avenger*. Please relay them to the appropriate members of the command crew, Krista."

"Thank you, Captain. Coordinates relayed to Lieutenant Haltar Sen, Ensign Dagon Jax and Senior Navigation Officer Simon DeLong."

"Load all torpedo tubes with the new M-99B missiles, Krista. And set the proximity triggers to fire the warheads at three hundred meters."

"Yes, Captain," Krista replied. "Orders relayed. Is there anything else?"

"No! Thank you, Krista."

"My pleasure, Captain."

He nodded, looked at Manda, then tapped on his datapad and contacted Dr. Jyra Dowd. Well or not, Haltar Sen was needed on the bridge to help Jax at the helm.

Seven minutes later, they dropped out of the Slip into NGC884 to be greeted by a Swarm cluster of thirty-three first-generation ships and six of the new second-generation —larger, faster, more heavily armed and more formidable than the earlier versions. They were deployed in a crescent formation three hundred kilometers out from the Slip gate. Not a large cluster, but made the more formidable by the addition of the six second-gen ships, three at each end of the crescent.

Manda's new coordinates would take the *Avenger* directly through the center of the formation. Not good, because it laid the ship open to a classic pincer attack as the wings of the crescent enfolded them.

Morian, now back on the bridge, stood at the rail and stared at the hologram. *Hmm...* he thought. *Thirty-nine...*

"All ahead full," Morian said calmly. "Flank speed for sixty seconds, if you please, Mr. Jax."

"All ahead full, Captain," Jax replied, and Morian felt the gentle surge as all six fusion engines went to full power.

Haltar Sen had joined Jax at the helm. He'd reported to Morian that he was stiff, his muscles cramping, but the meds Dr. Dowd had pumped into him were already beginning to take effect; he would be able to do his job and help Jax outmaneuver the enemy cluster.

Morian watched the time tick down, then said, "On my mark, reverse all... *MARK!*"

There was an audible "whoosh" as the engines shut down and then went into reverse, slowing the great ship almost to a stop.

Avenger was now in the dead center of the enemy formation, and the Swarm ships were already beginning to close the jaws of the crescent.

"Krista. Fire tubes one through twenty-four and reload," Morian snapped, bypassing the weapons station.

Instantly, twenty-two M-99 torpedoes left their tubes as the AI responded almost before Morian had finished giving the order.

"Tubes one through twenty-four away, Captain," Krista said, her voice emotionless, as always. "Reloading. Ready to fire in twenty-seven seconds."

Morian, Haal and Jadern, at the command rail, watched the hologram as the torpedoes, fired from the bow, rear wings and port and starboard sides, streaked away at speeds approaching Mach 17.

And then, the hologram was crisscrossed by more than one-hundred-fifty wavering blue streaks of plasma fire from the enemy ships. One by one the green dots representing *Avenger's* torpedoes began to wink out, but not all of them.

"Krista. Fire tubes one through twenty-four and reload."

Again, the ship shuddered as Krista fired the second salvo.

By then, the enemy had destroyed fifteen of the first twenty-two torpedoes. The remaining seven, however, had reached their preset proximities and had fired their warheads with devastating effect. Each 99B warhead carried six laser-guided, 120mm depleted uranium projectiles.

Morian and the entire bridge crew watched the hologram as, one by one, the blue dots began to disappear: three, then two more, three more... four.

"Oh yes!" Omario Kingston shouted, jumping up from his seat and pumping his fist. The rest of the crew began to cheer as they watched the enemy fleet being decimated. Even Morian was smiling.

"Yaaay!" Jadern shouted and then turned and slapped Morian's shoulder, then realized what he'd done.

"I... I'm sorry, Captain. I was—"

"It all right, Michael," Morian said, smiling as the second round of torpedoes closed in on their targets. By then, fourteen ships in the enemy fleet had been destroyed, including two of the new second-generation ships, and the remainder of the fleet had turned and were streaking away in all directions. Seven of them were not quite fast enough and one by one, over a period of less than thirty seconds, they exploded in balls of brilliant blue fire.

And then, as quickly as it had begun, it was over. What was left of the enemy fleet had disappeared from the hologram, heading into the system toward the twin suns.

Morian looked at Manda, smiled and said, "You're quiet. Not what you expected?"

She shrugged, smiled back at him and nodded, but she didn't reply. Morian knew she must be exhausted. The heavy weight of guiding *Avenger* across fifteen Slipstream jumps and more than a thousand light years distance was beginning to tell. She looked... drained. He reached out to her and could sense that her head was aching. Unfortunately, rest was not an option. They... she, still had two jumps to navigate before they could reach their destination.

"I'll give Jax the coordinates that will take us back to NGC869," Manda said wearily as she stepped away from the rail.

"Easy, Commander," Morian said. "Only three more jumps, right?"

She nodded and descended the steps to the well deck.

Ten minutes later they were in the Slip and Morian had ordered the shutdown.

"Sixty-nine minutes to exit, Captain," Haltar said.

Morian sighed. He'd hoped it wouldn't take that long. He wanted to exit and make the final two jumps to Typhon as soon as possible.

He shook his head and turned to Manda who was back at the rail. "Are you ready to tell me what happened?" he asked.

She nodded and said, "I need to sit down, Captain."

"My ready room, then," he replied and led the way off the bridge.

"Sit," he said as he dropped into his seat behind his desk.

She did, and the words came rushing out of her mouth. "It all changed," she said. "My vision." She licked her dry lips, her hands clasped together in her lap, and continued. "We weren't supposed to encounter any resistance when we entered Typhon's systems. Ten... fifteen enemy ships at the most... But that all changed. Now..." She shook her head in dismay. "I see chaos. Hundreds of enemy ships; too many. We won't survive. *Avenger* will be overwhelmed. If we don't do something she'll be destroyed... with all hands." Her face was pale. She bit her lip and stared helplessly at him.

Morian rubbed the stubble on his chin, looked at her, then closed his eyes, shook his head and sighed. He checked his chron. *We need to find a solution to this now,* he thought. "Krista?" His voice was strained.

"Yes, Captain?" the ship's AI responded instantly.

"Have the senior staff report to the conference room immediately."

"The order has been transmitted, Captain."

Chapter Thirteen

Avenger

Strategies

Slipstream

Morian waited as the senior staff arrived in small groups, including Jadern, Volkov, Fargo, Haltar Sen and Jax, Danis, and even Major Dubois who arrived with a gnarly smirk on his face. He took a stance at the rear of the room, close to the foot of the table facing Morian at the far end. He stood with his arms folded, feet apart. Dubois was either ready to do battle or to state his case and run.

Morian stood with his hands behind his back at the head of the table, looked around the gathering and said, "Please, sit down." He nodded at Sen. "I appreciate you stepping up, Haltar." He reached out to him hoping to make sure his senior helmsman was well and able to continue.

Sen's mind was a darkened space. Morian could tell the older man was hiding something, and there was a weariness in his eyes that Morian hadn't seen before.

"Of course, Captain," Sen replied.

Morian nodded, his concerns unabated. He took his seat, then turned to Manda who was seated at the table next to him and said, "Tell them what you just told me, Commander. Leave nothing out."

And she did. She let it all out and after several minutes, she leaned back in her chair, wiped her eye with the back of her hand and said, "That's it!"

"That's... not good," Danis said, acknowledging the understatement. "What are we going to do?"

"There must be something we can do," Jadern said, breathing deeply. "Are these visions you have... Are you seeing the inevitable future, or can it be changed?"

"I believe the elements—the Swarm presence, the location of the Slip gate and so on—are set and can't be changed," she replied. "If we exit the slip as planned, we *will* be destroyed. The question is, can we change *our* plan, develop a new strategy? So, now that you all have the information," Manda said, "we need to decide if we take the Slip to Typhon, or not."

She looked at Morian, and he gave her the okay to continue. "If we go, we have no choice. There is but one Slip gate into Typhon space." She quickly tapped on her datapad. "Haltar, I just sent you modified coordinates," she said.

Haltar glanced at the captain.

Morian nodded and said, "Go lay in the course, Mr. Sen."

"Wait," Kingston said. Sen paused at the door. "Has it occurred to anyone that this could be a trap?"

Fargo nodded nervously and said, "Is it possible the Swarm could have implanted the vision in your head, Commander Haal?"

Manda made a face, thought about it for a moment, then said, "It's possible... I suppose. Anything is possible, but I don't think that's what happened—"

"Neither do I," Morian said, interrupting her. He nodded to Sen, dismissing him. "The vision is Commander Haal's own. I'm convinced of it."

"So how do we change the outcome?" Jadern said, unable to hide the exasperation in his voice.

They all looked at the captain, and Morian looked at Manda.

The room was quiet. Everyone was still. Everyone was staring at Manda. Everyone wanted answers, but Manda didn't have any. Worse, she felt as if she was being interrogated, that what was happening was her fault. It wasn't. She'd just saved the ship and all their lives, for now. She opened her mouth to speak, but Corin Fargo beat her to it.

"Can you run a series of scenarios in your head?" Faro asked her. "See if you can find an option that might work?"

Several people nodded as Fargo was speaking. "Yeah, could you try that?" Kingston asked.

"Unfortunately," Manda said, her face pale, brow furrowed, "it doesn't work like that. Not for me, anyway. When I have a vision, it's... I can only project what will happen if we go down a certain path. I can't pick and choose... It's based on a course and a decision that's already been made. And as there is only one route to Typhon..."

Everyone at the table was looking at each other, restless, uneasy.

Arms still folded, Major Dubois spoke up. "Maybe I have something that will work... or at least give us a chance."

Morian looked at him and said, "Go on, Major. If you have a solution, let's hear it."

Dubois nodded, then said, "I saw a trick when I was aboard the USF *Luna* a few months ago that might work. You said that the Swarm will attack immediately upon our exiting the Slip. Is that not correct, Commander?"

"Yes, that's correct," Manda said. "As soon as we enter Typhon space. There will be no time for us to react."

"Well, then, in that case I think this could work; give us at least some breathing space."

Dubois looked at the officers assembled around the table and began to explain. "A ship can fire missiles prior to leaving the Slip. The *Luna* has proven that, but... it must be done at just the right moment," he said, wagging his forefinger. "The missiles can do their job and take the heat off the *Avenger*."

"That sounds like it might work," Kingston said thoughtfully.

"I agree," Morian said. "Not that we have a choice. Let's do it. To your stations, everyone. We don't have much time."

He waited until everyone had left the room and said, "Krista, load all thirty-two tubes with the new 99Bs and set the proximities to two hundred meters. Load Big Charlie with twenty-five-kilogram canister and prepare to fire all weapons on my mark. Then keep loading and fire at will until I give the order to cease. Bring point defense online the instant we exit the Slip and fire at will."

"Yes, Captain. Understood. All tubes are loaded and ready to fire on your mark. Point defense is standing by."

* * *

Morian sensed that everyone had mixed feelings about the plan, but they trusted the captain's decision nonetheless.

Morian, too, was anxious, though he'd never show it. He'd never done anything like it before, though he had heard rumors, and also knew there was plenty that could go wrong. Dubois was right: the timing was crucial.

Jax was continuously wiping his hands on his flight suit. Haltar, stoic, was seated at his side, ready to give help or support if it was needed.

"Six minutes and thirty-seven seconds to exit, Captain," Jax said.

Haltar Sen waved Manda over. "You're positive what you saw is correct?"

"Yes..." She hesitated. "As positive as I can be. I... just don't know anymore."

Sen nodded and rechecked the coordinates just to be sure.

Morian stood up from his command chair, stepped up to the rail and gripped it lightly with both hands. "Krista. On my mark. Fire all torpedo tubes and Big Charlie and reload and fire at will."

"On your mark, Captain," Krista replied.

Morian counted down two of the remaining five minutes to exit. "Five... four... three... two... *MARK!*"

The great ship shuddered as thirty-two M-99B torpedoes left the tubes, and under the recoil of the ship's giant railgun, the so-called Big Charlie. Twenty-three seconds later, she shuddered again, and then again. By the time she exited the slip, Krista had fired five salvos of M-99B torpedoes and five twenty-five kilogram canisters.

But Morian was worried. They were firing blind and Krista, as close to sentient as she was, without targets to lock onto, was limited.

Manda had, as best she could, worked around the blind spot problem by feeding Kingston specific coordinates as to where the Swarm clusters might be. "Might" being the operative word. If asked, Morian knew she would have replied that she was relying mostly on educated guesswork.

"Slipstream exit in T-minus thirty seconds," Krista said. "Continuing to fire all tubes on exit. Point defense is online and will open fire as targets come to bear."

Jax had a petrified look on his face, sweat showing on his uniform.

"Five, four, three..." Krista continued to count down.

Time itself seemed to stand still. Everyone sat rigidly upright in their seats as they stared at the churning blackness of the holo display.

Morian leaned against the rail.

Avenger exited the Slip into open space.

The hologram blinked into life showing Typhon space in real time. Typhon's sun, Eta Persei, some twelve-hundred-twenty light years from Orso, was in the upper western quadrant of the system. Typhon was represented on the holo by a round, purple orb at the dead center of the display.

A green icon representing *Avenger* appeared, surrounded by hundreds of blue dots. Hundreds more were in orbit around the planet, and even more were orbiting the sun. Manda had been right. Had they dropped out without her warning, Morian had no doubt they would have been destroyed. As it was, she was already taking fire from the closest enemy ships.

But space, for more than five kilometers in every direction, was littered with the debris of a hundred or more enemy ships, destroyed by the one-hundred-sixty torpedoes fired from within the Slip.

Morian watched the forward view screen as dozens of enemy craft came streaking in, seemingly from every direction.

Her forty-eight point defense railgun turrets opened fire with eighty-eight-millimeter dutrinium orbs. Enemy ship after ship exploded under the withering hail of fire, but not all. Some got through. He watched as bolt after bolt of plasma from more than a dozen ships hammered the shields, slowly breaking them down.

He gripped the rail, slowly shaking his head, then realized what he was doing and stopped. He couldn't let the crew see his doubts.

The great ship shuddered violently as she took a plasma bolt to her upper port bow and another to her keel, and Morian watched as one of the point defense turrets went spinning off into space.

He gritted his teeth. "Krisa," Morian commanded. "continue to fire all tubes. Shields, Mr. Kingston? Damage report, Mr. Volkov?

"We took a hit to deck seven, port side, forward, and another to deck five," Volkov said. "We also lost turret sixteen. Zero hull breach. The new armor is holding... so far."

"Forward shields are down to fourteen percent, Captain," Kingston said. "I'm diverting power from reactor four to bring them back online. Shields overall are at eighty-two percent."

Morian nodded and continued to watch as the carnage continued to grow. The enemy ships close enough to fire were being decimated by the hail of dutrinium being hurled at them.

They all watched as the green streaks representing the salvos of torpedoes continued to reach their targets. Their internal targeting systems automatically locking on. And they watched as the warheads exploded and the torpedo icons blinked out, as did more and more of the blue icons representing Swarm ships until there were too many to count.

The bridge crew heaved a collective sigh of relief and began to cheer.

"Stop that at once!" Morian snapped. "I appreciate your enthusiasm, but we're not out of it yet. Watch your stations. Ms. Fargo—"

He interrupted himself as he watched the ninth wave of torpedoes streak toward their targets, and he actually smiled when he saw one of Big Charlie's canisters explode in the center of a large cluster, taking out a third of their number.

"Krista, stand down," he continued quietly. "Ms. Fargo, continue to fire as we go. We need to clear a pathway and find a way to the planet."

"Aye, Captain," Fargo replied, her eyes glued to her targeting hologram.

"All ahead half, Mr. Jax. Take us out of this mess."

Jax, still in a state of shock, merely nodded and tapped the screens; the six fusion engines responded and drove the ship forward. The inertia dampeners kicked in, so the bridge barely felt the punishing G-forces as the *Avenger* rapidly accelerated through Mach 40—almost fifty-thousand kilometers per hour—following the preset coordinates Manda had given him.

He felt Jadern clap him on the shoulder and say, "Well, Captain, that went well, I think."

Morian smiled. Jadern never failed to impress him with his propensity for understatement.

"A little too soon to celebrate, don't you think, Michael?" he replied.

"True, Captain. But a wise man once told me to always look on the bright side," Jadern said, giving Morian a knowing look.

"And who, pray tell, was that?" Morian asked.

"It was you, captain. It's what you told me when I was first assigned to *Avenger*."

* * *

Danis, Morian reached out to his sister, *Be ready. According to Manda's predictions, we're in for a bumpy ride.*

Should I deploy the whole squadron? she said.

No. Just you and your three best pilots. We're going to make a run for it. You'll act as escorts. Take up a position above and to the rear of the bridge. Sorry, I don't need to tell you how to do your job. The ship should be able to handle the brunt of the work...

Agreed, Captain, she said. *We'll deploy whenever you give the word.*

Morian took a deep breath. He could feel the adrenaline surging through his sister's body.

Good luck, Danis. Don't take any unnecessary risks. I want you back here in one piece.

You bet, brother. Keep the big baby safe. See you shortly.

"I'm still waiting for my thank you, Captain," Dubois said, breaking into his thoughts.

"I'm sorry," Morian said. "I didn't realize you were on the bridge." *Does this man always need his ego stroked?* he thought, forcing a smile. "Yes... That was quite a trick. Thank you, Major."

Major Dubois chuckled to himself. "I'll be expecting a drink once this is all over. Your finest Orsonian brandy, I think."

Dubois didn't really catch the look Morian gave him, nor did he catch on to the fact that Morian wasn't in the mood to chit-chat.

"Of course, Major... Yes, that can be arranged." He checked his chron. It was just after six o'clock in the evening, standard time. Typhon was still six hours ahead and the route fraught with danger. It would be close to one in the morning when the Marines went planet-side.

"But, what is that old saying on Homeworld?" Morian continued. "'We're not out of the woods yet.'"

Dubois, to Morian's surprise, didn't respond. He simply nodded, clicked his heels and bowed his head, then turned and left the bridge.

* * *

"Gian, Jackknife, Ozzie," Danis snapped. "We're on escort duty. Prepare for imminent deployment. The rest of you stand down but stay in your ships in case you're needed."

Danis checked her systems, then said, "Zilvo. Cockpit check, please."

She'd managed to convince Grell Dunn to stay behind and work on his TK skills. She could sense something of an attitude shift in him. He seemed more... compliant and willing to learn. But she knew he wasn't ready for a full battlefield deployment. So she had her robot copilot in the seat behind her.

"All systems are operating at one hundred percent, Domino," the AI replied.

The fingers of her left hand fluttered over the controls as she brought her grav-engines, targeting, weapons, and proximity systems online. The hologram to her right appeared and she was shocked by the sight of the battlefield, the hundreds of blue ships, and the carnage created by *Avenger's* defensive activity.

She felt the sudden surge as Jax brought the six fusion engines to full power. As soon as the ship achieved flank speed, she would deploy.

"Ranger escort," she snapped. "Stand by to follow me out."

She felt the rush as the ship's fusion engines shut down as *Avenger* achieved Mach 40. *Here we go...*

The decompression warnings sounded, and two minutes later the hangar doors opened.

"On me," she snapped as she lifted the F32 off the hangar deck on its grav-engines and circled out into the black, followed by Gian, Jackknife and Ozzie Yalta, Ranger 10.

The second she exited the hangar, Danis shut down her gravs and brought her four fusion engines online. Then she circled *Avenger* and maneuvered into position above the port wing with Gian on her left. Jackknife took a similar position over the starboard wing with Ozzie on his left.

Almost immediately, her proximity alarms began to sound.

"Adjusting target range," Zilvo said. "Incoming! Sixty enemy craft. Range seven hundred kilometers and closing."

"Thanks, buddy," Danis said, mostly to herself. It was good to have her little robot back as copilot, for a while, anyway.

"Domino to Ranger Flight," she said as she flipped her engines and put the F32 into a blistering vertical climb, followed by her three comrades. "Let's show these blue bastards what we can do."

At five kilometers out, she shut down the power to her two starboard engines, throwing the F32 into a wide looping turn, then went to full power on all four engines and streaked back toward the incoming enemy cluster.

"Domino to Rangers. Fire missiles on my mark... *Mark!*" And eight Mark 7 Harpoon missiles streaked away toward the incoming enemy craft, still too far out for *Avenger's* point defense system to engage.

She watched her holo as the missiles closed with the enemy swarm—still too far out for visuals. Almost together, all eight missiles reached their pre-set proximities and fired their warheads. On her holo display, Danis watched as the blue dots began to blink out. She counted fifteen destroyed. *Not bad,* she thought.

"Domino to rangers. Fire two." And again, eight missiles sped away toward the incoming enemy ships

"Avenger to Domino," Omario Kingston said, his voice urgent. "Priority one! Return to *Avenger* and dock, best speed."

"You heard him," she said to her team, "Let's go home."

As she made the turn and flew for home, she reached out to her brother. *What's going on, Richard?*

You probably don't want to know, he replied. *Just get back aboard as quick as you can.*

* * *

Morian closed his mind to Domino, took a new grip on the rail and stared at the hologram, feeling the ship shudder beneath his feet as the point defense turrets fired sporadically.

Dubois had been right. His out-of-the-box tactic had indeed cleared a way through the cluster. How much damage *Avenger* had taken, though, was yet to be determined.

He gazed at the giant hologram, an atlas of the entire Eta Persei System.

He adjusted the view slightly, rotated it, still centered on the purple icon that represented the planet Typhon.

The sun, still in the upper western quadrant, some three-hundred-fifty-four million kilometers from Typhon, was surrounded by blue dots: too many to count visually.

He looked up at the display floating above the hologram; it was in flux, numbers changing by the second. The number of Swarm ships around the sun now numbered eleven-hundred-eighty-four. Swarm ships destroyed on exit from the Slip, including those Danis had just destroyed: two-hundred-eleven, leaving two-hundred-seventy still in proximity of the exit Slip gate. Swarm ships within five-thousand kilometers of Typhon: nine-hundred-twelve. Swarm ships in geosynchronous orbit around Typhon: one-hundred-sixty-three, most of them over the two population centers: New Hope and Bariettaire.

He stood alone at the rail. Manda Haal was in her seat next to the captain's chair. Michael Jadern was on the well deck talking to Omario Kingston. Haltar Sen and Dagon Jax were at the helm. *Avenger* was approaching one-quarter light speed and heading away from the sun into the eastern quadrant of the system—a route that would take them far away from the cluster of Swarm ships around the sun and to the dark side of the planet.

Inwardly, he shook his head and continued to stare at the hologram.

Getting in without being detected was going to be only the first hurdle. The second would be getting his Marines on the ground and off again while remaining undetected.

Morian knew that Kyne Minnah and his tiny group of

survivors were somewhere in the desert eighty kilometers, or thereabouts, to the northwest of New Hope.

"Mr. Kingston," Morian began, "Mr. Sen, Commander Haal, Commander Jadern. Conference room, now. Krista, ask Major Dubois and Commander Morian to join us, immediately."

Five minutes later, the seven officers were seated around the table in the conference room.

Morian generated a hologram in the center of the table, a much smaller twin to the one on the bridge, and expanded it to show more detail.

"As you can see," Morian began. "We are here." He pointed to the green dot that represented *Avenger*.

"We are some nine-hundred million kilometers from Typhon, here." Again he pointed, this time to the purple dot that represented *Avenger*.

"The enemy presence around Typhon is centered here and here," he continued. "We will approach the planet from the dark side. What I don't understand is why there's such a concentration of enemy craft in Typhon's space. The planet is conquered. The population virtually wiped out. My last transmission from Prince Elio, just before we left, said there are only thirty survivors, including Kyne Minnah. So why the huge enemy presence?"

"This Kyne Minnah," Kingston said. "Who and what is he?"

"Some kind of tech wizard... as far as I know," Morian replied. "And he has some captured Blue tech... Hmm. Perhaps he's the reason. No matter. We have more pressing problems to deal with."

Chapter Fourteen

Strategies

Typhon System

"**A**re we not out of the woods yet, Captain?" Dubois' tone was one of relief and sarcasm.

Morian stared at him. He didn't understand how the man managed to maintain his brash attitude at such a time.

"Not quite, Major," he said as he watched the holo display. *Avenger* inched closer to Typhon. "We still have several major problems to overcome. Not the least of which is getting you and your Marines on the ground and off again—"

Manda coughed, interrupting him; a long, hacking cough and then cleared her throat.

"Are you sure you don't need to go to the med bay, Commander? You really don't look well." It was the third time Morian had asked her.

She nodded weakly and drank some water from her hydro pack.

"No. I'm fine, really," she said, obviously not wanting to be relieved and sent to Dr. Dowd. "I still feel a little light-headed but much better than I did. And I have a slight headache, but that's something I'm becoming accustomed to." She smiled weakly at him.

"So, Captain," Jadern said, deftly changing the subject, "we're at flank speed and some six hours out from Typhon. Have you formulated a plan of action for when we arrive?"

"Not one I'm happy with," Morian replied, "which is why you're all here."

Morian tapped the hologram and changed the view to one of the planet Typhon. "This is the most current map I have of Typhon," he said. He touched a spot on the hologram with a fingertip; a red dot appeared. "As far as we know, Kyne Minnah and his group have gone to ground in this area here." He tapped again and the view expanded.

"As you can see, it's desert country—desolate, rugged and, during daylight hours, extremely hot. The location, though we don't know exactly where, is about eighty miles northwest of New Hope. Prince Elio has supplied the frequency upon which we can contact him. It's centuries old short-wave so, we hope, the Blues won't be monitoring it."

"Short-wave?" Jadern asked, looking at Sandra Lowry.

She smiled and said, "It's an archaic form of radio communication dating back to before The Purge. It's quite simple. It operates on the frequencies between the AM and FM bands. It has the unique characteristic of traveling very long distances, making it the perfect medium to someone like Kyne Minnah. It's old tech, but it's reliable. I have manufactured a radio transmitter and receiver for you to use. It's..." She made a face, then continued, "kind of primitive, but it should work, provided Kyne's still alive... and he's listening."

"See if you can contact him, Sandra," Morian said. "If he's listening, you should be able to get a fix on his position."

She nodded her head and said, "I'll give it a go, but the unit is low powered; only ten watts, and we're still a long way out."

"Please, do your best. I need his location."

Lowry nodded, stood up and left the room.

"You mentioned other problems, Captain," Jadern said.

"I did," Morian replied. "Most of them relating to getting in and out undetected."

He changed the holo view back to the Eta Persei System. The green dot that was *Avenger* was notably closer to the planet. The blue clusters of Swarm ships hadn't changed, which he took to be a good sign, one that seemed to indicate they were sailing undetected. *Avenger's* engines were shut down. She was sailing under her own momentum using only passive scanners. Only her thrusters were firing now and then, making tiny course corrections. She was, in effect, running silently.

"We'll approach the planet on the dark side and establish a low, geosynchronous orbit. Lieutenant Jax, you will shuttle the Marines to the surface where they will deploy and, we hope, rescue the survivors without incident. You will then ferry them back to the ship and we'll take them home. Easy!"

He grinned at the assembled officers. Not one of them looked quite so confident as he did.

"What about the Slip gate?" Sen asked. "It will be guarded... surely."

Morian looked at Manda, his eyebrows raised in question.

"It's on the far side of the planet from the exit gate."

She gave Morian the coordinates. He tapped them into the holo display and a yellow dot appeared.

"Stars!" he said before thinking, and he tapped again and brought up a number. "One-hundred-eleven. That's... not good. We'll have to draw them away somehow.

He shook his head, pursed his lips, then said, "Well, that's a problem we can address later. For now..."

It was at that moment that Sandra Lowry returned.

"Ms. Lowry?" Morian said.

"I spoke to Minnah. The connection wasn't good, but it worked. He and twenty-nine souls are waiting for us." She tapped the holo and changed it back to a view of the planet, expanded it and touched the display. "He's somewhere here, in the desert."

Morian tapped the holo and expanded it further to show an aerial view of the region. It was a vast, mountainous desert area of rocky peaks and canyons, desolate, dry and... unapproachable.

"Now we know why Minnah chose it," Danis said. "It would be difficult to put an F32 down there, much less a shuttle."

"Commander Morian is right," Jadern said as Morian zoomed in on the area. "There's no way the shuttle can put down there."

"No," Dubois said thoughtfully. "He chose that location wisely. Some of those mountains are more than ten kilometers high. If we can't put down there, neither can the Swarm. Mr. Jax? You're the shuttle pilot. What d'you think?"

"I can try, but—" Jax replied, shaking his head before Morian interrupted him.

"No!" he said. "You can't try. This is too important. If you try and fail... We can't afford that. What other options do we have? We need to be in and out quickly before the Blues discover us. What's the nearest location you can put down?"

Jax looked at the terrain, slowly shook his head and then said, "Here... maybe."

"Morian stared at the spot to which Jax was pointing, shook his head and said, "That's fifteen kilometers. Not quick and probably not possible."

"Captain," Dubois said, taking his usual arms-folded-feet-spread-apart stance. "May I suggest something?"

Morian raised an eyebrow; he was surprised that the man asked permission at all. "Of course, please do."

"We could do a suborbital drop," he said, nodding once like it was already decided. "We have the appropriate gear. We also have personal grav-packs. Here's what I suggest. I will take half my Marines—thirty, plus myself—and we'll make a drop from inside the atmosphere at an altitude of say, twelve thousand meters. That will enable Jax to make the drop and be in and out quickly."

"And this is safe?" Morian asked as he stared at him in a mixture of fascination and horror. The man was either an idiot or a hero or a daredevil, or all three. Morian had heard the horror stories about such stunts. One human error, and the drop suit would not operate correctly. The great fear with this: hypoxia sets in quickly, blood vessels in the brain constrict and burst, then death. Morian winced at the thought.

Dubois puffed out his chest even more. "I wouldn't suggest it if I didn't think we could do it. It's what we've been trained for, Captain... Look," he said, sucking his teeth. "It's safer than if we were to take the shuttle down among those peaks. I've been in similar situations, and I can tell you this. It is far more dangerous than a drop suit. And... Who knows if—I'm sorry—*when* the Swarm ships will show up? This way, we go in covertly. We grab the survivors and we get them out of there. Quickly and quietly, as you requested." He ended his speech with a nod. He was satisfied with himself.

"What about extraction?" Manda asked. "How are we going to get all those people back? What do you suggest for that, Major Dubois?"

"The drop team will be equipped with grav-packs," he replied. "We'll take enough extra packs for up to thirty-five. The shuttle will fly in at a low altitude—after we provide the coordinates—and we'll... We'll fly up and board it. Simple."

The officers stared at him open-mouthed, as did Morian. But the truth was, he, Morian, could think of no other way to carry out the mission.

Morian sighed, checking his chron and said, "We're three hours out." He nodded, took a deep breath, looked at the Marine Major and said, "All right, Dubois. I don't like it. It's risky, but I don't see an alternative. We'll do the drop. Get your Marines ready."

"Commander Morian, you, Jackknife, Gian and Ossie, stand by to support the shuttle and the Marines."

Danis nodded reluctantly.

Everyone filed out of Morian's office except Manda and Danis who pulled the captain to one side and began speaking earnestly to him.

* * *

An hour later, Danis was in her brother's ready room, awaiting Major Dubois.

"So you've made up your mind to do this?" Morian asked.

"You know I have," she replied.

Morian sighed. When his sister was determined to do something, there was no changing her mind. Of course, he was captain and he could order her not to go, but he trusted her, and he knew she was capable. He would always care about her safety, though. And that was never going to change.

Danis could feel the protective cloak emanating from her brother. Even without the use of Psy she could feel it, and she smiled at him; she knew her brother very well.

"You know," she said. "I haven't heard you use that phrase in quite a while." She leaned back in her chair, stretching her arms.

"What phrase?"

"You know the one: 'Grace, good luck, and gumption.' Daddy always did have a way of saying things, didn't he?"

Their father, also named Richard, had been a pilot himself, though discharged after a bad training accident that involved civilians. It led him to drink. Synthol became his best friend, and eventually, it had killed him.

"He did," Morian said with a sigh.

Danis knew how much their father's guidance had meant to her brother. It had meant so much to her, too. Richard and Danis were twins, but they'd never been treated equally. Danis had always been the girl, the one that needed to be protected by her older-by-four-minutes brother.

In some ways, their mother, Gloria, would always see Danis as a girl. Her mother was very old school and set in her ways, more interested in when her daughter would find a mate to settle down with and have children than Danis's flight simulation stats. She'd been able to holo chat with her mother two standard days before the *Avenger* set off on her mission to Typhon:

"Can you believe these kids today?" Gloria asked her daughter. "No manners... 'What the vac' this and 'what the vac' that. Their mouths should be sanitized."

Danis just nodded. She knew how much her mother loathed the phrase, "What the vac?" The word "vac" meaning vacuum... Her mother felt like if "vac" was said enough times, the Slipstreams would close in on themselves, form a giant black hole, and all within them would be lost. It was a little extreme, but that was how she felt...

"They should be thanking the heavens above for even existing at all. All this alien madness going on." Then the conversation turned inevitably to Danis's love life, or lack thereof. "I know you," Gloria said. "You're my daughter and I see in your eyes that you have feelings for somebody."

Danis wasn't ready to talk about Elio... or Jackknife... or whatever she was feeling, because she was still trying to sort through it all herself. Her mother would just have to wait on the love story.

"So, how was that holodrama you were telling me about?" Danis quickly changed the subject. *Mom will be fine*, she thought. Women, if they chose, could have a baby well into their seventies, *I'll be fine...*

Major Dubois stepped into the ready room, interrupting her thoughts. "What's so important, Captain?" he asked impatiently. "I'm getting my Marines geared up for the drop."

"Well, Major," Morian said, looking at his sister, "this relates to that."

Dubois saw where Morian was looking, at Danis, and he raised an eyebrow, confused.

"Well, what is it?" he said after waiting for someone to say something. "Don't we have a schedule to keep here?"

"Tell him, Danis."

She stood up, turned and faced Dubois, then said, "The captain's already signed off on it," she said, emphasizing her brother's title, "but I'd like to ask your permission to join you on the drop."

She was scared out of her wits by the idea, but she made sure that none of that leaked through. Her hands were behind her back. She squeezed them together.

Dubois opened his mouth to speak, then shut it again quickly with a *pop*, then said, "Join the drop, you say? You mean that *you*, untrained and ill-equipped, want to join a platoon of highly trained Marines on a suborbital drop?" His eyes creased as he smiled. He obviously thought it was funny. Then the smile was gone. "Absolutely not," he snapped.

Chapter Fifteen

Impositions

Typhon System

Danis blinked several times. She hadn't expected Dubois' words to sting as much as they did. But she kept her composure, wiped her sweaty hands on the pants of her USF suit, and looked Dubois directly in the eyes. "No, I'm not a trained soldier," she admitted, locking eyes with him. "But I've led a platoon of Marines in combat before. So I think I can handle it."

It was true. Back in the Pricus System on the planet Tor, she was the one who had to take the lead. She had no idea how she got through it, but she'd learned from the experience.

"I've faced the Blues. I've killed Blues face to face. I'll be an asset."

But Dubois wasn't moved. "I don't see how you'll be much hel—"

Morian raised his hand, cutting him off. "It's settled, Major. She's going with you."

And that was the end of it. Dubois nodded, saluted, turned on his heel and left the room without saying another word.

Morian sighed, glanced at his datapad. "W're behind schedule," he said.

He cleared his throat. "Gian, Jackknife, Ossie and Skyla will fly fighter escort."

"Skyla?" Danis asked.

"Yes, she's a good pilot and wasted in the copilot's seat, and her TK is strong."

She nodded, took a deep breath. "That's good. Thank you."

She was about to take her leave when Richard stopped her again.

Wait... he reached out into her mind. *There's something else.*

* * *

Danis saw what he was thinking, and she couldn't believe it.

You can't be serious! It was difficult for her to contain her anger.

"You want me to take Grell Dunn on the mission? You've got to be kidding. Apart from the fact that he's an untrained civilian, he's... he..." She ran out of words, waving her hands in the air in exasperation. "He's a..." She shook her head and lowered her voice when she realized how hyped up she was becoming. "He's privileged, spoiled... and you want to take him into battle, on the ground, against the Swarm?" She stood with her hand on her hip. "Captain," she added finally.

"It's not what I want," Morian said. "Actually, I advised him against it. Very strongly."

"And?" she said, her blue eyes shooting daggers at him. "What happened, Captain? You just allowed it to happen?"

"Much like when Prince Felder was aboard," he said, "my hands are tied. Mr. Dunn wants to go... He threatened to have his family back out of the Freyja Operation."

And then she understood. Dunn's family was funding most of the operation. Morian was entirely at his mercy.

"Wow," she said, knowing she was going to have to deal with it. "So he's going to join us on the drop, too, is he? Dubois will have a fit."

"Yes. There's no other way."

Danis just shook her head. She was wiped out by the enormity of the responsibility he was putting on her. She was unsure she could keep herself alive, much less a bumbling civilian.

She looked at her brother, not knowing what to say. She took a deep, shuddering breath, then resigned herself to the situation and said, "So that's it, then? My job is to basically babysit Dunn."

Morian smiled. His sister knew him so well. "I'm sorry, Danis. It has to be done."

* * *

Danis waited for the elevator doors to open, then stepped out into the hangar to the sound of Major Dubois' angry voice.

"Why do I have to get stuck with these people, Nortak?" he asked, sounding frustrated. Ilia Nortak was a Marine lieutenant. "First it's the queen of the fighter squadron, now it's a civilian. Neither of them are trained to make a suborbital jump and the civilian is overweight."

Dunn was there, listening to Dubois rant, and he was clearly intimidated. Danis was no little insulted that Dubois put her in the same box as Grell Dunn.

"Major Dubois," she snapped as she approached the small group. "I suggest you stop blathering and look to your command. It is what it is, so I further suggest you accept the situation and try to make the best of it."

Dubois stared at her for a moment, seemed about to speak, then nodded and turned and walked away to the crew room.

Danis turned to Dunn. He looked as if he wanted to turn and run. His forehead was covered with sweat.

If he can't handle the sight of me, how will he be able to cope on the ground against the Swarm? She looked stoically at him as he timidly approached.

"Hello, Commander." He reached out a hand as if he wanted to shake hers, then he dropped it, letting it dangle beside him. "I assume the captain informed you of my inten—"

The look she gave him cut him off mid-sentence. "Yes, I was made aware," she said, her hands behind her back.

"I want you to listen to me, Grell. If you insist on continuing this folly, I want you to understand that once we're on the ground, there will be no coming back until we're extracted. Understand?"

He nodded, eyes wide and shoulders hunching, as if trying to make himself smaller.

"If you give me any trouble, any trouble at all, any backchat, while we're down there, I will shoot you dead."

Again he nodded, locked his jaw, but said nothing.

"If I even get an inkling that you're planning to do

something foolish, your little trip of self-discovery will be over. I don't care how much money your family is pouring into the Freyja Operation, is that clear?"

"Y-yes, Commander," he managed with a gulp.

She hoped what she'd said would scare him off.

"You understand what I've said and that I mean it?"

"Yes, Commander."

"And you still want to go?"

"I do," he replied without hesitation.

"Good," she said with a curt nod. "Go suit up. You're in for a long drop."

Dunn left and Gian joined her with a doleful expression on his face.

"You all right, Joker?" she asked gently.

"Yeah," he said shrugging. "I just wish I had you flying next to me. To have my back, y'know?" He looked up at her. "I know we all made the same commitment to fight the enemy to the death, but this... It's insane, Commander. You must know that."

"You don't need to worry about me, Gian," she replied. "I'll be fine. I have Major Dubois to protect me," she said sarcastically, looking around the hangar.

He nodded his head toward the shuttle. "You're going down there in that thing, and then you're going to jump out of it." He shook his head, locked eyes with her and said, "You know I'm going to worry about you. If you get yourself killed..."

"It will be all right, you'll see." Before she could continue the thought, Gian stepped forward, grabbed her and enfolded her in a long hug. "I'll always have your back, Gian. You know that," she whispered and patted his back lightly.

"And I'll always have yours."

He released her, took a step back, raised a hand to his eye and wiped away a single tear. Then he sniffed and said, "Um... got something in my eye." And quickly put on his helmet.

"Ha, yeah, that's what it is," she said, smiling at him and giving him a double thumbs up. "Go get 'em, Tiger. It's time for me to prepare for the drop." *Both physically and mentally,* she thought.

She went to the crew room to find a Marine already helping Dunn into his drop suit and Balto waiting to help her.

"Commander," he said brightly, smiling at her. "You ready?"

She smiled nervously and said, "Let's do it."

He doesn't seem nervous... she thought as she reached into his mind to find that his heart was racing.

"You done this before?" she asked as he helped her into the armored suit.

He pursed his lips, then shook his head. "Make a suborbital drop, you mean? Not in the field. Only in sim training." He grimaced. "I kept scoring in the high sixties, so that's why I'm here."

The drop suit was bulky.

"These probes," Balto said, "at your upper left arm and lower spine will read your vital signs and inject you with meds if they detect something is wrong."

Danis could feel the knot-like patches on the inside of the suit. "Not exactly comfortable," she said, squirming in an effort to make them sit better.

He grinned and said, "The shuttle will take us down to ten kilometers. From there... we're on our own. We jump in groups of three. You'll be in my group, along with Rammo."

He nodded in the direction of a young Marine, already suited up at the far side of the crew room.

"Hey, Rammo," Balto shouted. "C'mere."

The Marine strode heavily across the room and joined them.

"This is Commander Morian," Balto said. "You, me and her will make the drop together. Let's show her how it works."

He grabbed Danis by the arm and pulled her in close and linked arms with her. Rammo stepped up and completed the circle. "We have to stop meeting like this, Commander," he joked. "People will begin to talk."

"Belay that, Marine," Danis said, smiling at him. "Any more of that and *you* won't be *able* to talk at all."

"Yes, ma'am!"

"So that's it?" she asked as they released each other and stepped apart. "That's all there is to it?"

"Not quite," Balto said. "We'll leave the rest until it's time to make the drop." He handed her a helmet.

"I guess it's time, then," Danis said.

Balto nodded. "Good luck, Commander."

Chapter Sixteen

Into the Black

Typhon Space

The plan was for *Avenger* to approach the dark side of Typhon from a position some fifteen-thousand kilometers out, taking advantage of the virtual eclipse to hide their approach. Then *Avenger* would establish a low geosynchronous orbit in the planet's mesosphere at an altitude of one-hundred-twenty kilometers that would keep the ship on the dark side of the planet, in its shadow, and hopefully out of sight of the Swarm clusters.

Unfortunately, it was high summer over New Hope. That, and Typhon's rotation of seventy-seven hours local, made for long days and short nights: fifty-six long hours of daylight.

Again, unfortunately, the sun was only just beginning to rise over New Hope, making it impossible for the drop to be made at night. They could not afford to wait for nightfall.

Morian would be unable to keep *Avenger* in orbit for such an extended period without being discovered.

The plan, then, had to be to go in and out as quickly as possible. Therefore, the drop had to be made in daylight, which meant that the shuttle would be exposed for most of its approach.

Danis took her seat in the shuttle alongside Balto and Rammo, along with twenty-eight Marines, Dunn—who'd been grouped with two Marines—and, of course, Major Dubois.

She was encased from head to toe in the armored drop suit, a grav-pack attached to the back of the suit, her nerves in tatters. *What was I thinking?* she thought. *This is madness. I won't survive the drop, much less the extraction. We're all going to die.*

"Five minutes to deployment," Krista said.

The hangar doors opened. The Marines inside the shuttle were deathly quiet. The shuttle's grav-drives came online and the ship lifted silently off the hangar deck.

"Five... Four..." Krista counted down, and then Jax took the ship out into the black of space.

Danis watched the port at her side as four F32 fighters zipped past them and took up positions on either side and above and below the shuttle. She saw Jackknife, on the port side, close to the cockpit, wave at Jax and grin.

For forty minutes they flew in the planet's shadow, heading east around the planet, the shuttle's hull glowing dull red from the friction of reentry. The planet itself was a vast black disc. Slowly, they descended through the mesosphere, then the stratosphere until they achieved an altitude of ten kilometers, still heading east around the planet.

Seventy minutes after leaving *Avenger,* the shuttle broke out of the planet's shadow into blazing sunshine.

Danis activated her transitional visor and the light dimmed.

She looked down out through the port. The terrain far below was the color of golden sand; the tall mountain peaks cast stark shadows in the early morning sunshine.

Danis heaved a trembling sigh. It was almost time.

She reached out into Dunn's mind. *Oh, please God protect me!* he thought.

Her heart was racing along with Dunn's. *So much for adventure,* she thought.

"Five minutes to drop," Dubois announced. "Everyone ready?" It was not a question to which he expected an answer. Nor did he get one. He looked at Danis and nodded, and she saw him wink at her through his visor.

She nodded back, took a deep breath and begged her knees not to wobble.

"On your feet, Marines!" Dubois commanded.

Jax opened the rear cargo ramp. The wind howled. The vortex threatening to drag them out.

"On my go!" Dubois shouted and then began to count down: "three... two... one... Go!"

As one, in groups of three, they leapt off the ramp; Dunn and his group third from last, followed by Danis and her group then, finally, Dubois and his group.

Danis, Balto and Rammo—Danis between them, all three linked together at the waist in a row—ran headlong off the ramp into the wind. Danis couldn't help the terrified yelp that escaped her lips. Balto and Rammo somehow managed to link themselves together, so they were now in a huddle as they'd practiced. The green light flashed in her helmet, indicating the friction-reducing force field generator on Balto's chest was active, protecting the group as they fell toward Typhon.

Danis felt physically sick. Her head was swimming. She tried to look down, but that only made it worse. She was in free fall and there was nothing she could do about it. Twice in her career she had to abandon a damaged fighter. But that was different. She was in space—no free fall there—and in a suit designed to ensure her survival for up to twelve hours or more. But this: she was plummeting toward the ground at more than two-hundred-twenty kilometers per hour. And, try as she might, she couldn't dispel the fear that was threatening to overwhelm her.

"Administering medication," the AI voice in her helmet intoned.

Danis gritted her teeth as the probes pierced her skin. The meds began to take effect almost immediately. Her eyelids fluttered. The nausea and the pain subsided. She began to feel more alert.

The long fall continued, seemingly for hours, and it was no wonder. They'd been falling for almost thirty minutes when they entered the clouds. The force fields shut down and the suits' anti-grav generators kicked in, and their fall began to slow.

Danis's group, falling feet first, began to spin, slowly. The wind howled around them. Then they were through the clouds and could see the ground spinning slowly below them.

She reached out to Dunn. He was sobbing, but somehow she didn't feel sorry for him.

Danis looked down. It seemed the ground was rushing up to meet them at an incredible rate, and suddenly she was certain she was going to die.

She tried to reach out to her brother, but all she could think about was the rocky surface rushing toward her.

She felt the anti-grav generators pushing her, slowing

her breakneck descent and then... suddenly... she was on the ground. Her legs buckled. She fell to her knees, dragging the two Marines down with her and she began to laugh.

"Oh, man," she said breathlessly, "that was one hell of a rush."

Balto and Rammo also laughed. It was their first time too.

Balto unclipped them and they fell apart, rolling on the rocky floor, laughing together.

Danis lay on her back, trying to catch her breath, staring up at the towering peaks.

Chapter Seventeen

Assassins

Orso Royal Palace

It was almost ten o'clock in the morning standard time when Tenilo decided to take a walk, to clear his head and to think. The echo of his footsteps, and those of the guards following at a respectful distance, had a calming effect on him.

He was on edge, and so was Elio. They feared that someone could carry out another attack on the king, at any moment, and they didn't know how to prevent it.

He found King Wulfrick Tudor in one of the palace's many parlors. He was in a state of deep concentration, reading a holo-book. He sighed audibly when he saw Tenilo and began to rise from the sofa.

"Wait, please," Tenilo said as he quickened his pace.

The king slowly sat back down, his posture hunched.

"Must you ruin what little pleasure I'm allowed, Mr. Tenilo?" the king said. He sounded tired and annoyed.

He was wearing a sky-blue suit trimmed with gold and a slim golden circlet on his head.

"You already have my wife locked away, only God knows where," he continued, flailing the air with his arm, then let it drop back down in his lap in an attempt at a dramatic gesture. "To interrogate her on some bizarre and unfounded accusation."

Tenilo's eyes widened "Unfounded?" he said, taking a step closer to King Wulfrick. "So is it a coincidence that this terrible thing happened to the king the moment you and your wife arrived on Orso?"

"I assure you, sir—"

King Wulfrick was cut off by a sudden noise outside in the corridor and he jumped to his feet.

"What's that noise?" he asked, backing away.

The door burst open and a group of six men rushed into the room, all dressed in black and wearing masks.

Tenilo and the king backed into a corner while Tenilo's four elite guards turned to face them; the other four being shared by Elio and King Orson.

The battle, severely one-sided, lasted but a few seconds. Prince Felder's bodyguards were highly trained and equipped not only with the new Q5 laser pistols, but also with personal magnetatron shields.

"Come with me!" Tenilo said after the last of the six would-be assailants had fallen. "We must go to the infirmary to protect King Orson."

King Wulfrick looked shocked. He jumped up from the sofa and followed Tenilo and his guards down the long corridors to the infirmary.

What's happening, Tenny? Are you all right? Elio reached out to Tenilo.

We were attacked, Tenilo replied. *In king Wulfrick's quarters. There were six of them. My guards beat them off. We're on our way to the infirmary. I suggest you stay where you are. Keep your guards around you.*

Keep me informed, Tenny. Make sure the king is safe.

I will, my prince.

The guards outside the King's room snapped to attention. Tenilo, his guards and King Wulfrick, with Tenilo's permission, pushed past them into the room to find King Orson much as before, lying peacefully on his back, hands by his side, eyes closed.

"What is this?" Dr. Myster said after he rushed into the room. "Why are you here? The king must not be disturbed."

Tenilo quickly explained what had happened and then said, "Nobody is to be allowed into the room other than myself, Prince Elio, you and medical staff expressly authorized by you, doctor. Is that understood?"

Dr. Myster nodded and said, "Of course."

"The guards will remain outside until further notice. Make sure they are not tested, Dr. Myster. They are authorized to use deadly force."

Tenilo took one last lingering look at King Orson, then nodded to Wulfrick, and they turned and walked out into the corridor, wondering just what they were up against.

Invaders. Inside a royal palace. Unprecedented. He tapped his datapad as he walked and contacted his personal ship's AI. "Send T-1 to these coordinates," he directed it.

T-1 was a project he'd been working on for more than a year. The prototype had been completed just two months earlier. It was something he'd dreamed about since his early childhood, but it wasn't until just after the Swarm attacked the Eta Persei System that Prince Felder had granted him the funds to begin development. T-1, an advanced AI robot that looked eerily like him, Tenilo,, was the result.

"I suggest, your grace, that you stay with me for the time being," Tenilo said to Wulfrick as they walked quickly along the corridor to his quarters. "At least until we know the present emergency is over."

The king nodded, breathing hard, trying to keep up.

Five minutes later they were ensconced in Tenilo's suite next to Elio's. Where Elio was, Tenilo didn't know.

There was a gentle knock at the door.

Tenilo nodded to one of the guards. The guard opened the door, gasped, turned to look at Tenilo, then at the visitor, then again at Tenilo. His eyes wide.

"Sir... It's... It's you."

Tenilo smiled and said, "Come in, T-1."

Wulfrick gasped as the robot stepped into the room, did a double take, then a triple take.

"Who on Odin is that?" he asked, bewildered.

"T-1," Tenilo said, smiling widely, "this is King Wulfrick of Odin. Please introduce yourself and explain."

T-1 bowed his head slightly and said in a voice not unlike Tenilo's, "Good day to you, your grace. I am, as Mr. Tenilo said, T-1, a class nine AI automaton, fully sentient and capable of processing in excess of one billion snippets of information per second. As you can see, Mr. Tenilo has created me in his own image. I am, according to my creator, the ultimate PP, personal protector. My outer shell is constructed from a ductile dutrinium alloy and I possess a personal forcefield."

All the while T-1 was talking, Tenilo was smiling as he observed the looks on the faces of the king and the four guards.

"Your grace," he began when T-1 had finished. "We are about to enter a new pha—"

The door slammed open. Five black-clad men rushed into the room, guns blazing. Tenilo's guards, taken completely by surprise were gunned down.

The intruders turned to Tenilo. Hesitated. Stared wide eyed at the two look-alikes and then chose the wrong one.

During that slight moment of hesitation, T-1 had activated his shield. Five blasts of white laser fire slammed into his shield. The shield glowed brilliant white. T-1 stepped in front of Tenilo, shielding him, then stepped forward and with a sudden flurry of fists, so fast Tenilo couldn't follow them, he killed four of the attackers and severely injured the fifth.

T-1 bent over the lone survivor, pulled back his fist and was about to deliver the coup de gras when Tenilo shouted, "Don't kill him! I need him alive."

T-1 paused, relaxed, stood up upright, then rubbed his hands together in an oddly human manner and shut down his force field.

Tenilo stepped forward and removed the man's mask. He was young, no more than twenty. The scowl seemed to Tenilo as if it had been etched on his face. His thick brown hair was plastered to his forehead. The man was drenched with sweat.

"Who are you. Why are you here? Who gave you the order to attack me?" Tenilo asked him.

The assailant bared his teeth and opened his mouth as if to speak, but before he could, he sucked in a deep breath and closed his eyes, his face contorted in pain. He clutched his throat. His eyes opened. His eyeballs bulged. His body shuddered, then went rigid until finally he went limp and his hands dropped away from his neck.

Tenilo checked his pulse. The man was dead. He stood up, sighed and stared down at the body.

He tapped his datapad and contacted Ugo Tan.

Tan was interrogating Queen Zara in the military complex adjacent to the palace.

"If you don't mind, Marshal, I'd like you to bring the queen to the infirmary. I have a few questions I'd like to ask her. Something has happened."

"Why, what happened?" Tan asked.

"I'll explain everything when you get here," Tenilo replied. Then he looked at the robot and said, "We'll take the intruder to the infirmary. I want to know how he died."

T-1 nodded, picked up the body and followed Tenilo and Wulfrick out into the corridor to the infirmary.

* * *

"Without an extensive battery of tests," Doctor Myster said, "I can't say for sure what killed him, but my educated guess would be is that he died from a similar Psy attack as that perpetrated upon the king."

Tenilo turned to Wulfrick and was about to speak when Elio walked into the examination room.

"Where are your guards, my prince?" Tenilo asked him.

"There are enough here. We have plenty," Elio said. "I told them to watch the perimeter. What the..." he said, his eyes wide, when he spotted T-1.

Tenilo glanced at the robot, then said, "I'll explain later. First, I need to speak to Queen Zara. Ugo Tan is bringing her..."

Elio glared at King Wulfrick. "Ugo Tan is not here. He's with the queen," he said, looking back at Tenilo, then at T-1 "They're in her quarters, in the palace, with her entourage."

Tenilo nodded, then turned to Wulfrick. He was about half a meter shorter than the king, but he stood his ground and locked eyes with him.

"Is the queen responsible for these attacks and the attack on King Orson?" Tenilo probed the king's mind, waiting for an answer. He got it almost instantly.

Wulfrick shook his head vigorously. "Those attackers looked like they wanted to slit my throat," he said. The muscles tightened in his throat as he gulped. "Why, for heaven's sake, would she... or I be a part of such a thing?" He breathed in deeply. "We have nothing to do with this... My wife has nothing to do with this. She's an ambitious woman, yes. But she would never, *ever* stoop to something so vicious."

Tenilo nodded. He believed the king when he said his wife had nothing to do with it, but did she? Only an interview with her would tell.

"Where are your guards, Tenny?" Elio asked.

"They are dead. We, the king and I, were attacked in my quarters. They were taken by surprise." He glanced at his lookalike and said, "T-1 made short work of them. This one... he survived but was the victim of what we think was another Psy attack. I need to talk to the queen."

Elio saw what Tenilo was thinking. "I'm going with you," he said.

Ugo Tan met them at the door to the queen's quarters and ushered them inside.

"She refused to leave the palace and insisted on her own guards," Tan said apologetically. "As far as I can tell, she's clean. We found nothing untoward. She does, however, possess an advanced level of Psy."

Tenilo nodded. "I'd like to talk to her."

Tan nodded and together they entered the queen's

parlor, Elio leading the way, to find her seated and surrounded by a phalanx of more than a dozen uniformed guards.

One of them, a slim woman, stepped forward and, using TK, tried to stop Elio from reaching the queen. Elio pushed back. The woman was strong. He pushed harder. She staggered back—

"That's enough," Queen Zara snapped, rising to her feet and pushing through the guards.

"Prince Elio, Mr. Tenilo..." She hesitated when she saw the two of them. "What do you mean by this intrusion?"

She stood in front of her guards facing Elio with her arms folded across her chest, and Elio quickly realized what a formidable woman she was.

The guard with the TK was panting, her brows furrowed. Her TK at minimum level. She was obviously prepared to guard her queen to the death.

The queen looked at her, nodded once, and she slowly took one step back. Her eyes remained locked on Elio.

"Why are you here?" the queen asked, her eyes on one Tenilo then the other. "This place was supposed to offer me and my husband refuge and hospitality. And what do I get?" She shot a look at Ugo Tan. "Accusation upon accusation. Outrageous! And which one of you am I supposed to be talking to?"

Tenilo took a half step forward. "I am Tenilo, your majesty. T-1 is my... alter ego, shall we say?"

"I know who you are," she snapped. "Please get on with it, whatever it is you want. I'm tired."

Tenilo reached out and probed the queen's mind and was surprised when she offered no resistance. She was outraged... and she was telling the truth. She had nothing to do with the attacks, on the king or himself. He was baffled.

"Why were you so secretive?" he asked frowning. "Why did you block me, Queen Zara?"

"You see these halos?" she waved her hand at her guards. They were all wearing slim, golden halos on their heads, as was she. "They're not just for nerve jacking. You see, I've heard about the Canis file as well. So, I had a team of engineers work on a halo that, in theory, would prevent a Psy attack." She smiled proudly. "I let you in, Mr. Tenilo, because I need you to know that while I still press my claim to the throne of Orso, I had nothing to do with the attack on the king, or anyone else."

Tenilo looked at Elio. Elio nodded. The Queen was ambitious, and competitive. So much so that she'd kept her invention a secret. Selfish as she was, Tenilo was relieved to learn that the queen was innocent.

"And don't worry, my prince," she said turning her gaze to Elio. "I won't make this intrusion and the defamation of my character a bigger issue than it already is... Here, put these on." She handed Elio and Tenilo each one of the halos. "And don't take them off."

Elio bowed slightly and thanked her. The queen could have made it an *enormous* issue. She could have taken it to the courts where a long, drawn-out battle would have ensued. And she would have had a case: defamation of character, false imprisonment, a malicious act against a royal...

The queen smiled at him. "I'm a forgiving woman, Elio, and we have much bigger things to worry about. I will help you find the Psy assassin," she said, her chin held high. "Nobody gets away with trying to kill my husband."

Chapter Eighteen

Survivors

Planet Typhon

Danis lay still for what seemed like minutes but was in fact only seconds, trying to lower her heart rate, breathing deeply, but Balto was already up on his feet and making ready to move out.

"We need to get going, Commander," he said earnestly. "We're exposed. We have to find the rest of the team."

She struggled up onto her elbows, sat up and removed her helmet, then squinted up at him silhouetted against the early morning sunshine.

She scrambled to her feet, looked around at the forbidding terrain and said, "Where are they, the others?"

Balto glanced at his datapad. "Spread out from here to kingdom come," he replied, "but, so I'm told, that's not unusual. Major Dubois is half a klick that way," he said, pointing east along what appeared to be a narrow canyon.

"We should go. Grab your helmet and don't lose it. You're going to need it for the extraction. Here, let me show you."

He grabbed the helmet from her, stepped behind her, clipped it to her belt then stepped back in front of her.

"The suit is not designed for walking, but like the helmet, you're going to need it. It is air-conditioned... here, let me." He took a step forward and tapped an armored glass screen on her chest. She immediately felt the cool air surround her body, and she couldn't believe how good it felt.

"You can adjust the temperature here, like this." He looked down and tapped the screen on his own chest. "See? Easy! So, you ready?"

"I guess," she said. The uncertainty in her voice made him narrow his eyes and look at her. "Oh, don't look at me like that," she said. "I'll be fine. Lead the way."

Balto nodded, then turned to Rammo and said, "You ready, brother?"

Rammo nodded and they set off along the rocky trail, Balto leading, followed by Danis with Rammo bringing up the rear.

They hadn't traveled more than a couple of hundred meters when they were joined by three more Marines, then several hundred meters further on by another group of six.

Ten minutes later, at the foot of a rocky outcrop, they found the rest of the team, including Dubois and Grell Dunn, surrounded by seven dutrinium alloy equipment cases. Danis knew that one of them contained K15 8mm railguns and another had twelve gravmules.

"What's in the rest of the containers?" Danis whispered to Balto.

"Our way home," he muttered.

"Huh?" she asked him.

"Gravpacks. They clip onto the back of the suit, which is why I said you'd need it and the helmet. They'll lift us to an altitude of one-point-five kilometers where, we hope, the shuttle will be waiting to pick us up."

Danis looked at him, horrified. "You have to be kidding me," she said, taking an involuntary glance skyward.

"Don't worry," he said. "It's no big deal. I've done it twenty-two times... in training, and I'll be right there with you." He grinned at her.

Danis, however, no matter what he could have said to reassure her, did worry. She couldn't help it. It wasn't that she was afraid to die; it was the manner in which she could potentially die that bothered her.

To die in battle, in an F32, in a blaze of fire was one thing. To contemplate a fall onto the rocks from such an altitude was quite another.

Still, she couldn't allow Balto or Dubois, or any of the others to see how she felt, so she smiled at him, winked and said, "Every day's a new adventure."

"That it is," Balto said, grinning at her.

"You made it, then, Commander," Dubois said as he approached the pair. "Good. Stay safe. I don't need the extra paperwork. You know how to operate one of these?" he continued as he tossed her a K15 rail-rifle.

"I think I can manage it, Major," she replied dryly and worked the action, loading a round into the chamber. Then she tapped the power stud. The weapon whined as it powered up. She checked the charge and the magazine, nodded, powered the weapon down and nodded again.

"Good enough, Major?" she asked.

He smiled slightly and said, "Very good, Commander. Take good care of her, Balto." Then he turned and walked away, smiling widely as he heard her snort.

By then, the gravmules had been attached by powerful electromagnets to the equipment cases which, in turn, had been tethered together, line astern.

Dubois, like some ancient wagon master, circled his arm in the air, pointed forward and shouted, "Yoah," and then stepped off smartly in an eastward direction. And so they began the long trudge to the end of the canyon.

"Does he know where we're going?" Danis whispered to Balto.

Balto laughed. "Oh yeah," he replied. "He's been in touch with Kyne Minnah using that radio thing, whatever it is."

And on they marched... well, not quite. The terrain was rocky, uneven, and many of the Marines stumbled; even Dubois lost his footing and almost fell, which caused Danis no little amusement.

And then there was Dunn, overweight and seriously out of shape, and Danis could tell he was losing the will to continue, but he trudged along regardless. He'd taken Danis's threat to heart.

"Stop! I hear something," Nilo Pistach, the Psy-op working with the Marines, said breathlessly. "We have company."

"What company?" Dubois snapped, annoyed that she hadn't provided more information.

"I don't know," the Psy-op replied. "Back that way. She turned and pointed back the way they'd come.

Danis turned, listening. At first she heard nothing. Then, in the distance, echoing off the canyon walls, she heard heavy footsteps coming towards them: "Clunk, clunk, clunk."

"Take cover!" Dubois shouted. "Prepare to defend your positions."

Danis and Balto hunkered down behind a rocky outcrop and watched as the equipment cases sank gently to the canyon floor behind a pile of rocks. The rest of the Marines also found cover, and the last thing she noticed before the Blues arrived was Dubois grabbing Dunn by the arm and hauling him out of sight.

The Blues appeared some hundred and fifty meters back down the canyon from where they'd taken cover.

They were approaching quickly, crushing the rock under their heavy, armored boots.

Danis saw the familiar pale blue glow of the Blues' forcefields, but that was all that was familiar about them. They were larger and more humanoid than those she'd encountered before. Their armor looked "different" was all she could think of. *They must be Stompers*, she thought.

"Stompers?" Danis whispered to Balto.

He nodded. "Oh yeah."

"They're different!"

"These suckers regenerate," he said.

"What protection will these suits offer?" Danis asked as she powered up her K-15 rifle.

"Against plasma weapons?" Balto asked. "None. They're drop suits, not battle armor. They are armored, but only against atmospheric friction."

Danis nodded, took a deep breath and readied herself to receive the enemy.

It was at that moment that one of Dubois' Marines decided to find a better position, upped and ran across the canyon floor and dived for cover behind a pile of rocks. He was just a little too late.

One of the Stompers spotted him. Its reaction time was in nanoseconds. It fired almost instantly. A bolt of brilliant blue streaked along the canyon, almost at the speed of light.

The Marine, who was already in the air, was hit just below the knees, severing his legs. He landed under cover of the boulders, alive, rifle still in hand, the wounds cauterized by the plasma; the man would live.

"Fire!" Major Dubois yelled, his voice echoing among the peaks and valleys.

Twenty-nine Marines and Danis opened fire on the now rapidly advancing Blues. Danis counted six of them; four of the new Stompers and two smaller Stalkers. It was the first time she'd seen them, the Stompers. *Stars!* she thought, *they're huge...* Involuntarily, she ducked as a bolt of blue fire sizzled over her head and hit the canyon wall only a few meters behind her, showering her with pulverized, blistering hot shards of rock and dust.

The noise in the canyon became unbearable as thirty K-15 rifles opened fire togeher and the walls contained the earsplitting din of the sonic explosions as thousands of projectiles broke the sound barrier. The Blues immediately returned fire, adding blinding blue flashes of light to the cacophony.

One of the Stompers went down, then another, then a stalker; its upper body shattered under the impact of dozens of 8mm projectiles, but they kept moving resolutely forward, the Stompers' shields stopping most of the dutrinium slugs. But the more they were hit, the more their shields began to degrade until, eventually, the projectiles broke through and slammed into their armored shells.

The first thing that Danis noticed when this happened was that the Stomper's armor was no longer shattered on impact. It appeared malleable. The armor seemed to give, absorbing the impact, then recovered and regained its original shape. Sometimes, though, if hit more than once, the slugs would break through. When that happened, the

Stomper would appear to seize up, then topple over and appear to be dead, *if that's the word,* she thought. But then she saw one of the downed Stompers slowly rise to its feet and begin to walk forward as if nothing had happened.

Damn! she thought, glancing sideways at Balto. *He's right. They're regenerating. We're not going to be able to stop them.*

There was an almighty explosion somewhere behind them, then another, and another and then a series of explosions.

"What was that?" she said to herself as she strained her neck to see.

"Get down, damn it!" Balto shouted, grabbed her free hand and pulled her roughly sideways.

A searing bolt of blue plasma slammed into the rock behind which they were hiding.

"What are you trying to do?" he yelled at her. "Get yourself killed? Keep your damn head down."

She gripped his hand, squeezed it, nodded and mouthed, "thank you."

She lay with her back against the rock and glanced sideways across the canyon, where she could see Dunn curled up in a ball on the ground behind a large boulder with his hands over his head.

Suddenly, Dubois landed heavily at her side, between her and Balto, breathing hard.

"Are you all right, Commander?" he shouted at the top of his voice, trying to be heard over the sound of continuous gunfire.

"I am!" she shouted. "They're regenerating."

"I see that!" he yelled, hunkering down. "We have to get out of here."

"What are we going to do?" Danis yelled.

He just shook his head. He obviously had no idea.

He glanced at Balto, who had his back against the rocks and was struggling to reload; Dubois grabbed his shoulder roughly, which only made Balto fumble the more.

"Get it together, son!" Dubois shouted.

Then, out of the corner of her eye, Danis saw something moving high above. At first she couldn't make out what it was, but then...

People! she thought.

She grabbed Dubois' arm and pointed.

"Look," she shouted. "People."

There were four of them. Three men and a woman. They were making their way down through the rocks. As they came closer, she could see that one of them, an old man, was carrying a small octagonal device. It glistened in the sunlight and sparkled in the blue flashes of plasma. It was obviously made from some kind of metal, and it looked heavy, but it didn't seem to weigh the man down.

They descended through the rocks until they were no more than fifty meters above the canyon floor, where they stopped. The old man's three companions ducked and took cover. He remained standing, held the device over his head and appeared to go into some kind of trance... and then, the device floated out of his hands.

He has TK, Danis thought.

The old man opened his eyes, stared at the group of advancing Stompers, and the device flew toward them so fast it became a blur.

"Come this way," the woman shouted, waving her hand. "Come. Quickly.

One by one the Marines began to jump to their feet, two of them carrying their wounded comrade. Seven of them lay dead, four severely wounded. Major Dubois' little army had been reduced to twenty-five, including Danis and Grell Dunn.

"What about the equipment cases?" Danis asked as she, Dubois and Balto prepared to head for the hills.

"They're all gone," Dubois said.

"Those explosions?" she asked.

He nodded. "The Blues scored a lucky hit."

"What are we going to do?" Danis yelled. "What about the extraction?"

"We'll think about that later," Dubois replied. "There'll be no extraction if we don't get out of here. Come on."

He grabbed her arm and together they ran, followed by Balto, and began to climb.

"What about the dead?" Danis shouted. "We can't leave them..."

"We don't have any choice," Dubois shouted. There are too many, and we have to get the wounded out. Come on. Move it, Commander."

They hadn't gone more than a dozen meters when they came under fire. They ran on, ducking and dodging, rocks exploding around them.

"Get down!" the woman shouted.

And they did. They ducked down behind a rocky outcrop some thirty meters up the steep climb.

Danis lay there breathing hard. Dubois and Balto were on their knees peering down into the canyon. She scrabbled up and joined them.

Now she could see the Blues, ranged in a semi-circle, firing at the Marines as they ran to the canyon wall to begin their climb to what they hoped would be safety and a way out.

They watched as two more Marines fell: one cut in half, the other headless. The third went down just as he reached cover, his right arm missing at the shoulder. He jerked violently for several seconds and then lay still.

"DAMN! *Damn, damn,*" Dubois shouted and raised his rifle and sent a stream of slugs at the nearest Stomper.

Danis and Balto—his weapon empty—watched as dozens of dutrinium projectiles hammered the Stomper's forcefield. It dimmed under the relentless stream of gunfire, then shut down and slugs smashed into its armored chest. For a second the armor held, then suddenly a hole appeared as more and more slugs hammered into it. Slowly it toppled over backward under the force of the withering fire and lay still. And Dubois continued to fire until, at last, his weapon went silent. He'd emptied an almost full, two-hundred-round magazine.

He fell back, exhausted, tears tracking through the dust, sweat and grime covering his face.

"I think you got him, sir!" Balto shouted.

Dubois looked at him and shook his head but didn't reply.

"What's he doing?" Danis shouted, looking up at the old man some twenty-five meters away up the rock wall.

He was holding up both arms. Another of the group, one of the men, was at his side, holding his datapad in front of his face.

The old man brought his hands together over his head and closed his eyes.

Danis looked down into the canyon. The device was hovering some fifteen meters above a group of four Blues— three Stompers and a Stalker.

She looked up at the man with the datapad. He spoke something she couldn't hear and, when she looked down into the canyon, the device was spinning, glowing, and it appeared to be emitting some sort of forcefield. It was a shimmering blue. It ballooned, expanding, pulsating like a giant jellyfish until it enveloped all six Blues.

The forcefield's color intensified around the device, from pale blue to deep purple at the center with lighter reds and pinks towards the edges.

The ground under and around the Blues began to vibrate as the forcefield continued to intensify. The dust rose from the canyon and became an undulating carpet surging around the aliens' feet and then, quite suddenly, the Blues' forcefields flickered out. Their weapons went dark and they crumpled and fell to the ground.

The forcefield snapped off. The old man opened his eyes, spread his arms, and the device returned to him, much more slowly than it left.

The old man took a deep breath and wiped the sweat from his brow. The other man—the one with the datapad— patted him on the back and said, "You did well, Mozzley."

"We need to get out of here," the woman said to Dubois, "More are coming. Please follow us."

Danis could see Dubois was devastated by the loss of his men—ten dead and four severely wounded.

One behind the other, they followed the four people up the mountain to the ridge. Dubois came last, making sure that everyone still alive was present and accounted for.

* * *

"You," Danis said to the man towards the front of the group. "You're Kyne Minnah, aren't you?"

He looked at her and smiled.

There was no mistaking him: a tall, slim man, aged about forty with a mop of sandy-colored hair and a long, trailing mustache. She recalled the file picture she saw before the drop. "Prince Elio sent us here to rescue you. How many of you are there?"

Kyne pursed his lips, then sighed heavily. "Yes, I'm Kyne. In all, just thirty. We've been searching for more survivors but..." He shook his head. "No luck so far. The capitol's completely destroyed."

So many lives lost, Danis thought. *They can't be the only ones...*

But from the looks on their dejected faces, that seemed to be the case. Kyne nodded to one of the people in his group. "That's Yarrow."

Yarrow held up his hand weakly in a half-hearted wave; his fingernails were caked with dirt.

"He worked at a Dutrinium processing facility before... before all of this started."

"I think we were attacked so aggressively because they want the Dutrinium for themselves," Yarrow said, scratching his scalp.

Danis didn't want to burst his bubble. She knew the truth. *They're not after just our minerals. They want it all. And they want all of humanity annihilated.*

Danis had pondered the Swarm's mission many times over the past months since the Swarm's initial attack, and she'd discussed it with her brother and friends. Humankind had always naively and arrogantly thought they were God's gift to the galaxy—the one intelligent species meant to rule and dominate. *Are the Slipstreams really causing a rift in the universe itself?* she wondered. *Is the Swarm justified in their quest for a reset? We humans have always felt justified... Or is the Swarm just greedier than we are?*

"That's Tara," Kyne continued with his introductions, bringing Danis back to the present.

"And this is Mozzley."

The old man, clearly more than a hundred years old, managed a small smile. His face, heavily lined and tanned dark from a life under the sun, was brightened by a pair of sparkling, iridescent blue eyes. What little hair he had left was pure white and wispy and probably should have been shaved off decades ago.

"He's— " Kyne started to say, but Mozzley finished.

"Retired... These kids have lugged me into their schemes." His forehead glistened with sweat.

Dubois pointed at Yarrow, who had the octagonal device tucked under his arm and said, "What is *that*? How did it... do what it did?"

Yarrow held it up for the others to see.

"Neat, right?" Kyne said, obviously proud of it. "It's just a modest prototype, but it works." He stood up straighter and put his hands on his hips. "I intend to develop it further, if we get out of here alive."

"It's much better than the last version," Tara said.

"Humph, the last version was garbage," Yarrow mumbled.

Kyne eyed him coldly but didn't comment.

"Yes, but what is it exactly?" Major Dubois said, followed by a loud exhale.

"It's an EMP generator," Kyne said.

"An EMP?" Danis asked. "An electromagnetic pulse generator. I thought those went out with the Purge."

Kyne nodded. "They did, but you see, I have... well, you'll see. Anyway, it came to me that these things—the Blues—all run on some kind of power. I haven't quite figured out what yet, but I thought, maybe... well, I put that thing together. It generates an EMP within a limiting forcefield that can be directionally oriented. And before you ask, it will not work against their ships. I already tried that with the one we have. The ship has lost most of its power source but what little it does have seems impervious to an EMP. Why, I don't know. I need access to Avenger's AI." He shook his head, seemingly lost in thought.

Yarrow tapped the side of the device with his knuckle. "It's dead right now... It uses a lot of power. It's only good for one use and then takes a while to recharge. It needs a better power source."

"I made it from scraps of an old robot and... other stuff I managed to cobble together," Kyne said. "Frankly, I'm surprised it's still working at all."

Balto's eyes were wide. "Damn, how did you—"

"It's a long story," Kyne said, holding up his hand and shaking his head. He looked as if he was tired just thinking about it.

Tara rubbed the back of her neck, leaving a streak of sweaty grime behind. "We could have dozens of those devices, and it wouldn't matter," she said despondently.

"Why? What do you mean?" Danis asked.

The sun's rays were bright, and Kyne shielded his eyes. "The Swarm is planning to attack Orso."

"Hundreds of thousands of them," Mozzley said.

Kyne shook his head but said nothing and started walking again, heading east along the canyon crest with Danis and Dubois at his side, followed by Yarrow, Tara and Mozzley. They, in turn, were followed by Balto, Rammo and the rest of the Marines.

"How do you know they're planning to attack Orso?" Dubois asked Kyne.

"He's a hacker," Yarrow said. "When he was messing around in the wrecked ship, he figured out how to hack into the Swarm's network."

Dubois looked at Kyne. "They have a network, the Blues?" he asked.

"Is that so hard to believe?" Tara smiled mirthlessly. "They're light years more advanced than we are. Of course they have a network, and they're evolving quickly. Those Stompers are newer tech. So is the crashed ship."

"Kyne thinks the core draws its power from the Swarm's alternate reality and also acts like a sort of beacon," Mozzley said. "I tend to agree with him."

"They're building something just to the north of the city," Kyne said. "Some kind of communications center, I think. It's huge and you can feel the power vibrating through the ground beneath your feet. It's almost finished. I'd like to take a look at it. I think maybe I could... learn something that could help the war effort."

"And what might that be?" Dubois asked skeptically.

Kyne rubbed his hands together, as if anticipating what he'd find, and said, "I won't know 'til I get inside, now will I?"

"And you think you'll be able to hack into its communication system?" Danis asked.

This time, Kyne smirked as he walked resolutely on. "Probably not, but it's worth a try, isn't it?"

Danis didn't know quite what to reply to that, so she said, "Where is it and how long would you need?"

"It just to the north and west of New Hope," he replied, "maybe fifteen clicks from the wrecked ship. How long would I need? Without a suitable AI, months. Our only real option is to crack the core. I think Avenger's AI might be able to do that. If so, we should be able to link directly with the comm center."

"So you don't actually need to get inside it then, the comm center?" Danis pressed him.

"Yeah, I do," he snapped. "I need to know exactly what we're up against and I can only do that from inside, but first, I need to go get the core. It's in our cave close to the crash sight. By the way, how're you figuring on getting us out of here anyway?"

"That's yet to be decided," Dubois said. "So let's get to it, shall we?"

"The sooner, the better," Danis said as she looked back to check on Dunn. He was breathing hard, but he was keeping up and Danis couldn't help but smile at his newfound tenacity.

Chapter Nineteen

Extraction Plans

The Avenger

Haltar Sen, seated at the helm, had managed to hold himself together since Jax had left to drop Danis and the Marines over Typhon, but an hour later it had become obvious to all that he was suffering.

Commander Haal was about to go to him, but Morian beat her to it.

"What is it, Haltar?" she heard him ask. "Are you sick?"

Sen shook his head and said, "It's just exhaustion, Captain. I just need a few minutes."

"I appreciate your courage, Haltar, but that's not good enough. I've been watching you, and I think it's something more than exhaustion. Come." Morian helped him to his feet. "Off to the med bay with you."

Manda looked at the overhead chron. It had been more

than an hour since Dagon Jax had returned from making the drop. Tentatively, testing her developing Psy ability, she reached out to him and could tell, even though his thoughts seemed to be jumbled, that he was in a state of deep depression.

So much devastation... was all she could manage to read before she experienced a debilitating dizzy spell. Quickly, she removed herself from his mind, but the dizziness continued for several seconds before her head cleared and, in a vision using her Sight, she saw them exiting the Slipstream.

She shook her head. It cleared, leaving her swaying slightly on her feet.

"Not you, too," Morian said as he joined her at the rail. "Are you all right, Commander Haal?"

"Yes, sir. I'm fine. There's a large Swarm cluster approaching from the east. We have less than ten minutes. We need to summon Jax to the helm, now." And with that, she opened a shipwide channel, ordered Jax to the bridge immediately, ran to the steps, descended to the well deck and began to pace back and forth at the helm waiting for Jax to arrive.

"Ms. Fargo," she snapped. "Load tubes two through thirty-two with the new M99s and prepare to fire a broadside; proximity setting one-hundred-fifty meters. Then reload and prepare to fire again. These are the coordinates... Bring all starboard point defense systems online and prepare to fire... Where in God's name is Jax?"

She was just about to sit down at the helm herself when Jax burst in and ran to his station: his by default since Sen was in sick bay.

She waited for him to sit, then snapped, "Turn ninety

degrees starboard and roll eleven degrees port and hold your position." Then she ran back up to the command rail where she joined Morian, and together they watched... nothing.

For almost four minutes they watched, and then "Fire all!" Manda shouted. And sixteen M99 torpedoes left the starboard tubes and streaked away toward the dark horizon of the planet and... nothing.

Morian looked at her, the question in his eyes.

"Wait," she said, staring at the screens. "They're coming."

Morian looked at the hologram, watching the green threads tracing eastward around the planet.

He glanced up at the screens. Still nothing. The a group of nine Swarm ships appeared, blue silhouettes against the backn of space. The trickle became a stream until there were more than a hundred Swarm ships streaking toward them, straight into the teeth of the oncoming torpedoes.

One hundred and fifty meters out, the sixteen warheads exploded, sending ninety-six 120mm, laser-guided projectiles into the cluster at close to one-quarter light speed. The effect was devastating. The Blues were taken completely by surprise. Seventy-two two of their ships were hit by the projectiles and exploded in balls of brilliant fire. Eleven more were destroyed as a result of their close proximity to others when they exploded.

"Fire tubes six through twenty," Manda snapped. And eight more torpedoes streaked away toward the surviving enemy ships. And they watched the hologram as one-by-one they blinked out of existence until the last one had disappeared.

The threat was over. Tentire action had lasted less than five minutes, during which time the Swarm had not fired a single shot. By Manda's count, she'd fired twenty-four of the new M99B torpedoes and destroyed one-hundred-twenty Swarm ships.

"There's nothing like the element of surprise," Manda muttered to herself, after taking a deep breath of relief.

Morian, who hadn't said a word, stood at the rail with his hands behind his back, staring at the giant hologram, apparently in a state of disbelief.

He turned to Manda, looked at her, shook his head and said for all to hear, "I... don't know what to say, Commander, other than well done. That could have been catastrophic. On behalf of myself and the rest of the crew, I thank you."

She nodded. She was relieved that he wasn't angry with her for usurping his command, but there hadn't been time. Had she waited to explain, the outcome may well have been, as Morian said, catastrophic.

She was also relieved that she'd been right, for there was always a chance, no matter how small, that she could get it wrong.

"D'you think they had time to transmit a warning to the rest of the fleet? She asked. "If they did..." She didn't bother to finish the obvious conclusion.

"There's no way of telling," Morian replied. "Let's hope not."

Jax leaned back in his seat at the helm, closed his eyes, and rubbed his temples, then opened them again and contacted Manda on a closed channel. "Forgive me, Commander. Am I right in assuming that Lieutenant Sen's going to be in the med bay for the rest of the mission?"

Manda hadn't told him of Haltar's location; clearly, he'd made an educated guess.

She turned away from Morian and said softly, "I'm not sure, Ensign. Would it be a problem if he was?"

Jax took a breath, looked up at her and smiled. "No, ma'am. You can't... y'know... *see*?"

Manda rolled her eyes and said, "I told you it doesn't work like that. Haal out."

Jax turned his attention back to the helm. Manda shook her head, but the truth was, his question had aroused her curiosity.

She turned again to Morian and said, "If you'll excuse me, sir, I'd like to go to the med bay to check on Lieutenant Sen."

Morian, at the rail with his hands clasped together behind his back, looked at her and nodded.

When she arrived in the med bay at Sen's door, she found it closed, which was unusual, and she couldn't help but wonder why.

Not wanting to disturb Dr. Dowd in the middle of a consultation, or worse, an evaluation, she reached into Haltar's mind with her still burgeoning Psy, then opened her own mind and listened:"...can't keep this a secret for much longer, Haltar," Dr. Jyra Dowd said.

"I know." Haltar flinched as he reclined. He closed his eyes. "The Captain's becoming suspicious. I'm going to have to tell him something. How bad is it, Doc?"

"The disease is progressing," Dowd replied.

"But the injections have been helping," Sen said.

Manda could feel the pain coursing through his body. She drew in a deep breath. What she was learning wasn't good— not for Sen, not for the ship. She was now in possession of important information, information that had a direct bearing on the running of the ship, and that put her in something of a quandary. First, she was eavesdropping on a doctor/patient conversation and two, she knew she couldn't keep it to herself; she'd have to inform the captain.

"Yes, but they'll only do so much good," Dowd said. "Your joints are swelling aggressively. You're already experiencing muscle spasms. And you're fatiguing more quickly, too."

Sen chuckled. "That all comes with age, doesn't it?"

"You're a stubborn one," Dowd replied.

Manda blinked and closed the connection. She'd heard everything she needed to hear. *Poor Haltar,* she thought as she walked slowly back along the corridor toward the elevators, wondering what to do about what she'd heard.

Her thoughts were suddenly interrupted by an onslaught of thoughts broadcast from the planet's surface, to anyone who could receive them, by Nilo Pistach, the Psy civilian on the ground with Danis and the Marines: *Have a forcefield generator. Took out a whole group of Swarmies! On our way to Minnah's alien crash site. Second generation... ship. Kyne... Tech... Attack... Orso... Thousands of Swarm... Enemy fleet... Gravpacks destroyed. Need ground extraction. Communication center... Will... location and time. Will... you know ASAP!*

Nilo's thoughts were sporadic, weakened by the great distance, but the meaning was clear enough. The Swarm was going to attack Orso in force, and Minnah had some new tech.

"Thousands?" she whispered to herself. They'd never faced anything like that. *Nothing* came close.

"Now here this! Now here this," Krista's monotone voice reverberated along the corridor. "Senior bridge officers to the conference room. Senior..."

"Stars," she said as she stepped into the elevator.

* * *

Morian was already seated at the head of the table when Manda stepped into the conference room; she was the first to arrive.

She noted the grave expression on his face and, if she'd read Nilo's thoughts correctly, she thought she knew why.

"Sit down, Commander," Morian said. "You received Pistach's message, I assume."

"I did. I hope you received it more clearly than I did."

He shook his head. "It was garbled, but I got the gist of it. The Swarm is planning to attack Orso, and the away team is stranded on the surface and are going to need to organize an extraction. How's Sen doing?"

"I couldn't see him," she replied, hoping he wouldn't read her thoughts. "Dr. Dowd was with him."

Morian nodded but didn't pursue it.

Five minutes later, almost the entire bridge team was present and Morian began the briefing.

"I've just received important intel," he said. He leaned forward in his chair, his hands clasped together on his desk. "The Swarm is planning to attack Orso. Apparently, Kyne Minnah, the object of this mission, has somehow been able to acquire this information and he has also acquired tech that could be vital to the outcome of the war."

The room was quiet. They all sat there numb, staring at him.

"From what I can understand from the garbled Psy message I received from Major Dubois' PsyOp, they are stranded without a way to get off the planet." He looked at Jax and said, "Mr. Jax, that will mean a surface extraction. For how many, we don't know. Nor do we know the time and place. Not yet, anyway. Is there anyone other than you that can make such an extraction?"

"I can do it, Captain," Jax said.

"I'm sure you can, Ensign, but unfortunately Mr. Sen is in the med bay, so you will be needed here."

Jax's face paled. "Um... neither of the other two shuttle pilots have the experience. They're just shuttle pilots. One of the fighter pilots, perhaps; Gian Vastum or Jackknife."

Damn! Morian thought. *And Danis is on the ground. I shouldn't have let her go.* He nodded at Jax and changed the subject.

"The PsyOp also indicated that Orso will be attacked by..." He shook his head in disbelief, then continued, "thousands of Swarm ships."

There was a collective gasp from several of the officers seated at the table.

Jadern raised his hand. "That, Captain, is hard to believe. How did Minnah get this information? Could the Swarm be setting a trap?"

"Could they be feeding him false information? Could the numbers be false?" Fargo asked.

"What if they're not even going to Orso? What if they're feeding us false information, as Corin said, and are really planning to attack another system?" Sandra Lowry asked, frowning.

Morian shook his head and held up his hand. "It could be any of that. We just don't know, and we won't. Not until we retrieve Minnah, and that we must, at all costs," he said, flattening his hands on the table. "But all we have to go on is that they are presently headed cross country to investigate some sort of Swarm communication center. I've already approved the mission." He smiled as he continued, "Actually, they took it upon themselves without my approval, which is fine because we need all the intel we can get and if Minnah can get it... Well, we'll see. In the meantime, Orso needs to be warned. Mr. DeLong. Send a probe through the Slipstream network to the palace. Prioity One. Fastest rout possible. How long with it take to get there?"

"Approximately twenty-nine hours, Captain," DeLong replied.

"Very well. Do it now. Send 'To Prince Elio Lorne. Marshal Ugo Tan. New Intelligence. Minnah has found the wreck of a new Swarm ship. Details unknown. Minnah also warns of an impending Swarm invasion. Target Orso. Numbers unknown but estimated to be in the thousands. Suggest you prepare to defend yourselves and both slip gates. Signed Richard Morian, Commodore commanding USF Avenger.

"In the meantime, the rest of you stand by to make the extraction. The shuttle will be accompanied by a fighter escort. You will organize that, if you please, Commander Haal. The rest of you... Stand by. Any questions?"

Everyone started talking at once.

"One at a time, please," Morian said, holding up his hand.

The room went quiet.

"No?" Morian said, then he tapped his chin.

"How many survivors are there?" Jadern asked.

Morian lowered his head, shaking it slowly and said, "No more than thirty."

Everyone took a moment of silence as the news hit them. Typhon had been completely destroyed, more than five million souls had been lost, and the same thing could happen to Orso.

"Very well," Morian said, rising to his feet. "Back to

your stations. Commander Haal, please move forward with the extraction plan."

Manda nodded, thinking hard. She knew that the only person that could be trusted with the extraction was Dagon Jax. She needed Haltar Sen back at the helm.

She was the last to leave the conference room, and when she did, she headed straight back to the med bay.

* * *

She found Haltar out of bed, dressed and about to leave. He was standing with a slight stoop, holding a hydro pack and a caffegen tab in the other. He seemed surprised to see her. He straightened his stance but couldn't conceal the pain it caused.

"Commander," he said, and he popped the tab into his mouth and washed it down with a couple of swallows from the hydro pack. "It's... nice to see you. Is there a problem? I see from my datapad that Jax handled the ship quite well." He seemed proud and sad at the same time. "And I see we have new orders." He was referring to the extraction plan.

"Yes, no," Manda said. "Haltar, you need to tell the captain the truth."

His eyes widened, then he nodded slowly. "So you know," he said sadly and looked away. "I've been trying to keep my condition at bay for the longest time," he said, "but it's a degenerative disease," He shrugged.

"Jax is good," Manda said. "But he's not you, not yet, and we need him to fly the shuttle. We need you at the helm, Haltar."

Sen smiled. "I love that boy. He has a passion you don't often see these days." His eyes watered, glistening in the harsh light of the med bay.

"You have to tell Dagon," she said again, then put her hand on his shoulder and looked down into his eyes. "You have to prepare him."

He nodded, then looked up at her and said, "You're right, of course." He sighed. "I will, but first I must tell the Captain." He flinched, and Manda couldn't tell if it was from pain or the thought of not being able to fly anymore.

Chapter Twenty

Psy Hunt

Orso Royal Palace

It was almost an hour later. Marshal Tan had made some excuse and had left the room. Tenilo was waiting patiently with Elio and T-1 for Queen Zara to open her eyes.

She opened them slowly until they were mere slits, her face set, her mouth open slightly. "I feel... something," she muttered, raising her chin, her brow furrowed in concentration. There's a strong presence coming from..." She closed her eyes and rubbed her temples. "*Beneath!*" She pointed to the floor with a long forefinger. "What is below?"

"Below?" Tenilo asked, looking at Elio.

"Tunnels," Elio said. "Catacombs if you like. They were created when the palace was built more than three hundred years ago. No one goes there. To my knowledge they haven't been used in decades."

"That's where we must look for your assassin," Zara said. "He is searching for someone." She looked at Tenilo.

Elio nodded, looked at his small contingent of guards, checked to make sure their modified halos were functional, then said, "Follow me."

"You, too, T-1," Tenilo said.

The robot nodded and joined the group.

They made their way along several corridors, down two flights of stairs, then turned right and continued on until they reached an elevator set conveniently next to one of King Orson's many offices. The elevator took them down three more levels.

They stepped out of the elevator into a cylindrical walkway. It was indeed a tunnel, but not in the true sense of the word. The walkway was lined with a smooth, white ceramic material that glistened under the overhead lights.

"Why are the lights on?" Tenilo whispered to Elio.

Elio shook his head, then said, "I can feel it. Someone is reaching out." He lifted his hand to his halo.

"*Don't!*" Queen Zara sounded the warning, reaching out with her Psy so Tenilo and Elio would hear her. *If you do, you'll die. Go straight until you pass two corridors, then go left.*

And then? Tenilo asked as they started down the path.

I don't have Sight. He felt the snap in her thoughts. *I just feel the presence.*

Tenilo looked at Elio and said, "I can feel it too. Can you?"

"Yes, I can, too," Elio replied.

The guards took the lead, clearing the corridor and each room as they moved slowly forward.

After a while, following the queen's directions, they

made a left turn and found themselves confronted by a locked metal door.

One of the guards stepped forward, raising his weapon, but Elio held up his hand. "Hold your fire," he said. "Preserve your ammunition and step back, please."

Elio held up both hands, palms out facing the door, stared at the lock and concentrated.

The door screeched in protest. The metal around the lock buckled. The doorframe—also metal—twisted, creaked, then, with a crack that sounded like a railgun shot, gave in and swung inward, crashing against the wall.

"Ah!" someone yelled. There were armed soldiers on the other side of the door and they rushed forward, laser weapons blazing.

T-1, his forcefield activated, stepped forward as the assailants opened fire. The opening was too narrow for more than one person to fight effectively. All Elio, Tenilo and the guards could do was stand back and let T-1 deal with the soldiers.

Please, don't let me die down here, underneath this palace, Tenilo thought as he slid down the wall and hunkered down in the corridor, shut his eyes and clapped his hands over his ears.

"Get down, my prince!" he heard one of the guards shout.

He imagined Prince Elio obstinately moving forward, using his TK to help in the fight. *Don't get yourself killed,* he projected to Elio, his thoughts filled with fear and sorrow. *Who will rule Orso then?*

I'm sure we'll arrange something. The reply came, still in his head, but not from Elio.

Tenilo tried to shield the unkind thoughts that streamed

through his mind, but he was sure the queen was still monitoring them.

With a laser pistol in each hand, T-1 stepped forward through the open doorway into a hail of laser fire. His forcefield glowed brilliant white under the onslaught. Impervious to the laser fire he was taking, he fired his weapons only six times, each time with devastating effect, and each time he fired, a soldier died; his aim was impeccable.

Having done his work, T-1 turned around, stepped back out into the corridor, and said, "The way is clear. Would you like me to take the lead?"

"It's all right, Tenilo," he heard Elio call out. "It's over. You can get up now."

Elio held up his hand for the group to wait, then stepped past T-1 through the doorway from one corridor into the other.

Tenilo and Elio bent down beside one of the dead soldiers. Tenilo was stunned when he saw that they were, all six of them, Orso Special Forces.

"What in star's name is going on here?" Elio said.

"Prince Elio, please allow me to explain." Someone shouted at the far end of the corridor.

The man had his hands up and began walking toward them.

As far away as he was, Tenilo recognized him immediately. He was stunned, dumbfounded. Walking slowly toward them was Marshal Ugo Tan!

Ugo Tan stood beside the fallen soldiers, lowered his hands to his sides, and bowed his head.

"It would seem I have some explaining to do, my prince," Tan said quietly. "Perhaps it would be better if I showed you. If you would, please, follow me." He gestured with his hand, then turned on his heel and walked away, back the way he'd come.

Elio looked at Tenilo. Tenilo nodded and, together, they set off along the corridor following the marshal; T-1 and the guards close behind them.

After several twists and turns, they arrived outside a pair of double doors.

Tan waited for them to catch up, then leaned forward and put his eye to the scanner to the right of the doors.

There was a buzz and a double click, and the two doors slid open to reveal a vast room with brilliant white walls.

The room had been divided into a half-dozen containment areas with taniglass windows and doors; each contained a group of people: men, women and children. Each containment area featured several large holo displays flashing images that made no sense to Tenilo. The people, all in some sort of state of distress, were babbling to themselves or to others. Some appeared to be clutching their heads in pain. Some had nosebleeds while others were heaving, drenched in sweat. To Tenilo, it was sickening to behold.

Elio looked around slowly, taking in everything. His mouth hung open. Tenilo could sense that he was both stunned and disgusted by what he saw. Elio turned to face Tan.

Tan drew himself up in front of the prince and lifted his chin. He was a tall man, but not as tall as Elio.

"What is this?" Elio asked. "What are you doing down here?" His voice was low, his tone harsh.

"This is an intelligence cell," Tan said. His voice remained level. "An undercover operation, if you will." He gestured towards the containment cells. "These people are Seers."

So many on Orso? Tenilo thought as he shook his head, obviously in a state of total disbelief. *How could this be?*

"Who authorized this?" Elio snapped. "Who authorized you to torture these people?" Elio's hands were balled into fists at his side as he waited for an answer.

He's the commander-in-chief of Orso's military forces, Tenilo thought. *Perhaps he took it upon himself.* But deep down, Tenilo already knew the answer. An operation such as this was too big even for Ugo to do on his own.

Tan locked eyes with Elio and reached out to him. Tenilo reached out to Tan and heard him say, *Your father...*

Tenilo saw the secret meetings between the two great men flash through his brain. He listened in as Elio responded, *How could I have missed this?*

It was decided to... The link was broken. Tan was blocking both of them.

"Your father, the king, authorized all of this. Much of it he oversaw personally," Tan said, waving his hand in a sweeping, back-and-forth motion. "He authorized it after the first Swarm attack—back when the ability of Sight was little more than a rumor. And he was right. What we've learned will..."

"But it's insane," Tenilo said, interrupting him.

Tan looked at him dismissively and said,

"Insane, you say? "There's something else you should see."

"Wait," Elio said as Tan started to walk away. "Why were we unable to read these minds down here before we entered this room? All we could get were echoes, vibrations." He looked at Tenilo. His face was unreadable.

Tan laughed and said, "It was a difficult endeavor, and expensive," he said without looking back. "Like those little halo inventions you have on your heads, we had engineers mind proof this whole section." He stopped outside another door, leaned in for the scanner and the door opened.

"Obviously, it isn't perfect," he said as he stepped inside."

On the other side of the steel door was a single cell. The man inside was seated, restrained in what once would have been called a zero-gravity chair. His eyes were closed. There were IV's in both his arms. His breathing was steady but shallow. He appeared to be in a meditative state.

"Is that...?" Elio began to ask.

"Yes, that is the Psy assassin, as you've all been calling him," Tan said, his voice emotionless. "He can find and kill without leaving this room but..." he pointing at the machines pumping liquids into the man, "only with the help of certain proprietary drugs."

Tenilo looked at Elio. He could see the rage boiling up inside him.

With a guttural cry, and using his TK, Elio lifted Ugo Tan high into the air and threw him across the room to slam against the wall.

Ugo writhed on the floor in pain. "My prince..." he gasped.

Tenilo took a step back. Never had he seen the prince so furious.

"What are you doing, you maniac?" Elio shouted and threw up his hands, palms and fingers open wide. "You tried to kill my father."

He tightened the muscles in his fingers as if he was strangling someone.

Ugo Tan rose slowly off the floor, his head tilted back, his hands clawing at his throat, choking. For several seconds Elio held him there, seemingly suspended by his neck, his feet dangling, kicking.

Then Elio let him fall, took a deep breath and stared at him.

"Your father... had to be... removed," Tan gasped, needing his bruised neck with his fingers.

"You're not implying, that my father, the king, would want *himself* killed?" He raised his voice. "Marshal! Answer me, or so help me, or I'll squeeze you until you burst..."

And Tenilo believed him, absolutely.

"The Seers," Tan said. His eyes looked as if they were about to pop out of his head. "They say we're about to be invaded. Orso, my prince. Orso is about to be invaded. Any day now. Your father couldn't, can't do it... You... my prince, are the only one that can." He coughed and licked his lips "Only you can lead the USF to victory against the Swarm... for Orso... For all of the Sovereign Systems. For all humanity. You, my prince, will save us all."

* * *

With trembling hands, Elio raked his fingers through his hair. "And you didn't think," he said, his voice cracking, "to just discuss the fate of humanity with my father before you tried to assassinate him?" He looked at Tan in utter bewilderment. "He would have gladly stepped down!" Elio knew that his father was a stubborn man, but he was not so callous and set in his ways that he would remain in power if it meant the destruction of the human race.

Ugo Tan struggled up onto his knees, still massaging his throat. "I could *not* take that chance, my prince," he said quietly, shaking his head.

Elio couldn't believe what he was hearing. If his father

died because of what this man had done, or if he'd been rendered brain dead, he'd kill Ugo with his own bare hands.

Ugo cleared his throat and stood up, his legs wobbling. He appeared about to collapse again, but he didn't. He managed to stand relatively still, drew himself up to his full height, came to attention, lifted his chin and said, "There was another premonition." He turned his head to look at Tenilo and opened his mind: *I wanted to dispose of you too. The Seers say that you will betray mankind one day.*

Elio had also received Tan's thoughts. He looked at Tenilo. He could feel his friend's mind reel, filled with denial, anxiety and dread.

"I would never!" Tenilo said aloud, his voice trembling.

Elio, though he'd known Tenilo for many years and they'd become friends, couldn't help but consider what Tan had said. If Ugo Tan had taken the unthinkable step of trying to assassinate the king, then Elio knew that he truly believed what the Seers had predicted. That being so, Elio had no alternative but to consider Tan's accusation. But at the moment, Elio couldn't even begin to think about what Tenilo *might* do in the future. He had to concentrate on the here and now.

To Elio, this operation, this intelligence cell, was an abomination, a blight on the kingdom, and it had to be eradicated.

"I want it all..." He waved his hand in the air. "Shut down, now," he said, then turned and shouted, "Guards! To me!" His voice echoed throughout the cell and into the corridor.

The guards rushed in.

"Arrest him." He pointed at Ugo Tan. "Immediately! For the atrocities he committed down here. For crimes against humanity and for conspiring to murder the king."

Ugo Tan locked eyes with Elio, smiled weakly and said, "That won't be necessary, my prince."

He bowed slightly, showing great respect for the prince, shuddered violently and then fell to the ground, dead.

Elio turned to the man in the cell. "You!" he shouted, pointing at him.

The man's eyes were still closed, but he was smiling. The clear liquid in his IVs changed to a deep lavender. His body went stiff. His lips bared his teeth. His body arched against the restraints, and he began to thrash around.

Elio tried to break open the cell door with TK, but it was no use. It was impenetrable.

The man continued to thrash around for several seconds, his eyelids fluttering. His eyes opened wide, showing only the whites. He went still, his body stiff, arched against the restraints. Then he went limp. His head lolled to the right, his mouth half-open, tongue protruding slightly on his bottom lip, his eyes wide open, sightless, seemed to be looking straight at them.

He was dead.

* * *

"Get these people out of here," Elio said to the sergeant of the guards. Take them to the med bay and have them detoxed, fed and settled into comfortable quarters. I'll see to them later." He turned and looked at Tenilo. "Come," Elio said. "We must speak with the Tudors." And with that he turned and walked out of the chamber without a backward look at either Ugo Tan or the dead Psy assassin.

Tenilo and T-1 followed Elio to the royal couple's suite. On the way, Tenilo answered Elio's few comments by saying as little as possible, part of him terrified that the

Seers' prediction might be correct. *How could it be?* he thought. *What could I possibly do to turn against my own kind, and why would I help the Swarm?* He was deeply troubled by what Ugo Tan had said, no matter how much he tried not to think about it.

"Don't worry, my friend," Elio whispered. "I don't believe a word of it."

Tenilo smiled at him. The prince's words brought him little comfort. But it did ease his mind to know that Elio believed in him.

They entered the royal suite to find that the king and queen of Odin were expecting them.

"From your moods," Queen Zara said, folding her hands delicately in her lap, "And from what little I saw of what happened down there, I see we have much to discuss."

Elio nodded and said, "Rather than offer a long-winded description of those events, your grace, I think it would be prudent if I open my mind to you and let you see for yourself. Don't abuse the privilege. If you do, you will never have the opportunity to do so again."

The queen smiled and nodded sardonically.

Elio sat, took off the halo and closed his eyes.

Less than a minute later, the queen said, "Thank you, my prince. That was... both informative and alarming. Tell me, what do you intend to do with the Seers?"

"I haven't had time to think about that yet," Elio replied.

"If I might make a suggestion?" she said.

"Of course."

"I have no doubt they will be useful in our fight against the Swarm, so I suggest you set aside a suite of comfortable rooms for them here in the palace and have them attended by a team of properly qualified doctors. Also, have them monitored around the clock by someone you can trust implicitly."

"I will not condone the use of drugs or torture," Elio snapped.

"Nor should you," the queen replied. "But make use of them, you must."

"I agree," Elio said and looked at Tenilo, his eyebrows raised in question.

Tenilo shook his head and said, "No! Not me, my prince. I am compromised by the Seers' prediction. I cannot be seen to be trusted. You must find someone else."

Elio nodded thoughtfully.

"Why would he have himself killed?" King Wulfrick asked, referring to Ugo Tan.

"We don't know," Tenilo said.

"Yes, we do," Elio snapped. "He took the coward's way out. He didn't want to face the consequences of his heinous acts of high treason."

"Perhaps," Tenilo said, "but perhaps he did it to protect something else. Perhaps there's something bigger going on."

"And what would *you* know about that?" the king asked, shooting Tenilo a dark look. "You're right, young man. You can't be trusted. Why am I not surprised that a Galactic Easterner would conspire to destroy us all," he spat the words at Tenilo.

"That's enough, your majesty" Elio snapped. "I trust Tenilo. I have known him for a long time. He has worked tirelessly to advance the war effort. Further, we know from past experience that the Seers' visions are often incorrectly interpreted and taken out of context. As of now, we have more important things to think about—the imminent invasion of Orso, for instance."

"The Swarm will be here soon, then?" King Wulfrick asked.

"If the Seers are correct," Elio replied, "yes; we can expect them in overwhelming force. I am sending an emergency communique to the general staff ordering a full-scale mobilization of all USF forces, and I expect your full support."

Wulfrick glanced at Zara. She nodded, but said nothing.

"Of course, your highness," Wulfrick said, bowing his head slightly.

An hour later, Elio received the message sent by Captain Morian, confirming the impending Swarm attack.

Chapter Twenty-One

Planet Typhon

Above the canyon

Near New Hope

Danis and the Marines under the command of Major Dubois, being led by Kyne Minnah's small group, were nearing the end of the canyon and the Swarm ship crash site. *I hope it's worth it*, she thought as she tripped over a large rock, fighting to retain her balance. The truth was, she was exhausted. For more than three hours they'd stumbled over the rocky terrain. They were all tired except, so it seemed, Kyne Minnah—obviously a man on a mission. She watched him as he leapt easily over a large rock and landed effortlessly.

Oh yes, she thought. *It had better be worth it... Positive thoughts, Danis, positive thoughts. How does that pre-Purge era saying go? Don't put all of your eggs in one basket? Hah! We already have, and we can't afford to drop the basket. Not now,* she thought as she stumbled again. *Damn it! Hell, we can't afford to break even one egg!*

She stopped walking, paused for a moment and bent forward, her hands on her knees. She took a deep breath, stood upright, put her head back, hands on her hips, stretched her back and stared up at the cloudless blue sky, the sun a great yellow ball to the east, the rocky canyon peaks shimmering under the relentless sunshine.

She shook her head, took another deep breath and stepped resolutely onward, now trailing Dubois and Kyne Minnah by several dozen meters. She quickened her pace in an effort to catch up. The drop suit was more of a hindrance than protection. She made her mind up to get rid of it the first chance she got.

By then, Kyne Minnah and his group, unhindered by the cumbersome drop suits, had taken the lead. Even Dubois had fallen behind. The rest of the Marines, in single file, loaded down with equipment and the four wounded Marines, were strung out in a long line behind Danis. She was sure if they didn't get some relief soon, they'd begin to drop out.

She paused again, turned and looked back, wondering how Dunn was doing. She spotted him in line with the Marines some eight men back from Lieutenant Nortak at the head of the column and doing surprisingly well.

Poor, Grell, Danis thought. *All of this running for his life may do him some good. Build some character, perhaps.*

She smiled to herself, turned again and stepped resolutely forward, the heavy K-15 railgun slung across her back.

"How much further, damn it?" she heard Dubois ask.

"Not far. Just leave it to me," Kyne said, not picking up on the annoyance in Dubois' voice.

"We'll be there soon," Tara said.

"We've got about another kilometer to go," Yarrow chimed in. He looked at Minnah and said, "Right, Kyne?"

"Yes," he said, adjusting the strap of his backpack. "As I said, not far now. Wait 'til you see it. It's amazing."

And so the trek along the canyon ridge continued until, at last, Kyne held up his hand and called a halt.

Danis, now thoroughly fatigued—fighting a battle in space was one thing, but this—noticed that the canyon had narrowed considerably.

"See that?" Kyne said and pointed. "There. See it?"

Danis stared down into the canyon, but all she could see was rocks, rocks, and more rocks. *They must have been falling from the canyon walls for eons*, she thought. *What's he pointing to?*

And then she saw it: the wreckage of a Swarm ship. She would have seen it sooner had it retained its blue halo. As it was now, the ship's light gray color appeared as a dull shadow among the rocks at the end of the box canyon; even from a distance she could see it was much larger than the ones she'd encountered in the past.

Balto gasped. "Even broken and flightless," he said, shielding his eyes from the sun, "it's still quite magnificent."

"That it is," Yarrow said, nodding pensively. "Hah, terrifyingly so."

"Look out!" Dunn yelled out from somewhere behind her.

Suddenly, Yarrow seemed to leap into the air as Dunn used his TK to hurl him out of the way as a searing blast of plasma shattered the rocky floor on which he'd been standing.

Yarrow hit the ground hard, but managed to roll when he landed, saving him from injury. He looked at Dunn, who was standing some ten meters away, staring wildly around at the group of Blues marching resolutely toward them: three Stompers and a Stalker.

"Take cover!" Dubois shouted.

Dunn didn't need to be told twice. He scurried like a rat behind a large boulder and dropped to the ground shaking like a leaf.

Kyne ripped off his backpack and ran for cover.

Danis slipped the K-15 off her back, powering it up as she ran, stumbling for the nearest large boulder, which happened to be at the edge of a ridge, and experienced a moment of dizziness as she looked over the edge and down to the canyon floor more than one-hundred-fifty meters below,

She glanced at the wrecked ship. From where she was, she had a clear view. It was no more than five hundred meters away. *So close, yet so far,* she couldn't help but think. But thinking wasn't something she had time for. They were under attack.

She peered over the top of the boulder. The Blues, now less than four hundred meters away, were striding steadily forward, each surrounded by a shimmering blue forcefield and each carrying a heavy-looking plasma rifle.

The Stalker was the first to die, under the combined, withering fire of the K-15 railguns.

As the heavy slugs slammed into it, first its forcefield failed, then its silicon-based armor shattered into thousands of pieces.

The three Stompers continued to walk forward, plasma

beams like brilliant blue searchlights flickered this way and that, crisscrossing one another, looking for a target, but they found none; the Marines were far too well trained to leave themselves open, and they continued to hammer at the Stompers.

The Stompers, however, were different from their Stalker handler. Their forcefields were more resilient and their armor, made from a ductile, silicon-based material, was able to better withstand the withering fire from thirty rail-guns, and Danis suddenly realized they were in trouble.

The Marines, hunkered down over a wide area, were hammering the three Stompers continuously, and they were effective. One after another they fell, only to rise again minutes later.

"They won't die!" one of the Marines yelled and rose to his feet firing a continuous stream of slugs at the nearest Stomper, now less than one-hundred-fifty meters away.

Danis shot a glance at Kyne, now under cover just a few meters away.

He shrugged.

She reached out to him and entered his mind. *Can't you do something? What about your device?*

The answer was discouraging. *The Swarm's a constant force*, he answered. *Ever-evolving. My device, as you call it, is useless. It needs charging. Can't you do something?* he thought. *Don't you have TK?*

No, she replied. *I have only Psy. What about your man, Mozzley?*

He's exhausted. What about that guy you brought with you? He has TK.

She looked at Dunn, then at the advancing Stompers, then back at Dunn. He was hunkered down behind a large boulder, his hands over his ears.

Dunn, Danis reached out to him. *Get up. You have to do something. You're the only one who can. We're all going to die if you don't.*

Dunn looked at her, made a face and shook his head.

Get up now, damn it! That's an order. It's why you were allowed to come. You were able to lift a shuttlecraft in the hangar. Now do something or you're going to die, along with the rest of us, right where you are.

Dunn reluctantly struggled to his feet, peeked over the boulder, took stock of the situation and then... something seemed to come over him.

He stepped out from behind the boulder, raised his hands, palms out, fingers clawed, took a deep breath and... It was at that point one of the Stompers fired at him.

A brilliant bolt of plasma streaked toward Dunn at the speed of light, only to be met by the irresistible force of his TK.

Danis, to that point, had no idea just how strong Dunn's TK was, and she watched as the plasma beam flowered like a stream of falling water hitting a rock.

The Stomper continued to fire a continuous stream of plasma and Dunn continued to deflect it until, after several seconds, the Stomper gave up and began to walk forward again, closing the gap.

But Dunn wasn't done. He took a deep breath, filling his massive chest, and concentrated on the leading Stomper.

As if jerked backward by an invisible tether, the Stomper flew into the air to land more than five-hundred meters away.

Dunn switched his attention to the two remaining Stompers. They had stopped walking and were bringing their weapons to bear, but before they could fire, they both streaked upward, vertically, to a height Danis estimated to be at least two hundred meters and then Dunn hurled them away as if they were toys. And then he just stood there. Transfixed. Then he turned, looked at Danis and smiled.

"Everybody!" Kyne yelled as he leapt to his feet. "Follow me. Run!"

Chapter Twenty-Two

Swarm Ship

Planet Typhon

80km Northwest of New Hope

In single file they followed Kyne Minnah as he ran like a frightened dreen down a narrow, rocky path to the canyon floor. Once there, they continued their hectic dash toward the rock wall towering above the wrecked ship.

"Follow me," Kyne yelled again as he dodged left and ran toward a cleft in the rock wall.

Two minutes later they were all safely inside the entrance to Kyne's cave, breathing heavily.

The run down the path into the canyon was not, by itself, taxing, but it was dangerous—had anyone stumbled they would certainly have fallen to their death—and the exertion of running in the drop suits made it that much more arduous.

"We must stay out of sight," Kyne said to Dubois, Nortak and Danis. "They'll be back. Your man didn't destroy them. We have to post a lookout. They'll be on the canyon ridge, maybe even the canyon floor."

"See to it, Nortak," Dubois said.

The lieutenant nodded, tapped two Marines on the shoulder, and they followed him back out into the sunshine.

"My people are back there, waiting for me." He nodded toward the darkness inside the cave.

Dubois stared at him for a long moment, then said, "We have to get out of here, back to *Avenger*. We need an extraction point—"

"I need to get into that communications center before I can leave," Minnah said, interrupting him.

"And where might that be?" Dubois asked. "And how do we get out of this godforsaken canyon with those... those machines up there?"

"The same way we came down," Minnah replied. "My EMPG will take care of the Stompers, once it's recharged. I can operate it remotely, but Mozzley's TK isn't strong enough to raise it the distance required."

"I can do it," Dunn said, taking several steps forward.

"Good," Minnah said. "It will take at least an hour to fully charge. Before we go, I need to fetch some things from the shipwreck." He looked at the group standing with him.

"Tara, you and Commander Morian see to organizing our people for evacuation, please," Minnah said.

She looked at him and nodded.

Minnah continued, "Explain what we're doing and that we're getting out of here. Mr. Dubois, I suggest you have your men get rid of those suits. We have a long hike ahead of us."

"You heard what the man said," Dubois shouted at his

Marines. "Move, move, move! Get rid of the suits and see to your weapons. What did you think? That you're on R and R?" He paused, looked at Minnah, then continued, "How long before you can rejoin us? I need to know where this communications center is and how we're going to get there."

"Thirty minutes. No more than that," Minnah replied.

"D'you need an escort to the shipwreck?"

"Hah, no. I'm better off alone. I know how to stay out of sight."

Dubois nodded, turned to Danis and said, "I'm coming with you and Tara. I want to see what we have to contend with."

Minnah turned to Mozzley. "Put this on charge for me," he said, taking the octagonal device from his backpack. "I'll return soon."

Mozzley nodded. "Stay safe, my young friend."

"Always." Minnah grinned at him, then turned and trotted out into the blazing sunshine.

"Keep 'em in order," Dubois said to Nortak, who'd just returned from posting the lookouts, then he turned to Tara and said, "Lead the way."

And the small group, led by Tara who was followed closely by Danis and Dubois, then Yarrow with Mozzley bringing up the rear, walked into the darkness of the cave.

They hadn't gone far when the way began to lighten and soon they found themselves the underground cavern, well lit and cool.

The survivors—there were twenty-six more of them; twelve men, eight women and six children ranging in age from nine to fourteen—were all busy with various tasks, most of them packing to get ready to leave.

"Gather round everybody and listen up," Dubois said, clapping his hands. "My name is Major Dubois, USF

Marines. This is Lieutenant Commander Morian of the USF *Avenger*. We're here to take you…" He paused, looked at Danis and said, "Where are we taking them?"

Danis shrugged, thought about it and then said, "We're taking you home to Orso."

"That's not our home," one of the women shouted. "This is our home."

"I know, I know," Danis said loudly, holding up her hands to quiet them, "but you can't stay here. You have to come with us… for now. Until it's safe for you to return."

"And when will that be?" the woman shouted.

"What's your name?" Danis asked.

The woman looked at her, hesitated for a second, then said, "Nelda. It's Nelda Creek."

"Well, Nelda," Danis said, "the truth is I don't know when you'll be able to return. Right now, nobody does. But you can't stay here."

The woman stared at her, a sulky look on her face. Then she nodded and turned away.

"So please," Danis said, "pack your things and be ready to leave in an hour. Take only what you need. We have a long trek to the extraction point.

It was almost an hour later when Kyne Minnah rejoined them, his backpack full of… what, he didn't reveal.

"Mozzley," he said as he sat down on a makeshift stool, "did you charge the EMPG?"

"It lacks but a few more minutes for the cycle to complete," Mozzley replied.

"Major. Commander," Minnah said, looking from one to the other. "It would seem that I'm wrong. The Stompers have not returned, not that we can see. So, I think it's safe to leave this place. How many are we?"

"Including the commander and myself," Dubois

replied, "twenty-one of us, including the four wounded, and thirty of you, making fifty-one in all. How far do you intend to lead us?"

Minnah lowered his chin, stared at the cave floor for several seconds, then looked up and said, "Speaking from memory, ten, maybe eleven kilometers."

Dubois stared at him, stunned. "Are you serious? That's a march of... on this terrain, and in broad daylight, in the sun, with civilians? At least four hours. We should call it off and find a viable extraction point as soon as possible."

"I understand all of that, Major, but I must insist. We have to know what they're doing. You know that. Am I not right, Commander?" he asked and looked at Danis.

Much as she hated to say it, she knew Minnah was right.

"Yes," Danis said simply.

"And you think you can hack into whatever it is?" Dubois asked.

"Perhaps," Minnah replied, looking up at him.

"Perhaps? Perhaps?" Dubois snapped. "That's not good enough, Minnah. You're suggesting I, that is we"—he glanced at Danis then continued—"drag fifty odd people halfway across Typhon because you think that *perhaps* you can hack into some half-completed alien... artifact. What if you can't? What then?"

Minnah smiled up at him and said calmly, "Then I'll destroy it."

"Destroy it? How?" Dubois demanded.

"The same way I destroyed the Stompers. With an EMP blast."

Dubois stared down at him, pursed his lips, blew out a loud blast of air, then looked at Danis and said, "And you're going along with this?"

"I don't see any other option," Danis replied. "If it is what Kyne thinks it is, we need to destroy it, whether he can hack into it or not. And, as an officer and a soldier, you know that, don't you, Major?"

Dubois glared at her. Then his face softened and he smiled and nodded. "That I do, Commander."

He looked around, spotted Nilo Pistach and beckoned to him.

"Can you contact *Avenger?*" he asked.

"I can."

"Very well then," Dubois said. "Do so now, and request extraction in one hour. Give them the coordinates at the northwest perimeter of the oasis."

Then, without waiting for Pistash to answer, he turned again at Minnah and said, "Come on then. We don't have much time. Let's get this show on the road. I want to be back on *Avenger* in time for dinner tonight."

Chapter Twenty-Three

Planet Typhon

Near New Hope

The trek to the top of the ridge was much harder going than it was coming down. By the time they reached the top they were all breathing hard, and Dubois called a five-minute rest.

He and Danis stood together gazing out over the bleak terrain. For the most part it was flat, featureless. But in the far distance, Danis could just make out several tall buildings shimmering under the hot sun, which she assumed to be New Hope.

To the left she could see green trees made tiny by the distance. Between them and the trees lay only desert, unforgiving and desolate.

She took a deep breath, unslung her rifle, and sat down on a nearby rock, and she couldn't help but wonder if they would make it across, especially the children.

Dubois did not sit down. Instead he paced slowly back and forth until finally he stopped and shouted for all to hear, "That's it. We'll rest again in an hour. Move out!" Then, more quietly, "Let's go, Commander."

A little over three hours later, the group stumbled into what turned out to be an oasis: green trees surrounding a small, spring-fed pond.

Dubois called a ten-minute rest and, after refilling their hydro packs, they flopped down to rest, all except Danis, Dubois and Minnah.

"Come," Minnah said. "Now you'll see." And he led them to the eastern edge of the trees and pointed. Less than two kilometers away a tall structure, obviously still under construction, shimmered a deep, indigo blue.

"That's what I've been telling you about," Minnah said.

Dubois stared at the structure for a long minute, then said, "You're right, Minnah. That's something special. It's... big. You think that gizmo of yours can shut it down?"

Minnah shrugged, then said, "We won't know until we try. But I am looking forward to trying. These bastards deserve whatever we can dish out. I don't know what's in there... For all we know it could even be some kind of gateway from their reality to ours. Whatever it is, we have to take it out."

"I agree," Danis said. "I suggest..." She looked around, then pointed and said, "This is as good a place as any for an extraction point, so I suggest we leave the civilians and the wounded here, with the exception of Dunn... Mozzely's... If we have to make a run for it, he won't make it. How far is it?" she asked.

"Fifteen... sixteen hundred meters," Dubois replied. "Say fifteen to twenty minutes, unencumbered."

"So," Danis said thoughtfully. "We leave the civilians

here. Twenty minutes there. Twenty minutes back. How long do you need, Kyne?"

He shook his head, thinking, then said, "If I can hack into whatever's in there... five... ten minutes. If not... No time at all. We'll hit it with an EMP, but there's a problem. Look."

They looked. Even at that distance they could see a half-dozen blue figures moving around in different directions.

Dubois stood for a moment, saying nothing, obviously thinking hard.

"We need a diversion," he said finally. "What's that? Over there?" He pointed to a group of several ruined buildings some three hundred meters left of the alien structure.

Minnah shook his head. "Looks like a farm... maybe."

"How many shots have you got in that thing?" Dubois asked.

Minnah made a face. "It's fully charged. Five, maybe six, but if we're going to destroy the complex, I'm going to need it all."

Dubois nodded, looked at Danis and said, "How about your boy? D'you think he could do what he did again?"

She thought for a moment, then looked at him and nodded.

"Minnah," Dubois said. "I'm not sure we can take those Blues. We don't have the ordnance. All we have are our rifles, two TKs and that gizmo of yours. I think we can get within a hundred meters or so without being seen, but the final hundred is across open ground. Not only that..." He looked around and then continued, "We need to get in, get out and bring in the shuttle for extraction. That, we can do on the far side of the oasis. Are you sure you need to get inside that thing?"

"Yes. I need to at least see what they're doing."

Dubois shook his head, then said, "All right. Here's what we'll do. You, Commander, will take Nortak and six of my men and the TK and make for the farm, or whatever it is. Tell Nortak he's going to need concussion grenades—"

"Those are no good against the Blues," Minnah said, interrupting him. "I know. We tried."

"You think I don't know that, Minnah?" Dubois snapped. "Now shut up and listen."

He turned again to Danis and continued. "I'll take six more men and go with Minnah. You let me know when you're in position, and on my mark, Nortak will set off a half-dozen grenades. He will need to make as much noise as possible. That should draw the Blues to you where, hopefully, the TK can deal with them, or at least keep them occupied."

He looked at Minnah and said, "There's no way of knowing what obstacles we'll have if and when the Blues take the bait, but I'm giving you no more than fifteen minutes and then I'll drag you out if I have to, and then we hightail it back here where, I hope, the shuttle will be waiting for us."

He looked at his chron, then said, "Let's go and organize the extraction. I've had enough of this godforsaken planet."

Chapter Twenty-Four

Impending Attack

Orso System

Elio was frustrated. Since the assassination attempt on his father, he felt as if he'd been in an endless cycle of meeting upon meeting. And there was yet another one pending and only the stars knew how many more he'd have to attend—not just attend; he was now the chair. *If father remains in his current state*, he thought, *I don't know what I'll do. This is not what I envisioned.*

Even though they'd never truly seen eye to eye, if he was to take the throne, he swore he would make his father proud. His mother, too. He looked up at the ceiling and prayed she was looking down upon him now that he needed her strength and support.

He donned his halo and jacked into the meeting, savoring the familiar tingly sensation as the probes connected with his nervous system. He took a deep breath

225

and assumed a calm but authoritative demeanor as his avatar stepped forward and took his father's seat.

The marshals were gathered around the large, round table, a ring of solid oak with a holo generator at its center.

Tenilo was seated to his right, the king and queen of Odin to his left. Sasha Crowe and Tiger Wok were seated together to Telino's right.

Elio took a deep breath and started his speech. "Good day to you, my friends." He leaned forward, placed his hands flat on the tabletop and continued. "I'd like to thank you all for attending on such short notice. You will have noticed that Marshal Ugo Tan is absent. Sadly, I regret to inform you that he has... passed away. The cause of his death is yet to be determined."

King Wulfrick coughed, then cleared his throat but said nothing. His face was flushed.

Queen Zara gave Elio a discreet, knowing look. Only she, King Wulfrick, Tenilo, and the infirmary's Dr. Myster knew what really happened, and he had been sworn to secrecy. Elio did not intend for anyone, other than his small group, to know anything about the circumstances surrounding Tan's death or the part he played in the attempted assassination. Or, for that matter, the Psy assassin and the secret cells in the tunnels. He would allow nothing that to take the focus away from the important matters at hand.

The marshals were, understandably, shocked and surprised to hear the news, but no one interrupted Elio as he continued.

"These are dire and momentous times," Elio said as he slowly rose from his seat, a steely glint in his eyes.

"Ladies and gentlemen, I have learned, from two impeccable sources, that we—that is the Orso System—is soon to be invaded by a mighty Swarm fleet and will soon be engaged in a battle the likes of which humankind has never experienced. We cannot stop it coming; we cannot even slow it down." He stood with his feet apart, his chest out, back rigid, hands behind his back and continued, "We will meet our enemy head-on. Not because we can, but because, if humanity is to endure, we *must*. It will take all of our resources, weaponry and courage, but we *will* defeat them."

He opened his mind and absorbed the mixture of apprehension, fear, and... hope. And he wondered if even a fraction of what he'd said contributed to that hope.

Marshal Sian Tali raised her hand to speak. At only one-point-seven meters tall, she was considerably shorter than most of Orso's ruling class. She wore her dark brown hair cropped short. Her almond eyes were a glittering, iridescent blue, the result of more than seventy years in space culminating in her promotion to Fleet Marshal. Her white, body-hugging uniform was trimmed in gold. Elio had noticed long ago that she wore a perpetual pout on her lips, which caused people who didn't know her to perceive her as sullen, the exact opposite of what she actually was. She was assertive.

"Please, Marshal," Elio said, giving her leave to speak.

"You say the Swarm is planning to attack Orso, as they did Tor, Odin, and Typhon. In what numbers? And how many ships and how much time do we have? And one more thing, your highness; who will you appoint to replace Marshal Tan?" She nodded politely and sat down.

Elio could feel the tension rise. King Wulfrick and Queen Zara flinched at the mention of their home planet.

Sian Tali was the commander of the Second Eastern Fleet.

"Good questions, Marshal Tali," Elio replied, sitting

down again. "And they lead me to what I'd like to discuss next."

He relaxed, placed his hands on the ornate chair's arms and kneaded the plush covering with his fingers. Even in the virtual world, the chair in which he was seated was ostentatious: purple velvet embroidered with gold. It reminded him of his father's throne. He loathed the grandiosity of it all, but it was the way of the royals. And even though it wasn't a life that he would have chosen for himself, he was bound by duty to accept it in totality.

"Yes, the Swarm intends to attack Orso," Elio said, "and soon, and in numbers unlike anything we've seen before. Perhaps in the hundreds of thousands. And, according to the intelligence, they will attack within the next forty-eight to seventy-two standard hours, which means we'll be unable to evacuate the planet."

"Hundreds of thousands?" Marshal Andrew McAlan whispered. He was the oldest of the assembled marshals. He was ninety-eight years old, but looked no more than sixty with only a single streak of silver hair in his jet-black waves.

"It can't be," another marshal said.

"Is that even possible?" Marshal Tali asked.

The rumble of conversation spread throughout the room.

Elio cleared his throat. "If you please, ladies and gentlemen," he said, holding up his hands to quell the noise. "I know this is all very disconcerting. And yes, Marshal Tali, it's more than possible, and time is running out." He looked around the table at the silent, frowning faces. "As to your final question regarding Marshal Tan's replacement," he continued, "I, myself, will temporarily assume the role of Commander in Chief."

Again, he looked around the table, expecting objections. He received only one.

Duke Rutta closed his eyes, heaved a heavy sigh, and said, "I'm sure your intentions are good, your highness, but it's my considered opinion that we need someone eminently more qualified to fill Tan's position... Marshal Tali, for instance."

Before Elio could answer, Tali raised her hand and said, "With all due respect, Duke Rutta, I disagree. Prince Elio's position as regent and the fact that he has not one, but two of the gifts—Psy and TK—and that he has the respect and confidence of most of us gathered here today, more than qualifies him to lead our system and her allies during these tumultuous times. He certainly has my confidence."

"Mine, too," Marshal McAlan said.

"And mine," Queen Zara said, much to Elio's astonishment. "This discussion is a waste of precious time. I suggest we put it to the vote and be done with it. All who agree that Prince Elio assumes the role of commander in chief, say 'Ay' now."

The vote was twenty-seven to two for Elio, with only Dukes Rutta and Paulus voting against.

"Thank you," Elio said, trying to keep the relief from his voice. "Let's get on with it." He paused for a moment then rose to his feet again, clasped his hands together behind his back, stepped away from the table and began to pace, thinking hard, then said, "I need statistics, please. Marshal Clien?"

Clien was in overall command of the ten orbiting battle stations, Orso's last line of defense.

"All stations are fully armed and operating at one hundred percent, your highness. We're ready."

"You have the new M99 torpedoes?" Elio asked.

Clien nodded and said, "We do, your highness. Each battle station has been supplied with one thousand of the new torpedoes. We could, of course, use more but..."

"We'll get you more," Elio said. He nodded, stopped pacing, turned to face the table, and said, "Marshals?"

The marshals began checking their datapads.

Tali raised her hand. "The one-hundred-seventeen ships in my fleet are, with two exceptions, fully armed and battle ready," she said. "My flagship, the USF *Vagabond*, has a full complement of ten squadrons of the latest F32C fighter—one-hundred-twenty-six in all, plus four squadrons of six B29 fighter bombers and two CX4 gunships. She has one-hundred-twenty 88mm railgun turrets and one-hundred-eight torpedo tubes. Her armor, thanks to Commodore Morian, has been upgraded to the new mino-dutrinium alloy: two meters thick. She has in her arsenal one-point-two million 88mm railgun projectiles and eight thousand of the new M99 torpedoes." Tali paused and scrolled through her datapad.

She continued, "No damage to hull... Minimal damage to shields on the port side, third quadrant. The ship is oper-ating at ninety-two percent capability." She looked up at Elio and said, "There's much more, your highness, but I won't go on. It would take far too long. Suffice it to say the Second Fleet is ready. I will have a full report on your desk within the hour."

"Thank you, Marshal," Elio replied. "How many of our ships have the new armor? Does anyone know?"

Tenilo raised his hand.

Elio looked at him and nodded.

"To date, the refitting is still ongoing, Tenilo said. "Sev-enty-six percent of the work has been completed. Of the sixteen USF fleets comprising twenty-one-hundred-ninety-seven ships, plus ancillaries, of which fifteen-hundred-forty have the new armor.

"Between them, they are able to field forty-eight Minotar-class carriers with four-hundred-eighty squadrons of twelve F32A, B and C fighters, five-thousand seven-hundred, give or take. They also have one-hundred-ninety-two squadrons of six B-52 fighter bombers: one-thousand-one-hundred. For a total of seven-thousand-two-hundred attack fighters.

"The combined fleets also include forty-seven battleships, two-hundred-sixty-eight heavy cruisers—each with a squadron of F32's—six-hundred-thirty destroyers and twelve-hundred-four fast frigates."

Tenilo paused, took a breath and continued.

"The factories across the systems are producing the new torpedoes in large quantities and we are sending them to the fleets as they come off the assembly lines. The factories on Freyja are also producing them in large quantities. And the Freyjan shipyards are launching new Avenger-class heavy cruisers at the rate of three a month." He looked up at Elio, who was standing behind Queen Zara.

"Thank you, Mr. Tenilo," Elio said. "Next?"

Marshal Hans Fairway sighed and went next. Public speaking was not the man's strong suit. "Captain Able Reins of the USF *Moongazer* received two shipments of the new M99 torpedoes..."

And so it went on and on until finally Elio held up his hand and called a halt.

"It would seem, then," he said, "that we have assembled the largest force in our history, but will it be enough, and will you be able to get here in time?"

He turned to Tiger Wok and Sasha Crowe and said,

"Where exactly are you, my friends, and how long will it take you to get here?"

Wok frowned and said, "I'm afraid the news I have is not all good. We are on our way from the shipyards on Freyja. Unfortunately, we are still some twenty standard hours out from Caerus…" He paused for a moment, then said quietly, "I must also inform you that a third of the Free People's fleet, those that were assigned to protect Orso, have gone rogue and returned to Freyja. The rest of us, one-hundred-thirty-two ships of varying classes, will be there as soon as we can."

Wok's statement caused chaos around the table. Voices were raised. Shouts of consternation, derision and insult were flung at the two avatars led primarily by Dukes Rutta, Paulus and Marshal Fairway. All to no purpose. Wok and Crowe remained seated, their arms folded across their chests until finally, Wok had had enough.

"I repeat, we'll get there as soon as we can." And with that, Wok first and then Crowe, removed their halos and left the meeting.

"Well, that was helpful," Elio said sarcastically, looking around the assembly. "Why would you insult an ally who, through no fault of theirs, is unable to meet the Swarm's schedule and is doing their best? Shame on you, Duke Rutta. You, too, Marshal Fairway. You are a military man. How could you?"

"They are pirates," Fairway replied. "In any other circumstance we'd be hunting them down. Now we have to pander to them? I don't think so."

"Hear, hear!" Duke Paulus snapped. Rutta remained silent, smirking.

"Silence!" Elio snapped. "Any more of this… this unruliness and I will relieve you of your positions. They are *not*…

pirates. They are free people. Now let's continue... If you please."

Marshal Wayfair raised his hand to speak again, and Elio acknowledged him with a nod.

"My prince," he began, "might I enquire as to what part you intend to play in the battle?"

Elio locked eyes with him and said, "I intend to take command. Is that a problem, Hans?"

"I was thinking that perhaps it would be best if you stayed at the palace... where it's safer."

"No, no, no," Elio said, shaking his head. "Thank you for your concern for my welfare, Marshal, but I will take command, in the field."

"Well," Fairway said, scratching his nose, "if you're certain, your highness."

Marshal McAlan looked sharply at him and frowned, but said nothing.

"I'm not just sure, Marshal. I'm absolutely certain," Elio replied hotly. "My flagship, *The Invincible*, is an A-Class carrier, completely refitted with the new armor." Elio smiled. "What kind of leader would I be if I stayed here at home when our system is engaged in a great battle, a battle for the existence of humanity? No, I will take command of the USF forces and trust my sister, Captain Sasha Crowe, and her fleet to fly with me... No, Duke Rutta, they will not abandon me," he said aloud, responding to a snide thought from Rutta's mind. "I trust Sasha, and that's the end of it. *And, I might add*, he thought, reaching out to Rutta, *I will deal with you when all of this is over*." Rutta blanched and the color drained from his face.

Elio paused, took a deep breath and said, "I think we're talking. Now, let's get to work. I expect you all to be here, with your fleets, within the next twenty-four hours. The sooner, the better. This meeting is now closed." And with that, Elio removed his halo and sat down, his mind in a whirl.

He felt as if he was trapped in a thriller-coaster sim ride. So many ups and downs, twists and turns, and a crushing G-force pressing down on him, and he so desperately wanted to stop the program, but he couldn't, because what he was experiencing wasn't virtual reality, it was real, and it was terrifying. It was all on him.

If he failed...

Chapter Twenty-Five

Orso Space

USF Invincible

Five hours later, Elio stepped out of *The Queen's Pleasure* onto the *Invincible's* vast, portside hangar deck where he was met by Vice Admiral Hiro Yoshimura, along with Captain Marcus Vincente Diego and a company of officers of varying ranks ranging from ensign to commander.

"Welcome aboard, your highness," Yoshimura said as he stepped forward, bowed slightly and offered the prince his hand.

Elio took it, shook it and smiled at the diminutive admiral. A man small in stature but large in reputation, he wore his straight black hair long over the gleaming white collar of his uniform. His eyes were disturbingly black, but his smile was genuine and welcoming.

The admiral then went on to introduce his senior officers. That done, Elio introduced Tenilo, now standing slightly behind him and to his left.

Elio had tried to convince him to stay back at the palace, but Tenilo was not to be persuaded.

"No, my prince," he had said. "That I cannot do. Not now. Not with all that's going on and with what's about to happen. I will stay at your side, come what may."

Elio assumed it had to do with over-anxiousness about the Seers' prediction. Was Ugo Tan telling the truth, or was the prediction something he'd made up because of his dislike for Prince Felder's envoy? Elio didn't know. What he did know was that it had devastated his friend to think that he might turn against his own kind. Elio, however, had no such doubts. He was convinced Tenilo would be loyal to the end.

Yoshimura took Elio on a tour around the flight deck and the row upon row of F32 fighters.

Invincible was the same class of carrier as Marshal Tali's flagship. At almost two kilometers long and half a kilometer wide with fourteen decks, they were behemoths.

"May I escort you to the bridge, your highness?" Yoshimura asked.

Elio nodded, and together the three of them boarded a gravrail car that whisked them quickly almost the entire length of the carrier.

The senior officers saluted him as he stepped onto the bridge, an immense complex at the center of which was a giant hologram more than twice the size of that on the *Avenger*.

Elio didn't care for the formalities, but again, it was protocol and his status couldn't be changed. It was just the way of things.

"Welcome, Prince—" the chief helmsman, Commander

Rogan Cline quickly corrected himself. "I mean Captain." Cline was a big man, muscular, fit. Elio had known him for several years and had always teased him that he should have been commanding his security detail instead of flying one of the largest starships ever constructed.

Elio hadn't really been able to appreciate the extent and complexity of the great ship's refit until then, but seeing it with all its new hardware and tech made him smile. He was reminded of the feeling he got on his twenty-first birthday:

His mother had been so excited, blindfolding him before taking him down to the palace's hangar. "You ready?" she'd asked as she squeezed his shoulders. Elio didn't have Psy or TK then, but he could feel his mother's glee. Her excitement matched or even exceeded his own.

"More than ever," he'd told her, rubbing his hands together.

She tugged on his blindfold, and when he opened his eyes, she yelled, "Surprise!"

And there it was, glistening in the middle of the hangar, an XR2 space yacht, custom-built especially for him. He remembered how stunned he was.

"I... I... don't know what to say." He could barely get the words out. "Thank you so much, Mother."

Right on cue, Dinka, his first robot, the one that had died on Typhon, glided out with a platter holding glasses of champagne, imported from Homeworld, once known as Earth.

"Does father approve?" He hesitated as he reached for his glass. Elio had wanted a yacht since he was eighteen. He'd been taking lessons at the military flight school adjacent to the palace since he was fifteen, all thanks to his mother's encouragement. He loved space and how free it made him feel. Free and unbound by royal life.

King Orson, his father, of course, had thought it all a waste of time and money. "You should be focused on your studies, diplomacy, commerce, the economy," he'd said. "You'll be king one day."

How many times he'd heard that, Elio couldn't count. The only reason why Elio wasn't sent off to a "proper" boarding school, as his father had called it, was because his mother insisted that he stay home and learn from a phalanx of tutors, including Marshal Ugo Tan.

"Oh, bah," his mother said as she picked up her glass. "Don't burden yourself with what your father might think. Just be happy. You'll be involved in his world soon enough." And she was right.

"I couldn't be happier, Mother," he'd said. And it was true. His mother had always known how to bring a smile to his face.

"Good," he remembered her saying as she raised her glass. "Cheers to you, my son." And she touched her glass to his. "Nothing gives me greater pleasure than to see you happy and content. Happy birthday, Elio."

And it was at that instant he knew what he was going to name his new yacht: *Queen's Pleasure*.

Elio couldn't help the wave of emotion that came over him whenever he thought of his mother, but he quickly composed himself.

His datapad buzzed. It was a message from Sasha. She and Tiger Wok were now only fifteen hours out from Caerus.

The message read: *You need to see this right away.*

"If you don't mind, Admiral, I'd like to postpone my tour of the bridge for a short while. I'd like to see my ready room, if you please."

If I'm to die, he thought, *let me do so protecting my people.*

The admiral had a chief petty officer show him and Tenilo the way and asked him to contact him whenever he was ready to continue his tour of the ship.

His ready room was a large utilitarian space to the right and rear of the bridge. It contained a large drexon desk with a holo generator at its center and chairs enough to seat ten. It was, in fact, little more than a working office.

He waited until the automatic door closed, then told Tenilo about the message, activated the holo and contacted Sasha.

"Sasha," he said. "It's good to see you, sister." He enlarged the hologram until he could see her face in closeup. The only way that he could tell he was looking at a hologram was the occasional streak of light that flashed through the image. Her coloring was almost perfect; it was almost as if they were nerve-jacked into a virtual meeting. "I got your message," he said.

"It's bad, Elio," she replied. "The Swarm is massing in deep space just beyond the two Slip gates in the Pallas System. We're about to make the jump to the Kapalia System. Elio, I've already lost nine flyer pilots."

"Flyers" were the IMPF's term for fighter pilots. Jack-knife had been one such flyer before becoming a fully-fledged citizen of Orso.

Sasha shook her head and quickly moved on. It was clear that she didn't want to hear him tell her he was sorry, so Elio didn't bother to tell her, but he was.

"Look here," she said as she enlarged the hologram just to her left. "There are so many of them. Do we even have a hope of defeating them?"

Elio stared at what appeared to be an ocean of blue.

Thousands of blue dots, each representing a Swarm ship. It was a terrifying sight.

"Stars," he whispered. His heart beating so hard it felt as if it would burst through his rib cage.

"There are almost a hundred-thousand of them, Elio," Sasha said, "and the numbers are climbing with no signs of slowing down."

"You need to get out of there," Elio said. "How many are you?"

"Between Tiger and me, one-hundred-thirty-two ships of the line ranging from twenty-four tubes to sixty-four. My ship, the *Golden Condor*, is a forty-eight-gun heavy cruiser, completely refitted and rearmed with the new M99's ."

Elio pursed his lips. "How long before you get here?"

"If we don't run into more trouble... eleven hours."

Elio nodded. "Sasha, you'll join my fleet. My flagship is the *Invincible*. I have to go. I need to get this out to the fleet. Contact me as soon as you enter the Orso System. Stay safe, sister."

"You, too, my brother. Crowe out." And the hologram flickered and then was gone.

Elio looked at Tenilo and said, "I'm not sure I can do this, Tenny. The numbers..."

"You have no choice, my prince," Tenilo replied. "The Seers said you're the only one that can lead us to victory. You must have patience. It will come to you."

"I hope you're right, my friend... Now, I need a few minutes alone, if you don't mind."

"Of course, my prince," Tenilo said, gave a slight bow of the head and then left the room.

Elio closed his eyes and thought for a moment, then contacted the ship's AI, Selina.

"Selina?" he said, hoping he'd gotten the name right.

"Yes, Captain Lorne," she replied. "What can I do for you?"

"I need to send a message to the commanders of the combined USF fleet. It goes as follows. 'From the Commander in Chief Elio Lorne to the combined fleets. I have just received intelligence that the Swarm fleet is massing at the Pallas System Slip gates, which means they could be here in less than fifteen hours. You are to deploy your fleets around the Orso Slip gates and maintain your vessels on high alert. Be aware that one-hundred-thirty-two ships of the Free People's fleet will exit the Slips in approximately ten-hours thirty-seven minutes. Do not. I repeat, do not open fire on them. The intelligence indicates that the enemy numbers already exceed one-hundred-thousand. Keep an open channel and await further orders. Lorne out.'"

"Understood, Selina?" he asked the ship's AI.

"Yes, Captain," Selina answered quickly. She then repeated the message and said, "Is there anything more you'd like to add, Prince Elio?"

"No, that will be all, thank you."

"Understood. Your message has been sent to the fleet commanders."

Elio nodded absently, knowing it meant nothing to the omnipresent, all-seeing AI and continued to sit at his desk, his mind whirling.

He wished that Captain Morian was with him. Morian's calm in the face of danger was truly a gift. Then his thoughts turned to Danis, and suddenly he longed for her to be with him, too; not because he thought she needed to be there. It was a selfish wish. She always seemed to know exactly what to say in his moments of self-doubt. Every time he looked at her, he felt as if her striking blue eyes could see into the depths of his soul. The image of her beautiful face faded to be replaced by a frantic collage of thoughts steaming through his mind. *What if this is the end? What if I never see her again? What if I never get to tell her how I really feel?*

The more he thought of her, the more his heart raced. The feeling deep in the pit of his gut when he thought of her was something he'd never experienced before. More than butterflies... More than the weight of ten G's pressing down on him. More than...

His father had wanted to marry him off since he was in his late teens. "You need an heir," he said constantly. He'd gone out on dates with countless women just to appease the king. And he'd connected with some of them, *but nothing like this*, he thought, and then smiled to himself. *Damn it! I think I'm in love...*

Chapter Twenty-Six

Extraction

Typhon System

venger was hiding in stationary orbit forty-four thousand kilometers out on the dark side of the planet and she was running dark and silent, most of her systems shut down, with Krista using only passive scanners to keep a watchful eye out for enemy craft.

Commodore Morian was in his ready room talking to Haltar Sen.

Manda Haal was in her quarters.

Jax, who had returned from the drop more than sixteen standard hours earlier, was at the helm.

Commander Michael Jadern was at the rail staring at the view screens, the giant hologram having been shut down because it was generated by detectable active scans. The forward screens were, for the most part, black. Those showing the surrounding space showed only the vast starfield. All was quiet.

"Ms. Fargo?" he said, more from boredom than necessity.

"Yes, Commander?"

"What's the state of our inventory?"

Fargo nodded, tapped an icon on her console and said, "M59 missiles at sixty-two percent. M8 Rapiers at eighty-seven percent. M99s are at eighty-three percent. M12 Sabers... ninety percent. 88mm kinetic rounds are at eighty-four percent. 120mm at eighty-two."

Jadern nodded and tried not to look concerned. "Let's cross our fingers that and hope it will be enough, Lieutenant," he said and grabbed the rail with one hand.

Fargo nodded and turned again to her console.

"Mr. Kingston?" Jadern said.

"Shields are shut down, Commander, but are fully functional. Life-support is at one hundred percent. Point defense is at one hundred percent. Nothing to worry about."

Jadern smiled and said, "Ms. Lowry?"

"Nothing to report, sir. All systems are functional."

And so it went on as Jadern continued to inventory the ship and its dormant systems.

* * *

"You know I should write you up for not telling me sooner?" Morian said.

He was tired, in need of sleep. The bags under his eyes looked as if they'd made a permanent home there. His voice was mild; the look on his face was one of concern.

"Yes, Captain. I..." Sen paused, shook his head and

sighed, not knowing quite how to finish. He squirmed uncomfortably in his seat and looked at him.

Morian clasped his hands together, leaned forward, set his elbows on the desktop and said, softly, "Look, Haltar. We've known each other for how long? Since I was a teenager? You pretty much taught my father everything he knew. You're one of the best starship pilots I've ever known. And I doubt I'll meet another like you... or person, for that matter, but..." He paused and looked earnestly at Sen.

Sen nodded slowly. "Thank you, Captain. I appreciate your kind words," he said, looking down at his lap, then looked up again and said, "but I know what you're going to say." He sniffed.

Morian raised an eyebrow. "Oh, is that so? You have Psy now, do you?"

They both laughed, and the mood lightened.

"On a serious note, though, Haltar, how are you feeling?"

"I—"

"Don't lie to me, Haltar," Morian interjected.

"I don't feel so good, Captain, but I'm not incapacitated, not yet. I can still carry out my duties. We're in a serious situation and young Jax... while he's one of the best pilots I've met in a long time, he's not ready yet. You still need me. I won't let you down."

"Good enough, Haltar. It's not over 'til it's over. For now, at least, the helm is yours, but please keep me informed. I can't have you passing out in the middle of an emergency. Be smart enough to consider the welfare of the ship... and to know when to step down."

Sen nodded, took a deep breath, managed a small smile and said, "Thank you, Captain. You have my word."

Chapter Twenty-Seven

Planet Typhon

Alien Communication Center

Diversion

Captain Morion was on the bridge languishing in his command chair, slumped down, legs outstretched, one elbow on the arm of the chair, his chin resting on his hand; he was thoroughly bored. For twenty-six hours and seventeen minutes, *Avenger* had been running silent in the shadow of the planet while they waited to hear news of the extraction from his sister on the ground with the away team. He was anxious to get them back on board and head for home as fast as possible.

Manda Hall was in her seat at his side. Commander Jadern was wandering the well deck, stopping here and there to chat with members of the bridge crew, including

Haltar Sen—now cleared for light duty by Dr. Dowd—who was seated beside his protégé, Dagon Jax.

Gian, Jackknife and the rest of Ranger Squadron were in the crew room, relaxed, bored, but ready to fly at a moment's notice.

The ship's combat crews—missiles, point defense and Big Charlie—were all at their stations, weapons loaded.

The entire ship was in a state of quiet readiness, waiting; for what, they didn't know.

Captain Morian!

Morian almost leapt out of his chair, startled by the sudden intrusion into his mind.

Yes, this is Morian. Who are you?

Sir, this is Nilo Pistash, Major Dubois' PsyOp. He's asked me to contact you to arrange the extraction one hour from now at these coordinates.

Stand by, Morian sent to Pistash as he entered the coordinates into the system.

"Krista," he said, "I need a route and an ETA for the shuttle."

"If the shuttle leaves immediately at flank speed, it should be on the ground in exactly forty-four minutes and thirty-two seconds USF standard time," Krista replied.

"Very well. Load the coordinates into Shuttle One's navigation system."

"Aye, Captain," Krista replied.

"Mr. Jax," Morian snapped. "You're on. You need to go now, immediately. The away team needs extraction in one hour. It will be tight, but if you don't run into trouble, you should be able to make it."

"Aye, Captain," Jax said, leaping up out of his seat and making a run for the bridge doors and then the elevators.

Mr. Pistash? Morian reached out again to the PsyOp.

There was a moment of silence and then, *Yes, Captain. I'm still here.*

What's going on down there? Do you have Minnah and the survivors? Why is it taking so long?

Yes, sir, we do have Minnah. Unfortunately, our grav-packs were destroyed during a Blue attack and we had to hike out. We've been walking for more than three hours. That's why it's taken so long.

So why another hour? Morian asked angrily. *Why did you not call for extraction sooner?*

Um, well, Minnah insisted on checking out some kind of alien structure. He thinks they're building a communications center. He thinks he can hack into it. He says it's of vital importance that he tries. If he can't, he intends to destroy it. He has some kind of weird tech that sends out some kind of pulse... That's all I know, Captain.

Casualties, Pistash, Morian said. *You say you were attacked. How many casualties?* he asked, dreading the answer.

Four wounded. Ten deaths.

Morian froze. *My sis— Commander Morian. Is she...?*

No, sir. She's just fine. She's leading the diversion party.

Diversion party? What are you talking about?

It's a long story, Captain. The short version is that Commander Morian and the one of the TKs will create a diversion to draw the Blues away from the complex while Major Dubois and Minnah enter the structure. If all goes well, they should all be at the extraction point on time.

One of the TKs? Morian asked. *We sent only one.*

There's one with Minnah. An old guy. Must be at least a hundred-twenty, but he's strong. I'm sorry, sir. I have to go. Major Dubois is waving at me.

Take care, Pistash. Tell Dubois the shuttle is on the way.

"Krista, I need a shipwide channel."

"You have it, Captain."

"Now hear this. Now hear this. This is the Captain. Ranger Squadron, prepare for immediate launch. Your mission is to escort Shuttle One to the extraction point. The ship will maintain silent running and remain at general quarters until the shuttle and its escort return. Morian out."

"From that," Manda Haal said, "I take it you heard from the away team."

"I did," Morian said and sighed. "They're off on some crazy mission dreamed up by this... this... I don't know what he is, except he's some kind of genius and prince Elio's friend. It's going to be a very long two hours until the shuttle returns... if it returns," he said somberly.

* * *

Seven decks below the bridge, Dagon Jax ran to his shuttle, fully aware of the organized chaos going on around him as the fighter pilots ran to their ships.

Without stopping, he ran up the ramp, threw himself into his seat, strapped himself in, tapped the icon to bring up his hologram, navigation systems and comms, brought the grav engines online, and finally contacted hangar operations.

"Shuttlecraft One ready to depart."

"Copy, Shuttlecraft One. You're a go as soon as the doors go green. You are to maintain comms silence for the duration except in an emergency. Good luck, Dagon."

The doors began to open, and ten seconds later, Jax lifted the shuttle off the hangar deck. It rocked slightly. *"Damn!"* Jax muttered to himself as he flexed his fingers and tried to calm his nerves.

He took a deep breath and flew the craft smoothly out into the black, cut the gravs and engaged the twin fusion engines and looked around. The sun was hidden behind the planet and he found himself in almost total darkness facing the silhouette of Typhon's enormous black disk, its rim glowing bright gold in the light of Eta Persei beyond.

It was breathtaking, but Jax had no time for sightseeing. He checked his trajectory and the preset coordinates, and increased his speed to Mach 15, then tried to relax as the inertia dampeners enfolded him.

He glanced to his left and saw Lt. Hawkins in Ranger 6 some fifty meters away with two more F32s in formation. He looked to his right and saw three more. Their flight leader, Lt. Draman in Ranger 9, smiled and waved. Jax could only smile back and nod.

Then, instinctively, he tried to duck as three more F32s —Jackknife, Joker and Dreamer (Skyla)—flashed overhead, seeming only meters away, to drop into formation in front of him. The three of them would escort him all the way down to the extraction point. The rest of the squadron would stay on the edge of the atmosphere and wait.

The craft reached Mach 15. The engines shut down. The inertia dampeners eased their grip on his body and he was free. The thrusters made some slight adjustments to his course, then he settled down to what would seem to be an endless ride down to the extraction point.

He checked his chron. *Thirty-two minutes,* he thought. And then his thoughts turned inevitably to his future and that of Haltar Sen. He changed the hologram and brought up a view of the great, dark bulk of *Avenger,* almost a kilometer and a half long, floating in the black far behind him. His stomach churned and his mind filled with self-doubt. He sucked on his bottom lip as he stared at the apparition, and he shook his head. He'd never flown anything larger than a Class R shuttle, and now, *they expect me to—*

The thought was interrupted by the clamor of the shuttle's reentry warning. The shuttle was about to enter Typhon's atmosphere.

Jax took a deep breath, exhaled, pushed the doubts from his mind and concentrated on the stats. The thrusters engaged, causing the shuttle to slow dramatically. Its dutrinium armor began to glow and the thrusters increased power and adjusted the angle of descent.

The shuttle's nose dipped, and suddenly Jax was presented with an astonishing view of Typhon's surface far below. The shuttle was still eclipsed by the planet but was rapidly entering its western hemisphere, now a giant golden crescent. He checked his chron again, for at least the fifth time. *Twenty-one minutes to touchdown. I wonder how Danis is doing.*

Ten minutes later, the shuttle broke out of the shadow and into the blazing sunshine, slowed even further and began to level out. Jax shut down the autopilot and checked his displays. He was at an altitude of thirty-thousand meters and descending. He cut the thrusters, engaged the fusion engines, took manual control and continued his descent to fifteen-hundred meters, leveled out and reduced speed to six-hundred knots, just shy of the speed of sound, and the shuttlecraft and its escort flew low across the desert toward the extraction point.

So far, so good! Jax thought.

* * *

Forty-five minutes earlier, Major Dubois, Lt. Nortak, Kyne Minnah and Danis, along with Grell Dunn and twelve

Marines, had left the oasis at a fast trot toward what Minnah hoped was a Swarm communications center under construction. And they had taken cover some three hundred meters out under a rocky outcrop.

"That's your objective," Dubois said to Danis and Nortak, nodding in the direction of a group of stone-built structures some three hundred meters away to the right. "We don't have much time. You know what to do. Let's get to it. We'll advance to that pile of rubble and split up. You'll make a run for the farm. As soon as you get there, you'll set off the concussion grenades. Don't wait. Just do it. That should draw the Blues away. At that point, Minnah and I, with our group, will make a run for the building, enter it, Minnah will do whatever it is he does, and we're out of there. Understood?"

They all nodded.

"Then let's do it," Dubois said, and they ran, bent low at the waist, across the open ground to what once had been an impressive home.

"Go, go, go," Dubois urged, and Danis, followed by Nortak and his six Marines, ran headlong toward the cluster of farm buildings with Dunn puffing along behind them.

Danis, closely followed by Nortak and the Marines, dodged behind the first building she came to and stopped and dropped to her knees, breathing hard.

She waited for the two TKs to scramble under cover, then nodded to Nortak. He nodded back, turned to his men, snatched a grenade from his belt, and snapped, "Grenades." Then he twisted the top of his grenade, activating it, and tossed it as far out into the desert as he could. It exploded even before it hit the ground with an almighty bang and a shockwave that riffled the dust around their feet. One by one, six more grenades flew through the air to explode out in the desert.

They waited for the dust to settle, then Nortak stepped out from under cover and began waving his arms and shouting.

"Hey, you blue sons o' bitches," he yelled at the top of his voice. "Over here. We're over here. Come and get us."

He was rewarded almost immediately by a sizzling bolt of blue plasma that tore a hole in the wall of the building just to his right.

"*Stars!*" he yelped, holding his ear as he dove for cover and grabbed his rifle. "That was way too close."

"Here they come," someone shouted.

Danis peeked around the corner of the building. There were nine of them—three Stalkers and six Stompers—marching resolutely toward them.

"Spread out and engage," Nortak shouted and opened fire on the nearest Stalker. Seconds later, a second railgun opened fire, then a third, until all seven Marines and Danis were pouring streams of 8mm solid dutrinium projectiles at the oncoming Blues.

The Stalker under fire from Nortak and two more of his men went down in a mighty explosion of blue fire, then a second and then finally the third. The Stompers, however, seemed to be impervious to the heavy slugs, and they kept on coming, spears of blue plasma flickering this way and that from their weapons.

Danis looked around, searching for Dunn. He was hunkered down behind a pile of rubble that had once been one of the farm outbuilds.

"Grell," she shouted.

He barely heard her over the racket made by the railguns. His hands covered his ears as he stared at her.

"Do something," she yelled at him.

He shook his head and seemed to shrink even lower.

"Damn it! Damn it! Damn it!" she shouted and then leapt to her feet and sprinted across the open space, rifle in hand, chased by flickering beams of plasma.

She threw herself over the pile of rubble, rolled, jumped to her feet, scrabbled over to him, stood and kicked him in the ribs.

"On your feet, you useless..." she shouted as he lay there doubled up in pain.

Slowly he rose to his feet.

"Good," she shouted. "Now do something."

"But..." He caught the look on her face.

Reluctantly, he stepped forward, glanced at the oncoming Stompers, looked around, found what he was looking for and concentrated.

A large piece of masonry that must have weighed all of fifty kilograms rose slowly into the air, hovered for a second, then took off as if it had been fired from a railgun.

The effect was devastating.

The projectile slammed into the nearest Stomper's chest area. Its armor buckled, and at the same time, the alien was lifted off its feet more than two meters into the air and propelled backward more than twenty meters to crash onto its back where it lay, its appendages outspread, apparently lifeless.

"That's more like it," Danis yelled. "Do it again and keep doing it. Don't let me have to come... to... you... again."

She stared in horror as the Stomper began to move: first its right arm, then both its legs as its buckled armor began to morph and reform back to its original shape. Slowly it sat up, reached for its weapon, rose to its feet, stood for a moment, then began to march steadily forward again.

The next ten minutes were total chaos as the Marines continued to pour an almost continuous stream of railgun fire at the advancing Stompers and Dunn continued to hurl gravcar-size chunks of masonry at them.

Time and again the Stompers were hurled back only to rise again and continue their forward march, slowly reducing the defender's cover to dust with their plasma weapons, and slowly closing the distance between them and the defenders. Finally, Danis ran out of ammunition and ran to Nortak.

"It's no use," she shouted as Nortak slammed his last mag into his weapon. "We can't hold them. I'm out of ammo. They'll overrun us in a matter of minutes. We have to get out of here."

"We can't," Nortak yelled, his back to the wall. "It's more than a hundred meters to the nearest cover and open ground all the way."

"Then what are we going to do?" Danis yelled. "We can't stay here."

All Nortak could do was shake his head and shrug his shoulders.

"Have you heard from Dubois?" she asked. "We need support, and we need it now."

Again, Nortak shook his head. "Not since we left him. I tried to contact him twice." He flinched as a section of the wall above his head exploded and rained dust down upon them both. "But he's not answering."

Danis stared at him, took a step sideways and peeked around the corner of what was left of the building. The leading Stomper was less than forty meters away.

She activated her datapad and tried to contact Dubois herself.

"Morian to Major Dubois. Come in!"

She listened. Nothing.

She tried again, "This is Commander Morian to Major Dubois. We are about to be overrun and need support. Come in."

No answer.

She looked at Nortak. He shook his head and made a face. "Looks like we're on our own, Commander. I guess now's as good a time as any to die."

She stared at him in horror as his words sank in. *Oh, dear God,* she thought. *Can it be true? Is this really how it ends? No! It can't be.*

Again, she peeked around the corner of the building. The nearest Stomper was now less than thirty meters away.

She opened her mind and reached out to her brother, but either because the distance was too great or the fact that *Avenger* was still in shadow on the far side of the planet, her attempt failed. Suddenly, for the first time in her life, she felt... helpless and alone.

* * *

Dubois and Minnah watched as Nortak and his group ran to the farm buildings and took cover, and then they waited.

Seconds later, the first concussion grenade exploded, quickly followed by another and another. And they watched as the nine Blues turned as one in the direction from which the noise of the explosions had come, and then, just as Dubois had hoped, they all set off across the open space, weapons at the ready.

Dubois waited until they'd cleared the structure, then waved his group forward. They ran across the last hundred meters to the great structure the Blues had erected.

Fortunately, there were no walls or doors to negotiate.

Why would there be? There's no one here to keep out, Dubois thought as he looked upward at the edifice towering hundreds of meters above their heads. It was roughly pentagonal at the bases, perhaps two hundred meters in diameter, tapering upward almost to a point, and it appeared to be constructed all in one piece. The walls were smooth, seamless, and a deep, translucent blue, as if they were made of glass.

"Come on," Dubois said. "We don't have much time. Let's get this done." And, together, the eight men ran through the doorless opening into the structure. Twenty meters in, Dubois called a halt. They were in what appeared to be a vast cathedral, the ceiling more than one hundred fifty meters above their heads. In the center of the cavernous interior, a second structure, a smaller mirror-image of the first, towered almost one hundred meters toward the pointed ceiling. It, too, appeared to be constructed from the same blue glass, but its interior was glowing, pulsating rapidly in places, fluttering in others, casting a rainbow of different shades from deep blue to pale violet against the outer walls.

"What the hell is this?" Dubois muttered, more to himself than anyone else.

"I don't know," Minnah replied. "I thought..." Slowly he turned a full three-sixty, staring at... what, Dubois had no idea.

"Well?" Dubois said. "We're here. What are you going to do? Whatever it is, you'd better do it quickly."

Minnah, seemingly impervious to Dubois, stepped forward, put his hand on the glowing structure and closed his eyes. For a moment he stood there, silent, then he opened his eyes, shook his head, took several steps back, shook his head again, turned to Dubois and said, "I think I was right. This is some kind of communication device. How it works... I don't know. The technology is... I've never seen anything like it."

"Can you hack it?" Dubois asked, looking warily around.

"I don't think so," Minnah replied. "There are no terminals... nothing. Just... it."

"What about the gadget? Will it work? Can you shut the damn thing down?"

"I don't know," Minnah replied.

"Well what the hell do you know?" Dubois snapped. "For God's sake, do something and let's get the hell out of here before they find us."

"I'll see if I can shut it down."

He took the octagonal device from his backpack, crouched down and, as he set it on the floor, the glowing core tumbled out of the backpack and rolled toward the pulsing structure. The structure reacted immediately. The intensity of its light show increased. The pulsing and flickering increased until it became one vast, slowly pulsating violet pentagonal pyramid.

Minnah ran forward, grabbed the core and jammed it back into his backpack. Then he stood back and stroked his fingers over his datapad. There was an earsplitting bang that seemed to shake the floor beneath their feet. The pyramid emitted a blinding flash of violet—almost white—light and then went dark.

Dubois, Minnah and the six Marines stood stock-still; Minnah's eyes and mouth wide open.

"Is it dead?" Dubois asked, finally.

Minnah shrugged. "I don't know. Looks like it. It obviously doesn't like the EMP. At least we learned that much."

"Then grab that thing and let's get out of here."

Minnah nodded and did as he was told. They ran out of the structure to the trees from whence they'd come.

Once they were under cover, Dubois called a halt and tapped his datapad, intending to call Nortak, but the pad didn't respond. He tapped again. Same result.

"What the hell?" He looked at Minnah.

Minnah shook his head and said, "It's the EMP. Nothing electronic will work. They're fried. We need new ones."

"Damn!" Dubois snapped. "Then how can I contact my people and the commander?"

Minnah simply shrugged and said nothing.

Dubois made a split-second decision. "There's nothing we can do here. We're going back to the extraction point. We need to get you out of here if no one else. Come on, go. Run, damn it."

Minnah took a deep breath, exhaled, then said, "Right. Let's—"

He was interrupted by a deep humming sound overhead.

* * *

Danis looked at Nortak and said, "This is it, then?"

He smiled at her, nodded, and said, "That it is, Commander. I don't know about you, but I'm going out with a bang."

"Yeah, that," she said and looked down at her empty weapon. "I guess I'll throw rocks at them— "

She was interrupted by an almighty explosion of gunfire. It was so loud she could feel the ground shaking beneath her feet.

A shadow passed overhead. She looked up and was

instantly filled with elation. Hovering less than a hundred meters above was an F32 fighter, spewing eight hundred 55mm rounds a minute from each of its twin railguns.

The noise was beyond description as Danis, Nortak, Dunn and the six Marines stepped out into the open and watched as the F32 chopped the six Stompers to shreds. Heads, arms, legs, weapons and torsos were flung into the air, spinning wildly to land spread out over a wide area.

The F32's guns quit firing. The silence was deafening. Danis' ears were ringing. She was shaking from the effects of more than a thousand concussive, sonic explosions when the heavy slugs had broken through the sound barrier.

The F32 spun slowly above their heads, then sank to the ground on its grav engines. The canopy slid open and a voice shouted, "Hey, Danis. You need a ride?"

"Gian," she yelled and ran to the fighter.

Chapter Twenty-Eight

Planet Typhon

Extraction

By the time Minnah, Dunn, Dubois and his twelve Marines arrived back at the oasis some twenty-five minutes later, the civilians, the wounded and all but four of the Marines they'd left behind were already aboard the shuttle and the three F32 fighters were on the ground.

When Danis saw them coming, she stood up in the rear seat of Gian's fighter and waved them on.

"Come on," she shouted. "Get a move on. We need to get out of here. Now!"

Dubois, leading the small column, waved dismissively at her, marched to the shuttle's open ramp and stood to one side and watched his people enter one after the other; he was the last one to board, casting a backward look at Danis, still standing watching, and gifted her with a sardonic smile and a lazy salute.

The ramp closed, and even before the locks snapped shut, the shuttle lifted off, stirring up a massive cloud of dust.

"You ready, Commander?" Gian asked as the canopy closed over their heads.

"I am," she replied. "Take us home, Joker. I'll handle the comms."

"Right... So, this is a first," he said.

"What is?" Danis asked.

"Me, outranked by my copilot."

She smiled, then said, "Don't get comfortable, Gian. This is a one-off."

"Hahahaha!" He had a big smile on his face. "Hang on, Commander. Here we go."

His fingers fluttered over the controls like those of a concert pianist. The F32 lifted off and rose rapidly to a height of one hundred meters on its grav engines, at which point Gian turned the nose up, engaged the four fusion engines, cut the gravs, increased the power and the F32 surged upward.

Danis felt the familiar comfort of the inertia dampeners as they enclosed her, dissipating the bone-crushing G-forces as the fighter rose through the stratosphere until it reached Typhon's escape velocity when Gian cut the power and the fighter continued onward and upward.

The G-forces subsided. The inertia dampeners released their grip, and Danis breathed deeply, happy to be back in space. *This is where I belong*, she thought.

"This is Domino to shuttlecraft," she broadcast. "Come in."

"This is Shuttlecraft One," Jax replied. "I have you on visual."

"Status?" Danis said.

"All present and accounted for. ETA to *Avenger* forty-eight minutes."

"Thank you, Jax. Domino out!" She paused, then said, "Domino to Jackknife and Dreamer. Close in on Joker. Arrowhead formation. Fifty meters. We'll follow Jax in. Domino out."

Again, she paused for a second, then said, "Domino to Ranger Squadron. Form flights of three and spread to one-thousand meters. Listen up, all. We're now forty-two minutes out. After what happened down there, the Blues know we're here, so we can expect company. Keep your wits about you. Domino out."

She watched the hologram in front of her and to the right as the ten fighters closed in around the shuttle, and she smiled; space, as far as she could see, was clear.

Ten minutes later, however, that was not the case. They had still not quite reached the dark side of the planet when a blue blip appeared at the edge of the hologram, and then another and another and... suddenly there were twenty-one blue dots in flights of three, approaching fast, traveling at nearly twice the speed of the shuttlecraft.

"Domino to Ranger Squadron," Danis snapped. "Incoming on vector three-nine-one. Prepare to engage." She closed the channel and said to Gian, "You want me to take it from here, Gian?"

"Er... no! Not hardly. This is my ship, Commander, and you're my guest. I'll do the flying, if you don't mind."

She smiled to herself. She'd expected no less from him.

"Very well, Joker. You do realize I don't have TK, so you're on your own?"

"That's just the way I like it, Domino. Now leave me the hell alone. I have Blues to kill."

He opened a channel and said, "This is Joker to Jackknife and Dreamer. How d'you want to do this?"

"We split to one-twenty meters," Jackknife replied, "and we hold formation until we can't. You copy?"

"I copy," Gian replied.

"Me, too," Skyla said. "Whoa, here they come."

And, as if out of nowhere, six Blue fighters appeared on their forward screens, brilliant blue bolts of plasma flashing from their gun platforms.

Gian's shields lit up bright blue as he took a hit.

"Stars," Danis heard him mutter as he cut power to the two starboard engines and increased the power to the upper port engine, throwing the ship into a wild, twisting dive to starboard.

He held the dive, verbally counting off the seconds, "Eight, nine, ten!" Then he reengaged the starboard engines, rotated all four one-hundred ten degrees and poured on the power. The F32 went into a long, skidding climb at close to Mach 40. The inertia dampeners kicked in and Danis was clamped into their folds as she watched the hologram rotate and the F32 make a long, looping turn that brought it up onto the tail of the two leading Blue craft.

"Target lock. Missiles away," Gian yelled.

The fighter shuddered. Two M-7 Harpoon laser-guided missiles streaked away toward the two Blues.

Danis watched, her eyes flitting back and forth between her forward screen and the hologram. The Blues had obviously detected the missiles because they immediately increased speed and turned away, each in a different direction. But the two missiles followed them, slowly closing the distance until they reached proximity at fifteen meters and the warheads exploded, each firing six, 88mm depleted uranium slugs at the fleeing Blues.

One after the other, the two enemy ships exploded in brilliant balls of blue as the slugs pierced their shields and impacted their hulls at almost seven thousand meters per second. One minute they were there; the next they were gone.

"Yahoo!" Gian yelled over the open channel. "That's the way to do it!"

For the fourth time in as many minutes, Danis had to smile to herself. Gian, her protégé, had come along from the arrogant, know-it-all youngster she'd taken under her wing six months earlier. Though she had to admit she was less than comfortable sitting there behind him in the rear seat, unable to do anything to help.

"Dreamer. Watch out," Jackknife shouted. "You have two at seven o'clock low and closing."

"I know. I know," Skyla snapped. "You think I don't know? I know, damn it, and I can't lose them. Oh stars; one of them has a lock. Do something, Jackknife, before—"

She broke off. Danis watched, her heart in her mouth, as Skyla's fighter seemed to stop dead as she reversed all four of her F32's engines and increased power to maximum.

The two Blue fighters were taken completely by surprise and hurtled past her at a speed approaching Mach 65. That according to the display floating above the hologram.

"Gotcha, you blue bastards," Skyla shouted as she reversed her engines and poured on the power. "Target lock. Missiles away. Whoo hoo. Oh yeah. There you go," she yelled as both Blue ships disappeared in two blinding flashes of brilliant blue fire.

But it wasn't all going their way. Danis watched as first

the icon representing Ranger Seven blinked out, then Ranger Nine. Both were gone, destroyed.

She slammed her fist against the metal hull, skinning her knuckles, and she cursed. "Damn, damn, damn!"

"I hear ya," Gian shouted. "What's our ETA?"

"For the shuttle..." She glanced at the readout. "Eleven minutes... If she makes it."

"What's the status of the enemy? Uh-oh. Here we go again. We have one on our tail. Switching to guns," Gian yelled as he pulled the fighter up into a long, looping, textbook Immelmann turn that put him on the tail of the single Blue.

The F32 shuddered as Gian opened fire with his twin 55mm railguns.

Danis watched as the twin streams of slugs streaked away and disappeared in the darkness until... Suddenly, the Blue ship veered violently to port, its port weapons platform severed at the root, spinning away in a cloud of debris.

Gian continued to close the distance. The Blue ship's shields collapsed. It began to spin slowly, end over end, and then it imploded, collapsing in on itself. The spin increased, and Gian turned away.

"As I was saying," Gian said. "What's the enemy's status?"

"Eleven destroyed... to our three. We've lost Rangers Seven, Nine and Ten... What the hell?"

Suddenly, without warning, one of the blue icons blinked out and simultaneously, she saw through the canopy window a flash of blue fire. The Swarm ship was gone. Destroyed, but none of the Ranger Squadron fighters were anywhere in the vicinity.

Two minutes later, there was a second flash and another blue icon disappeared from the hologram.

What the hell is going on? she wondered. *Who—*

"Avenger to Ranger Squadron. Domino. This is Commander Kingston. Do you copy?"

"This is Domino," she replied. "Was that you that just killed two Blue ships?"

"That it was, Domino. Cost us two M-99s. Those are expensive little suckers. Hope it was worth it. You should know the shuttle landed safely five minutes ago. We have you at four minutes out. You are to return to *Avenger* on vector two-six-three. Bring your people home, Commander."

"Roger that, Avenger. We're on our way."

"Better make it quick. We have more incoming. Seventy-eight craft on vector three-five-zero: speed Mach 34. You have three minutes before they engage. We'll do what we can to protect you. Avenger out."

Danis opened a channel and shouted, "Ranger Squadron. We have more incoming. Turn to vector two-six-three and return to *Avenger*. Immediately."

"Damn it, Commander," Jackknife shouted. "I'm hit, and I didn't see it coming. I've lost my upper port engine and I'm in a spin!"

"I see you, Jackknife," Gian yelled. "I'm on my way."

"I see you, too," Skyla said.

"Jackknife," Danis shouted. "Are you all right? Do you need rescue?"

"If... I can... stop the... spin," Jackknife replied, his voice strained. "And if she doesn't blow... Ah, there we go. She's.... she... Whew! I thought for a minute... Hold while I compensate... Compensating... Oh, this is not funny. I can barely hold her straight. Uh-oh! I have one on my tail—"

"I got him," Skyla yelled. "Get out of my way, Gian."

And Danis actually flinched and ducked as Skyla's F-32

flashed by so close she could see her smiling face. And she watched as she swept over Jackknife's ship, her throttles wide open, streaking head-on toward the enemy craft. And then, in less time than a blink of an eye, she was on it; she dropped two laser-guided Rapier torpedoes, killed her upper port and starboard engines and hauled the F32 upward in a one-eighty and streaked away, just as the Swarm craft exploded behind her.

"Whoo hoo," she yelled. "That was close. Hey, Jacko. You doin' okay? You'd better be. I just saved your ass. You owe me dinner tonight."

"My pleasure, sweetheart," Jackknife replied.

"All right," Danis snapped. "That's enough. You pull a stunt like that again, Skyla, and I'll ground you. You almost took our canopy off... *Stars!* Incoming, incoming. Go to vector two-six-three immediately and return to *Avenger*. Jackknife! Can you make it?"

"Well, I sure as hell can't get out and walk," he replied. "Yeah, I'll make it." Then he added under his breath, "*Somehow.*"

Danis watched the hologram as Jackknife struggled to make the course correction.

"All right," he snapped. "I'm on my way in. Those hangar doors better be open."

"We're two minutes out," Danis yelled.

"We have visitors, Danis," Gian said quietly. "There are hundreds of them. Oh, wow."

Danis looked out through the canopy. *Avenger* was in sight, looming closer by the second, her great bulk a stark silhouette against the stars. Her point defense guns were blazing as dozens of Swarm ships streaked by.

Suddenly, she could see the light of the open hangar

doors. One by one the survivors of Ranger Squadron swept inside until only she and Gian and Jackknife were left.

"Go, go, go, Gian," Jackknife shouted. "Get yourself inside, now! If you don't, you may not be able to. I just lost my lower port engine. And I'm crabbing and going in hot."

Gian didn't bother to answer. He increased the power slightly, adjusted his trajectory, shut down his fusion engines, engaged his gravs and flew effortlessly into the hangar under *Avenger's* blazing gunfire.

By the time Gian landed and he and Danis had exited the fighter, most of the passengers, now all wearing pressure suits, had disembarked leaving only Jax, Dubois, Nortak and Dunn. All four were on the ramp, watching as Jackknife made his run for the hangar.

Danis, Gian and Skyla, on the other side of the hangar, watched in horror as Jackknife made his approach. He was several hundred meters out and coming in fast, portside on, and under fire from five Swarm ships.

His shields were holding, but the F32 was rocking violently.

Above the hangar doors, point defense Turrets Seven, Nine, Eleven and Thirteen were hammering the five Swarm ships with thousands of 88mm railgun rounds.

First one enemy ship exploded, then another. Another had its starboard weapons platform shot away and was already spinning wildly when it was hit almost immediately by a stream of fire from Turret Thirteen and exploded in a great ball of blue fire.

Jackknife was almost at the hangar doors when another Swarm ship, under fire from three of the four turrets, suddenly lurched to port, flipped end over end and dropped out of sight, leaving only one Blue fighter so close on Jackknife's tail the point defense guns had to shut down for fear of hitting him.

Less than two seconds later, Jackknife's wounded F32 lurched sideways into the hangar, its nose slamming into the armor-plated hull, causing it to spin as it hit, wheels up, onto the hangar deck, metal on metal screeching under the impact. The fighter skidded, spinning slowly across the hangar deck, and slammed into Shuttle Two where it came to rest.

The explosive bolts fired, sending the canopy spinning upward into the dark reaches of the hangar. Jackknife leapt out of the cockpit, landed on the wing, jumped to the deck and ran for cover as the Swarm ship that had been on his tail entered the hangar, its guns blazing, raking Jackknife's now defenseless F32, its shields and systems shut down, with blast after blast of blue plasma.

Danis looked wildly around, knowing there was little anyone could do. The interior of the hangar was defense-less. If someone didn't do something, and quickly, *Avenger* would be destroyed from the inside.

She spotted Dunn, still standing on the shuttle's ramp, staring at the huge blue ship, seemingly transfixed.

"Dunn!" she yelled over the crackling plasma fire. "Do something!"

He looked at her, then at the Swarm ship, then back at Danis.

"*Do something!*" she shouted as loudly as she could.

His mouth dropped open. He took a step back, then looked at Danis again.

"*For God's sake, Grell!*"

Dunn, his eyes open wide, stared at the enemy craft and, so it seemed to Danis, he straightened up a little. He closed his eyes, his feet together, arms by his sides and, for several seconds, nothing happened. The enemy, having completely demolished Jackknife's F32, turned its attention to a second fighter and was proceeding to destroy it.

Then, as Dunn concentrated, lifting his hands slightly, palms up, the Blue fighter began to rock, its nose tilted upward, its plasma weapons raking the dutrinium-clad roof, lighting the entire hangar electric blue.

The Blue ship began to move. Backward. Slowly at first, then faster and faster and then, suddenly, it was outside, beyond the hangar doors, its weapons still blazing. The crew chief hit the big red icon with his fist and the hangar doors began to close, but not before the Swarm ship got off one last shot, severing Dunn's right arm cleanly just above the elbow.

For a minute, he stood there. Obviously not realizing what had happened to him.

The doors slammed shut. The hangar began to pressurize. Danis ripped off her helmet and ran to Dunn.

He opened his eyes. His face was pale. He looked down at what was left of his arm and passed out.

Danis caught him and lowered him gently to the ramp.

She looked up at Dubois, who was still on the ramp with Nortak and Jax, and said, "For God's sake, Major. Don't just stand their goggling. Get the medics down here... *Now!*"

The medical team arrived minutes later, and Danis watched as they placed Grell Dunn on a gravgurney, gave him an injection, inserted an IV, and then whisked him away to the med bay. He seemed to be in good spirits, considering the loss of his right arm. He smiled weakly at her and raised his left hand. Fortunately, he hadn't lost any blood; the wound had been cauterized by the plasma.

Chapter Twenty-Nine

Avenger

Typhon Space

Behind Enemy Lines

The battle continued to rage around *Avenger* as Captain Morian, standing at the command rail, watched it happening in real time on the hologram.

The stats, changing by the second, indicated the number of enemy craft was at one hundred forty-eight and continuing to rise.

He gripped the rail, turned his head to look at Manda Haal who was standing beside him and said, "What do you see, Commander? Anything?"

Slowly, she shook her head, made eye contact with him and replied, "Nothing. I see nothing."

"Is that like... we're dead nothing, or are you just not seeing anything?"

She smiled and said, "I'm not seeing anything, Captain."

The ship shuddered violently and rocked under the impact of a massive hit.

"Damage report, Mr. Volkov," Morian snapped as the ship righted itself.

"Minor hull breach. Deck nine, sector seventeen," Maxim Volkov, *Avenger's* Chief Engineer, replied. "Damage control is working on it now."

The ship shuddered again.

"That was Turret Twenty," Volkov said, anticipating Morian's next question. "We've lost her. The gun room is self-sealing, so no breach."

"Status, Ms. Fargo," Morian snapped.

Corin Fargo, Chief Weapons Officer, replied quickly, "Shields are ninety-three percent, Captain. Turrets Twenty, Twenty-four, and Thirty-one are down... Captain. I think they're targeting our engines."

"How far to the Slip gate, Mr. DeLong?"

"Twenty-seven minutes, sir."

Morian looked again at Manda Haal, shook his head and said quietly, "Too long."

She nodded and closed her eyes.

Morian watched her, hoping.

She opened them again and shook her head, "Nothing!"

Morian nodded and turned again to the hologram, then glanced up at the stats rolling above it.

"Two hundred and eleven," he muttered, more to himself than to his first officer. "We're not going to make it, Manda."

"We're not done yet, sir," she said.

"Not yet, but we will be, and soon... How many more hits—"

The ship shuddered, then shuddered again. He looked at the tactical readout. With the exception of the three damaged turrets, all forty-eight point defense turrets were hammering at once, spewing thousands of rounds per minute at the Blue hoard.

"How's our ammunition holding, Ms... Far... go?" he said as the deck juddered beneath his feet.

"Eight-eights are down seventeen percent to eighty-three percent, Captain. M-99s are at eighty percent. The enemy is too many and clustered too close for us to fire at them without risking blowback."

Morian nodded. *That's the only problem with proximity warheads,* he thought. *Set them at too short a distance, less than twenty meters, and you risk premature explosion and possible damage to your own ship.*

"After shields are down to forty-two percent. Reactor two containment is failing. Shutting it down and diverting power from reactor three to after shields," Volkov shouted.

Again, the ship rocked. Morian looked at the forward screens, then the starboard, port, above, below and aft. The screens were alive, flickering with blue beams. The brightness made his eyes hurt. He averted his gaze... *We can't take much more of this,* he thought.

"How much longer, Mr. DeLong?"

"Thirteen minutes," DeLong replied.

Too long! Morian thought. *Much too long.*

"Captain! Something's happening. Look." Manda Haal grabbed his arm and pointed at the hologram.

Morian looked and, at first, didn't believe what he was seeing. The blue icons were grouping together and, "No, they can't be," Morian said in astonishment. "Why would they? Manda, they're leaving. Will you look at that? They are. They're leaving. Why?"

The answer to Morian's question was, of course, unanswerable. Inexplicably, they were gone, heading toward the Slip gate.

More importantly, he thought, gripping the rail with both hands as he stared at the hologram. *Where are they going?*

He watched as the last of the blue icons disappeared from the hologram, swallowed up by the Slipstream.

"ETA Slipstream, if you please, Mr. DeLong?" he said thoughtfully.

"Nine minutes, Captain."

"I need you to plot a course straight to Orso. Flank speed. And I need an ETA."

DeLong was quiet for a moment, his fingertips dancing over his holographic console.

"Best speed... Twenty-eight hours nineteen minutes, Captain."

"And if those Swarm ships are also going to Orso, how far behind them will we be?"

Delong let out a deep breath, stared at his console, ran his fingertips over the holographic display, then said, "Five hours thirty-seven minutes."

Morian shook his head. Past USF experiences had long ago confirmed that the Swarm traveled the Slipstream at speeds thirty percent faster than the USF craft. And no one could understand why. *Perhaps Minnah's core can provide the answer.*

Morian nodded and said, "Set the course, Mr. Delong." Then turned to Manda and said, "I need to freshen up. I'm going to take a quick hydro. Call me if anything... Well, call me. You have the bridge, Commander."

"Aye, Captain," she replied.

But he didn't move. Instead, he just stood there, hands on the rail, staring at the hologram, a now serene global view of the entire Eta Persei star system with the planet Typhon, a giant orange and blue ball seemingly only a few thousand kilometers distant; it was, in fact, more than two-hundred-fifty thousand kilometers behind them and growing smaller by the minute.

In truth he knew they'd been lucky. He doubted they could have beaten them off. *They left as if they'd been ordered away. But where are they going? Orso! They must be going to Orso.*

He sighed, shook his head, turned from the rail and left the bridge to the sound of the five-minute warning.

"Now hear this," Krista's calm, musical voice echoed throughout the ship. "Now hear this. Slipstream entry in five minutes. I say again. Slipstream entry in five minutes."

As Morian stepped into his quarters a few moments later, he felt the slight shift of the deck beneath his feet, his stomach lift and a momentary sensation of nausea as the ship entered the Slipstream.

Twenty minutes later he stepped out of the hydro feeling refreshed, much relieved and a little light-headed.

He dressed quickly in a fresh, navy-blue flight suit trimmed in gold. He wore it open at the neck over a white T-shirt. He clipped the black and gold datapad around his left forearm and felt the familiar tingle as the nano probes pierced his skin and attached themselves to his nerve endings, connecting him to his ship and all of its systems, including the med bay that constantly monitored his vital signs.

Finally, he looked in the mirror, ran his fingers through

the black stubble on top of his head and wondered, not for the first time, if he should shave it.

He smiled at his reflection in the mirror. The gold stars on his collar glittered, as if they were winking at him. *Shave my head? I don't think so.*

He stepped away from the mirror and called his sister on a closed channel.

"I'm sorry I haven't had time to talk to you since you got back," he said, looking at his chron. It had been almost three hours since the squadron had returned. *Has it really been that long?* he wondered. "Everything went well, I understand. You found Elio's friend."

"I did," she replied. "It was... quite a trip. Not one I'd volunteer to make again. You know I lost three pilots and four ships on the return journey?"

"Yes, I heard, and I'm sorry. Do you have replacements?"

"For the F32s? No," Danis replied. "Pilots? I have three, including Jackknife. His F32 was destroyed on landing. They're spacing it now. He's having that old single-seat Veridian serviced and armed and intends to fly it. Oh, and Skyla did well. I'm thinking of promoting her. That would fill the final spot. But until we can get replacements, we're down to eight ships and Jackknife's antique. What d'you think? About me promoting Skyla, I mean."

"I think you're squadron commander and must do what you think best. If that's promoting Skyla, so be it. Um... How is Minnah? Does he really have some alien technology?"

"He does," she replied. "And he's invented something, a device, that generates a directed EMP that can knock out the Blues. He used it to knock out what he called a communication center. He also has what he thinks is a functional core taken from one of the Blues he calls a Stomper. We ran into some of those—Stompers, I mean. If it hadn't been for Gian, I wouldn't be talking to you now. He saved our lives. How about you? You sound... subdued."

"I'm fine. I just... Something happened out there, Danis. They had us. We were about to be overwhelmed and then... they just quit and left. I don't get it. Even if they were leaving for the Orso System, why not wait until they'd finished us off? Look, I'm calling a meeting in about an hour. I need to talk to Minnah. I'd like you to be there."

"No problem," Danis replied. "That gives me time to grab a hydro and change into something more fitting... I feel as if I've been in this flight suit for a week. An hour, then?"

"Yes. An hour."

He closed the link and was about to open a channel to his senior officers when there was a knock at the door.

"Who is it?" he said as the door slid open.

"I'm Kyne Minnah," the man said as he stepped inside. "I need to talk to you, Captain."

Morian looked at him, at the wild mop of yellow hair, the piercing green eyes, the unusual clothing, and he wasn't impressed.

"I don't have time to talk now, young man. Whatever you have to say can wait. We're about to—"

"I'll tell you what you're about to," Minnah snapped, interrupting him. "You're about to be destroyed along with the entire, combined USF fleet, Orso and God only knows how many billions of people if you don't listen to me. Now do you have time?"

Morian was stunned. Never in his life, and certainly never as a USF officer, had he been interrupted and spoken to so rudely. Any other time he would have retaliated with a strong reprimand, but these were extraordinary times.

"I have already sent a message to Orso advising them of an impending attack, Minnah," Morian said, controlling his temper. "What more d'you want me to do?"

"As did I, Captain, but you don't know the half of it," he said, sitting down. "I've just spent the last several hours in the lab with your AI. Krista, I believe you call her... Perhaps I should begin at the beginning. Several months ago I, along with several survivors, managed to destroy several Blues. Our objective was to capture one of the energy cores that drive the Stompers. And we did. I brought it with me, along with... Oh never mind. You see, I believed the core was more than just a source of energy. I believed it might be the key to their entire actuality, their life force... even their reality. And I was right. I now believe it's how they communicate and how they move from one reality to another. I believe it holds the answers we've been looking for."

He paused, locked eyes with Morian, then continued, "There's no way to hard wire into the core, but I was originally able to make contact with it using eniotronic waves. The language itself is problematic and is going to take some breaking, but their mode of communication is basically a form of spatiotemporal binary code. Of course, I was able to work most of that out myself back in New Hope using my own AI. And I found that that thing has been, and still is, receiving and sending vast amounts of data, most of which, again, is going to take time to decode. However, one stream of code was, and still is, being received, with slight variations, over and over, so I concentrated on that and after—"

"Mr. Minnah," Morian said. "I don't have time to sit here all day listening to your blow-by-blow account. If you have vital information, please tell me and let me get back to work."

Minnah stared at him, then nodded and said, "As you

say, Captain. As you already know, I was able to decode that stream, and the gist of it is that the Swarm is planning to invade the Orso System in strength. Their objective is to pierce our defenses there and destroy our fleets. If they succeed, Captain, it's likely the entire Sovereign Star System will collapse, and humanity will be eradicated from the galaxy."

Morian nodded. "Again, Mr. Minnah, we already know this."

Minnah smiled wryly and said, "I know that, too, Captain, but what you don't know is that Krista and I intercepted a second communication stream, and the news is devastating. They are planning to augment their main invasion with a surprise flank attack. A massive Swarm cluster is already in the Orso System, in deep space, out beyond the gas giant Athena traveling at near-light speed toward the Caerus. This means the USF fleet will be fighting at the Slip gates, not knowing they'll be flanked by a second massive Swarm fleet coming in from deep space."

"Sovereign Stars!" Morian muttered. "How much time do we have?"

"The most up-to-date data puts them some twenty-three billion kilometers from Caerus, traveling at point-eight light speed so..." He closed his eyes, waved his hand in the air, then opened them again and said, "Twenty-six hours forty minutes."

Morian looked at him in amazement. "How did you do that?"

Minnah smiled at him. "It's what I do, Captain."

Morian shook his head, then tapped his datapad. "ETA Orso, Mr. DeLong?"

"Twenty-seven hours two minutes, Captain."

"Is that the best we can do?"

"It is, Captain."

For a moment Morian sat there staring at Minnah, then said to DeLong, "Thank you, Simon," and closed the channel.

"We're not going to make it in time," he said.

"I heard," Minnah replied. "What are you going to do?"

For the first time in his life, Morian was stumped for an answer. His mind was blank. He stood up, went to his credenza and poured two glasses of Nayan Synth, then carried them back.

"Drink?" He offered one to Minnah.

Minnah took it and said, "Thank you, Captain. This will be the first in almost eighteen months."

Morian nodded absently, then said, "Enjoy," and sat down again.

"How many jumps do we still have to make to Orso?" Minnah asked.

"Including this one, thirteen. Why d'you ask?"

"And that's the fastest route?"

"So my chief navigation officer tells me. Again, why d'you ask?"

"I take it the problem lies in the distance between the jumps?" Minnah asked.

Morian nodded. "All but one, Omicron Ceti, according to my first officer—she's a Seer—are clear of Swarm ships. We lose almost three hours there. As it is, the main Swarm fleet will reach Orso some four hours before we do. And we'll arrive twenty minutes too late to warn them of the second enemy fleet."

"Why?"

"Why what?"

"Why would you lose three hours in the Omicron system?"

My Seer tells me there will be upwards of a hundred Swarm ships between the two Slip gates. I have to avoid them. I can't afford to take any more damage."

Minnah nodded and said, "But you have the advantage, Captain. You know they're there, but they don't know you're coming. There might be something you can do."

"Oh, and what might that be?"

"You can calculate the most direct course between the two gates, then fly at maximum speed between the two gates and enter the Slip without slowing."

Morian shook his head. "The last captain to try that tore his ship apart. I can't risk it."

I think the risk *is* worth it," Minnah said. "Think, Captain Morian. Think of the risk-reward. You fly the safe route home, and the USF fleet is taken by surprise and possibly destroyed. You take the risk and win; you save the fleet. If you take the risk and lose, the outcome is unchanged, but at least you tried."

"Thank you, Mr. Minnah," Morian said, rising from his seat. "I'll consider what you suggest. Now, if you'll excuse me, I have a meeting to prepare for. I'd like you to attend."

Minnah stood and said, "My pleasure, Captain. When? Where?"

"The conference room in twenty minutes."

"I'll be there... Thank you for listening to me."

Morian waited until the door closed behind him and then opened a channel to his senior officers. "Attention. We'll assemble in the conference room at 15:30 hours. I expect everyone to attend with a full status report. Morian out."

* * *

"Thank you all for being so prompt," Morian, standing at the head of the conference table, began. "Before we begin, I'd like to introduce you all to Mr. Kyne Minnah, the reason for our mission to Typhon." He nodded at Minnah, who was sitting one seat from the end of the table. "If you would introduce yourselves, please, starting with you, Mr. Kingston."

Kingston nodded. "Omario Kingston, Lieutenant Commander. Chief Tactical Officer."

Lieutenant Commander Michael Jadern, Executive Officer.

And so it went on around the table until it came to Danis.

"Hello, Kyne," she said. "You already know who I am. Welcome aboard."

Major Dubois, who was sitting next to Danis, merely nodded and said, "Minnah."

"Good," Morian said. "Now that's out of the way, we can continue. As you know, the main Swarm offensive will begin when they enter the Orso System by one or both of the two Slip gates at least four hours ahead of us. We are now less than twenty-seven hours and thirteen jumps out from Orso, and that's a problem. What you don't know... What I just learned from Mr. Minnah is that a second Swarm fleet is in deep space, some twenty-three billion kilometers from Caerus, approaching from the dark side of Athena. Their intent is to flank the USF fleet at the Slip gates."

Manda Haal, who was sitting next to him, looked up at him and said, "We have to warn them—"

"And that's why we're here," Morian said, cutting her off. "We must warn them, but we can't; not without risking the ship and all of our lives. As it is, we'll arrive some twenty minutes *after* the second Swarm fleet begins its attack."

"We can't send a probe," DeLong said. "It wouldn't get there in time. So... what are we going to do?"

"Um, how is that possible?" Jadern asked. "How did this second fleet enter the system? They can't have made an interstellar crossing. The nearest star system is more than five light years from Caerus. It makes no sense."

"I would suggest," Minnah said, "that there must be an undiscovered Slip gate out... beyond, or within, or at least close to the Oort cloud."

"How they got there," Morian said, "is of no consequence." He looked at Kyne and said, "The problem is the delay in the Omicron Ceti System. We'll lose three hours there because we have to avoid the Swarm cluster between the Slip gates."

He paused and looked at Manda. "Any change in your prediction, Commander?"

She looked up at him and slowly shook her head.

He sighed, tilted his head in frustration, and continued. "Then we have no choice. We must warn the fleet, which means we have to cut the time we spend in Omicron. It's the only way."

"Captain, I estimate at least one hundred Swarm ships will be present between the two gates," Manda said.

"I know," he replied. "And if we stand and fight... who knows the outcome. That would be a fight we can't afford to lose."

"So... I hope you're not suggesting what I think you are," Kingston said.

Morian nodded. "Mr. Minnah has suggested we exit the slip into Omicron under power—thus taking the Swarm by surprise—and make a run for the gate. If we do that. And if we're successful. We'll cut our journey by at least ninety minutes, giving us a good hour to warn the fleet. The main attack at the Slip will be well underway, but we'll be in time to warn the fleet about the second force."

"And if we're not successful?" Kingston said. "To my certain knowledge, such a thing has only been tried once before and with disastrous results."

"That, I believe, was an attempt made by a Captain Edwick Mason some ninety years ago," Minnah said. "Ship design, materials and construction methods have changed dramatically since then. I believe it can work. I also think, if we are to give the fleet—and humanity—a chance, we have no choice."

"I would remind you, Mr. Minnah," Maxim Volkov, the ship's chief engineer, snorted. "This ship *is* almost ninety years old. At what speed d'you suggest we enter the Slip?"

Everyone turned to look at Minnah. He squirmed uncomfortably in his seat, then shrugged and asked, tentatively, "Mach 30?"

Everyone, even Morian, cringed.

"Are you insane? That's almost thirty-seven thousand kilometers per hour! Impossible," Volkov said, shaking his head like a wet dog. "The stresses will tear the ship apart."

"Then what do you suggest, Mr. Volkov?" Morian asked.

"I... I... not more than... Mach 5."

Morian looked at Minnah. He was slowly shaking his head.

"What if we split the difference?" Manda asked.

"Are you saying that would work, Commander?" Morian asked. "Is that what you're seeing?"

"No... It was just a suggestion."

"Mr. Minnah?" Morian asked.

"Mach 30," he said firmly.

Volkov threw up his hands and said, "We're doomed. She won't take it."

"We have to try," Morian said quietly. "We have no choice. Mach 30 it is. Thank you. Dismissed. Commander Morian, I'd like a word, if you please."

He waited until the room cleared, then went and sat beside his sister and said, "You're not looking well, Danis."

She shook her head, then looked at him and said, "I'm fine, just a little tired. The mission was exhausting."

"I want you to go and see Dr. Dowd," he said. "I need you in peak condition when we break out into the Orso System. I have a feeling it's going to be a nightmare."

She looked at him and said, "I'm fine—"

"No arguments," he snapped, cutting her off. "Go. Now."

* * *

Danis reluctantly left Morian seated at the conference table and made her way to the elevators. She tapped the icon and waited, but just as the doors opened, she saw Major Dubois approaching, so she held the doors for him.

"Going down?" she asked.

He nodded and stepped into the elevator without saying a word, his face creased in a frown.

The elevator stopped, the doors opened and Dubois stepped out first, still not having spoken to her.

"Hold on, Major," she said as he began to walk away. "What is wrong with you? You've been a bear ever since we embarked on the shuttle for Typhon. Is it something I said that's upset you?"

He stopped, stood still for a moment, then turned to face her.

"No, Commander. It's nothing you said; it's what you did. You pulled rank and forced yourself into an extremely dangerous situation, as did that fool Dunn. And while I appreciate the help you both were able to provide, I still believe your presence could have seriously compromised the mission. Neither you nor Dunn are combat trained which means someone has to look after you. In your case, that was me... I'm sorry, Commander. That's how I feel. However, I will not include my personal feelings in my mission report, but I would ask that in the future you stick with what you do best and leave the ground combat to the professionals."

"Whew!" she replied. "That was unexpected."

"Look," he said. "I have a PsyOp embedded in my command. He's combat trained. He knows how to handle himself in a sticky situation. Having seen Dunn's capabilities and those of old man Mozzley, I could use a TK, but he, or she, would have to be properly trained. In the meantime, Commander, I have the greatest respect for you and what you do. It's not my nature to be surly. Give me time and I'll get over it. Now, if we're done, I have a report to write."

And with that, he turned and walked away, leaving Danis staring after him, the wheels grinding away in her head. *Hmm,* she thought. *That makes a lot of sense.*

Chapter Thirty

Orso System

USF Battle Fleet

The Floodgates

The bridge of the USF Super Carrier *Invincible* was vast and, for the most part, silent.

Prince Elio was at the command rail with Vice Admiral Hiro Yoshimura, Captain Marcus Diego, and Tenilo, all staring at the giant view screens and the towering hologram hovering over the well deck. All were dressed in pressure suits—except for their helmets—as were the other thirty-two members of the bridge crew.

Before them, to port, starboard, above, below, and aft, more than three hundred USF capital ships and twenty-hundred ships of the line, including those of the newly arrived IMFP fleet, were spread out over an area that covered many thousands of cubic kilometers completely encircling the two Slip gates. The great ships were supported by more than seven thousand fighters and fighter bombers. It was the largest fleet ever assembled in the annals of human history, and it was a breathtaking sight.

Two hours earlier, Elio had issued orders for the fleet to go to General Quarters, launch fighters, and prepare to fire on the Swarm as their enemy exited the Slip gates.

Two hundred meters off *Invincible's* port bow, Sasha Crowe's Defender Class cruiser, *Golden Condor,* floated serenely, her bronze minodutrinium armor glistening in the weak light of Orso, the system's Class F Blue-white star, her gun ports open. Her forty-eight point defense turrets all aimed toward the Western Slip gate. Two hundred meters to starboard, he could see Tiger Wok's *Red Dragon,* a sixty-six-gun heavy cruiser. They had arrived from Freyja with a fleet of one-hundred-thirty ships less than an hour earlier.

Some half-a-kilometer aft of *Invincible,* her one-hundred-forty-four fighters and fighter bombers were clustered, their pilots patiently waiting.

"It's an impressive sight, don't you think, your highness?" Captain Diego asked.

Elio nodded thoughtfully. "I wonder if it's enough," he replied. "Do we have an update on the enemy's numbers?"

"Last I heard, still upwards of a hundred thousand," Diego said. "We've heard nothing from the Seers, and nothing from *Avenger* since she left the Eta Persei System more than twenty-four hours ago."

Elio nodded. "It's the waiting," he said. "The not knowing that's nerve-racking. The calm before the storm, as they say."

"If the numbers don't change," Yoshimura said, shaking his head, "we're outnumbered almost twenty to one."

Elio smiled at him and said, "Better than I thought...

What you have to remember, Admiral, is that while they may have the advantage in numbers, our weapons are more effective, and we have a lot of them. Far more than a hundred thousand. Their shields are almost ineffective against our 88mm and 120mm railguns and the new M99 torpedoes."

"For now, anyway," Tenilo interjected. "But we know they are constantly evolving. And we already know they have a new ship. We need information. Minnah and Richard Morian have it but can't get it to us, so we're in the dark. We need to develop some sort of faster-than-light communication system."

"We have probes that can travel the Slips," Diego said.

"True," Yoshimura said, "but they are barely faster than our ships. It can take days for a probe to travel from the rim to Orso. Mr.Tenilo is right. We need something better."

"Perhaps when this is over," Diego said.

"If we survive," Yoshimura muttered, staring at the vast, undulating section of space that was Orso's Western Slip gate.

He shook his head and glanced at his chron, then at the rolling data above the hologram. "Where are they?" he said.

"Maybe they're not coming," Diego said.

"Oh, they're coming," Elio said. "I can feel it in my bones."

He lifted his arm, touched an icon and opened a channel to his sister.

"Sasha?"

"Hello, brother. Are you as bored as I am? Where the hell are they? My bridge is as quiet as a hospital morgue. Have you heard anything from *Avenger*?"

Elio laughed, shook his head in amusement and said, "Hello, Sasha. No. I don't know, and no, I've heard nothing more from Richard, but he can't be more than four hours out. How are you holding up?"

"Oh... I'm fine," she replied, "but this waiting; it's unsettling to say the least... Wait! What's that? Something's happening. Something's coming through the gate. They're here. Stay safe, my brother. Crowe out."

Elio stared at the gigantic forward screen. Something was indeed happening. The swirling black nothingness, more than six kilometers in diameter, was speeding up and changing color: deep purple at the center to brilliant violet at the rim. A single Swarm ship emerged as if spit from the maw of a giant worm. It was followed by a second, a third, five more, seven, ten until the trickle became a stream and then a vast river of blue as hundreds then thousands of enemy ships, their blue halos shimmering, flooded out into Orso space.

"Helmsman!" Elio snapped. "Bring her about. Turn eighty degrees to port and roll seven degrees. Weapons officers! Tubes two through one hundred. Stand by to fire on my command. Point defense standby. Lorne to Commander Air Group. They're here. Prepare to defend the ship."

And the great ship began to turn. Slowly at first, until her starboard broadside was facing the Slip gate and the enemy.

"Fire tubes two through one hundred," Elio said quietly, and he immediately felt the mighty ship shudder beneath his feet as fifty M99B proximity torpedoes left her starboard tubes at speeds in excess of Mach 10.

"Reload and prepare to fire again," Elio snapped, then he, Yoshimura, Diego and Tenilo held their breaths as they watched the missiles, and those from more than a hundred of the leading ships of the fleet, track across the hologram toward the incoming Swarm fleet. It reminded Elio of an old vid titled *Gladiator,* recorded and digitalized long before the Purge, in which showers of fire arrows rained down on the attacking gallic horde.

And each of them silently counted the seconds to proximity and the first explosion: eight... nine...

"Yay," Diego shouted, throwing up his hands in excitement as first one, then a split second later, all fifty torpedoes exploded, their shaped charges each throwing six laser-guided, 120mm depleted uranium projectiles at the enemy ships. And then the entire bridge crew began cheering as one by one the blue icons on the hologram began to blink out.

It was a small victory. Within minutes, the flood had turned into a tsunami as thousands upon thousands of Swarm ships exited the two Slip gates located more than a million kilometers apart.

Tenilo watched as the leading capital ships began to move forward, launching salvo after salvo of missiles from their bow tubes, point defense blazing, railguns hammering, and all to great effect, but the sheer number of enemy ships exiting the Slips was unimaginable. They kept coming so quickly that the rolling stats above the hologram became almost unreadable and, instead of individual blue icons, they merged into huge blobs, clusters of hundreds of blue-haloed ships. The enemy descended on the USF fleet like a swarm of locusts.

The hologram became a seething globe of blue. The fleet dispatched thousands of torpedoes, the railguns hundreds of thousands of 88 and 120mm rounds, destroying incalculable thousands of Swarm ships, and still they poured out of the Slip gates. Within thirty minutes the numbers had passed one hundred thousand and were still climbing. And it was only the beginning.

Tenilo reached out to the members of *Invincible's* crew and was almost overwhelmed by the influx of hot-blooded thoughts, bravery, fear and impending doom, but there was nothing he could do. He closed his mind to the masses and concentrated on Elio. He reached into his mind to find it in turmoil, an assemblage of disconnected thoughts of crisis, tactics, strategy, concern, reticence, and diffidence thrashing around his brain like a whirlwind. And he knew that Elio, too, could feel the fear of the men and women on his ship.

Fear not, my prince. Stay calm. Think. You can do this.

Get out of my head, Tenny. This is not the time. And Elio closed his mind to him.

Tenilo breathed deeply, sucked in a huge breath of air, and looked nervously around. So far *Invincible* had seemed immune from attack, partly because of her huge fighter escort and partly because of her two-hundred-twenty point defense turrets. But then, the sheer numbers of enemy ships began to tell. *Invincible* came under fire from multiples of enemy craft, clusters of them. And, big as she was, she shuddered under the recoil of her many heavy weapons.

The deck seemed alive beneath his feet. He could feel the vibration throughout his body. His eyes burned from the intensity of the screens, now overloaded as the ship's shields flared in cataclysmic eruptions of blue fire, absorbing blast after blast of blue plasma.

The minutes quickly turned into an hour, and still the battle raged unabated. The enemy casualties were numbering in the tens of thousands, but the USF fleet was also beginning to take casualties.

* * *

Elio was beginning to feel as if his brain would burst. With his eyes glued to the hologram, he was trying to direct the battle single-handedly—ordering ships forward as he ordered wounded ships to the rear. He was playing a monumental game of chess, a game he doubted he could win.

He felt a hand on his shoulder. He looked to his left.

"You can't do it alone, my prince," Captain Diego said. "The fleet is too big to micro-manage. You have to trust your admirals and captains. If you don't, you'll confuse them. They've been trained for this. Trust them. Send the fleet a message of encouragement and get the hell out of our way."

Elio stared at him in astonishment, opened his mouth to speak, but was interrupted by a thought from Tenilo.

He's right, my friend. You must step aside and let the professionals do what they do best.

The ship shuddered, rocked under their feet, under a combined attack from a cluster of at least twenty enemy craft, some of a type Elio had not seen before. They were similar in design to the ones he'd dealt with on Typhon in the early days of the Swarm invasion, but much bigger. They were faster, more maneuverable; their weapons were heavier and fired beams of plasma broader and more intense.

They attacked line astern, one following the other, all four weapons aimed at the bridge. The assault was relentless. *Invincible's* nineteen laser-guided bow guns hurling thousands of rounds a minute took out seven enemy craft in their first pass, but the remaining Blues got through the barrage and, one after another, seemingly solid bolts of blue plasma slammed into the forward shields protecting the bow and the command bridge.

The seven destroyed enemy ships were quickly replaced by at least a dozen more, and the cluster swooped in for a second pass.

Elio, his hands gripping the rail, his jaw locked, stared at the forward screens, at the flashes of brilliant blue fire, the exploding enemy craft, the debris spinning by at speeds beyond Mach 10 and, for a moment, he was rendered speechless.

For several minutes the shields, under continuous, heavy enemy fire, held until, after more than a dozen direct hits, they slowly began to degrade.

"Forward shields at seventy-two percent and cratering," Diego snapped. "We have to do something. Now."

Elio took a deep breath and said, "Wait until they make their next pass and then fire all forward tubes."

He looked at Tenilo. Tenilo nodded. He glanced at Diego.

"What are your orders, my prince?" Diego asked quietly.

The ship rocked. The screens lit up brilliant white as the forward shields took hits from all four weapons of a second-generation Swarm ship.

"Forward shields at forty-six percent," Diego shouted.

"Divert power from reactor nine to the forward shields," Elio said.

"I think it's time to get into our helmets, my prince," Diego said, reaching for his own.

Elio nodded and said, "Give the order, Captain."

"Prince Elio," the communications officer called out. "I have an incoming, fleet-wide transmission from *Avenger*."

Chapter Thirty-One

Omicron Ceti Space

Into the Black

Avenger exited the Slip into Omicron Ceti space, some six-thousand kilometers from the gate that would take them to the next system, to find it seemingly deserted.

Captain Morian, at the command rail with Manda Haal at his side, had been prepared to order Haltar Sen to go to full power immediately. Instead, he ordered him to wait and then turned his attention to the hologram and ordered a passive scan of the area of space between *Avenger* and the Slip gate.

"Where are they?" he muttered. "Have they left, too?"

"Passive scans indicate a large cluster of Swarm ships congregated around the Slip gate, Captain," Sandra Lowry replied.

Morian nodded, looked at the hologram and said,

"There they are." Then he looked at Manda and said, "You're right again, Commander. Well done. Now for the hard part." He looked up at the data readout and continued, "There are one-hundred-two of them. They don't seem to be moving. I don't think they know we're here. Hmm... Six-thousand kilometers at Mach 10... that's thirty minutes. All ahead slow, Mr. Sen. Increase speed to Mach 10 and hold. Rig for silent running. Passive scans only. Bring the ship to battle stations, Commander."

Manda nodded and opened a shipwide channel. "Now hear this..." she said and ordered the ship to battle stations.

Morian waited until she'd finished, then called the bridge officers to attention.

"For those of you who were not present at the meeting of the senior officers," he began, "I want to inform you that we're about to try something that's been tried only once before... with disastrous results." He paused and looked at each of the twelve officers in turn.

"We need to shave at least two hours from our arrival time in the Orso System. That means we don't have time to take the long way, or to fight the enemy clustered around the Slip gate." He paused, then continued. "It's been suggested we charge the enemy formation, break through and enter the Slip at... Mach 30."

The statement drew a collective gasp from the bridge crew. The normal entry speed was less than one hundred kilometers per hour, in fact.

"I have no idea what the consequences will be," Morian continued, "but we have no choice. If we make it through to Orso in time, we may be able to save the fleet from almost certain destruction. If we don't... well, nothing ventured, nothing gained, as they say. Any questions?"

Morian waited a beat. "No? Good. Ms. Fargo, load

tubes one through four and nineteen through twenty-two with M99B torpedoes. Set proximities to five hundred meters. Bring all point defense turrets to standby. We go to Mach 30 in..." He checked his chron, "seventeen minutes."

Those seventeen minutes were the longest in Morian's life. The waiting as the ship crept forward seemed interminable. Barely a word was uttered among the bridge crew, and those that were, were spoken in whispers.

As the final seconds ticked away, Morian rose to his feet and approached the rail.

"They've spotted us," Lowry shouted. "They're turning. They're coming!"

"Mach 30, if you please, Mr. Sen. Ms. Fargo, stand by to fire torpedoes."

Sen turned to his console, his back straight, and his fingertips fluttered over the holograph. The ship surged forward. The inertia dampeners engaged but not before Morian had taken an involuntary step backward.

"Fire torpedoes," Morian snapped, gripping the rail, leaning forward as if to get a closer view of the forward screens.

"Torpedoes away," Fargo all but yelped.

"Bring point defense online as the guns come to bear," Morian said.

The Swarm cluster was taken completely by surprise.

Avenger achieved Mach 30 less than ten kilometers from the Slip. Two seconds later, eight M99B torpedoes streaked from the tubes and impacted the cluster. Eleven Swarm ships exploded in blinding balls of blue fire as she blasted on through without slowing, all forty-five remaining railguns firing, taking out eight more enemy craft as she went.

Morian's facial muscles tightened. He gripped the rail

so tightly his knuckles turned white as the vast maw of the Slip gate grew closer and closer until... suddenly, the view screens went dark and the hologram became an undulating ball of blackness.

For several seconds nothing happened... and then the entire ship began to shake.

"Reverse engines, Mr. Volk—"

But Volkov had anticipated the order. The engines whined under the strain and... nothing happened. *Avenger* continued its mad dash through the Slipstream without slowing, seemingly unencumbered by the laws of physics.

The shaking increased. The command rail began juddering violently. The bow began to drop. *Avenger* began to roll to port.

"Cut the gravity, Mr. Volkov," Morian shouted.

Volkov disengaged the artificial gravity generators, and while almost all of the bridge crew were restrained in their seat, Morian's feet lifted off the deck as the ship continued to roll, shaking and shuddering.

"For God's sake, Volkov," Morian shouted. "Do something! Cut the engines."

Volkov disengaged the engines, then shouted, "There's nothing I can do, Captain. I told you it wouldn't work. Much more of this and she'll come apart at the seams."

The shaking continued to increase to the point where Morian became convinced that Volkov was right.

"Hull breach!" Volkov shouted. "Deck seven. Sector nine. She's breaking up!"

And then, they broke out into normal space, bow down at an angle of twenty-two degrees, rolling at a speed of three revolutions per minute.

"Engage thrusters," Morian shouted. "Stop her rolling.

Bring up the bow. Damage control to the hull breach. Damage report, Mr. Volkov."

For several minutes, the bridge was in chaos as they tried to assess the damage. Fortunately, *Avenger*, having gone through a recent refit, was in better condition than most of her peers and seemed to have weathered the storm. The hull breach was minor and quickly sealed, the artificial gravity generators were brought back online, and the engines reengaged.

Finally, when everything had settled down once more, Morian asked, "Where are we, Lieutenant Sen?"

Sen was quiet for a moment, then looked up at Morian and said, "We're in the Beta Fornacis System, two jumps out from Orso. We seem to have skipped one."

"ETA Orso?" Morian asked.

"Two hours, eleven minutes."

Morian nodded and looked at Manda, who'd joined him at the rail. He let out a sigh that only she could hear.

* * *

"ETA, Mr. Sen?" Morian asked some ninety minutes later.

"Thirty-nine minutes to Orso's western gate, Captain," Sen replied.

Morian nodded. *If Minnah's right, and I have to assume that he is, the invasion began almost an hour ago,* he thought. *That second fleet can't be much more than ninety minutes out. It's going to be tight...* "Battle Stations, Mr. Jadern."

"Battle stations. Aye, Captain," Jadern replied and broadcast the order.

"Lieutenant Fargo. Load all tubes with M99B torpedoes. Proximity settings at five hundred meters. Target the exit and prepare to fire in... thirty-one minutes. Then reload and keep firing until I tell you to stop."

"Aye, Captain," Fargo replied.

He went to his command chair, sat down, opened a private channel to his sister and said, "Danis. How are you feeling?"

She heaved a long shuddering sigh, then said, "I'm feeling that today will be a good day to die, my brother."

Inwardly, he shook his head. He knew the odds of survival were close to zero, but he couldn't accept it.

"No," he replied. "Today is a good day to live. What's the status of your squadron?"

"We're nine, including that pile of Veridian scrap Jack-knife insists on flying."

For what must have been the tenth time in the past hour, he glanced at his chron, then said, "We'll exit the Slip in twenty-eight minutes. I need you to launch the squadron the second we're clear of the enemy fleet, which, if I've calculated correctly, should be a little more than twenty minutes after we exit. Don't wait for my command. Just do it. Understood?"

"I understand... Richard, if we... if we don't meet again, I want you to know—"

"*Don't* say it," Morian interrupted her. "We'll get through this. Both of us. I know it."

"Is that what Manda told you?" she asked jokingly.

"No. It's what I know. Believe me. I've been around longer than you have."

"Ha! Four minutes longer... I love you, big brother. There. I've said it."

"I love you, too, Danis. Now go prepare yourself and your pilots. Stay safe out there. I'll talk to you when this is over. Morian out." And he closed the channel before she could answer.

He glanced at his chron again. *Twenty-three minutes. Stars... This waiting...* He gazed at the undulating black mass of the hologram, lost in thought, not really seeing it, his eyes unfocused. *How many?* he wondered. *How many will die today? Millions? Billions?*

"Fifteen minutes to exit," Sen's monotone voice echoed around the bridge and shipwide.

The bridge was deathly quiet. The minutes continued to tick by. Morian, still in his command chair, continued to stare at the hologram, half hypnotized by the undulating black mass.

"Ten minutes to exit."

Morian stood, stepped briskly to the command rail, gripped it with both hands, rocked himself back and forth, once, twice, then steadied himself, looked around the well deck and said, "I won't try to tell you all not to worry, that we'll survive the next several hours. You know better than that. The chances are that we won't. Our job is to get the message to the fleet that they are about to be flanked. We *must* do that at all costs. Ms. Lowry, prepare to send the following message fleetwide, priority one."

He paused for a second, then continued, "This is Commodore Richard Morian commanding USF *Avenger* to all fleet and ship commanders. There is a second Swarm fleet traveling at near-light speed in deep space from beyond Athena. They will be in position to attack our flank in less than sixty minutes. Numbers are known to be in excess of twenty-five thousand. I say again."

He looked over to Lowry. "Send that the second we exit the Slip. Send it on a loop for twenty minutes."

Lowry nodded, then repeated the message back to him.

He nodded, but said nothing. He was already deep in thought.

"Exit in five minutes," Sen said.

Morian took a deep breath and said, "Shields up! Commence firing torpedoes, Ms. Fargo."

Two minutes later *Avenger* burst out of the western Slip gate into normal space and... a sea of enemy ships, thousands of them.

"All ahead full," Morian shouted as he watched the trails on the hologram of the more than one-hundred-forty M99 torpedoes streaking away in front of them. Fargo had managed to fire three salvos before they exited the Slipstream. "I want every ounce of speed you can get, Mr. Volkov, and I want it now! Keep those torpedoes coming, Fargo. Point defense, fire as your guns come to bear."

They were approaching the enemy from the rear, and Morian's goal was to fly right through the middle of the Swarm fleet toward the USF fleet. *Avenger's* top speed was one-quarter light, but that took hours to achieve. The best he could hope for was Mach 75.

He watched the screens. The torpedoes were having a devastating effect. So closely grouped was the enemy that almost every projectile hit home as *Avenger* streaked through their mass.

He stood alone at the rail, watching. He glanced up at the Machometer. They were approaching Mach 60, more than seventy-three-thousand kilometers per hour and still accelerating.

"Message sent to the fleet, Captain," Lowry said, looking up at him.

He nodded but said nothing, continuing to watch as hundreds of enemy ships were either disabled or destroyed by broadside after broadside of torpedoes and thousands of rounds of railgun projectiles as they made their mad dash through the enemy fleet.

At first, the enemy appeared to be oblivious to their presence, but after several minutes they seemed to realize what was happening, and suddenly the screens lit up brilliant blue as the Swarm ships began to fire on them.

Again, Morian glanced up at the Machometer and was surprised to see that *Avenger* was approaching Mach 84, more than one-hundred-thousand kilometers per hour, too fast for any enemy ship to achieve target lock, and better than he'd hoped for.

"Ms. Fargo, cease firing all. We do not want to hit any of our own ships."

"Aye, Captain," Fargo replied and broadcast the order.

Less than five minutes later, they were through not only the enemy fleet but also the USF fleet.

"Reverse engines, Mr. Volkov," Morian ordered. "Slow to Mach 4 and bring her around, Mr. Sen."

"Morian to Domino. Copy?"

"Domino. Copy."

"Belay that order to launch fighters. We're now aft of the USF fleet and making the turn to join them. Stand by to launch on my command. Copy?"

"Copy that, Captain," Danis replied

"Ms. Lowry, I need to find the flagship."

Chapter Thirty-Two

Orso Space

USF Invincible

The Battle for Caerus

"Prince Elio," Lieutenant Lewiston, *Invincible's* communications officer, said, "I have a fleetwide transmission from *Avenger*, from Commodore Morian. They have just entered Orso space through the western Slip gate and making all speed through the Swarm. It's urgent, sir. It's looping."

"Let's hear it, son," Admiral Yoshimura said.

"Aye, Captain," Lewiston said and played the message:

"This is Commodore Richard Morian commanding USF *Avenger* to all fleet and ship commanders…"

When the message finished playing, Elio looked at Yoshimura and said, "A second Swarm out beyond Athena. How can that be? There's no Slip gate out there… is there?"

"Not that I know of, but Orso is a binary system and the perimeters have never been completely explored. More to the point, my prince, if what Morian says is true, we're in serious trouble. We're managing to hold them on this front, but if we're outflanked..." He didn't bother to finish. Instead, he stared at the hologram and the large yellow orb that represented Athena.

"There's nothing there yet," Captain Diego said.

"Increase magnification," Yoshimura ordered.

The orange orb increased in size until it was more than a meter in diameter.

"Stop!" Yoshimura said, holding up his hand.

He stared at the blackness of space surrounding Athena and, for a moment he saw nothing. Then he grabbed Elio's arm and pointed.

"There," he said. "D'you see?"

Elio stared at the spot Yoshimura was pointing to, pulling his arm free from his grasp. It was hard to see, but sure enough, it was there; a hazy blue smudge, maybe four centimeters in diameter, and it was moving slowly toward Caerus, Orso's capital planet.

"I see it," Elio said, nodding. "Morian said there are more than twenty-five thousand. Could that be true?"

"I'm afraid so," Yoshimura replied, "and if they're traveling at near-light speed as he says, they'll be in Caerus space in less than an hour."

"You can't be serious?" Elio said as the color drained from his face.

"Oh, I'm serious, my prince. What are your orders?"

Elio hesitated, almost overwhelmed by the sudden onset of an intense feeling of inadequacy. He looked at Yoshimura, sucked in his lower lip, turned again to stare at the blue smudge, took a deep breath and said, "Hiro, you say we're holding them here. Do you really believe that to be true?"

Yoshimura shrugged, then seemed to make up his mind, nodded and said, "Yes, your highness. Our strategic advantage in weaponry has given us the advantage. At a rough count, I estimate we have destroyed or disabled almost a third of their number. Our losses are minimal by comparison: two carriers, three battleships, thirty-two heavy cruisers and one-hundred-eight destroyers and frigates. How many fighters we've lost... I don't know, but more than a thousand. Those numbers may sound... unacceptable, and they are," he added hurriedly, "but they are small when compared to the losses sustained by the enemy."

"So what are you saying?" Elio asked, unable to take his eyes off the blue smudge.

"I'm saying... we have the edge, and that we can win this battle, but to do so, we must deal with this second fleet. And that means we have to face them—on a battlefield of our choosing."

"And where would that be?" Elio asked skeptically.

"Here!" Yoshimura pointed to an orange and blue orb.

"Are you mad, Admiral?" Elio snapped, turning to face him. "That's Caerus, our home planet. Why would we fight them there?"

"Because of these, my prince." And one by one, he pointed to the ten giant battle stations orbiting in deep space around the planet.

Elio was silent for a moment as he stared at the stations. Then he nodded and said, "Perhaps you're right. But what of the fleet? How many ships do you think we can spare and still maintain the upper hand over their main force?"

"Not as many as I would like," Yoshimura replied, "but they are no longer entering the system, which means two things: One, there are no more coming, and two, if we can gain control of the gates, we can stop them from receiving reinforcements. But first we have to deal with these interlopers, and we don't have much time. They are already decelerating."

Elio nodded and made up his mind. "We'll take my sister, Sasha Crowe, and her fleet, and we'll detach Marshal Tali and her fleet, along with carriers *Juno* and *Acheron*, and with battleships *Royal George*, *Resolution* and *Defiance*. I also want *Avenger*. They've earned the right to be there at the end. If it had not been for Morian, the enemy would have outflanked us. As it is, he's provided us with a chance to win this thing."

Yoshimura stared at him, his mouth turned down at the corners, then he nodded and said, "I agree, but I think you should talk to Marshal Tali yourself. The order would be better coming from the commander in chief rather than a mere vice admiral."

Elio smiled at him, then turned to the rail and said, "Mr. Lewiston. Open a private channel to Marshal Tali."

"Good day to you, my prince," Tali said. "I assume this is about the message I received from *Avenger*."

"It is, Sien," Elio replied, "and I need your help. It's my intention to meet the new enemy fleet before they can outflank us. I need your fleet. Please withdraw and stand by to receive further orders from Admiral Yoshimura."

"As you wish, Prince Elio. I'm happy to comply. Please tell the admiral I'll be pleased to receive his orders."

"Thank you, Marshal, and good hunting. Lorne out!"

"You heard that, Admiral," Elio said. "You're the tactician. You can handle it from here. I'll stay out of your way. Send a message to the combined fleet commanders stating our intentions and make way to meet the enemy immediately. I will talk to Captains Morian, Crowe and Wok." Then he turned away, went to the command chair and sat down with Tenilo at his side and made the call to Sasha.

* * *

"I've just received a priority one communique from Prince Elio, CIC USF Combined Fleet," Lowry said to Morian over a closed channel. "It's a bit... well, you'll see for yourself. It reads, 'Elio Lorne to Commodore Richard Morian commanding USF *Avenger*. Richard. Welcome home. You are to make best speed to join *Invincible*.' That's it. There's nothing more, except that the message provides *Invincible's* coordinates and course direction."

So, he's done it, Morian thought, smiling to himself. *He's beaten them and taken control of the kingdom. Good for him.* "Send the coordinates and course direction to Lieutenant Sen, please, Ms. Lowry. Then send to *Invincible*: Message received and understood. Will join you shortly."

He tapped his datapad and spoke to Sen directly.

"We're to join Prince Elio. Lowry's sending coordinates. Best speed, Mr. Sen, and I need an ETA."

"Aye, Captain... ETA *Invincible*, sixteen minutes twenty-two seconds."

* * *

Elio remained seated in the command chair, his legs outstretched, his left elbow on the arm of the chair, his fist supporting his chin, and he watched as the blue smudge continued to grow as the two fleets drew closer together.

Tenilo was seated to his left. Yoshimura and Diego were standing together at the command rail talking quietly to one another. They all were watching the view screens and the hologram.

"*Avenger* has arrived, your highness," Lewiston said. "She's five hundred meters off the port bow."

Elio sat up straight and said, "Open a channel to Captain Morian and put it on my holo, Mr. Lewiston."

There was a moment of silence before the holo generator to Elio's right came to life. He was looking at a half-life-size image of Morian's head and shoulders.

"Richard," Elio said. "It's good to see you again, my friend. We don't have much time, but I wanted to... I was becoming worried about you. How was your trip? Fruitful, I hope."

"Yes," Morian replied. "You could say that, but at a cost. We lost four F32s, three pilots and ten Marines and we rescued Minnah. He's quite a character."

"That he is," Elio said. "He's also a genius, but we don't have time for that now. We'll catch up later. I must thank you for your timely warning. Without it... it doesn't bear thinking about. As you know, we're to intercept the new enemy fleet. You are to accompany us. Contact in sixteen minutes. I want you on my port flank. My sister Sasha will take the starboard flank. Her fleet, and that of Marshal Tali, is deployed in a crescent formation with *Invincible* at the center. Do you have any questions or... thoughts?"

"None that I can think of," Morian replied. "Other than, as you say, we don't have much time."

"Yes, go. We'll talk later." He closed the channel and Morian's image disappeared, leaving Elio feeling... alone.

He gazed at the spot where Morian's image had been, then sighed, pushed himself to his feet and joined Yoshimura and Diego at the rail.

They were now just outside Caerus' exosphere approaching Battle Station 7.

Yoshimura called for an open channel and broadcast to the stations to stand by and open fire on the enemy at will, then turned to Elio and said, "There they are!" and pointed to the three forward screens.

Elio looked. The images looked small on the giant screens, but they were quickly growing larger. He swallowed hard, trying to rid himself of the lump in his throat, and looked at the hologram. They were approaching fast, in a vast, globular cluster. He glanced up at the data scrolling above the holo.

"More than twenty-seven-thousand," he said to the offiers standing next to him. "To our three-hundred-twenty. Is it even possible?"

"Between us, we have almost as many M99s as there are enemy ships," Yoshimura replied. "So yes, it's possible."

"I hope you're right, Admiral... Here they come."

Chapter Thirty-Three

Caerus Space

Battle Stations

The new Swarm fleet attempting to make a surprise attack was deployed in a vast globular cluster spread out over more than ten cubic kilometers. They filled *Invincible's* screens. On the hologram, the formation was more than a meter in diameter, a semi-transparent, shimmering ball of thousands of blue icons: twenty-seven thousand six hundred, according to the data.

Ranged before them, the portion of the combined USF battle group dispatched to meet them and deployed in a reverse crescent formation more than ten kilometers across, its wings pointing toward the enemy, was tiny by comparison. To port, the faded yellow and deep blue and green planet Caerus, almost three meters in diameter, its ten battle stations represented by red icons, dominated the hologram. It was a scene that defied the imagination, awe-inspiring, terrifying.

At the command rail, Admiral Yoshimura, flanked by Elio and Captain Diego, was on an open channel talking to the entire fleet.

The USF fleet stood stationary in space, flanked by Battle Stations 7 and 9. The Swarm fleet had slowed from near light speed to Mach 10 but was still approaching, the distance between the two fleets closing rapidly.

Then, unexpectedly and without warning, the Swarm formation began to change. Large numbers of ships began to break away, heading in different directions, but the main bulk of the formation continued to advance.

Elio stared at the array of giant screens. To port and just to the rear, he could see the great, bronze-colored bulk that was *Avenger*. To starboard, Sasha's *Golden Condor* was similarly positioned. He glanced from screen to screen, taking in the supercarriers *Vagabond*, *Juno* and *Acheron*. The battleships *Royal George*, *Resolution*, *Defiant* and more than three hundred smaller ships, along with upward of a thousand F32 fighters and a single eighty-year-old Veridian, waited for what could be the last battle of their lives.

Fifteen minutes earlier, Danis had been ordered to launch her squadron and was now in position clustered around *Avenger*.

Invincible's fourteen squadrons of fighters and fighter bombers were ranged in two wings of seventy-four. Both forward of her bow: one below and the other above.

"Distance to targets, ten thousand meters and closing," the chief tactical officer warned.

"Hold your fire," Yoshimura ordered to the fleet.

"Seven thousand meters," the chief tactical officer continued, "six... five thousand... four thousand..."

"Fire!" Yoshimura shouted, and more than two-thousand-five-hundred M99B torpedoes streaked toward the oncoming Swarm. The result was swift and deadly.

More than a third of the torpedoes failed to reach proximity, destroyed by bolts of shimmering plasma. Many of those that did reach proximity were destroyed before they could release their warheads. But more than a thousand exploded five hundred meters out from the enemy fleet sending more than six thousand laser-guided 88mm depleted uranium slugs into the heart of the enemy formation.

The result was devastating; more than three thousand enemy ships were either destroyed or disabled in less than thirty seconds.

"Fire!" Yoshimura shouted. And a second barrage of torpedoes streaked from the still stationary USF fleet with similar results. But there was no time for a third salvo. The enemy had closed to within a thousand meters. Space was filled with thousands of fingers of sizzling blue plasma.

More than a thousand of the USF fleet's F32 fighters streaked forward to engage the enemy and were instantly embroiled in fierce, wide-ranging dogfighting, railguns spewing thousands upon thousands of 88 and 55mm kinetic rounds at the oncoming hoard.

The USF fleet's initial onslaught had been devastating, destroying or disabling more than six-thousand enemy craft, more than twenty percent of their number, but it wasn't enough. By sheer weight of numbers, the Blues began to break through the fighter screen. The first few were quickly destroyed either by short-range Saber missiles carrying exploding warheads containing 55mm dutrinium shot, or by point defense fire.

Slowly, the enemy continued to advance into the jaws

of the crescent, and as they did so, they came under withering 88mm and 120mm enfilading fire.

And then, so it seemed, the dam collapsed and *Invincible* was under attack by a hoard of blue-haloed craft, crisscrossing back and forth, giant fingers of plasma raking her shields.

"Don your helmets," Yoshimura shouted to the bridge crew. "You, too, my prince," he said through gritted teeth, "and it's time for you to leave the bridge and go to the safety of the secondary bridge."

Elio looked at him as if he'd just been insulted.

"That's not going to happen, Admiral," he snapped. "My place is here, at the head of our forces. Tell me. What can I do to help?"

"I insist you leave the bridge, your highness. There's nothing you can do here. Go to the secondary bridge where you'll be safe should we be breached."

"I repeat, Admiral. That's not going to happen. To do that would be to betray the crew and mark me as a coward. You don't seem to understand, sir. I've fought the swarm hand-to-hand on Typhon and in Typhon space. And, while I'm no tactician, I'm probably more qualified to lead the fleet than you are. So, I repeat, this is where I belong. I'll hear no more about it."

Yoshimura looked at him and sighed. "As you wish, my prince, but I do think Mr. Tenilo needs to be taken to safety."

Elio glanced at Tenilo who was shaking his head, then said, "I agree. If you would escort him to the emergency bridge, Captain Diego... and while you're there, please prepare for the worst. Activate the backup bridge crew and have them stand by."

"But—" Tenilo began.

"No buts, Tenny. You're far too valuable. We can't afford to lose you. Besides, Padric would never forgive me."

Diego and his charge left the bridge while Elio turned to reach for his helmet, as did Yoshimura. They checked each other's suits and then turned to the hologram and the screens. The views were beyond comprehension. The bulk of the Swarm had broken through the crescent, and the hologram was a giant hornet's nest of blue icons wheeling, streaking this way and that between the ships of the USF fleet now taking heavy fire.

The two battle stations were also under attack but appeared to be holding their own against incredible numbers, hurling hundreds of missiles and thousands of 120mm rounds per minute at the whirling Blues, with deadly effect.

Invincible, now under sustained attack by upwards of fifty enemy craft, many of them second generation, also seemed to be holding, but as Yoshimura continued to direct the battle, all Elio could do was watch.

Several times he was able to use his TK to ward off incoming second-generation fighters, but his view through the screens was distorted and there was little more he could do, other than watch and wait.

He flinched as the forward shields lit up under the impact of a bolt of plasma, then another and a third, and then the second-generation Swarm fighter fell to *Invincible's* point defense guns as dozens of 120mm rounds slammed into its shields. For a second the blue halo glowed bright, but then it failed and went dark, and the heavy rounds hammered its hull. Elio expected to see it explode, shatter into thousands of glass-like shards, but it didn't. Instead, at first, it seemed to absorb the heavy projectiles. Then it began to spin, slowly at first, then faster and faster,

Invincible's heavy guns continuing to pound it until, finally, it exploded in a huge ball of brilliant blue fire.

Those new ships truly are different, he thought, then turned his attention to the *Juno.* She, too, was taking heavy fire, as were the battleships *Resolution* and *Defiance.*

A little to *Juno's* port and to her rear, the heavy cruiser, *Caesar,* suddenly went dark as her shields failed and her bridge exploded in a ball of orange fire. The explosion rippled along her hull. Dozens of escape pods appeared, many of them destroyed by enemy fire before they'd traveled a hundred meters from the exploding hull. And then, one of her fusion reactors blew and the great ship disintegrated in a cataclysmic explosion that sent massive chunks of minodutrinium armor hurtling through space, several of them impacting enemy fighters, ripping them apart.

Elio watched, his face pale, as ship after ship fell to the enemy fleet.

The battleship *Royal George,* a mighty ship more than sixteen hundred meters long, appeared to be drifting, dead in space. Her bow open to the vacuum, her engines dead, her shields flickering, all but a dozen of her turrets still firing.

The battleship *Resolution,* just a thousand meters to starboard, her shields lit up, all two-hundred-twenty railguns firing, was under withering assault from more than a hundred enemy fighters, wheeling and dodging, raking the mighty ship from bow to stern with sustained bursts of plasma. Space, for a thousand meters around her, was littered with the debris of more than a hundred fighters—both her own and those of the Swarm. And still she continued to fight, her F32 fighter squadrons diminishing by the minute.

Stars! Elio thought. *How much more can she take?*

But his own ship, *Invincible*, wasn't doing much better. She was, by then, almost an hour after the battle had begun, under constant attack. Cluster after cluster of enemy craft swooped in at speeds beyond Mach 20, raking her with plasma and then wheeling away. Her F32 fighters trying to protect her often found themselves fighting not just one enemy craft but two or more, sometimes as many as five. Of her one-hundred-forty-four fighters, seventy-seven were known to be disabled or destroyed. Twenty-two of her point defense turrets had been stripped away from her hull. Thirty-two of her two-hundred-twenty torpedo tubes had been damaged or disabled. Two of her eight engines had been damaged and had to be shut down. Her shields were fluctuating between eighteen and eighty percent.

The carrier *Juno*, two-thousand meters to port, was under constant attack by a Swarm cluster of more than a hundred enemy craft. The carrier *Asheron*, fighting a thousand meters to starboard, was also under heavy attack.

Marshal Tali's carrier, *Vagabond*, all guns blazing, seemed to be doing slightly better. The great carrier was surrounded by the wreckage of hundreds of enemy craft, along with many of her own fighters. In addition to almost all of her railguns, she was firing broadside after broadside of Rapier and Saber missiles with devastating effect.

Space, from one end of the crumbling USF crescent to the other, was rapidly becoming a vast debris field, a graveyard of thousands of Swarm and USF ships. The remains of more than ninety USF ships, large and small, almost a third of the fleet, were scattered across the battlefield. Many hundreds of escape pods were slowly drifting away from the conflict, their emergency location beacons flashing.

But the crescent tactic, degraded as it was becoming, was working, and while the great capitol ships were obviously the Swarm's primary targets, the smaller ships were doing much better. The destroyers and frigates were everywhere, using their speed to great advantage.

Off the port side and five hundred meters to *Invincible*'s stern, *Avenger* was indeed more than holding her own, as was Sasha Crowe's *Golden Condor*.

Chapter Thirty-Four

Caerus Space

Avenger

Like Elio, there was little Morian could do once the battle had begun. What he *could* do was monitor the action from the command rail where he was standing with Manda Haal and Michael Jadern on either side, having turned operations over to Omario Kingston and Corin Fargo, the ship's senior tactical and weapons officers.

Danis and her squadron had launched when they joined *Invincible* and, having already returned twice to rearm, were now gone, fighting somewhere off *Avenger's* port bow near the center of the great crescent formation.

Though small in comparison to *Invincible, Avenger* was indeed holding her own. Whether or not that was because she was taking less fire than the flagship, Morian didn't know. What he did know was that his ship had destroyed more than sixty first- and second-generation Swarm ships and, to that point in the battle, had suffered only minimal damage. What he didn't know, and neither did Manda, was that that was about to change.

He was closely watching at the screens. Despite the fleet's mounting losses and taking into account the incalculable effect the two battle stations were having on the enemy fleet, he estimated they were slowly gaining the upper hand. So engrossed was he, he failed to notice the cluster of nine second-generation ships approaching from the rear at more than Mach 20. Kingston, however, did notice.

"*Incoming. Aft!*" he shouted. "Divert power from reactors one and six to main aft shields."

He was less than a second too late. The leading Swarm ship opened fire with all four of its weapons on *Avenger's* two port engines, long, sustained blasts from its new, heavy weapons. It was followed almost instantly by a second ship and then a third. Both leading Blues were destroyed by point defense, and the third was disabled. With its starboard weapons platform severed at the root, the Blue ship went into a violent spin and slammed into the fourth in line, destroying both of them.

Avenger's shields flared momentarily, taking the brunt of the first Blue's barrage, but then failed as a second Blue pounded engines one and two with all four of its weapons, then raked the unprotected hull, scouring out a furrow more than twenty meters long and half a meter deep in her armor as it passed. The power from the two reactors surged and the shields came back up. Of the remaining five Swarm ships in the cluster, one slammed into the shields and exploded; two were destroyed by point defense fire, and two managed to unload on *Avenger's* shields and then get clean away.

"Damage report, Mr. Volkov," Morian snapped.

"Engine two is offline. Engine one is damaged but functioning at seventy-two percent. We have no hull breach. Captain, those weapons are ten times more powerful than anything we've seen before."

"Shields, Mr. Volkov?" Morian asked, ignoring the comment.

"Main shields are at eighty-two percent and holding, but we can't take—"

"Very well, Mr. Volkov," Morian snapped, interrupting him before he could finish his statement. "That will be all. Report to me immediately."

Volkov arrived on the command deck less than sixty seconds later. "Aye, Captain?" he muttered the question.

"I must ask you to keep your thoughts to yourself, Chief," Morian said. "We do not want the crew to learn the possible consequences of whatever may befall us. Panic is the last thing we need in the middle of a battle, don't you agree?"

"Aye, Captain. It won't happen again. Thank you, sir."

Morian nodded. "Dismissed, Chief. No hard feelings."

"No hard feelings, Captain." He saluted, turned on his heel and returned to his console on the well deck.

Meanwhile, the battle continued to rage around them. The constant clatter of the railguns and the flashes of brilliant blue as the shields absorbed blast after blast of plasma were beginning to wear on him.

He opened his mind and reeled under the onslaught of last-minute thoughts from a thousand dying humans: fear, panic, regret, even acceptance. He shook his head, tried to clear his mind and reached out to his sister.

Danis... where are you? Are you all right? Danis... Danis... But Danis didn't reply.

* * *

Danis, with Grell Dunn in the co-pilot's seat, her mind closed to all but what was going on around her, had launched her squadron only minutes after *Avenger* had joined Elio's fleet. That had been more than three hours earlier, and since then, she and her squadron had been fighting for their lives—and losing.

Of her ten pilots, only five remained; half of them were gone, including Skyla. Only she, two junior grade lieutenant pilots, Rangers Four and Six, Gian, and Jackknife in his ancient Veridian remained.

"Domino to Ranger Squadron." *What's left of it,* she thought dolefully. "Report your status."

"Ranger Six. No damage. Missiles gone. Railguns at eighteen percent."

"Ranger Four here. Same. Railguns at twenty-three percent."

"This is Joker. Engine One out, as you well know. Missiles all gone. Railguns... Hahaha... six percent. You can mark me up for nineteen of those suckas!"

"This is Jackknife. I'm almost out of everything. Need to rearm." Danis thought he sounded... dejected. *And no wonder,* she thought. *He was in love with Skyla.*

All eight of her own missiles were gone and her railgun ammo was almost depleted. So, for the third time, she ordered what was left of her squadron back to the ship to rearm.

"Back to the ship, Rangers," she said. "Let's go load up and get back at 'em."

She switched channels and called *Avenger*. "Domino to Avenger. Ranger Squadron returning to the nest to rearm and redeploy. You copy?"

"Come on home, Rangers," the hangar chief replied. "We're ready for you."

The five fighters swept into the hangar one after the other. The hangar crews pounced on them and rapidly replenished missiles and railgun ammunition. Hydro packs were quickly replaced, all while the pilots remained in their cockpits. Hand slaps were exchanged with the crew chiefs, and in less than fifteen minutes, the squadron was back in space again and almost immediately pounced upon by a cluster of nine enemy fighters.

"*Look out! Incoming!*" Danis yelled as her proximity screen lit up, flashing red.

Dunn, who'd been watching the screens, glanced up and out of the canopy. A group of three of the enemy fighters, some two-thousand meters off the F32's starboard bow, was hurtling toward them. He gritted his teeth, concentrated, closed his eyes and gripped the arms of his seat with both hands.

Danis was just about to reverse her engines and put the F32 into a steep dive when the leading Blue suddenly veered hard to starboard and slammed into the craft next to it; both of them exploded in a flaming ball of blue fire while a single Harpoon missile from Gian's fighter ripped the starboard weapons platform from the third.

"Yippee!" he yelled as his F32 flashed by Danis' rapidly slowing machine. "Take that, you slickery blue bastards."

He was rewarded by a bolt of plasma fired from a fourth incoming Blue that grazed his lower starboard engine.

"*Sovereign Stars!*" he yelled. "I'm hit. Engine four. It's overheating. I'm shutting it down."

"Domino to Joker. Shut that engine down and return to *Avenger* immediately. That's an order Gian. Get the hell out of here before you get yourself killed."

"Not on your life, Domino. I've been practicing for this in the sim. I can handle her with only three engines. It will give me a maneuverability advantage. And besides," he said, "I have to protect your sorry ass."

"That remark, Joker, will cost you dearly," Danis replied, smiling to herself. "All right. If you think you can handle it, but try to stay out of trouble." *Stars!* she thought. *As if.* "I'll be watching you. Domino out."

"Yes, ma'am," he yelled. "Here we come. Wooo hooo."

All Danis could do was shake her head and wonder what had become of the arrogant, insecure lad she'd taken under her wing all those months ago.

By then, Jackknife and the two surviving Rangers had dealt with the six remaining Blues, and her tiny squadron was grouped closely together, looking for an opportunity.

"Grell," she said as she studied her screens. "Those three incoming Blues; did you do that?"

"Um... I think so. Yes."

"Thank you. Well done," she said.

Dunn didn't reply.

Thirty minutes and two major engagements later, her mind cold, focused, locked down, her ammunition almost depleted, Danis and Grell were alone, circling the abandoned hulk of the battleship *Resolution*. The great ship was drifting, dead in space, her guns silent, her armor pierced in more than a dozen places, fires burning throughout her hull.

Danis had heard nothing from Rangers Four and Six in almost twenty minutes. Gian had lost another engine and was limping back to *Avenger* with Jackknife escorting him, and Danis was just about to follow them when she spotted something.

What the...? Who? Someone wearing a pressure suit was standing at the edge of an immense, ragged cavity in the battleship's port side.

Chapter Thirty-Five

Caerus Space

Invincible

An hour earlier, Elio, Admiral Yoshimura and Captain Diego—just returned from the emergency command bridge, having left Tenilo there with the backup bridge crew under the command of Lieutenant Commander Hans Timmerman—were together at the rail with the Admiral directing the battle.

By then, the battle had been raging for almost three hours but was far from over.

As far as Elio could see, the vast battlefield, more than five million cubic kilometers, via the screens and the hologram, was a gigantic debris field. The Swarm fleet had been reduced from more than twenty-seven thousand to—according to the data—just six-thousand-four-hundred-seven, and there was still no sign of them giving up.

By comparison, the USF fleet had lost almost half its

number, including the battleships *Royal George* and *Resolution*; both were dead in space, lifeless, drifting on the solar winds. The carriers *Juno* and *Acheron* were severely damaged; *Juno* so badly that Elio wondered if she could be saved.

The carrier *Vagabond*, Marshal Tali's flagship, seemed to be faring better. She'd lost many of her turrets and two-thirds of her fighters, but she was still fighting hard.

Elio's flagship, the *Invincible*, had lost an engine, thirty-eight of her two-hundred-twenty gun turrets, almost two-thirds of her fighter squadrons, and she was rapidly running out of ammunition. Stores of M99 torpedoes were down to nineteen percent. Railgun ammunition was down to twenty-two percent. Elio calculated that the ship had already fired more than two-million rounds.

"How much more of this can we take, Admiral?" Elio asked at last.

Yoshimura glanced sideways at him, smiled at him through his faceplate and said, "Why worry about it, my prince. There's nothing more we can do other than fight on." He turned again to lean on the rail and stare at the hologram.

"But can we win?" Elio asked.

The admiral stood upright, took a step backward and said, "That, my prince, only God can decide. They still outnumber us more than twenty-to-one and we're running low on ammunition. We need a miracle."

Elio shook his head and stared at the starboard screens, at the battleship *Resolution*. She was dark, dead in space, little more than a hulk. nineteen hundred meters of scrap minodutrinium. Her bridge was gone. Five of her eight fusion engines had been destroyed and she'd been holed more than a dozen times—that he could see—from stem to stern.

He turned to look at the screens on the port side of the bridge where the battle cruiser *Defiance* was under attack by at least a hundred enemy fighters intermingled with almost as many black and white USF F32s. On the screens, it looked like the ship was surrounded by a swarm of angry hornets.

"Incoming," Lewiston shouted.

Elio turned just in time to see a cluster of twelve enemy ships—six first-generation and six second-generation—coming in fast in two groups, both in line astern, side by side.

Invincible's fourteen laser-guided bow guns came to bear and began sending streams of 120mm kinetic projectiles at the two leading enemy craft. Within seconds, first one, then the other first-generation ships exploded; the debris flared as it hit *Invincible's* shields.

"They're leading with their weakest ships," Elio shouted. "They're drawing our fire so the bigger ships can close with us. We need to keep something in reserve. Hold fire on turrets one through seven."

"Belay that," Yoshimura growled. "There's no time for you to play games, my prince. Now stand away and let the professionals do what needs to be do...ne!"

There was an almighty flash of blue fire as four blasts of inconceivably powerful energy fired from a second-generation enemy craft slammed into the forward shields as the Blue craft swept by. They were followed by four more and yet another four.

"Forward shields are down to forty percent," Lewiston shouted.

BAMMM! BAMMM! BAMMM!

Again and again the shields took hit after hit.

"Shields are down!" Lewiston shouted.

He was cut off by a colossal explosion. The entire starboard side of the bridge imploded, blue streams of plasma searing the well deck as a blue craft sped by.

The doors sealed as the air in the bridge blasted out through the massive hole, taking most of the bridge crew with it, including Yoshimura and Diego.

Elio, who was holding the rail, tried to hang on.

The power went out. The entire bridge went dark and the hologram disappeared as the air rushed out into space.

For several seconds, Elio was able to hang on, his feet in the air, pointing toward the gaping hole. But then he felt his grip beginning to slip. Panic set in and he looked around wildly for some way to tether his body to the ship.

A huge chunk of the rail gave way and Elio found himself flying toward the hole. In a matter of seconds he was out in space, spinning wildly, end over end, not breathing as the shock of his predicament came to bear.

He could see almost the entire battlefield flashing by as he rotated. He closed his eyes, closed the darkened visor, opened them again, took a quick breath, reached with his right hand for the thruster controls on his belt and gently slowed the spin to a stop.

He looked frantically around. He could see *Invincible* now more than two hundred meters away, and the gap was widening quickly. He checked his heads-up display. He was moving too fast for his thrusters to do much more than slow him a little. Using his thrusters, he rotated until he was facing the direction of travel.

Ahead—he estimated the distance to be almost seven hundred meters—and some way below his trajectory, he could see the wreck of the *Resolution*.

He checked his speed. He was traveling at just over seventy meters per minute. *Ten minutes,* he thought. *I have to make it. If I don't, I'll be lost in space.*

He used his thrusters to adjust his trajectory and aimed himself at the center of the hulk.

It took every minute of the ten he'd estimated. He was still more than a hundred meters away and closing fast when the thrusters lost power and he found himself drifting out of control toward the abandoned battleship.

Stars! he thought. *I'm coming in too fast...* And, without even thinking about it, he used his TK to slow himself down. He landed with a thud, topside on the hull of the once illustrious battle wagon.

For several moments he clung to the armored hull, clinging on with his fingers and then he was floating, belly down, some twenty-five centimeters above the platework.

Slowly, he relaxed his grip, ready to grab on again if he began to drift. He waited several seconds, then nodded to himself. He checked his air. He'd already been in the suit for almost ninety minutes and was alarmed to see he had less than an hour and a half remaining.

He looked around. Space, in every direction, for as far as he could see, was littered with the remains of thousands of enemy and USF craft. And the battle was still raging around him. Hundreds of F32 fighters were engaged with thousands of the enemy.

In the distance, more than two kilometers away, he could see what he thought must be *Avenger,* or perhaps the *Golden Condor.* There was no way to tell for sure. Either one, she was too far away for him to attempt to reach her. And it was at that moment he realized he was done for. *Maybe so,* he thought, *but not without a fight.*

He looked down at the hull, made up his mind and

began to crawl, floating crabwise slowly across the top of the giant ship, stopping now and then to peer over the side.

Ten minutes later, he spotted what he was looking for, a giant hole in the ship's port side.

Slowly, drifting, using his fingertips, he floated over the edge of the hull and descended, headfirst, to the edge of the hole, grasped the sheared dutrinium, pulled himself inside and looked around.

He was inside what must have been one of the battle-ship's two hangars; its doors were gone, blown into space when the hull was breached, along with just about every-thing else, except for a dozen or so huge chunks of the ship's armor, floating inside the hangar like tiny asteroids.

He pushed himself off and floated across the hangar to the internal doors. They were sealed. He heaved a deep breath, then pushed himself off again and floated back to the rift in the hull, grabbed the edge and looked out across the battlefield.

A blue Swarm fighter streaked silently past, followed almost immediately by an F32, its railguns flashing as it spit hundreds of rounds at the rapidly disappearing Blue. To his right, not more than a half-kilometer away, two F32s were trying to outrun three second-generation Blues. So fast were they moving that they were gone almost in an instant.

And then he froze. Two hundred meters away, rising slowly, as if inspecting what was left of the *Resolution,* a first-generation Blue appeared.

For more than a minute they floated there, each seem-ingly appraising the other. The Blue's weapons platforms began to move, swiveling toward him. He looked wildly around, grabbed one of the hunks of dutrinium with his TK and hurled it at the enemy ship.

His aim was good. Before the Blue had time to fire its

weapons, it was hit by more than five hundred kilograms of solid dutrinium armor and it exploded in a flash of dazzling blue fire.

Elio grinned to himself, then quickly wiped the grin from his face. The explosion had attracted attention. Two more Blue ships appeared, both of them second-generation.

One after another, he hurled the remaining chunks of dutrinium at the two blue ships. One of them snagged his suit as it hurtled by. His stock was down to just two small pieces when the last of the ships seemed to simply die and drift away.

If he could have sat down to rest, he would have. As it was, all he could do was float there, just inside the ruptured hull, and watch as the battle raged on.

Again, he checked his oxygen levels and shook his head. *Twenty minutes,* he thought. *That was quick.* And then he remembered the snag to his suit and realized it must have been punctured and was leaking air. *Hah! So this is it, then.*

He tried to reach out, to anyone, but he received no reply until... *Elio? Is that you?*

Danis? Where are you?

And then he spotted the F32, one-hundred-fifty meters away, approaching from the bow end of the battleship.

Hold on, Elio. I'll come and get you. But first, I have to take Grell back to Avenger.

There's no time, Danis. My suit's punctured and I'm losing air... fast.

Danis, her mind in a whirl, thought franticly, then said, *Stand by, Elio. We can do this.*

"Grell," she said. "We have to save the prince. This is the only thing I can think of, but you're not going to like it."

Chapter Thirty-Six

Orso Space

Rescue

old on, Elio. I'm coming.

I'm almost out of air, Danis.

Hang on! I'm almost there.

"Grell," she said. "Make sure your helmet's secure. How much oxygen do you have?"

"Sixty-five minutes... why? What d'you want me to do?"

"We have to save Elio. There's not enough room for two back there so I'm going to leave you here and send the shuttle to get you."

"*No!*" he yelled. "You can't. I... can't."

"Man up! You'll be all right. Just stay in there and wait and I'll send them as soon as I get Elio to *Avenger*."

"Nooo... please. You can't. Please don't do this. I'll die. I know I will. Ple...ase."

Slowly, she maneuvered the F32 side-on to the gaping hole until it was almost touching the hull.

"Hold on, Grell," she said and hit the emergency canopy release. The explosive bolts fired. They blew the canopy off, upward and away, spinning wildly.

"Out you go, Grell. Grab Elio and help him inside."

"I, I, I, I..." he stuttered.

"*Get out, Grell!*" Danis yelled. "That's an order. If you don't, I'll eject you and then there'll be no rescue. Do it, damn it. He's dying."

Grell scrambled awkwardly out of the cockpit and jumped for the cavernous hole. And he didn't stop until he hit the far wall of the hangar.

Elio, she thought, reaching out to him, *come on. Climb in. We don't have much time.*

I... I...

Grell! He's barely conscious. You've got to help him. Use your TK. Hurry. Please... Please, Grell, help him!

She was almost sobbing with emotion as Elio hung, floating loosely just inside the hangar. And then he began to move as Grell gently pushed him to the fighter and lowered him into the rear seat.

"Oh, my stars," Danis gasped. "Thank you, thank you, thank you. I'll send help as soon as I can. I promise." Then, her fingers flew over the controls of her F32.

"Oh, my God," she muttered, tears rolling down her cheeks as she wheeled the F32 and streaked toward *Avenger.* "Don't you die, Elio. Don't you dare. Don't you die!"

"Domino to Avenger. Emergency. Emergency. I'm coming in hot with prince Elio. He's out of air. He's dying."

"Copy that, Domino. Landing bay cleared. Medical services are standing by."

Two minutes later she crashed, landing gear up, onto the dutrinium hangar deck, sparks flying as the fighter slid across the plating. The hangar doors closed and the bay began to pressurize. The second the F32 came to a stop, Danis ripped off her helmet, jumped up out of the cockpit onto the engine strut, waited for the green light, then ripped off Elio's helmet.

His face was white. His lips blue. He didn't appear to be breathing. She ripped off her gloves and felt his neck. She could barely feel a pulse.

"Help! Help me get him out of here," she yelled. "He's not breathing. He needs CPR."

She jumped up, straddled the cockpit, grabbed his suit and, with a supreme effort, hauled him out of the cockpit, laid him on his back on the strut and began to apply CPR through the pressure suit, tears streaming down her face.

She felt a firm hand on her shoulder. "Step away from him, Commander," the medic said. "We'll take it from here."

She fell away from him onto the strut, scrabbled backward, then slid off the strut to land on her feet on the hangar deck.

She backed away, her fist in her mouth, unable to take her eyes off the two medics as they worked to revive Elio.

For more than five minutes she stood there, and with each passing minute the fear for Elio grew until she was sure he wasn't going to make it.

She felt a hand on her arm. She turned, looked at Jackknife, began to sob, then wrapped her arms around his neck and buried her face in his chest, sobbing.

"Hey, hey," he said softly, his hand on the back of her head. "He's going to be all right."

"No, he isn't," she sobbed. "He's going to die."

"I said he's going to be alright," Jackknife said, pushing her away and looking into her eyes. "Trust me. I know. Remember?"

She gazed up at him, started to choke, shook her head, stood up straight, then stepped away from him, gathered herself together and said, "Are you sure? If he dies, I'll... I... I'll send you back to Freyja."

"Hah!" He laughed. "You think that would be a punishment? I'm sure. He'll be fine. See?" He nodded toward the F32 where they were gently lowering Elio's supine body onto a gravgurney.

She took a step forward to go to him, but Jackknife grabbed her arm and said, "Leave it. They're taking him to the med bay. You can see him later. Right now we have a battle to win... Where's Grell, by the way?"

She sucked in her lower lip, put her hand to her mouth and said, "Oh, m'God. He's still out there. On the wreck of the *Resolution*. We have to go get him. Now! We'll take Shuttle Two. Well, don't just stand there. C'mon." And she grabbed her helmet, turned and ran across the hangar, up the open ramp and into the shuttle.

Jackknife stood for a moment, sighed, shook his head and ran after her.

He was about to close the door when he heard someone shout, "Hey, wait for me."

He looked up and spotted Gian running across the hangar.

"This is Domino to operations requesting permission to exit the hangar and execute rescue of copilot Grell Dunn."

"Stand by, Domino... Permission granted."

The warning alert sounded. The green lights above the hangar doors turned red. The hangar depressurized and the doors opened.

"Damn," she said as she looked over the controls.

"Here. Let me," Gian said, slipping into the copilot's seat beside her.

His fingers fluttered over the controls. The shuttle lifted smoothly on its gravs and Gian flew her smoothly out into the black. Less than ten minutes later, the shuttle was gliding toward the gaping hole in the side of the great ship where Grell was waving his arms like some demented ogre.

Gian guided her alongside. Jackknife lowered the ramp and Grell leaped aboard, his arms flailing as he flew through the open cargo door and slammed into the far wall, bounced off, grabbed the back of one of the seats and hung on, blubbering with terror, while Jackknife closed the door.

The door closed, and Jackknife turned to him and said, "Get a grip on yourself, man."

"You don't know what it was like," he blubbered. "I thought no one was coming for me."

"Everything all right back there?" Danis shouted.

"All good," Jackknife replied, staring hard at the quaking Grell.

"Go," Danis said to Gian as she gazed out of the cockpit windows. "Whew. Will you just look at that."

The battle was raging around them unabated.

"I see it," Gian replied. "Let's hope we don't get spotted. This crate has no weapons."

"*Avenger's* taking heavy fire," she said. "You think we can get through?"

"Ahh!" Gian exclaimed as he cut power to the port engine and crammed the starboard engine and thrusters to full power, throwing the shuttle into a crazy, almost vertical dive to port, barely avoiding a blast of blue plasma thicker than a man's waist from a second-generation Blue that shot by so fast Danis almost missed it.

"Stars. Will you look at that?" Gian said as he righted the craft. *Avenger* was under attack by more than a dozen Blues, wheeling in and out and around her like flies, raking her with plasma fire, her shields flaring as they took hit after hit.

"Shuttle One to operations control," Danis said. "We're two minutes out and coming in. Open the doors and lower the shields on my mark."

"This is operations control. Request received and understood. On your mark."

She looked at Gian. He sucked in his lower lip, held it there with his teeth, and nodded.

"Go for it, Gian," she said.

He took a deep breath, eased the throttle forward, increased power to the thrusters...

Danis stared at the ship as she rapidly grew in size, waiting... waiting... "*Mark!*" she yelled and closed her eyes.

The shields to level one, section seven, snapped off. The shuttle slipped through, and the shields snapped on again.

Danis heaved a sigh of relief, grabbed Gian's arm and squeezed it. The shuttle settled gently down onto the deck.

Gian sat back in his seat, shook his head and said, "That... was the scariest thirty minutes I've spent since I boarded *Avenger* almost a year ago. How the hell Jax does it, I don't know."

Danis smiled at him and said, "You've come a long way, Gian. Your reactions are incredible. You've become a true fighter jockey, my boy. One of the best."

"Hey, I heard that," Jackknife said from the cockpit door. "He's still a rookie in my book."

Gian grinned up at him and said, "I'll give you a run for your money any day, old man. Sight or not!"

"That you would, son," Jackknife replied. "That you would."

"If you two don't mind," Danis said dryly, rising from her seat. "There's still a battle raging out there."

"Yes," Jackknife said, stepping to one side to let her through. "And it looks like I'm all that's left of Ranger Squadron. I have the only serviceable craft left."

"That old Veridian?" Danis said. "It's about time you gave up on that. She's about to fall to pieces."

"Ah, but she's a lovely old girl and she's served me well for more than twenty years. I'm not going to abandon her now."

"Well, maybe not, but you're done for today," Danis said. "I'm not going to let you back out there alone... Come on, Grell. Let's get you cleaned up. I'm sure you must need a clean pair of pants." *And I need to go see Elio,* she thought. *But I need to talk to Richard first.*

Chapter Thirty-Seven

Orso Space

Avenger

"The shuttle just landed, Captain. Commander Morian is back aboard," Lowry said.

"Status, Ms. Fargo," Morian snapped, wrenching off his helmet.

"M99 missiles at thirteen percent, Captain. Railgun ammunition seventeen percent. Turrets seven, eight... Twenty-three of the forty-eight turrets are out of action—"

"Enough!" Morian snapped. "Mr. Volk...ov?" The deck shuddered under his feet as *Avenger* took what Morian calculated to be her thirty-third hit.

"Engine one is still functioning at seventy percent. Number two is offline. Four is... Four's gone, Captain. I mean completely destroyed. We have multiple hull breaches on levels two, five, six, seven and eight. Reactors three and five have been shut down. Main shields are at thirty-eight percent. Captain, we..." Volkov caught himself and shut up.

The ship shuddered again.

"Incoming," Kingston yelled. "Off the port bow. Eleven o'clock."

"Divert power from reactor seven to the forward shields," Morian snapped.

"Reactor seven just shut down, Captain," Volkov shouted. "You already have all we've got."

"Here they come," Lowry shouted.

"Fire everything we've got left," Morian commanded. "Fire at will."

And they watched as missile after missile streaked away, heading toward the cluster of thirty incoming Blues.

One after another the missiles reached proximity and their warheads exploded, driving their deadly, laser-guided payloads onward. Blue ships began exploding as the heavy kinetic slugs hit home, flinging debris into *Avenger's* shields. The barrage took out all but nine of the thirty Blues. The rest continued their attack right into the teeth of her point defense guns.

Morian, breathing deeply, stared at the forward screens, flinching as a second-generation Swarm ship slammed into the shields and exploded. *Avenger* rocked under the force of the explosion. Four more enemy ships fell to *Avenger's* heavy guns, exploding in cascades of blinding blue fire. A sixth, both its weapons platforms shot away, hurtled toward the upper bow, glanced off the shields and careened off into open space. Two more fell to the big guns, but not before they managed to fire their weapons. The shields flared but held, barely, and Morian held his breath as the last enemy ship hurtled toward them through a hail of railgun fire and all four of its energy weapons fired.

Baarraam! Baarraam! The shields flared brilliant white, flickered, then disappeared, and the wounded second-generation Blue ship slammed into the hull and exploded. *Avenger* rocked under the impact.

Morian gripped the rail and looked to his left at Manda. She had her helmet on, but he could see her face was white. He reached out to her, grabbed her hand, glove to glove, and squeezed it.

She looked at him and nodded, pointed to her helmet and then to his. He shook his head. He'd decided if he was going to go, he'd go with his ship, and quickly... without his helmet.

"Shields down!" he heard Volkov shout. "Hull breach level nine, sector three! We're leaking atmosphere!"

Morian glanced up at the data rolling above the hologram and shook his head. *Still more than four thousand of them and we're... We're almost... We can't beat them.*

He tapped his datapad. "Attention all hands," he said over a shipwide channel. "This is the Captain. Prepare to aban—"

"This is Marshal McAlan commanding the Sixth USF Battle Group," the old man's voice broke in, echoing around *Avenger's* bridge and what was left of Elio's fleet. "The battle for the Slip gates is won. The enemy is in full retreat. The Ninth Battle Group is in pursuit. We are approaching your position at one-tenth light and will be with you in less than five minutes. Stand fast. McAlan out!"

Avenger's bridge crew was silent for several seconds, then Jax started yelling, then Jadern, then Fargo and then the entire bridge was on its feet, cheering and yelling.

Morian, at the rail with Manda, could do little more than stand there smiling, shaking his head.

Oh, my God, he thought breathlessly. *We're going to make it... Danis! Danis? I haven't heard anything from her.*

Then he reached out to his sister.

Danis. Where are you? Are you all right?

Danis, who was just leaving the hangar, replied, *Yes, Richard. I'm fine. I was just... Oh, never mind. How about you? I know the ship has taken a beating. Are you hurt?*

I'll survive, but the ship... I don't know. How about your squadron?

There was a long moment of silence before Danis replied. *They're all gone, Richard, except for Jackknife and Gian... Ironically, the only fighter that survived without major damage was Jackknife's ancient Veridian. Gian's F32 lost two of its engines and was so badly damaged on landing it had to be spaced. Mine... I had to make a hard landing; it's repairable, I think. The rest of the squadron... They're all gone, including Skyla.* At that, she paused. Morian could feel her pain. *Gian and Jackknife are fine,* she continued. *Oh, and so is Grell. I'll talk to you about him later... Look, Richard, I hate to cut this short, but I'm on my way to see Elio. He's in the med bay, so—*

That's fine, Danis, he interrupted her thought. *We'll talk later. Now go see the prince. I'm sure he'll be pleased to see you. Give him my best wishes and tell him we'll talk soon.*

He closed his mind to her and was about to turn from the rail when Lowry shouted, "They're here. Look!"

Morian looked up at the forward screens. Marshal McAlan's Sixth Battle Group had indeed arrived, and what was left of the enemy was already retreating, back toward the gas giant Athena. Morian couldn't help but wonder, and not for the first time, if there was a third Slip gate somewhere out there, in the outer reaches of the Orso System.

Chapter Thirty-Eight

Orso System

Time and Place

Danis, filled with trepidation, her nerves jangling, arrived at the doors to the med bay to find them guarded by two of Major Dubois' Marines.

"I'm here to see Prince Elio," she stated.

They looked her up and down, and she was instantly aware of the mess she must look.

"I'm Lieutenant Commander Morian," she said. "I brought him in."

They stood aside. She stepped forward, held the palm of her right hand to the scanner and the doors swished open. She stepped inside, walked quickly to the next security terminal, looked into the lens and waited.

It took only a second before the terminal said, "Welcome, Commander Morian. How can I help you this afternoon?"

"I'd like to see Prince Elio," she said.

There was a moment of silence while the terminal contacted the nursing station.

"You're cleared to visit prince Elio Lorne," the terminal replied. "Please proceed to suite C, Commander. Do you know the way, or would you like me to have someone come and get you?"

"I know the way, thank you."

"Thank you, Commander. I hope you enjoy your visit. Goodbye."

Danis shook her head as she walked the corridor to Elio's suite.

She stood for a moment outside the door, took a wipe from one of the breast pockets of her flight suit, wiped her face with it, restored it to the pocket, ran her fingers through her hair, took a deep breath and then knocked on the door and waited.

A few seconds later, the door swished open and she walked confidently into the foyer, where she was met by a nurse.

"Prince Elio's awake and is expecting you, ma'am. I should warn you, though... he may not seem quite himself. Dr. Dowd had to medicate him when he was brought in. You can go on through."

Again, Danis took a deep breath and stepped inside, her heart in her throat. It hadn't been more than a couple of hours since she dragged him out of the cockpit of her F32, and less than an hour since she suddenly realized just how much in love with him she was.

She found him half-asleep, propped up in bed and was horrified to see the color of his skin. His face was pale with a blueish tinge; the whites of his eyes networked with spidery red veins.

"There you are," he said as she stepped up to the bedside and sat down. His voice was weak, tired.

He held out his hand. She took it in hers. He squeezed it gently and stared up at the ceiling. "Thank you," he said. "You saved my life."

"I—" she began.

"Shush," he said, breathing slowly, deeply. "I would have died out there." He coughed, closed his eyes, heaved a deep breath, then turned his head to look at her. "What you did... I shall be forever in your debt."

"No," she said gently. "No... No, I just did what I had to do. I... I couldn't lose you."

"If you say you would have done it for anyone, I'll get out of this bed and... Thank you, Danis."

"It was my pleasure, your highness."

"That's something else I never want to hear from you again—your highness, my prince, or anything else other than my name, Elio. Do you understand what I'm saying?" He squeezed her hand and gave her a wink. "Well, maybe when we're in public. You know how these things are." He grinned at her.

Heat rose to her face. "I think I understand, Elio," she said as they stared at one another, her eyes welling with tears. "I couldn't bear the thought of life without you, not after I realized how much you mean to me." Danis wiped a tear from her cheek. "I feel like a silly school girl. I'm used to being in control." Danis looked down at their clasped hands. "Is it even appropriate for me to feel this way, considering you're a prince?"

Elio placed his other hand along her cheek, and Danis raised her eyes to his. The smile on his face and the look in his eyes made her heart stutter.

"It's more than appropriate," he said, squeezing her hand.

Danis felt overwhelmed, quickly changed the subject and began to talk about the Swarm's retreat.

"The *Invincible?*" Elio said, interrupting her. "What of her? Was she destroyed? All I remember is there was a huge explosion and then I was out, in space... Is she gone?"

Danis started to rise to her feet. "I don't know," she said. "I'll go check."

But he squeezed her hand and stopped her. "No, please. Stay. Sit down. It can wait. I was hoping you'd come," he said awkwardly, unable to look her in the eye.

She sat down, and he took her hand in both of his and closed his eyes.

"Elio..."

His eyes snapped open. "Yes?"

"I really do need to go, but I'll come back if that's all right. I'll find out what happened to your ship and—"

"No. Don't go. I don't want you to go. Not yet."

"But—"

"Sit down, Danis. That is a royal command."

Her mouth dropped open. "Oh really?" she said.

He sighed, then said, "Come here."

She was already as close to the bed as she could be.

"Closer," he said. "I need to tell you something, in the strictest confidence. Yes, like that," he said as she leaned over the bed, "but closer."

She leaned in closer, so close she could feel his breath on her cheek. Her heart was beating so hard she was sure he'd hear it.

He slipped a hand around her neck, pulled her to him, and kissed her, a long lingering kiss that took her breath away. Then he let her go and said, "You've no idea how long I've been waiting to—"

She slid her arms around his neck and kissed him again. Embarrassment suddenly overtook her and she tried to pull away, but he held onto her. He kissed each of her eyes, the tip of her nose, her neck, her lips. She collapsed on top of him. Then scrambled up, off the bed, bewildered. He grabbed her hand and pulled her back to him.

"Elio, we shouldn't," she said laughing. "Someone might come in and see us."

"I don't care. I love you, Danis. I always have."

She stood there beside the bed holding his hand in both of hers, her mouth open, unable to believe what she was hearing.

"I... I love you, too," she whispered.

It was at that moment there was a knock on the door. It opened. She dropped his hand, just a second too late, as Elio's father walked slowly in with the help of a cane.

"Don't mind me," he said, staring at her, scowling.

Danis bit her lower lip, bowed her head and said, "Your majesty... I..."

"Come, come, girl. Do you think I don't know what's going on here? And you, my son. It's about time you found someone and stopped fooling around playing those stupid games." He paused, then continued. "And I'd better not find out you're toying with her."

"Ah, um, er, no, Father. I'm not." Elio said, his face turning scarlet. "Father, when did you wake up? How did you get here?"

"I awoke yesterday, sometime after you discovered the our... Seers. Yes, I know you know. The Psy assassin? I knew nothing of that. I would have come sooner, but that fool Myster insisted I say in bed. He even had the temerity to sedate me. But then I was informed you were injured, neer to death so, much to Myster's dismay, I commanded a shuttle to bring me to you as soon as the Swarm retreated."

The king turned again to Danis and said, "I hope he thanked you for saving his life, Commander. If he didn't. Shame on him. I will. I thank you from the bottom of my heart for saving my son's life."

"But I... I..."

"It's all right, child. Relax. I don't bite."

"Hah, so he says," Elio retorted, then his expression grew serious. "It is good to see you up and about, Father."

"I brought you these," the king said, tossing a pair of modified halos on the bed. "Meeting. In an hour. Be there. Both of you." And he turned to go.

"Father," Elio said.

"Yes, my son?"

"What about *Invincible*? Have you heard? Is she gone?"

"She survived. Lost her bridge and the entire bridge crew, including Yoshimura and Diego. You're the only survivor, thanks to the commander." He turned again.

"And Mr. Tenilo?" Elio said.

"He survived," the king said as he walked slowly out into the corridor.

The door closed behind him. Elio looked up at Danis and said, "Now you *have* to stay, by command of the king, no less."

And he grabbed her hand and pulled her to him.

Chapter Thirty-Nine

Orso System

All Good Things

An hour later, Elio and Danis jacked into the meeting in his father's conference room to find they were almost the last to arrive. The king, Richard Morian, Tenilo, Sasha Crowe, Tiger Wok, several dukes and marshals, including Marshal McAlan, were in attendance. The only ones not in their seats were the Tudors, Wulfrick and Zara. They arrived a few minutes later.

After thanking the delegates for coming and making the introductions, King Orson declared the meeting open and followed by personally thanking Captain Morian for his efforts in delivering the information that secured the successful defense of the Orso System. The king also thanked Commander Danis Morian for saving his son's life.

"I would also like to thank my daughter, Sasha Crowe,"

he said, officially recognizing her for the first time, "and, of course, Captain Tiger Wok of the Free People's colony of Freyja for their invaluable help. Without their support... well, none of us would be here today. Thank you both."

Sasha smiled, nodded, then turned to look at Elio and winked at him.

"I must also thank you, Marshal McAlan," the king continued. "I have it on good authority that it was through your strong leadership that the Battle for the Gates was won. Not a single enemy craft made it through to any of our inhabited planets. You will assume the role once held by the late Marshal Ugo Tan as Commander in Chief of the Orso Military... Thank you, Andrew."

He paused for a second, then continued, "It would be remiss of me to forget the enormous loss of life our forces suffered today. The numbers are not all in yet, but we estimate them to be in excess of ninety-thousand officers, men and women. And, while we did win the day, we lost more than half the combined USF Fleet. Not a single ship escaped undamaged. The two battle stations involved were also severely damaged. Of the forty-eight carriers engaged, eleven were destroyed. We also lost eighteen of forty-seven battleships, one-hundred-nineteen cruisers, four-hundred-sixty-one destroyers and more than nine-hundred frigates."

He paused to let the numbers sink in, then continued. "Sadly, we also lost most of our fighters and their pilots... Of the seventy-two-hundred engaged in the conflict, six... thousand... five-hundred-and-forty-two good men and women lost their lives."

Danis sniffed and wiped her eyes. Elio squeezed her hand.

"Your majesties, ladies and gentlemen." The king stood up and banged his fist down on the table. "We cannot allow this to happen again. The Swarm is far from defeated. They will come again. We *must* be ready for them."

First one, then two of the people gathered at the meeting began to slap their hands on the table. More joined them until the entire assembly was banging and cheering.

The king held up his hand for silence, then said, "Duke Rutta, you are unusually quiet. Have I said something you disagree with?"

"No, your majesty," he replied. "I was just... I was wondering if this means that you're taking back the kingdom from the er..." Rutta glanced at Elio, then continued, "from the regent. If not, I would suggest that while the prince does seem to have—"

"That's enough, Rutta," the king snapped. "The answer is that I will not be returning anytime soon. My doctors insist I need more rest. In the meantime, I have every confidence in my son and his abilities. He will continue his duties as regent. Any objections?" He looked around the table as if daring anyone to speak. The only one who took the bait was Queen Zara of Odin.

She smiled and said, "I agree. I, too, have every confidence in the young man's abilities, but I also wish you a speedy recovery, your grace."

Danis squeezed Elio's hand and looked up into his eyes. They were watering. It was the first time he'd ever heard his father acknowledge him as a man.

The meeting continued on for more than an hour until finally, the king, obviously tiring, called a halt.

Had anything substantive been achieved? Elio didn't think so. What he did know was that he had a new enemy to contend with. Duke Rutta would not forget or forgive the very public rebuke he received from the king. He also knew that, with his father out of the picture, at least for a while, he had a vast amount of work and diplomacy to get through if they were to be ready in time. Yes, the Swarm fleets had been decimated, but their resources seemed to be unlimited. His father was right. They would be back.

He removed his halo and set it on the med bay bed; Danis did the same.

Elio looked at her and was about to speak when there was a knock at the door.

"Come in," Elio said.

The door opened and Richard Morian walked in, followed by Manda Haal, Michael Jadern and Tenilo.

"Tenny," Elio said, sitting up in bed. "You're all right! You survived."

Tenilo smiled at him and said, "It was fortunate that Admiral Yoshimura had the foresight to remove me from the bridge before it was breached. Yes, I'm fine. Thank you, your highness. I'm happy to see that you also made it through the battle relatively unscathed."

"It's good to see you're recovering, my prince," Morian said. "I was hoping we might have a few minutes of your time." He looked at Danis, who was sitting beside the bed.

Elio caught the look and said, "Of course, Captain. But Commander Morian stays."

"I see," Morian said, smiling. "Anything I should know?"

Danis looked confused, but Elio smiled and said, "At this moment, no. Now, Captain, what's this all about?"

Morian took a deep breath and said, "You probably don't know this, my prince, but you're in the med bay of what can only be described as a wreck. Avenger was severely damaged, so much so that I fear she will have to be scrapped. Mr. Tenilo, however, seems to have other ideas."

Elio looked at Tenilo and said, "Tenny?"

"Er... Um..." Tenilo closed his eyes, made a face and then continued, "Well, yes and er... no. True, two of her engines are gone, two more are offline, and half of her gun turrets are gone, but her hull breaches have all been sealed, and thanks to the way her plating is attached to the hull, I see her more as an opportunity than a wreck. I propose to have her towed to the shipyards on Freyja for repairs and a complete refit. I... also have a few ideas."

"And they are?" Elio asked.

"I—" Tenilo began, but Morian interrupted him.

"I asked him the same question, but he wouldn't tell me."

Elio frowned and said, "Why not, Tenny?"

"Because, my prince, they are just ideas. I haven't even worked them through for myself, but if I could have Avenger—and if my ideas prove fruitful—I think you will be pleasantly surprised."

Elio stared at him, then at Morian, his eyebrows raised in question. "Richard?"

Morian shrugged. "I see no harm in it. It's up to you, my prince."

"Very well," Elio said. "Everyone here knows how much Avenger means to me, and to you, Richard. You have your ship, Tenny. But what about you and your crew, Captain? The repairs will take months."

"Marshal McAlan has offered me the command of the heavy cruiser Intrepid. She's... brand new." Morian didn't sound too enthusiastic.

"Is that what you want?" Elio asked.

"Not really, but nor do I want to captain a desk for the next twelve months. So, with your permission, I will take the offer, but only on condition that I get Avenger back when she's ready."

"Permission granted," Elio said and clapped his hands together. "Ask McAlan to contact me, and I'll make sure he understands. Is there anything else?"

Morian looked again at Danis. She looked back at him, her face set. He smiled, nodded and said, "A month's leave for Commander Danis Morian?"

She opened her mouth to speak, but before she could, Elio said, "Are you serious, Richard? She saved my life. She deserves better... Two months, I think. More if she wants it."

"But what about my squadron?" she asked.

"As of this moment," Richard said, shaking his head slowly, "it sadly comprises only Gian, Jackknife and an ancient Veridian fit only for the scrapyard... I think they need a break, too. Don't you?"

Danis could only stare at him, speechless. *Oh, my Lord, Richard,* she thought, reaching out to him. *We lost so many people. What will happen to us now?*

To you, you mean? Something wonderful by the look of you two. Focus on the future now, little sister.

I heard that, Richard, Elio butted in, grinning at him. *Now take these people and leave us alone.*

Richard smiled at him, nodded, stood up and said, "Thank you, your highness. I see you have... *weighty* matters to consider. If you need me, you know where I'll be."

Elio reached out to them with his Psy as they left, trying to gauge how soon it would be that the entire ship knew about Danis and him.

"What was that about?" Manda asked as the door closed behind them.

"That, Commander, is probably none of our business."

Elio smiled and squeezed Danis' hand.

Epilogue

One month later

It had been a long day and Kyne Minnah was tired, hungry, and ready to go home to the apartment Elio had provided for him.

He'd been in his lab in the military compound on the north side of the Royal palace for almost ten hours, working on several of his pet projects, including the almost intact remains of a first-generation Swarm ship salvaged from the debris field of the Battle for the Gates.

Kyne, for the past three weeks, had been trying to connect with it, but with no success. *If I just had my core,* he told himself for the umpteenth time.

But he didn't. The core had been whisked away by the military scientists in the War Department complex. What they were doing with it, he had no idea. He couldn't really blame them for taking it. It was, or could be, as he had communicated first to Elio and then Morian, a game changer in the war with the Swarm. They had also relieved him of his EMPG, but that didn't bother him half as much as the loss of the core. *I can always make another EMPG*, he thought.

He stared through the compexglass window at the alien craft. Its systems were dead, as was its blue halo, its force field. However, Kyne knew from his research of the downed ship in the canyon that the ship was somehow still communicating with the Swarm. *How in the name of the stars do they do it?* he thought.

He sighed, shook his head, turned away, stepped back to his desk and sat down. Just a few more calculations to make and then he could call it a night.

An hour later, Kyne was alone in his office, the lab techs having already left for the evening. He'd just turned off the lights and was getting ready to leave when he heard something. He looked up at a speaker above the lab's window. *What was that?* he wondered. *Someone must have left the system on in the lab. Who's that? It's... Tenilo? What's he doing? Why is he in there?*

He was just about to open the door and go and ask him when something made him pause.

The lighting in the lab was dim, but not so dim that he couldn't see. He watched as Tenilo slowly approached the alien ship and put his hand flat against the hull, then closed his eyes.

For a moment, nothing appeared to be happening, then Tenilo's face twisted in anger. He opened his eyes, jerked his hand away, staggered two steps backward, stood for a moment, then muttered, "I don't know who you are, and I don't understand. But I *will* find you."

The End